D1447047

ASHBY HOLLER

By Jamie Zakian

ASHBY HOLLER

Limitless Publishing, LLC
Kailua, HI 96734
www.limitlesspublishing.com

Formatting: Limitless Publishing

ISBN-13: 978-1-68058-666-4
ISBN-10: 1-68058-666-1

Dedication

This one goes out to my farm family for being so awesome.

Chapter One

Sasha's palm glided along smooth skin, her fingers tracing a path left by her tongue only moments ago. The woman below her shuddered with every touch. Soft giggles tickled Sasha's ears, and locks of red hair filled her hand. It was almost enough to make her forget the evils that waited outside her door…almost.

"Sorry, Candy, but I gotta go."

Candy clung to Sasha's arm and tugged. "You still owe me."

"Yeah." Sasha shook free, grabbing her bra as she rose from the bed. "But I can't keep my mother waiting." She wiggled into her cargo pants, fastening the belt. "And you better sneak out of here the way you came in. If I get caught again—"

"I know." Candy sat up, scooting to the edge of the bed. "I still hate myself for hiding in the bushes when your mom had the club beat you down."

Sasha slid a tank top over her head just in time to cover her frown. "More like stomp my face into the gravel."

"It's 1984. You'd think people would be more open to—"

"Shh!" Sasha crouched between Candy's legs, gripping her by the waist. "My mom will never accept a dyke as a daughter or a sergeant at arms. You know how important this is to me."

Sasha leaned in, scooting farther between Candy's legs.

"You better hurry then," Candy whispered. "Your meeting starts in five."

"Shit." Sasha jumped up, stopping in front of the mirror to fix her smeared makeup. After tying a bandana atop her messy hair, she headed for the door.

"Wait," Candy said. She hopped out of bed, snatched a leather coat from the floor, and trotted across the room stark naked. "Don't forget your skin."

Sasha slid her arm around Candy's waist, pulling her close. "Thanks. Wear that white mini tonight. I plan on repaying my debt." She took her jacket from Candy's hand then shuffled through the door.

Wooden boards creaked as Sasha thumped down narrow stairs, away from her loft above the garage. A stillness clung to the air, sweeping across all fifty acres of the compound. Rare, to have the place to herself. No locals passed out in the bushes or brightly painted chicks waiting for the party to kick off. Just her, a wide stretch of gravel, and the sun gleaming off a line of eighteen wheelers. She walked past the four majestic rigs. Her vessels of escape, each gassed up and ready to haul pounds of marijuana from their warehouse deep in the hills of

Kentucky to them thirsty city folk.

She hightailed it to the clubhouse without a glance at her mother's huge Victorian house atop the hill. When she climbed the porch steps, her mother's voice hit her ears. Then she heard her mother drop her name, along with a few colorful words.

"I know. I'm fuckin late," Sasha muttered, storming inside the clubhouse. Her hip bumped the pool table and caused the little colored balls to clink against one another. She maneuvered around a scatter of stools, took a sip of someone's steaming cup of coffee thoughtfully left for her on the bar, and slipped into the backroom. Before the door could click shut, she dropped into her seat beside Vinny like she'd been there all along.

Thankfully, the room was abuzz with side conversations. The men on the other side of the long table chatted with her mother, except for Kev, who looked asleep behind his sunglasses. Sasha didn't look at the head of the table. It was best to avoid her mother's glare, at least not until after a few hits of a big fat joint.

She nodded to Rolo, who was fidgeting at the end of the table, then glanced at Vinny.

Vinny narrowed his eyes and Sasha shrugged. He leaned close, his blonde hair tumbling over his wide shoulder. "You smell like pussy," he whispered.

When she burst out laughing, the chatter stopped and eyes veered to her. She cleared her throat, straightened her jacket, and sat tall.

"Now that we're all here," her mother said,

hurling a glare that could shatter ice, "we can begin."

"Sorry I was late, but I have a good excuse." Sasha reached into the inside pocket of her jacket and pulled out an envelope. When she dropped it on the table, polaroids slid across the glossy surface.

"What's this?" Chewy asked, his gray beard gliding along the table as he scooped up a picture. No one else moved. They just looked at Chewy, as if waiting for a thumbs-up from their vice president.

"That's our esteemed sheriff, getting…rode by Candy." Sasha grinned, grabbing a joint from the ashtray.

"Ha! Literally," Chewy said through a smirk, and everyone reached for a photo.

"Yep." Sasha searched for her lighter, the joint flopping as she spoke. "He wanted her to ride him around the motel room like a horse, whip and all."

Vinny snapped his zippo to life, holding out the flame. Their eyes met as she neared the fire, and he winked.

"Well, goddamn," Chewy drawled.

"I knew he was a freak," Vinny said, eyeing the pictures scattered atop the table.

"Look at those titties." Otis shoved one of the photos into his pocket then grabbed another.

Sasha didn't have to look. Every inch of Candy's body was etched into her mind. She flicked her ashes, taking another deep puff. Kind bud, breakfast of champions. "This is good shit. Is it our new product?"

Her mother nodded, eyes still stuck on the vulgar images. "We got that bastard, our own little bitch with a badge."

Vinny glanced at a picture of the sheriff on his hands and knees and pushed it away. "Think his wife rides him around like that?"

"Doubt it." Sasha chuckled. "That fat old cow would break his back. And they didn't bone. Candy really tried then the sheriff pulled out a saddle, so she went with it."

"This is enough to get him off our backs," her mother said, gathering up the photos.

"Good pun." Chewy snickered.

"That poor girl." Otis leaned back in his chair, running his hand along his smooth chin. "We should thank her, throw her a proper clubhouse party. Ellen?"

Sasha looked at her mother, who nodded.

"Which brings us to the topic at hand." Ellen shoved the pictures back into the envelope before taking her seat. "We lost three members in last month's…scuffle with the biker dicks."

Groans and muffled obscenities rang out. Sasha glanced at Vinny, shrinking back as he continued to stare at her.

"Both of our prospects are at the table and we have three positions to fill, so we're still a man down." Ellen paused, clasping her fingers together. "It's no secret Sasha wants the sergeant at arms spot."

"Okay." Otis chuckled. "What's she, like, twelve?"

Sasha steered her gaze at Otis, mirroring his cocky leer. "Nineteen, asshole."

"No one could ever replace Ronny as Sarge, but

he did take Sasha under his wing," Chewy said, looking to the ceiling. "Rest his soul."

"I second that," Kev blurted, removing his glasses and rubbing his eyes.

"Were you sleeping?" Vinny asked.

"There's no vote in motion to second, you fucking idiot," Otis said.

Sasha leaned back in her chair. A *tap, tap, tap* shook the floor beside her, and she looked at Rolo, who was slouched at the end of the table. Sweat rolled down his cheek, the muscles of his jaw flexing. That one glance sparked her temper, pumping fire into her veins. She knew that face. Rolo had the same stupid expression when she caught him stealing from her lunchbox in the fourth grade.

Her elbows hit the table, and she leaned forward. "Rolo, you've been awfully quiet." She rose to her feet, her chair scraping against the floor. "And you've got that look."

Vinny jumped up, following Sasha to Rolo's side. She placed her hands on Rolo's jittery shoulders, squeezing hard. Rolo reached for her wrist and Vinny seized his hand, pinning it to the table.

"Get off!" Rolo yelled. He tried to stand, but Sasha moved her grip to the back of his neck, holding him down. His shirt hiked up and she caught sight of a black wire.

"You motherfucker." Sasha dug her nails into Rolo's skin as she slammed his head against the table.

Blood splattered the second Rolo's face struck

6

solid wood. He dropped to his knees, holding his nose, and everyone rose to their feet. Large men crept toward Rolo, swarming like the sharks they were, and Sasha stepped away to avoid the frenzy.

"Don't do it, man," Rolo said, crawling backward on the floor. "The fuzz is right outside."

Ellen ran to the window, peeking out, and Vinny kicked Rolo in the gut.

Otis pushed Vinny aside, kneeling down to clutch Rolo's throat. "I'm gonna ass rape you with a broom stick every day we're in the pen," he said in a growl.

Sasha pushed back a snicker and pulled a knife from the sheath on her belt.

"I don't see anyone out there." Ellen breezed across the room, opening a tall cabinet. She handed an assault rifle to Chewy then tossed one to Kev. "You, go check the perimeter."

Kev scampered from the room, and Sasha cut the shirt from Rolo's chest. She ripped a thin cable from his skin and then kicked him over. The cord led to a recorder, taped to Rolo's back, and Sasha pulled it off.

"It's not live. No one's listening." She handed the device to her mother and sheathed her blade.

A sinister laugh bellowed from Chewy's mouth. He sounded like an evil Santa. Vinny cracked his knuckles. It was about to get messy, hours-of-scrubbing-the-floor messy.

"He's your friend, Sasha. You vouched for him," her mother said, holding a dangerous glare.

Sasha glanced over her shoulder at Rolo. The compassion she felt for the man cowering in the corner enflamed her already blazing rage to a near-blinding status. This room was no place for the weak. She grabbed a handgun from the holster on her mother's belt and tucked it into her waistband.

"I'm taking him to the cellar," Sasha whispered into her mother's ear. "You need to get this place swept before we talk any more business."

When her mother's hand grazed her cheek, she fought to keep from flinching.

"That sounded just like your father. Go on."

Sasha backed away, turning to eye the seething men cornering the scrawny punk on the floor. "Guys, it's obvious Rolo doesn't want to be employed at Ashby Trucking any longer, so I'm gonna drop him off at his buddy's house." She strolled past furious faces and grabbed Rolo by his ripped shirt, yanking the sorry sack to his feet.

"I'll go with you," Vinny said, latching onto Rolo's other arm.

Chapter Two

Sasha climbed into her pickup truck. Rolo crammed against her side as Vinny slid onto the passenger seat, and she inched away. Rolo's body oozed treachery, and Sasha didn't want any of it rubbing off on her. She turned the key, the engine's roar rattling all the dashboard's loose bolts.

"You were staring at me," Sasha said, looking beyond Rolo to Vinny, "the whole meeting."

"I, ah…" Vinny shifted in his limited space, glancing out the window. "I worry about you."

"There's nothing to worry about."

"Are you gonna kill me, man?" Rolo sniveled. "'Cause you don't have to kill me, man. I got family in Canada. I can disappear. You'll never see me again."

Vinny leaned forward, looking across the cab. "I saw Candy creeping up your stairs first thing this morning, and I know you were out with her all last night. If Ellen catches you again—"

Kev popped from the bushes, running right in front of the truck, and Sasha slammed on the brakes. "Dude's a fucking spaz." She rolled down her window, resisting the urge to slap Kev on the forehead.

"I don't see shit," Kev said, hoisting his rifle on his shoulder. "This little prick's a liar."

"My mom needs you in the clubhouse. Might have a bug infestation."

"Might have," Kev grumbled, strolling away.

The truck rolled forward again, and her eyes coasted to Vinny. "I was out with Candy getting those pictures."

"Sasha, please," Rolo said with a whiny edge to his tone. "We've known each other since we were six."

"That's how I know you don't have any family in Canada. You did this to yourself. Go ahead, sit here and pretend you don't know what's up. I dare you." She drove up the hill behind her mother's house and into the woods.

Rolo rocked in his seat, clutching the ends of his ripped shirt. "Fuck, man. Fuck."

"Dude." Sasha parked in a small clearing and killed the engine. "If you piss yourself in my truck—"

"You'll what? Kill me more?"

A loud breath flowed from her throat. The guilt of this decision was starting to fade, which bothered her more than killing the man. She opened her door, and Vinny jumped from the truck. His large body blocked the passenger side. She leaned against the driver's door.

"Tell you what," she said, pulling the gun from her waistband. "I'll give you one chance to save your ass, since we're old friends. Tell me if you planted any bugs and I'll let you sneak off."

"You swear to fuckin' God, man?"

"Yeah."

Rolo looked between Sasha and Vinny, blood still dripping from his nose. "I was gonna put one in the meeting room today." He shoved his hand in his pocket, and Sasha raised the gun.

"It's cool." Slowly, Rolo pulled a small device from his torn jeans and handed it over.

"Why'd you turn on us?" Vinny barked, landing a solid punch on Rolo's chin. "We're the only real family you've ever had, you piece of shit."

"Man..." Rolo stared at his fidgety hands, his foot rapping the metal floor. "I don't have people lookin' out for me like you two. I gotta have my own back."

The twitch of Rolo's eyes, the way he kept rubbing his nose...Sasha had seen this act far too many times.

"You're all coked out," she said, her words laced with disgust.

Rolo's bloodshot eyes flew to Sasha, brimming with guilt, and she cocked back the gun's hammer. "Get out," she yelled, his body jumping in place.

"Aw, hell. You swore, Sasha."

Rolo inched closer, and she grabbed his arm, yanking him to the ground.

"I am letting you go, brother." Sasha gave Rolo a hard kick to the chest, then another to the gut when he rolled onto his side. There was nothing worse than a soft soul. If she could control her drug use, she expected everyone else to as well. "You're so

11

far gone, you sold us out to Satan's Crew for blow. Idiot, you're already dead."

Vinny rushed around the front of the truck, standing behind Sasha. "That's what he was doing?"

"Rolo?" Sasha glared down, the gun in her hand propped on her hip.

"Yeah, man," Rolo said to the leaves below him. "Women like you ain't never seen and eight-balls on tap. They said it could be my every day. All I had to do was…"

"Let them kill us and take our holler." Sasha crashed the butt of her gun against Rolo's cheek, knocking him flat to his stomach. "This was my father's mountain." She pointed the barrel at the back of his head, inching away.

"Get up," Vinny said. "You're going in the cellar, alive."

"Oh shit." Rolo hobbled to his feet, taking a small step. "I think I just pissed myself."

"You're lucky you did it out here, scumbag. You know, you always—"

Rolo bashed his forehead against Sasha's nose, flashing the world to red. She staggered back, and he kicked Vinny in the nuts before taking off in a sprint.

Tears welled in Sasha's eyes, rising up in attempts to soothe the sting of her face. She blinked back a watery haze. Vinny rocked on his knees while gasping for air, and Rolo ran across the hillside. Blood dripped down Sasha's chin as she raised the gun. With one eye closed, she held her breath and pulled the trigger.

Rolo tumbled to the ground before the shot could echo down the holler. Sasha reached for Vinny, and he pulled away.

"You okay?" she asked.

Vinny waved for her to go, his eyes low.

"Not so great having all that crap between your legs now, is it?" Sasha said with a grin. She trudged through tall brush, toward the whimper beneath a patch of ivy.

"You shot me!" Rolo screeched, flopping onto his back. His chest heaved as he blubbered and wiggled in the dirt. "My leg! Shit, man."

Sasha looked back at Vinny, who cupped his balls as he limped closer. The sun had slipped below the mountain's peak, leaving only thin rays to light the trees around them. This was taking too long. She had shit to do with someone far more attractive than the loser on the ground at her feet.

"If I give you a bump, will you jump in the cellar all by yourself?" Sasha asked, only half-joking.

Rolo stopped squirming, the howls ceasing to flow. His shifty eyes calmed, flying to her. "Yeah. Two bumps, big ones."

It might be hard to believe a man would jump to his death for a few lines of cocaine if Sasha hadn't seen people do worse for much less. Rolo's pleading eyes stared up at Sasha, and she almost unloaded her gun in his face. Instead, she dug through her pockets.

"Ellen probably heard that shot," Vinny said, stepping beside her. "What's up?"

"Hold this." Sasha handed Vinny the gun and pulled a small vial from her coat. Rolo hopped up

13

the moment he saw it, slithering forward. She poured a line of white powder on his palm, looking away as he snorted it up his nose.

"The other one," Rolo said through gasps, wiping his blood-smeared nose and licking his fingers.

"Fucking gross." Sasha bumped him another fix, cringing. "Your face could be an after-school special."

Vinny chuckled, grabbing Rolo by the arm. "Come on, narc."

They walked Rolo back toward the truck, stopping next to a metal storm door in the ground. Sasha fished a set of keys from her pants and unfastened the padlock. Hinges squealed as the door opened, and the stench of death wafting into the crisp air sent shivers down her spine.

Rolo cowered, staggering back. "Right, so—"

With a kick to the ass, Vinny sent Rolo plunging into the dark hole. After a second of yelps, a thud echoed from far below.

Sasha peered down, glimpsing only shadows. The seconds of silence provided a hint of relief. She hoped he'd died instantly. A broken neck was better than a slow death.

"Ahh, shit. Man," Rolo said, his voice sounding so far away. "Sasha, throw down the blow. Come on, please."

She tightened her grip on the vial. Stupid. That's what she was for feeling sorry for that piece of shit. "Kill yourself with the bones down there, 'cause we ain't coming back. Asshole."

Vinny closed the door on the screams that

bellowed from deep within the mine's shaft, and Sasha locked it tight.

"I think you should be my girl," Vinny said.

Sasha waited for the butt of his joke, but he held a straight face.

"What head did he kick you in, 'cause…?"

"I mean." Vinny stepped closer, tucking the gun into her waistband. "If we pretend, it would throw your mom off your pussy stink."

She giggled, walking toward her truck. "That's a super romantic offer, but I'm gonna have to pass. You need to be more chill. You're the one who's gonna get me busted."

Vinny followed Sasha to the truck, not saying a word the whole ride back. After parking beside the garage, she cut off the engine and turned to face him. His eyes were locked on her, a strange mix of icy warmth in his stare.

"Candy's gonna get you caught," he said in a bit of a huff. "With her bright red hair running up and down your stairs all hours." He took her hand inside both of his, holding snug. "*You* need to be more chill. I won't watch them stomp you again. It'll go down bad."

"Nah, you're right." Sasha pulled her hand away, patting Vinny on the arm. "I get it. I'll be more careful. C'mon." His eyes lingered on her. She didn't look; she could just feel them. "My mom is probably flippin' her shit right now."

***

Sasha pushed open the door to the backroom,

stepping inside.

"Well?" her mother asked, marching forward.

"I think we're cool. He had this on him." Sasha handed over the slim recorder then tucked the gun back into her mother's holster. "He was gonna plant it in here."

"Did you…?"

"Yeah, but there's more." Sasha sat at the end of the table, plucking a joint from the pile in the ashtray. Her gaze wandered around the empty room before the clink of a zippo lured her stare back. "Where is everybody?"

"Getting shit ready for Candy's party," her mother said, closing the zippo's lid once Sasha sparked the tip of the joint. "You must be pretty close with her, to get her to do…that."

"Not really." Sasha could hear the sound of jeans rustling behind her, and the scent of Vinny's cologne filled her lungs. "She's just another trucker slut trying to fuck her way into the club, but that won't work with me. No cock."

"Hey! Watch your nasty mouth, girl."

"Sorry, Mom," she said, her sarcasm rolling out thicker than the smoke curling from her lips.

Ellen plucked the joint from Sasha's fingers, taking a few quick hits. "So? You said there was more."

"Rolo was working for Satan's Crew, not the fuzz."

"Shit." Ellen sat on the edge of the table, hitting the bone again before handing it back. "Is that better or worse?"

Sasha shrugged, rising to her feet. "It's a hell of

a lot more fun to kill biker douchebags than pigs."

"Where are you going?"

"Shower, get ready for the party." Sasha headed for the door, passing Vinny the joint on her way out.

***

Drops of water splashed against tile as Sasha reached for a towel. It still bothered her, calling Candy a trucker slut. The girls who hung around the club coined the term themselves, saw it as a title of honor, but Sasha couldn't stomach separatist labels.

She wrapped herself tight in the towel and walked out of the bathroom. Vinny looked up from the corner of her bed, and she almost tripped over her own feet.

"What the fuck, dude?" she yelled, grabbing an empty pack of cigarettes from her dresser and chucking it at his head.

"Your mom saw me come up here."

"So?" Sasha stripped off her towel, using it to dry her hair. After a moment of silence, she looked at the bed and into a full-on gawk. "For real? Perv."

"God...damn."

"Jesus." She tossed the towel at his face then pulled on a pair of cargo pants. Once her bra was tightly fastened, she turned her glare back to him. "Blood going to your big brain now?"

"That's still just...yeah! Hey, come here for a minute."

"No way," Sasha said, crossing her arms.

"Just a little closer. I wanna see something."

Sasha crept forward, standing in front of Vinny.

17

He hooked his finger around her belt loop and pulled her onto the bed. He pressed his body against hers, his rough hand gliding along her side.

"Anything?" he asked, dragging his lips along her cheek.

Her spine was stiff. She felt something, all right, digging into her hip. There was also some awkwardness and a bit of impatience brewing in her chest, but he probably wasn't interested in that.

Slowly, Sasha shook her head. Vinny rolled off her, a long sigh sinking his chest. She'd been shooting Vinny down for years, but this was the first time she felt guilty. It was also the first time sparks filled her body when he rubbed up against her.

Sasha squirmed off the bed, grabbing a brush from her dresser. "So…?"

"Yeah. I'll see you later."

Vinny's shoulders slumped as he walked toward the door. She couldn't stand that look in his eye. The heavy layer of sadness that gripped his face kicked on her best friend instinct, and she rushed forward, blocking his path.

"I do like you." Sasha ducked to find Vinny's gaze, which was difficult since he kept dodging. "A lot. I just can't like you that way."

Vinny's hands landed on Sasha's arms, making a light slapping noise, and he moved her aside. "I'm gonna down a few shots and try to figure that out," he said, walking from the room without a glance back.

Chapter Three

Sasha parked in front of Candy's house, peering in the rearview mirror to adjust her bandana. The clack of heels lured her stare, but the sight of Candy working those hips in her headlights held it firm. She leaned across the bench seat, opening the passenger door. A tight skirt rode up Candy's thigh as she climbed into the truck. One of the many reasons Sasha loved this old pickup.

Candy slammed the rickety door shut, looked at Sasha, and leaned back. "What do ya think?" She held the flaps of her white leather coat open, showing off the skimpy black halter top beneath.

First, Sasha stared at the stretchy fabric, which clung to all the right places. That tiny white skirt wiped her mind clear, those matching thigh-high boots filling it back up with so many naughty thoughts. Then her eyes coasted along the hints of flesh that led to Candy's pouty lips, and she leaned in. "Delicious," she said in more of a breath then a word.

A cute giggle flowed through the cab as Candy

scooted closer. "So where are you taking me tonight? Dancing? They just opened a disco in Lexington."

"Ah shit."

"The club." Candy moved away, zipping her jacket. "You're ditching me, aren't you?"

"No." Sasha grabbed ahold of Candy's tightly coiled arms, wriggling them free. "There's a surprise for you tonight. It's just not what I had in mind."

Candy's body loosened, her lips curving up. A trace of lavender rushed into her nose, drawing Sasha toward its sweet scent. She grabbed onto Candy's silky thigh and squeezed. Tingles ignited under her fingertips, creeping beneath her skin and settling in her toes.

A horn honked down the block, and they both jumped.

Sasha shouldn't feel wrong for kissing her girl in the privacy of her own truck, but she did. The vinyl seat crinkled as she slid away from Candy, back behind the steering wheel. "We should get going."

***

Cars and trucks littered the compound of Ashby Trucking, a bonfire blazing outside the clubhouse. Sasha killed the engine, music and laughter replacing its rumble.

"There's a party tonight?" Candy flipped down the visor, checking her makeup in the mirror. "Nobody told me."

"Huh. Strange." Sasha jumped from the truck,

waiting by the front bumper.

Candy unzipped her coat, waving to a group of men before hurrying to Sasha's side. "Well, maybe we can just pop in then sneak out and chill somewhere," she said softly.

"We'll see." Sasha hung back, letting Candy enter the clubhouse alone.

Cheers overshadowed the thump of speakers, and Sasha stepped inside. She crept behind Candy, who spun to face her.

"The club threw me a party!" Candy said, her eyes brighter than her smile.

"A little thank you. Go. Have fun."

"Really?" Candy wiggled out of her tight jacket, backing away.

Sasha nodded, and Candy threw her coat into the corner.

"Somebody get this bitch a shot!" Candy yelled, disappearing into the crowd that swarmed her.

After a quick scan of the room, Sasha leaned against the wall. People slung greetings as they strolled by, and girls danced atop the bar, but her eyes followed Candy. The girl floated around the packed space, her flirty grin charming every person in its wake.

"You're staring," Vinny whispered over Sasha's shoulder, stepping beside her.

Sasha took one look at his smug face and returned her gaze to the crowd. Vinny blocked her view, grabbing her hand.

"Dance with me," he said, flashing a devious grin.

Guitars screamed through the speakers, and

drumbeats rattled Sasha's chest. "This isn't dancing music."

"So what? C'mon."

Vinny tugged her arm, and she dug in her heel.

"Don't leave me hanging." His voice verged the threshold of begging and she gave in, allowing him to guide her away from the wall. His hands fell to her waist, pulling her close. Amid rowdy voices, cackling women, and harsh guitar riffs, they swayed. When she glanced up and into his frosty blue eyes, the noises stopped. Only his hands on her body and those eyes remained.

"Your mom's watching us."

Bit by bit, Vinny moved Sasha in a circle. She caught a glimpse of her mother grinning and whispering with Chewy, which incited the urge to storm out the front door. Her body grew rigid, and Vinny gripped tighter, keeping her in a gentle rock. He leaned close, his breath tickling her neck.

"You should kiss me," he whispered in her ear.

Sasha flinched, and Vinny slid his hands to her back, holding firm.

"Don't pull away. It'll look shady."

Every party for the last six years, Vinny tried this shit. It was her fault for making out with him that one time when they were thirteen. The standard procedure of elbowing him in the gut and strutting away wouldn't work this time. This time, the sergeant at arms position was open, and the president was watching. Plus, Vinny had that goofy smirk, the one that lit his eyes in blue flames.

A peck from her best friend was a small price to pay to get her ass in that seat beside her mother.

Sasha glided her hands up Vinny's chest, skating her lips atop his. He kissed her like they were the only two people in the room. Her instincts screamed to pull away, but she didn't. She couldn't part from the only lips that spoke kindly to her, couldn't push away the one set of hands that never hurt her. When his tongue slipped into her mouth, she grinded into him. For being so free with his hands, she bit his bottom lip as she drew back.

"You're an asshole," she said before strolling outside.

***

Sasha sat on the wooden rail of the porch, leaning against a splintered post. Her stare drifted beyond the raging bonfire, ears tuning out laughter. It was that kiss. Her lips still tingled, body still hummed. Vinny did not kiss like that when they were thirteen.

"So, Vinny?" Ellen asked from behind Sasha.

Sasha turned to face her mother, getting a lit joint waved in her face instead of the usual wagging finger.

"It's not…" Her words bunched up when she caught the look in her mother's eyes. It had been a long time since anybody looked at her that way, with pride. "We're just messing around. It's not serious."

"That's cool." Ellen leaned against the railing and pointed to the window. "Looks like Otis is taking a shine to Candy."

"Really?" Sasha passed the joint back to her

mother and jumped off the rail. She peeked inside, zeroing in on bright red hair. Her stomach twisted as Candy nuzzled under Otis's arm, giggling.

"Guess the girl found her cock," Ellen said on her way back into the clubhouse.

Candy twirled her fingers into Otis's hair, and Sasha turned away. It should be her in there, inching between that girl's thighs. Floorboards thumped as she rushed off the porch. She hurried beyond a couple going at it against the side of a truck, lifting her hand to block the view of the dude's hairy ass. The club should respect her, no matter who she fucked. Her steps grew to stomps. She stormed past a bloody fistfight and toward the garage.

***

The rage of the party streamed through the window, disrupting the air with its buzz. Sasha got up from her bed and crashed the windowsill down, barely muffling the clamor. She dropped back onto her mattress, falling against the pillows, and a knock shook her door. Without parting her gaze from the ceiling or bothering to move, she yelled, "Fuck off."

The door scraped open, and heavy boots creaked the floor.

"I'm sorry," Vinny said, clinging to the doorframe. "That was a dickhead move."

Sasha sat up and peeled off her leather jacket. "Shut the door."

Vinny hesitated in the doorway, and Sasha

kicked off her boots. Like Vinny, her stoned mind hadn't caught on to her body's intentions, even after she striped off her top. "Come here," she said, throwing her shirt across the room.

Vinny slammed the door closed, dashing forward. His strong arms wrapped around her, and their lips connected. A tremble hid beneath his kiss, his touch, but that didn't prevent his hands from wandering. It was too late to stop now. Both their shirts were off, hearts racing. They surpassed the point of no return when Vinny's hand slid between her legs.

He guided her back to the mattress, and she tugged at his belt.

"I've been dreaming about this for years," Vinny said, kissing Sasha's cheek.

"Don't." The belt unlatched with a clink, and Sasha rolled on top of him. "Words just fuck shit up."

He drew her to his chest, course palms ravaging every inch of her bare flesh. She almost forgot the feel of a man. Large hands, rippling muscles, their bodies so hard yet soft at the same time, a false security.

Before Sasha could crawl from a lusty haze, Vinny had her pants off and glided inside her. She wanted it to feel right. Her life would be so easy if she could just like fucking him as much as she liked hanging with him, but each thrust brought a new wave of guilt. His gentle touch radiated affection, and she was using him.

Sasha pulled back, wrapping her fingers around Vinny's neck. "Harder," she said, squeezing.

***

Sasha walked out the door. The belt of her leather jacket clinked, and her boxer shorts rustled as she sat on the top step. A cool breeze gusted from high up the mountain, bringing shivers that ran along her spine. After lighting a cigarette, she pulled her bare legs inside the coat's flaps.

The emblem sown onto the back of her father's club jacket rubbed her skin. She couldn't see the crest that soothed her mind, but she knew it well. Her childhood was spent staring at the backs of club members who wore the same skins, each with the emblem of a Mack truck bursting through cherry-red flames. It was the symbol of Ashby Trucking, and it was ingrained in Sasha's mind.

Smoke rolled up in puffs as she watched people stumble to their cars. She tapped her cigarette, ashes sprinkling her toes, when Candy walked from the clubhouse under Otis's arm. Her door squeaked open behind her, and Vinny crouched down.

"What ya' doing?" he asked, following her stare to Otis's truck. Candy slid across the bench seat, her head dropping below the steering wheel and into Otis's lap. "Oh, shit. Sorry, Sasha."

She flicked her cigarette down the stairs and rose to her feet. Vinny stood up, reaching for her waist, and she slinked past him.

"I'll see you tomorrow," Sasha said, walking inside her room.

Vinny's voice flowed until Sasha shut her door on his babble. Her insides twisted, the ache a well-deserved punishment. Vinny got too close and

Candy too far, all because of her need to please the club. She flung off her jacket and walked into the bathroom, turning on the shower. The rush of water silenced her jagged thoughts. She climbed inside, catching her reflection in the mirror. A dash of sorrow, a hint of regret, and a pinch of shame, the recipe of her glare. The shower curtain crimpled under her grip, and she yanked it closed.

Once the water ran down her face, tears felt free to flow. There was something about the warmth, the way the droplets pelted her skin, that brought her pain to the surface. She stood there, under the downpour, hiding her tears under the water's gentle stream.

***

Vinny

Vinny strolled across the lot, twirling his keys on his finger. A zippo's click pulled his stare to the clubhouse. When spotting Ellen on the porch, he veered in her direction.

"Did you tell her?" Ellen asked, puffing on a hand-rolled cigarette.

"I tried to, but she shut the door in my face."

"You were up there for over two hours."

"Yeah?" Vinny rubbed the back of his neck, glancing away to hide his smirk.

"That's fucked." Ellen tossed her cigarette at his feet. "Sasha's gonna be totally blindsided at tomorrow's meeting."

"I know. I'm sorry, Ellen." Vinny glanced up at

Sasha's door. He'd run up there and deliver the bad news, but it would ruin everything they just did. Then he'd never be able to do all those amazingly dirty things to her again. "Can't you just tell Sasha in the morning?"

Ellen walked down the porch steps, pulling him from the commotion of a slowly dying party. "As her mother, I'd like to warn her, but as club president, it's…inappropriate." She paused as a group of men staggered to their trucks. "That's why I was counting on you. Just, whatever. Go home."

Vinny shoved his hands into his pockets, turning away.

Chapter Four

Sasha

A high-pitched ring pulled Sasha from a deep sleep. She slipped her head under the pillow, only dulling the phone's blare. When the noise finally stopped and a heavy silence returned, she closed her eyes. It was no use. She'd already glimpsed the light of a new day. Her brain wasn't shutting off now.

The phone screamed once again, and Sasha slapped the nightstand. She grabbed a lighter, a handful of cigarette butts, and an empty beer bottle before finding the phone. The ring stopped once she lifted the receiver. She considered hanging up, but the idiot in her pulled the receiver under the pillow.

"Hello," she grumbled.

"Hey. Did I wake you?"

Candy's silky voice sent a flutter from Sasha's chest to her gut and right into the deepest parts of her soul. "No. I was up." She moved the pillow aside, clutching onto the phone's wide mouthpiece.

"Crazy party last night, huh?"

"Are you dating Vinny?"

"What?" Sasha sat up, the phone's cord yanking its base from the nightstand.

"Ellen was telling everyone you two are a thing."

"Is that why you gave Otis a blowjob in the parking lot?"

"You saw that?" Candy asked softly.

"A lot of people saw that."

There was a long pause. Sasha could see Candy's cute frown and the girl's remorseful eyes clearly inside her mind. If they were face to face, she would wither against Candy's smooth skin. Hell, she almost crumbled through the phone.

"Sasha—"

A clicking noise cut off Candy's words, and Sasha groped for the phone's base.

"Hold on a sec." Sasha clicked a skinny red button, flashing over to the other line. "Yeah."

"Oh, hey. It's Vinny."

"So formal. Use the phone much?"

"I…umm…"

"What'd you want?" Sasha asked, almost hanging up before she even got an answer.

"I really need to talk to you before the meeting."

Sasha moved a wall of beer bottles away from the clock on her nightstand. "We got an hour. Just come over now."

"No, I can't. I—"

Sasha groaned. Vinny could babble for hours and never about anything major, which was why she clicked back over to Candy. "You still there?"

"Of course," Candy said in a throaty whisper. "I

always wait for you."

For just a second, a fleeting thought crossed Sasha's mind. She could jump in her truck, pick up Candy, and drive to San Francisco. They could open a flower shop or maybe sell makeup. It was a nice thought to have, for just that second.

"You busy tonight?"

"No," Candy said, almost before Sasha could finish the question.

"I'm gonna come pick you up later, like nine or ten."

"Should I wear something pretty?"

"Nah." Sasha tried to sound cool, but the frown stuck on her lips warped her words into ones filled with gloom. "I just wanna talk. You know."

"Oh. Yeah, I ah…see you then."

With a click, the line went dead. Sasha gathered up the phone and returned it to her nightstand, rising from the bed.

***

Light spilled into Sasha's room as she opened her door, forcing her back a few steps. The cigarette stuck to her chapped lips decided to waft its smoke right into her eyes, making the whole sunshine situation much worse. She pushed a pair of shades up the bridge of her nose, thumping down the narrow stairs.

"Caffeine," Sasha muttered, her feet dragging across gravel. She climbed the porch steps, and Kev blocked the clubhouse door.

"It's almost noon," Kev said, crossing his arms

to bar her from squeezing by him. "Are you just getting up?"

A mix of a grunt and a grumble erupted from Sasha's lips, coaxing Kev aside. Her eyes locked onto a steaming pot of coffee. The scent of liquid energy filled her lungs, and she hurried toward the aroma, nearly tripping when a tall blonde chick stepped in front of her.

"Hey, Sasha!"

"Hey, umm…"

"Robin!"

"Right." Sasha moved to the side, but the chick followed like a shadow.

"Are you busy right now?" Robin asked. "I was gonna step outside for a smoke."

Sasha glanced around the now-trashed clubhouse. The usual batch of women decorated the bar while most of the crew crowded into the backroom. Thankfully, none of them had noticed her.

"Sure. Just," Sasha pointed around Robin to the silver urn on the bar, "coffee."

"Oh! I'll get that for you." Robin turned, glass clinking. "No cream, five sugars. Right?" She peeked over her shoulder, a sly smile on her red lips.

"Yeah, that's right."

Robin handed Sasha a mug and headed for the porch. "Come on."

While sipping her coffee, Sasha enjoyed the sway of Robin's ass in tight leather pants. She strolled to the porch, sitting on the bench. In every attempt to be casual, she eyed the woman beside her. Feathered hair straight from a bottle, bright eyeshadow in hues of blue and green. A regular bleached Barbie.

"Are you going with Vinny?" Robin asked, cringing as if expecting a slap for an answer.

A chuckle burst from Sasha's lips. That seemed to be the question of the day. "No." Except that wasn't the game they were playing. "I don't know. Maybe." She lit a cigarette, passing it to Robin before popping one in her own mouth. "Why, you into him?"

"No," Robin said, a little too fast. "He's not extremely sexy at all." She batted her eyes, which wavered in fear. "Please don't beat me up."

"Why would I beat you up?" Sasha asked, taking another sip of her coffee.

"I didn't know about you two, and I was laying it on kinda thick last night before you got here. I might have touched his—"

"Whoa! I don't need to know all that. Vinny is free to do whatever he wants with whoever he likes."

"I get that." Robin scooted closer, leaning in and bringing the scent of Halston with her. "You have to be a different type of gal around these men, hard. Even if it really doesn't bother you, I'll still keep my hands off. Until you're done with him, anyway."

"Thanks," Sasha said through a grin. "I appreciate it."

"You're not scary at all. We should hang out some time."

Sasha flicked her cigarette across the lot, holding

back a snicker. "I guess we could chill, do chick shit. You like shooting guns?"

A giggle skirted from Robin's lips, but it didn't hold a candle to the ones in Candy's arsenal. "I never shot a gun, but I'd like to learn."

"Okay. Maybe after the meeting we—"

"Sasha." Vinny gripped Sasha's shoulder, and she flinched, spilling a drop of coffee on her pants.

"Goddammit, Vinny."

Sasha handed the mug to Robin, jumping to her feet.

"I gotta talk to you," Vinny said, tugging on her arm.

Sasha pulled away, brushing at the stain. "You're lucky these pants are brown, asshole."

The thump of boots rattled the porch. A chill traveled up Sasha's spine, locking her in place. She could only stand there and stare at the brick shithouse of a man who'd walked into the clubhouse, at the last face she saw before passing out after the lesson her mother had the club teach her when she was fourteen. Desmond Archer. Sasha crept forward, watching his long hair tap the holler's emblem of his leather jacket.

"Your brother's out of jail," she muttered, glancing at Vinny.

"I've been trying to tell you since last night."

"Fuck. Dez?" Sasha slumped against the doorway, watching Dez walk into the backroom. "He's gonna want the sergeant at arms spot."

"I know," Vinny said softly.

"He'll probably get it too. He has seniority over me."

"I know," Vinny muttered, his eyes low.

"Fuck, Vinny!" Sasha stormed inside, making a beeline for the backroom. Her mother released Dez from a tight embrace as she walked through the door.

"Sasha, look who's out," Chewy said.

Dez turned, stopping to stare at Sasha. His eyes scanned every inch of her body. She could almost feel the intensity of his glare, like the thickness after a lightning storm.

"Sasha? Damn, you've grown." Dez stepped closer, tugging at the flap of her jacket. "You're wearing a skin." He looked at Ellen. "She's at the table now?"

"Her and your little brother made prospect about three years ago. Wow, you really have been gone a while, huh?"

"Almost six years," Dez said, shooting Sasha a harsh glare. "Where's Ron?"

"Oh shit." Ellen grabbed a beer from the small fridge behind her, handing it to Dez. "We lost Ronny, Jay, and Mad Dog last month."

"What?" Dez grabbed the beer, downing half the bottle in one gulp.

"Satan's Crew tore through town, things got ugly. Here," Ellen gestured to the long glossy table, "take a load off."

Dez moved toward his old chair, and Kev grabbed his hand.

"Sorry, brother," Kev said, looking down. "I was voted master of mayhem after you left."

"Shit, Ellen. I lost my position."

Vinny and Otis walked into the room, shutting

the door behind them, and Sasha dropped into her seat before she ended up in a corner.

"Here it comes," she mumbled beneath her breath as Vinny sat in his seat beside her.

"Sorry, Dez," Ellen said, taking her spot at the head of the table. "But someone had to put the parties together."

"Nah, it's cool." Dez settled into the chair at the end of the table, casting Sasha a quick leer. "People, parties, it wasn't really my thing anyway."

Once everyone took their seats, Ellen lit a joint and passed it to Chewy. "Not much has changed," she said, looking at Dez. "Chewy is still V.P. Otis is road captain. We have the sergeant at arms and two runner spots open. Yesterday our vote was…interrupted, so you've got perfect timing."

Dez rubbed the stubble on his chin, eyeing the empty seat at Ellen's left. "Sergeant, huh!"

The room fell under a blanket of silence, all eyes shifting to Sasha.

"Am I missing something?" Dez asked, glancing around the table.

"You missed a lot," Sasha said, leaning back in her chair.

"Sasha's been gunning for that spot," Ellen said, biting back a smirk.

"Oh yeah?" Dez turned to face Sasha, and his grin dropped once he glimpsed her narrowed eyes.

"Sasha really stepped up when we needed it," Chewy said.

"She found the biker fags' warehouse and firebombed it," Kev added, shooting Sasha a grin. "And yesterday—"

"A little girl, protecting the club." Dez snorted, shaking his head. "You all trust her with your lives?"

"Let's start with something easier," Ellen said. "I nominate Vinny as runner."

Chewy nodded. "I second that."

"All in favor," Ellen said.

Sasha slouched in her chair as the patched members voted. Her eyes drifted over, into Dez's glare. It looked like he wanted to fuck her and fight her at the same time. Creepy, yet a tingle slithered beneath her skin, lifting the hairs on her arms. She turned to Vinny, who took a thin patch marked **'*Runner*'** from her mother's hand.

"I nominate Dez as sergeant at arms," Otis said, his stare fixed on his lap. "Sorry, Sasha."

Sasha looked at the faces around the table. They all avoided her glare except for her mother, who was brimming with satisfaction.

"I don't know if I'm ready to vote on this yet," Chewy said, stroking his long, gray beard.

"All right. Tell you what." Ellen fished two sets of keys from her pocket. "We got two runs today. Kev, you take Dez. Get him caught up." She passed the key with a red tab to Kev and slid the other set to Sasha. "And you can show Vinny the ropes."

Ellen rose from her seat, peering around the table. "We'll reconvene the vote later."

Sasha grabbed the key from the table. The key's metal ridges pressed into her palm as she squeezed her hand into a fist. Once the room cleared with only her mother remaining, she rose from her chair. Their eyes connected. Her mother lifted her chin

37

and crossed her arms. Sasha lowered her glare. Every member of the club knew Charles Ashby, the true but now deceased president of Ashby Trucking, wanted Sasha in that sergeant's seat. They also knew an argument with the new president would only end well for the new president.

Much like a punk would do, Sasha kept her gaze on the faded wood floor and walked out of the room.

Chapter Five

Ten minutes. They got ten minutes down the interstate before Vinny started tapping the steering wheel. Sasha kept her gaze out the passenger window. Colors melded as trees whizzed by. The whistle of the diesel engine warmed the ice in her veins, until…

"So…"

Vinny's voice cut into Sasha's one second of peace, and she exhaled loudly, but that didn't stop him from blabbering on.

"You let me do some really dirty things to you last night."

Her hand flew to her forehead, as if trying to create a barrier between them. It wasn't working.

"Things I've never done with anyone else before," he continued.

Sasha turned to face Vinny, catching a hint of puppy love behind his electric blue eyes. "You can file all those things away in your spank-bank, 'cause it's never happening again."

"C'mon. I *know* you had a good time."

Vinny's hand landed on Sasha's thigh, and she shoved it away. "Don't fuckin' touch me."

"Damn." Vinny lit a cigarette, hurling glares between puffs. "If you don't want to be with me, why'd you fuck me?"

Sasha shrunk into her worn cloth seat, as far away as possible. "I was lonely. I wanted hands on me. It didn't matter whose they were."

"Ouch." Vinny flicked his ashes out the window, staring at the road ahead.

Hurt spanned his face, and a weight tugged on Sasha's heart. The urge to comfort him drew her hand out. A pothole rocked the cab, and she pulled back.

"Gimme your skin," she said, reaching into the back compartment.

"Why?"

Sasha held up a mini sewing kit. "I'm gonna sew your patch on."

"I don't get you." In rough yanks, Vinny pulled off his coat. "At all." He delivered a harsh glare along with his jacket.

Her hands went straight to work, but the stitches couldn't mend the rift that now lay between them. "You need this patch on when we get there or we'll both get shot."

"You don't have a patch."

"Everybody knows me. I've done this run a million times."

"Whatever. Just tell me when to turn."

That bitter fringe in Vinny's voice, the stiff edge that cut the air...more reasons she hated herself for fucking her best friend.

"My plan," Sasha said meekly, without glancing up, "was to treat you like shit to keep from leading you on. I didn't want you to know I had a good time last night. I didn't want you to think we were…"

"That's a stupid plan." Vinny's tense body loosened, a hint of a smile lifting his cheeks.

"I like what we have. I really don't wanna fuck it up."

"Tell me about this run," he said, his tone, look, mood, all back to the normal, chilled Vinny mode.

"It's a seven-hour trek south to Gulfport. We park at a dock and wait for the boat from Cancun. You give the Mexicans the briefcase, and they load the trailer. One hundred pounds on a pick-up."

"Oh shit! Really?"

"Yep." Sasha glanced across the cab between throwing stitches, Vinny's eyes growing wider each time. "So if you ever get pulled over on the way back, you better have your finger on the trigger. The weed's stuffed in teddy bears and crated up, but you never know. Sometimes the fuzz is just another biker-douche in disguise. That's how they got Mad Dog."

"I didn't bring a gun."

Sasha dropped her hands, the needle piercing leather. "You went on a run without packing proper?" She lifted the flap of her jacket, the butt of a gun strapped into her holster. "I got ya this time, but—"

"This time?"

"Yeah. You'll be ridin' solo soon, so pay attention, especially when we deal with Felix."

"Where's the other truck going?" Vinny asked.

41

"They're doing a drop-off. They took the red truck, that's ten pounds, to our buyer in Chicago. I'll go with you on drop-offs until everyone's comfortable. They're always more intense than pick-ups." Sasha looped the thread, pulled tight, and snipped the end.

"There you go." Sunlight shined off the runners badge as she held up the jacket. "A patched member of Ashby Trucking. You should be proud. I'm…proud of you."

After dropping the coat in Vinny's lap, Sasha wrapped her fingers around the wheel. "Put it on."

Slowly, Vinny released his control over the eighteen-wheeler. He slithered into his second skin and pulled the collar snug against his neck. He rested his palm atop Sasha's hand, and his gaze fell to her for a split second.

Sasha slid from his grasp, moving back into her seat. It wasn't Vinny acting different. He always pawed at her, flashed playful grins, proposed lewd acts. It was her. Sometime between last night and this morning, she forgot how to be cool. Sasha spun toward her window. She'd give herself twenty minutes to get her mojo back before she started faking it.

***

Dez

"You guys are pretty serious about this Sasha bullshit, huh?" Dez asked, although it was a stupid question. It only took him one glance to see the fire in her stare, which burned so bright it made him want to follow it to the ends of the Earth.

Kev shifted into ninth gear, stepping on the gas. "Sasha's a lot different since Ellen had you and the guys..."

"Teach her a lesson."

"Yeah." Kev rubbed the side of his neck, his nose scrunching. "I guess. I still don't know what she did. It must've been major to earn a beat down like that."

"I'm not telling you," Dez mumbled from behind the flame of his zippo, a cigarette hanging from his lips.

"Nah, that's cool. I'm just saying, you got sent away the next day so you don't know what it was like for her."

Dez sat back, dropping his glare. He knew the aftermath of a beat down, received plenty as a child, though he never thought he'd deliver one to a child. The day one of Sasha's bones cracked under his boot haunted him. It would always haunt him.

"She had a broken jaw," Kev rambled on, as if chatting about the features on a new Ford pickup and not the damage Dez inflicted on a little girl. "Her one eye was swelled shut for days, and she had this limp, still happens when it's rainy, but Ellen wouldn't let Sasha see a doctor or rest. The next day, Ellen had her mopping the clubhouse floor. The girl couldn't even stand. It was—"

"I don't think this is what Ellen meant by getting me caught up."

"Oh shit." Kev looked at Dez, grimacing. "Sorry, that's a total downer. You probably wanna hear about all the hot tail running around the clubhouse these days."

"Fuck, finally. Now you've got my attention."

***

Sasha

Sasha peered in the side mirror of the big rig, scooting to the edge of her seat. "Cut the lights. Pull up to the dock and kill the engine."

Gravel crunched under the weight of a creeping semi. The engine clunked, its rumble giving way to a chorus of cicadas.

"Now what?" Vinny asked.

A grin swept Sasha's lips. The shake in Vinny's voice reminded her of the first time they boosted a car together, eight years ago. It was kind of cute.

"Now, we wait." She stared out the windshield at the last sliver of sun, setting fast beyond shaggy trees. "Keep one eye on the gulf, the other on your mirrors."

Sasha tucked her jacket behind her holster, glancing around. "This is private property. Cops don't come this deep into the swamp, so if you hear anything strange out here—"

"Finger on the trigger."

"Yep. The boat will come from that direction." Sasha leaned across the cab, pointing to the gentle waves out Vinny's window. Her chest brushed against his arm, and he turned to face her. Warm breath flowed over her cheek, and her throat clamped shut. She backed away, swallowing hard.

"You're supposed to be watching."

"Right." Vinny adjusted his perfectly fine belt, his eyes darting back to his window. "What am I watching for?"

"When the boat gets close, it'll blink its lights. Three times, once, then twice. Got that?"

"Yeah."

"Then you flash the running lights twice."

Vinny recited the information in a near whisper when a pattern of lights flickered from the dark stretch of water. The trees lit up as he pulled a knob on the dashboard and a boat's motor revved.

"You ready?" Sasha asked, opening her door.

While nodding, Vinny reached for the handle and missed.

"Relax." Sasha jumped to the ground. "They'll smell your fear." A grin spread across her lips as she strolled to the front of the semi. When Vinny stepped beside her, she slapped on a tough leer, nodded, and walked toward the dock.

A charter boat moored beside the concrete wharf, sending little waves to rush onshore. Dim beams of moonlight shimmered off an emblem of a falcon amid flames, the words *Gulf Runner Tours* scrawled in red along the bow.

"Is that my Sasha?" Felix climbed from the boat, his short stubby legs barely clearing its tall side. He stopped on the pier, smoothed the ends of his white suit, and slid his fingers along the brim of his matching hat. With outstretched arms, he traipsed forward. "My girl."

"Uncle Felix," Sasha said, her smile spreading wide.

45

After scooping Sasha into a tight embrace, Felix stopped to eye Vinny. "Who's this?"

Before Sasha could answer, a flood of men surrounded Vinny—rifles raised, guns cocked. Vinny froze mid-step.

"This is Vinny. He's our new runner."

The barrels remained aimed at Vinny's chest, his nervous eyes on Sasha.

"*¿Está la policía?*" Felix asked, staring into Vinny's eyes.

"I, uh." Vinny's cheeks turned red as he shrugged.

"You know. *El hombre*. The fuzz." Felix nodded, and the man beside him patted Vinny down.

"Nah, he's cool." Sasha inched back, allowing the men to roughly frisk Vinny. "Known the guy since second grade. Poor bastard hasn't stopped following me since."

"Smart man." Felix waved his hand, sending his men back to the boat. He placed his hands on Sasha's shoulders, rubbing softly. "To what do I owe the honor of your presence, my dear?"

"Just training the new guy. And I missed you, of course."

Felix chuckled, his chest heaving, as a line of men hauled crates to the back of the truck behind him. "I'm happy to see you, dear, but…isn't this a little beneath you?"

Sasha frowned, her gaze dropping to the still patchless breast of her jacket. "We've had some issues. Satan's Crew. You might be seeing a lot more of me."

"*Pinche maricon*," Felix muttered, his expression turning venomous for the briefest of seconds. "It'll be nice to see your face more often, but I'd like to see a patch on that skin."

"Tell me about it."

"Sometimes I don't know what Ellen is thinking. Ahh, if I were twenty years younger, I'd whisk you away from all this. But then, you're too good for me." Felix glided his thumb along Sasha's cheek, sparking a smile. "You know you can call me anytime if the shit gets thick. Your enemies are my enemies, no matter who they are. *¿Comprendes?*"

"*Si. Gracias.* You're too kind, Felix."

"Only to you, my dear, only to you."

The cargo door of the semi slammed shut. Men gathered by the dock, clinging to their rifles, and Sasha looked at Vinny. "The case," she said, motioning to Felix.

Vinny crept forward, handed over a black briefcase, and nodded.

"I don't know about this one, princess." Felix rubbed his smooth chin, eyeing Vinny. "Too stiff, fidgety."

After another round of hugs and soft Spanish words, Felix left Sasha's side and returned to the charter boat. Her smile faded as the little red light of the stern disappeared behind mist.

"How is that man your uncle?" Vinny asked, scanning Sasha from head to toe. "You don't look Mexican."

"He's not my real uncle." Sasha glared at Vinny like the dummy he was, walking toward her truck. "C'mon, let's hammer down. It's a long ride home."

Chapter Six

Ellen

A diesel engine rumbled the clubhouse floor, and Ellen rose from her desk. She peeked out the window of the backroom as Dez jumped from the shining cab of a semi. His tight jeans hugged every curve as he walked, bringing a smirk to her lips.

Cheers rang out from the bar, echoing through the doorway of the backroom. Ellen strolled to the threshold, staring into the bar. Women swarmed Dez by the pool table, rowdy locals filed through the open door, and speakers crackled to life.

In almost slow motion, Dez steered his gaze to her, and she dipped her head. He cut through the crowd, walking into the backroom, and she shut the door.

"How was your run?" Ellen leaned against the wall, crossing her arms. It was hard not to stare. His large muscles had doubled in size since he'd gone away, and those eyes of his seemed even bluer.

"Like skinning a biker," Dez said.

Her own chuckle caught her by surprise, and she flung off the grin.

"What's up, prez?"

"This vote might go downhill for you. Sasha has Chewy, Vinny, and Kev. You..."

"Don't you want your daughter to be sergeant at arms?"

"Yeah. Maybe in five years. She's not ready yet. The girl's sloppy, wild. She'll get herself killed." Ellen's stare sharpened, and Dez shifted. "I think Sasha will back down if she's challenged."

Dez squirmed in his chair, his jaw clenching. "You mean—"

"No. Sasha needs a heavy hand, just not that kind of heavy. You dig what I'm saying?"

A devious gleam ran through Dez's eye, followed by a snicker. "I got ya."

"Go." Ellen motioned to the closed door. "Enjoy your party."

***

Sasha

Sasha passed Vinny a lit cigarette. The last six hours flew by, thanks to his endless chatter about their past misadventures. She had forgotten half the dumb shit they'd done, until now.

"How much longer?" Vinny asked, wiggling in his seat.

"About an hour. We should catch the tail-end of your brother's party."

"Don't we have to unload this shit at the

warehouse?"

"No. Only the prez and road captain know the location of the warehouse."

"And you," Vinny said, glancing at Sasha.

"Right. That's different. When my dad was prez, he took me everywhere with him, even let me drive the forklift to unload the crates." Sasha turned her gaze to the window, leaning into a gentle breeze. "I stole one of those teddy bears when I was nine. Two years later, I found out what was in them, ripped the head off, and smoked that shit. It was all dry and flakey, nasty."

Vinny's laugh filled the cab, pushing a smile onto Sasha's lips.

"Is it weird," Sasha asked, stealing the cigarette from Vinny's mouth, "having your brother back around?"

"Sort of. Dez is crashing at my place for a few days until he gets set up. That'll be weird. I got used to living alone."

"You should tell him to beat feet. He treated us like shit when we were younger."

"Yeah right. He'd probably kick my ass then take my room." Vinny smirked, but a hint of fear shined through.

"Dez does have a mean right hook." Sasha peered across the cab, frowning.

"Yeah."

Brakes whistled as Vinny steered off the highway and onto their ramp. They merged onto a skinny road, heading up into the hills, and he sighed. "I can't wait to get out of this truck. My ass is numb."

***

The sweet smell of sticky bud wafted from the clubhouse, and Sasha closed her eyes, inhaling the scent deeply. Vinny stood beside her, leaning against the front bumper of the semi to join her in staring at the rowdy swarms of people trampling their clubhouse.

"Weed," Sasha said, stretching as she walked toward the voices that flowed over loud music.

Two men burst from the front door, tumbling down the porch steps while locked in a backwoods brawl. Sasha steered her gaze from flying fists and spurts of blood, looking at Vinny. "One in the morning and it's still jamming. Here, gimme the keys."

"Sweet. I gotta take a leak." Vinny thrust the keys into Sasha's palm and squeezed his way inside the clubhouse.

Sasha stepped around the bloody men on the ground and pushed through the growing crowd. She wasn't even two feet inside when her mother waved her over. Tiny leather skirts and near nonexistent tops surrounded Sasha, yet somehow she managed to walk through the room with her eyes high.

"It's all good," Sasha said, handing the keys to Otis and reaching for her mother's joint. "Felix says hi."

"I doubt that." Ellen yanked her hand away, blocking Sasha from the roach in her fingers. "Felix hates me. Always said—"

"You weren't good enough for his brother from another mother. I know. I've heard it."

51

Ellen snickered, passing the joint to Otis.

"Hey, Sasha, will you give me a hand unloading?" Otis asked between hits.

"Shit. I just got back, man."

Otis held out a tiny smoking stub of a joint. "Please."

"All right," Sasha said, as if she could deny a request from her road captain. "Just give me twenty minutes to get my head on straight."

As Sasha walked from the clubhouse, Dez caught her eye. He sat on the small couch, a cute blonde under each arm. Sasha slowed her steps, listening as she passed.

"My fist shattered the whole side of this guy's face. That's why they gave me seven years, but overcrowding…"

Sasha stopped short, her glare shooting to Dez. He flinched and she recoiled, then rushed out the door. She almost made it off the porch when Dez called out from behind her. "Sasha!"

"What!" Sasha spun on her heels, staring straight into Dez's eyes.

Dez strolled into the doorway, smirking as he leered down at Sasha. "You know how shit was handled in the old days, when two club members wanted the same position?"

Chatter lulled to a hush around the compound, and Dez raised a brow. He waited for something, Sasha to argue or maybe throw a punch, but she kept her lips shut and her face blank.

"They had to slug it out," Dez said, the words carrying chills. "I say we settle this the old-fashioned way." He lifted his arms at his side, and his stare locked on her face. "If you can drop my ass, the spot's yours."

Beside the echo of music, a stillness clutched the air. Her gaze never left his, but she could feel a hundred other eyes on her. Without a word, Sasha turned and walked to her little room above the garage.

***

Otis revved the engine of a rumbling semi as Sasha hurried down the stairs. Twenty minutes was not enough. One could only suck down two joints in that time, and she needed far more narcotics to regain normal operational status. Her eyes kept to the gravel as she walked to the idling semi, ears blocking out whispers. She should be fuming. Cartoon smoke should be streaming from her every orifice, but it wasn't. The fact that she wasn't angry bothered her more than the humiliation. The piece of her that harbored dignity must have shattered. That, or she was just too numb. Either one would get her eaten alive.

After climbing back in the truck, and once they left the compound, Sasha turned to face Otis. "So what's this really about?"

"What'd you mean?"

"You don't need help unloading. There's a forklift at the warehouse."

Otis glanced at Sasha, his eyes stern. "Candy's got loose lips."

"So I've heard."

The chuckle that flowed from Otis's mouth

twisted Sasha's stomach, and that lovely visual of Candy going down on him popped into her mind.

"That's not what I mean." Otis shifted into seventh gear, glaring at her again. "She talked about you, a lot, the way a chick talks about a dude she's into. Except you're not a dude. No matter how hard you try, you can't change what you are."

A light shiver quaked Sasha's shoulders, but she couldn't tell if anger or fear was the culprit. "And what am I?"

"Just a little girl who likes to play with all the other little girls."

Sasha moved back until her side hit the door. Fear. The shiver was caused by fear. "What are you gonna do?"

"What? You mean, like, tell Ellen?"

When Otis looked at Sasha, she nodded as words failed.

"Nah. Ellen would throw you in the cellar this time. I don't want to see you hurt. That's why I nominated Dez." His hand fell to her knee, and he squeezed. "You have some tough choices to make, kiddo."

"I know what I want," Sasha said. She'd spent many nights pondering her choices. "The club is all that matters to me, my whole life. I just wanna do right by you guys. You're my family."

Otis rubbed Sasha's leg before releasing his grasp. "Then you better straighten up, if you know what I mean."

"No more of that shit," Sasha said. "Women, men, fuck all that. It's just club business from now on."

"That's not gonna work either." Otis parked beside the warehouse, cutting off the truck's engine. "Club members have fun. If you're not having fun, Ellen's gonna know something's up."

"So, what? I just slut around until I find the magic cock?"

Otis snickered, turning to face Sasha. "Maybe. I got one right here you can try." He grabbed his crotch, grinning.

"You dirty old man," Sasha said in an even tone.

"Old." Otis's hand dropped from his lap, his smile fading. "I'm only thirty-eight."

***

A hush had claimed the compound by the time they returned. Otis climbed from the semi and into his pickup. After a quick nod, he drove off, leaving Sasha alone in the empty lot.

She walked toward the garage, noticing a light in her bedroom window. "Vinny," she said, hurrying across the lot. She took the steps two at a time, stopping to smooth down her hair before opening the door. When spotting Dez on the corner of her bed, she choked back a groan.

"Excuse you," Sasha said in a sneer, holding her hand out to the open door.

Dez grinned, rising to his feet.

"Leave," she said, since he was too dim to pick up on her hand gestures.

The frost melted from Dez's stare as he walked toward Sasha. He grabbed the door, his chest brushing against her arm. "I'm not going anywhere," he said, slamming the solid slab closed.

"What the fuck, Dez? Nobody's here to watch you put on a show."

"You'd do the same thing if some youngin' came in here flashing their shit."

"Youngin'?" Sasha took a deep breath. It was either that or slug Dez. He reached for her hand, and she pushed past him, yanking off her coat.

"This was supposed to play out different," Dez said, almost to himself.

"What are you talking about?" Sasha tossed her jacket into a corner, searching her nightstand for a joint.

"I went to jail because of you."

That stopped Sasha's fumble with the ashtray, and she stood up straight. "How do you figure? 'Cause the last time I saw you, before you got pinched, you were shattering the side of *my* face with that fist of yours."

"Yeah." Dez rushed toward Sasha and she backed away, bumping her nightstand. Bottles clinked as he froze in place. "I couldn't stand what I did to you. I couldn't stop feeling your bones break, so I took it out on some asshole in a bar."

"That's not my fault."

"I'm not blaming you," Dez shouted in a way that clashed with his words. "But I spent sixty-eight months thinking of ways to make it up to you. This sergeant at arms shit is fucking that up."

The air grew thick between them, and Sasha slithered away from the intense stare bearing down on her. Dez grabbed the sides of her arms, driving her back against the wall. She held her breath. Her coward of a mind fled, leaving her head empty and body trapped inside the fire behind Dez's icy blue eyes.

"You're reckless," he said, pressing against her. "Too smart for your own good. You'll hurt the club, hurt yourself."

"Let me go."

Dez squeezed tighter, grinding against Sasha harder. "Say it again, with more fear, and I will."

Sasha turned her head, skin rubbing skin. Their lips hovered over one another, generating an electric charge. Dez's hand glided along her cheek, sparking prickles of heat, and Sasha fell into his kiss. It all stopped. Her whirling thoughts, tight chest, aching heart, they all dwindled under his touch.

Dez spun Sasha toward the wall, her forearms slamming onto wooden planks. Hands traveled her body, teeth digging into the back of her neck. His fingers slid inside her pants, and a moan scraped past her throat. This was right. Rough, hard. That's what she needed. That's what she deserved.

Her tank top flew over her head, bra dropping to the floor. She turned, but her eyes wouldn't lift to Dez's face. Her hands, however, couldn't keep off the ripples on his chest as he removed his shirt. When her courage kicked on, Sasha looked up from the muscles in front of her. Dirty blonde hair tumbled from Dez's shirt, splashing over his wide shoulders, and a somewhat wicked giggle slipped from her mouth. Dez gripped Sasha by the waist, skating his lips along her neck. He pushed her to the bed, knocking a gasp from her lungs.

Sasha stared up at Dez, reaching for the button of

her pants.

"No," he said, dropping to his knees. "I want to." He tugged on her pants, peeling the fabric free from her skin. "It's been so long since I've tasted a woman."

Dez yanked Sasha to the edge of the bed, his head sinking between her legs. The deepest groan ripped from Sasha's chest. Sheets balled beneath her curled fingers, a tingly haze fogging her brain. Before she could gasp for air, he covered her with his body, enveloped her, invaded her. Softly, gently, Dez wrapped his fingers around Sasha's neck and lifted her onto his lap. His hold on her throat remained light, but he thrusted into her hard, making her arched back shudder.

Chapter Seven

Sasha rolled onto her stomach, slowly peeking over her shoulder. Through waves of brown hair, she watched Dez buckle his belt. When he sat on the bed and pulled out a sandwich bag of green buds, she scooted away.

"Don't you have somewhere to be or something?" she said, propping on her elbow.

Dez chuckled, opening his bag. "You got a tray and some papers?"

Sasha slinked out from behind Dez, hopping off the bed. After tossing on an oversized t-shirt, she grabbed a small silver tray and a pack of rolling papers. She stood in front of Dez, tray in hand. If not for the bag of weed, she would've tossed him out. Or just left. Dez took the tray from Sasha's grasp, gliding his thumb along her the edge of her hand. She yanked her arm away, sitting at the far end of the bed.

Shame, guilt, and awkward humiliation churned in the air, hanging over Sasha like a dark cloud. The noises Dez pulled from her, the way she

59

squirmed…she never felt so foolish. It'd be nice if he'd just split. His chilled expression, steady hands. It only added to the thorns of embarrassment that burrowed in her gut.

The aroma of kind-bud surrounded Sasha like a warm hug. Her legs uncoiled, and she leaned toward the scent. Dez slipped a joint between her fingers, and she took a big hit. The smoke carried a fraction of worries from her body as it left. It wasn't enough of a release, so she went in for another hit. Mid-puff, Dez's hand landed on her thigh. Thick smoke bunched in her throat, which chose now to seal shut, and she coughed.

"Are you dating my brother?" Dez asked.

The cough turned to a full-on hack, and Sasha pushed the joint into Dez's hand. "No."

Dez narrowed his eyes, staring at Sasha. "A lot of people were saying—"

"We're just friends." Sasha was trying for an honest tone, but her words came out through clenched teeth. "People, opinions, assholes, you know how that goes."

"Tell me about that firebombing," Dez said, passing Sasha the joint.

"What the fuck is this?" She took a few hits, each puff renewing her barbed edges. "You don't have to go through this uncomfortable after-sex chit-chat bullshit with me."

"You used to be all smiles, floating around this compound. What happened to you?"

Sasha leaned back, glaring. "I got thrashed by the people I trusted most in this world. And the last five years I've spent earning their respect back was blown by your little stunt at the clubhouse."

Dez held a blank stare, which grated Sasha's already flared nerves. She jumped up off the bed, heading toward the bathroom. "It's late. You should hit the road."

Once shut inside the tiny bathroom, a puff of relief sailed from her mouth. She froze, waiting until her outer door slammed before turning on the water. Twenty showers wouldn't wash the filth from beneath her flesh or cleanse the part of her that enjoyed his hold over her body. She had to try, though.

The faucet squeaked as Sasha cranked up the hot water. She stripped off her shirt, dropping it to the floor. A cloud of steam parted as she stepped into the tub, surrounding her as she stood under the scalding downpour.

***

The sun barely shined through the curtain, yet its beam was strong enough to wake Sasha from a deep sleep. For a good ten minutes, she just laid there. The courage to leave her bed never arrived, but her need for nicotine had ignited a burn in her stomach nine minutes ago. She rolled out of bed, glancing at the clock en route to her pack of smokes.

"Three! Jesus."

A lit cigarette dangled from Sasha's lips as she stretched. She glanced out the window, stumbling forward at the sight of red hair. Candy strutted across the gravel, putting the beauty of an autumn-crested hillside to shame, and Sasha's forehead bumped the cool glass.

Candy headed for the stairs, and Sasha opened the window. With one hand on the railing, Candy froze. Then her bright eyes gazed up, robbing the air from Sasha's lungs.

"I'll be right down," Sasha yelled as quietly as possible. She tore through her room. Dirty clothes flew through the air as she searched for semi-clean cargo pants. After slipping on a tank top, she scooped up her jacket and ran out the door.

The staircase wobbled, low creaks ringing out as Sasha galloped down the steps. She ignored Candy's smile and gestured to her pickup truck.

"Come on. I'll give you a lift home," she said, opening the passenger door.

"But I just got here." Candy slapped on a pout then climbed into the cab.

Sasha hurried to the driver's side, hopping in. "Nothing's going on today. There's no reason to hang around." She cranked the engine to life, tiny pebbles kicking up as she sped toward the front gate.

"What's the rush?" Candy asked, slumping in her seat. "I hang out here all the time. You're making this look shady."

The truck's tires chirped when hitting the pavement, and Sasha buckled down on the gas. "And you can keep hanging here…" Her fingers drummed the steering wheel, her gaze locked on the road.

"But?"

Sasha looked at Candy, darting her stare away at the slightest hint of skin. Those legs…she wanted to slip her hand between them so badly.

"But," Sasha said in a quaver, "we have to stop seeing each other."

"Is that what we're doing? I thought we were just fucking when you felt like it."

"And you have to stop talking about me," Sasha said, hardening both her stare and her voice. "This isn't a game. If people find out, you'll just get bounced from the clubhouse, but I'll get thrown in the cellar to bleed out a slow death. Do you understand?" She parked in front of Candy's house, turning to stare at the fidgety girl in the passenger seat. "Please tell me you understand."

"I understand. I'll zip it up, I swear." Candy sprang forward, clutching onto Sasha's arm. "My mom's out of town. Come inside. We can spend one last day together."

Sasha closed her eyes, breathing in the sweet scent of lavender as Candy leaned closer.

"I just wanna feel your fingers on me," Candy whispered, "inside me, one more time."

"No." Sasha yanked her arm away, pushing Candy back. "Just go. Forget I ever existed." The instant the words left Sasha's mouth, a chill crept into her spine. A light gasp streamed from the passenger seat, but Sasha kept her eyes down.

It wasn't until the truck rocked from a door slamming shut that she looked up at Candy walking away. A tear escaped her clutches, carving a cool path along her warm cheek. She put the truck in gear and drove away from the locks of flowing scarlet hair.

***

After about two hours of pounding shots at the local bar, a numbness overcame Sasha. A slash still scraped her heart, but at least she didn't care anymore.

"One more, Jack," she muttered, sailing her glass down the bar.

"You're pretty lit up, Sasha. You drivin'?"

"Holy shit!" Sasha slapped her hand on the faded bar, glaring at the man behind it. "I didn't know you started working for the fuzz, man. See, and I thought you were a bartender."

"Yeah, yeah." Jack poured another double of whiskey, placing it in front of Sasha.

Before the sting hit her throat, a hand crashed onto her shoulder.

"What's this, one of them trucker skanks?" a man slurred from behind her.

"Nah. She's got a jacket on," another said, his beer spilling at Sasha's side.

"Did you steal that jacket, darling? 'Cause I don't think a sweet little thing like you—"

The sloppy grasp on Sasha's shoulder slid down her back, and she jumped to her feet. The stool banged to the ground, and she slipped her hand into her pocket, fingers looping into brass knuckles. She glared as three men inched toward her.

One drunken flinch set off a chain reaction of fists. Metal pressed against Sasha's skin as her knuckles slammed into the corner of a jaw. A hit rocked her gut, another cracking her cheek, and she dropped to her knees. While teetering, Sasha barreled her brass-covered fist into a man's nuts.

Before the smirk could leave her bloody lips, a kick sent her crashing into the bar. Stools clattered atop her, clearing once boots stomped her side. Wads of blood made her choke back her cry, a whimper seeping out instead as she hacked between kicks. She hunched over, pulling a knife from her belt. The next leg that neared got a blade to the calf.

Howls stopped the beating, and Sasha hobbled to her feet. Two men sprawled to the floor, one gasping while holding his balls as the other screamed about the knife buried deep in his leg. The last man lunged toward Sasha, his fist high. She snatched a beer bottle off the bar and knocked the guy upside the head, dropping him to his back.

"Huh!" Sasha shrugged, guzzling the bottle in her hand. Her arm dropped, and the glass slipped from her grasp, shattering on the floor.

"Sorry, Jack," she said to the stunned man behind the bar. He flinched when she reached for her pocket. Slowly, Sasha pulled out a handful of cash. "For the mess." She laid a crumpled ball of hundreds on the bar and turned toward the front door. The room took a quick spin, blurring in shades of red. Her brain said walk and the legs followed, a neat little surprise. After ripping her blade from the man's leg, she staggered out the door.

***

Sasha parked beside the garage, and her mother rose from her bottom step.

"Jesus fucking Christ, seriously," Sasha mumbled. She rolled from the cab, her groan quickly turning into a wince. Her trembling hand left her achy side, and she stood almost straight, attempting a stroll toward the stairs.

"Jack called," Ellen said as Dez walked from the shadows. "Are you for real? Look at you, a fucking disgrace."

"What's he doing here?" Sasha glared at Dez, who stared back with only concern in his eyes.

"He was here when Jack called. You stabbed a man?"

Ellen stomped forward, whacking Sasha upside the head. "You know Dez went down for much less. You're in deep shit. Those assholes are on their way to the hospital. Questions, cops."

Another wallop hit Sasha's head, and she cowered down.

"You stupid little bitch," Ellen yelled.

"Enough," Sasha shouted, her hands up. "I'll fix it." She pushed past her mother, limping up the stairs.

Once inside her room, the urge to collapse into a corner came on strong. She shed her bloodstained jacket, crying out from the splinters of pain that accompanied every movement. She clutched the phone with her shaky fingers and dialed. As she fumbled with the receiver, she heard a man's voice on the line.

"Hello?" Sasha said. After flipping the phone the right way, she finally heard the voice clearly. "Jack."

"Sasha! You're in deep shit, girl. I told you, you

had enough."

"Listen. If you go to the hospital and get those guys to leave me out of this, I'll give them each three grand. And I'll give you five for your trouble."

"Really?" Jack asked, his voice making the phone vibrate against Sasha's ear.

"Swear to fucking God, but you gotta convince them all to take the deal."

"Shit, yeah. I'll call you back."

The line went dead, and Sasha moaned while hanging up the phone.

"You okay?"

Sasha jumped at the sound of Dez's voice, relaxing with a huff.

"Beat it," she grumbled, slumping to the floor.

"Let me see that." Dez knelt beside Sasha, swatting her hands from her side to lift her shirt. "Oh fuck!"

A groan carried Sasha forward, and she peered down at the fringe of a giant purple mark. She sagged back, snickering through the ache. "That ain't shit. When less than half your body's a bruise, it's been a good day."

"What the fuck, Sasha? You trying to prove something to me?"

"Not everything is about you." Sasha used the last of her strength to shove Dez, but he barely moved from her side. "I just wanted a regular drink, like a normal person, and these motherfuckers fuck with me. Now I'm getting all kinds of shit about it. This is bullshit."

Dez dropped to his ass, scooching so close their

hips touched. "Did you really take out three dudes?"

Sasha waved her hand, as if that could clear Dez's question from the air. "I don't know. There was a lot going on."

"You might've taken me." Dez looked into Sasha's eyes, then away.

"I doubt it. You weren't drunk."

"Neither were you." His next words failed, leaving his mouth open and chest raised.

"Yeah, well, I'm pretty fucking sober now. And it sucks."

Dez smiled, pushing a strand of blood-clumped hair from Sasha's face. "I'd kiss you, but your lip's all split."

"What, not attractive?" Sasha leaned back, shrugging.

"Come on," Dez said, climbing to his feet. "Let's get you out of those bloody clothes and into bed."

Sasha held her arm out stiff. "Joint. Need joint."

A chuckle lifted Dez's lips. "I got ya, man. Bed first."

"Yeah, all right." Sasha took Dez's hand, wobbling to her feet.

Chapter Eight

Sasha lay in bed, listening to the chirp of birds. The small amount of sleep she managed had cleared her drunken mind but did little to heal her sore body.

"Fucking chicks," she muttered, crawling from bed. No one but a woman could've sent her running to Jack's bar, practically looking for trouble. She stripped off her shirt, stepped in front of the mirror, and stared at her reflection. Shades of blue, purple, and yellow spanned her left side, from thigh to ribcage. Her face was only a tad better. Fat lip, puffy cheek, and a few scrapes.

"Little girl." She hit the glass with her scabbed knuckles, shaking the closet door and rocking the image that failed to match her mentality.

She dressed slow and careful. Each move inspired a new wave of sharp throbs. As she tied on her bandana, the phone rang. Piles of messy clothes tripped up her steps. She hopped to the side to keep from trampling her jacket and reached for the screaming receiver.

69

"Yeah."

"It's a go," Jack said in a rush. "They already told the cops a group of blackies jumped them."

"Jesus."

"I think they were a little relieved. I mean, who wants to admit they got beat down by a girl?" Jack said with a bit of a chuckle.

"What the fuck did you just say?"

"Oh shit. Not that you're a regular girl or anything."

"Every word is getting worse, asshole. I like you better when I'm drunk."

"Ha! I get that a lot," Jack said, glasses clinking in the background. "Anyway. They're all at my place now, waiting for the cash."

"All right. I'll be there in an hour or so, but I ain't coming alone."

"I've been a friend of the club a long time, Sasha. I don't want no trouble with you."

"Nah, it's more of a heads-up than a threat. Thanks, Jack. I'll see you in a bit."

Before Sasha could hang up the phone, a light knock rattled her door. "Grand central fucking station around here," she muttered. "What?" she yelled.

"It's Vinny."

A slew of grumbles erupted from Sasha's lips at the sound of his voice. She popped a cigarette in her mouth, flicking her zippo to life. "Come in."

The door crept open, and the chain of a wallet swung into its frame as Vinny peeked inside.

"Oh, you're up," he said, stepping inside the room. "I thought—"

"What? I'd be a blubbering pulp."

"No. I don't know." Vinny shut the door, kicking aside the mess to clear a path to Sasha. His eyes lifted to her face, and he grabbed her hand. "Sasha, I…"

Sasha backed away, shaking her head. Whatever dumb shit was about to tumble from Vinny's mouth, she didn't want any part of it. In the blink of an eye, his expression went from one of love to annoyance.

"Why didn't you call me?" Vinny yelled. "I would've chilled at the bar. I was so bored last night."

"I don't know. I—"

"And Jack's bar, really. Only inbred fucks go there. What the hell?"

A shrug was all Sasha offered. She couldn't tell Vinny how she ran to Jack's looking for a fight to dull the pain of losing Candy. It would make her look like more of a punk than she felt.

"At least you look okay," Vinny said, running his hand along Sasha's cheek. "Pretty bad shiner, but—"

"Oh my god." Sasha pushed Vinny's arm from her face, stepping away from him. "What are people saying?"

"You really want to know?"

"No." Sasha snatched her jacket off the floor, muffling a groan. "Did *she* send you up here?"

"Yeah." Vinny sat on the edge of her bed, fishing a semi-bent joint from his pocket. "Ellen was worried. She wanted me to check on you."

Something between a snort and a giggle vibrated

Sasha's chest. "Yeah right." She lit her zippo, holding out the flame. "What'd she really say?"

White smoke drifted up in puffs, and Vinny leaned back, inhaling. "She said to go kick your retarded ass out of bed and drag you to the clubhouse," he said through a long exhale, passing the joint. "Everyone's here, so we're gonna reconvene the vote."

"Great." Sasha headed toward the door, smoke trailing behind her. "Let's go, then."

"Yo, man. Quit bogarting my doobie," Vinny called out, following Sasha outside.

***

"Hey, slugger," Kev said, pretending to sock Sasha in the gut.

Sasha lifted her arms, backing away. "Aw, come on, man."

"Don't encourage her," Ellen said from the head of the table. "We don't drop loads in our own town."

After a few snickers and grins, they all took their seats. Sasha peeked at her mother. Cold eyes glowered back, and she dropped her gaze.

"Since everyone is here," Ellen said, sitting back in her chair, "I want to get this vote out of the way."

Sasha tapped on the table, cutting off her mother's next words. "Can I just say something before you vote?" She didn't think it was possible, but her mother's hard stare turned even fiercer. "The club is what matters, not alliances or bloodlines. I'm okay being a runner, for now, if that's what everyone thinks is best for the club."

While ignoring the stunned eyes leering from all sides, Sasha eased back.

"Okay then." Ellen placed a patch in front of the empty chair beside her. "Let's vote on a sergeant at arms."

"I nominate Dez," Otis said.

Kev looked at Sasha, his eyes wavering. She gave him a light nod, her head bobbing almost without her permission.

"I second," Kev said, his gaze low.

"All in favor," Ellen said, barely able to contain the giddy tone in her voice.

Chewy shifted in his seat, and Sasha kicked Vinny under the table.

Vinny turned, glaring at Sasha. She tipped her head, and his eyes narrowed, but he slowly lifted his arm.

"That's three to two. Motion passes. Dez." Ellen gestured to the chair at her left.

Sasha watched Dez strut around the table before sinking behind Vinny's wide frame.

"And I nominate Sasha for runner," Ellen said through a smile.

"Second," Otis added.

"All in favor."

Sasha rolled her eyes as people raised their hands. A patch slid down the table, brushing her fingers, but she didn't move.

"Good. Now we just need some prospects to take care of the bitch work." Ellen sent a set of keys with a green tab sailing down the table. It stopped beside Sasha's runner patch. "I need you to take a run. Is there any other business?"

Heads shook, lighters flicked, and Ellen rose. "Meeting adjourned."

Sasha stayed frozen in place as boots shuffled toward the door. Now the circle of pain was complete. Her insides felt as ugly as the bruise that stained her skin. A sigh breezed past her cracked lips just as the door clicked shut. She leaned forward, reaching for the skinny strip of fabric that represented her place in this world.

"That patch don't mean shit," Dez said.

Sasha flinched, spinning in her chair. Dez stomped forward, and her surprise warped to irritation.

"I might have the title," he said, giving her a hard stare, "but they all look to you."

After gathering the keys and patch, Sasha stood. Dez didn't budge. His solid body pinned her between the chair and table, so she glared up. "See, everyone remembers you as the bad-tempered bulldog who spilled a pint of blood on the clubhouse floor every weekend. Now you're the man responsible to make level-headed decisions for us all."

"You don't trust me?"

"I don't know you." She gave him a little shove from her personal space. "And the way you keep crowding me is—"

"Turning you on." Dez wormed his way back in front of Sasha, reaching for her waist.

She whacked his hand away. "Freaking me out."

"They won't follow me unless you do."

"I have your back. Do you have mine? I need my

sergeant at arms right now."

Dez's hands stayed at his sides, a serious gaze rushing in to replace his flirty leer. "About last night?"

"Yeah." A slump took Sasha back into her seat. "I can't take this to my mother, and I don't know which way to go."

"Gimme the dets."

"I got the guys to agree to a pay-off. They already lied to the fuzz so...is it better to pay up and hope they stay quiet, or should I just make 'em disappear?"

"Hmm." Dez sat on the edge of the table, crossing his arms. "That's a tough one. When's this supposed to go down?"

"Right now."

"Shit! You have a run to make. Green key. That's Little Rock, right?"

Sasha nodded, glancing at the clock on the wall. "I got about an hour before I have to peel rubber."

"All right, let's go over to Jack's and pay 'em. If we have to, we'll kill 'em later. You got the cash?"

"It's in my room."

"Go get it. We'll take a ride over there," Dez said as confident as any other sergeant before him.

Sasha stood, and her hand grazed Dez's leg. That little touch was enough to spawn shivers, which spread throughout her body. "You know, if I had made sergeant, I still would've come to you with this. That just proves I'm not ready. I can't even handle my own shit."

Dez grabbed Sasha's arm just long enough to stop her from walking away. "You'll be sitting at the head of that table before you know it."

"I hope not."

Sasha left the room, catching Vinny's glare all the way from the porch. The closer she got to him, the faster his foot tapped the wooden planks. His face, a ripe mix of disappointment and appall, invoked the urge to bolt out the back door, but she marched onward.

"What was that shit?" Vinny said the moment Sasha was in earshot. "You totally caved."

Without a glance, she walked past him, and he followed on her heels.

"You would've had it."

"Maybe I don't want it."

"What?" Vinny stopped for a second then scurried to catch up. "Yes, you do. Making sergeant is all you've ever wanted since we were kids."

Vinny shadowed Sasha up the stairs and into her room. "This is exactly what I'm talking about. I do not get you. Do you even get yourself?"

Sasha hurled a glower over her shoulder, pulling a briefcase from her closet. With her back to him, she flipped open the lid and stuffed handfuls of neatly packed hundreds into a duffle bag.

"What are you doing?"

"Shut up. I'm counting." She knew exactly how many stacks of thousands she needed, could easily talk while loading the bills, but really didn't want to. She couldn't explain herself. No, she didn't get herself at all.

After tucking the case back into the closet, Sasha dashed from the room. Halfway down the stairs, she heard the sound of her door slamming shut, and

Vinny was right behind her again.

"So I guess now we can't even be friends. You'll just live your secret life with duffle bags of money and I'll do my own thing."

"C'mon, man," Sasha said without a break in her stride. "I'm just going on a run."

"Since when does run money come out of your closet?"

Sasha stopped short. Her glare iced over as she spun to face Vinny. "Shut the fuck up." Turning, she hurried from her own bitchy vibe clinging to the air and toward the line of semis.

"Hey, Vince," Dez called out from beside a green Peterbilt. "Gimme a lift to Jack's bar."

"No," Sasha said. "Don't get him involved."

"What the fuck, Sasha?" Vinny sneered.

There was no reason for her to treat Vinny this way, aside from the fact that he wouldn't leave her the fuck alone about this sergeant bullshit. Her remorse-filled eyes shifted to Vinny, but he veered from her gaze.

"This way," Dez said, stepping next to Vinny, "you can take the rig and hit the road straight from the bar. My little brother can give me a ride back, after a few drinks."

"Whatever." Sasha opened the truck's door, tossed the bag into the cab, and climbed inside.

Chapter Nine

Five hours of open road and Sasha still couldn't shake those Archer brothers from her head. Her stomach churned when she left the bar after seeing them laughing and drinking together. If they found out about each other, everyone would hate everyone. A regular old cluster fuck, her specialty.

It wasn't until her client's massive warehouse rolled into view that her brain unscrambled. Little Rock, home tuff of the Los Lobos, probably the sketchiest, deadliest, and biggest buyers on the roster. This drop-off definitely warranted a sturdy game face and sharp mind.

Sasha drove through the wide bay door of the only structure untouched by graffiti on the block and killed the engine. The bay door slammed shut, and florescent lights blinked on. Her hand froze on the door's handle, gaze locked on the beautiful woman strolling toward her truck. She stared through the windshield, watching long legs prance, a tiny waist sway, and feathery black hair bounce.

"That is not Miguel," Sasha muttered, opening

her door.

When her boots hit concrete, a swarm of men surrounded her. Rifles greeted her chest, bullets loaded into their chambers, and her hand inched toward the butt of her handgun.

"What's up?" Sasha said, unsnapping the button of her holster.

"That's enough. Ease off," a silky voice said along with a train of obscene words in Spanish.

Men backed away, their guns lowering as the woman strolled closer. The gray fabric of her dress hugged every curve, from chest to thighs.

"I'm Carmen, Miguel's daughter."

"Oh shit, *Carmelita*," Sasha said, shoving back a grin. "He talks about you all the time."

"And you must be the infamous Sasha Ashby." Carmen pointed to the truck, and men shuffled to unload the cargo. With just a flick of her wrist, a briefcase flew forward.

"Infamous, huh?" Sasha took the case, chucking it into the cab. "I don't know about all that."

Heels clanked as Carmen sashayed to Sasha's side. "You have no idea. People see what you do, how you carry yourself. More and more women are being accepted within the ranks of the underworld, the right women."

The last crate of drug-stuffed teddy bears was carried from Sasha's trailer, joining the pile that now overflowed a corner of the warehouse. Sasha leaned against the front bumper of her truck, the entire rig shaking as its trailer door slammed shut. "Well, that's something, I guess."

Carmen waved her arm, and everyone cleared

the warehouse, leaving them alone in the cavernous room.

"I think," Carmen stepped closer to Sasha, a coy smile lifting her cheeks, "we have a lot in common."

Sasha stood up straight, leaning toward the luscious body that drifted just within her grasp. "Is that so?"

A knee slid between Sasha's legs, warm breath flooding over her neck.

"*Si, mamacita,* except I've never *been* inside a Mack truck."

Creamy brown skin ensnared Sasha's gaze, and all by themselves, her hands gripped Carmen's firm hips. "I think I can do something about that." Soft strands of thick hair swept Sasha's cheek as Carmen spun, heading for the truck's open door.

Sasha's teeth dug into her bottom lip. She unzipped her jacket, trailing the muscled thighs that moseyed to her truck's door.

***

Dez

Dez sat at the bar of the clubhouse, watching his brother walk back and forth. Vinny had turned away three fine women so far who'd practically thrown themselves in his lap to pace on the front porch. If the guy wasn't dating Sasha, something serious must be up. No man could've turned down that last blonde, not without a really good reason. Dez grabbed a bottle of whiskey, walking onto the porch.

"What's up, Vince?"

Vinny flinched then shot a poorly forced grin.

"You seem tense," Dez said, sitting on the bench and unscrewing the cap.

"Nah. I'm just…bored."

A long swig sizzled its way down Dez's throat, burning away a fraction of the stench left by his brother's bullshit. He lifted the bottle, dangling it between his fingers.

Vinny sat beside Dez, taking the bottle. "So where's the green truck go?"

"You got pretty close with Sasha, huh?"

"No," Vinny blurted, looking away then back. "I'm just trying to learn." He poked the patch on his jacket. "Runner."

"You're so different. Everything's different." Dez took the bottle, downing another gulp. "You and Sasha used to sneak into the clubhouse, steal joints, then go beat up the local kids. Now you guys are at the table and I'm…"

"You're our sergeant."

"Yeah. Go figure." After another swig, Dez handed over the bottle to keep from finishing the damn thing. "You've been passing on some prime tail all night. I hear that Debbie chick can suck the chrome off a bumper."

Vinny snorted mid-gulp, coughing a bit while banging on his chest. "It's true. Mouth like a vacuum, but I ain't really feelin' it tonight."

"Sasha?"

"What?"

"You two," Dez leaned back, lighting a cigarette,

81

"fight like an old married couple."

"It's starting to feel like that," Vinny muttered.

"So you guys are fucking?"

"No!" Vinny shook his head, waving his hand. "No, no. I'm stuck in the friend zone. Why are you asking about Sasha?"

Dez stared across the parking lot. Moonlight shimmered off the line of gleaming rigs. The sparkle of light shining off chrome left a warmth in his chest, better than liquor, like home. "I know the whole crew, and you're my brother. But Sasha...I can't puzzle her out. She's either really smart or really stupid. Or maybe even both at the same time, if that's possible."

Vinny smirked, nodding.

The bench shifted as Dez turned, eyeing the bottle. "I worry she'll hurt the club."

"No way. The club is her life. It's all she ever talks about, thinks about. You caught her on a bad week, with that bar shit and other stuff. That's all. She's calmed down a lot these last few years. Just give her a chance."

Dez rose from the bench, took the bottle from Vinny's hand, and flicked his cigarette over the railing. "Green truck goes to Little Rock," he said before walking back inside.

***

Sasha

Sasha grinned at the cute gasps that filled her cab. She kissed Carmen's thigh, earning a moan.

She nibbled on the woman's flat stomach, scoring her a giggle, and the tip of her tongue, running between soft breasts up to a silky neck, brought shivers to both their bodies.

"*Ay dios mío, mamacita*," Carmen cried out. "*Es una lengua mágica.*"

"*Gracias, muñeca.*"

"You speak Spanish?" Carmen sat up in the cramped sleeper cabin, gazing into Sasha's eyes.

"*Si. Un poco.* I spent some time in Guadalajara last year."

"Really! You are an interesting girl, Sasha Ashby. Come here, let me do you now."

Sasha grabbed ahold of Carmen's wandering hands. "Aren't you worried? Fernando's gonna tell your father we were in here alone for so long."

"I hide nothing, am ashamed of nothing. My father respects me for it." Carmen lifted the end of Sasha's tank top. "Is that what this bruise is about? Intolerant redneck fucks? Things are a lot different here in the city, mama."

Sasha stopped Carmen from fumbling with her belt. Thoughts of a brutal stomp-down and a visit to the cellar kind of killed the mood. "I should hit the road. Besides, I came like five times just watching your body quake."

"Ooh." Carmen fell against Sasha's chest, licking her lips. "There's that magic tongue again."

A heart beat against Sasha's chest, and it wasn't her own. It was faster, harder. The thump turned to a pound as she slid her hands down Carmen's back, clutching onto her ass. Their lips met, gliding, caressing, skating atop one another. It took every ounce of strength and the last bit of her willpower, but Sasha pulled herself from the sensuous woman's embrace.

She hopped into the front, lighting a cigarette while Carmen slinked back into her dress. Carmen's fingers slid along the back of her hand before she stole the cigarette from Sasha's grasp.

"All right, mama. Let's get you on your way," Carmen said through a billow of smoke.

Sasha opened her door, climbing out. She helped Carmen ease off the steel grate step, those high heels wedging in the rough slits.

Once on solid ground, Carmen smoothed back her already perfect hair then smirked. "You know, if we pooled our resources and cut out the overhead, we could run the largest syndicate in the midwest."

The words sent razor-winged butterflies whirling in Sasha's stomach. Her mouth opened, but her thought process hadn't caught up yet, so nothing came out. Finally, she said, "I'm not lookin' to run anything."

Carmen laughed, more of a wicked taunt, and crept closer. "You will. And when you do, I'll be waiting."

After a long, ravenous gaze, Carmen strolled away. "Next time, mama."

"Absolutely," Sasha said in more of a whisper. By the time she climbed back into her rig, Carmen was gone and the warehouse bay open. She backed her big rig out of the warehouse, weaved past abandoned buildings, and barreled down toward the freeway.

"Shit, seven-thirty. I'm so late." The engine

whistled as Sasha ran through gears, pushing for the south. She clicked on the radio, turning up the volume. Not even the wail of Def Leppard could drown out Carmen's words. They could monopolize all criminal activity in a five-hundred-mile radius, easy. It would mean…sacrificing everything.

A shiver ran down Sasha's spine. She shook it off, shifted into tenth, and settled back for a long ride.

***

Vinny

Pebbles skipped under Vinny's anxious pace. He looked at his watch, stopping to gawk. "Twelve-fifteen," he groaned. "Where the fuck are you?"

Voices drew his gaze back to the clubhouse. From across the lot, he watched Dez escort Debbie to his truck then drive off. Alone again, with only the chirp of crickets, Vinny resumed his circular gait. The rumble of a diesel engine echoed from the hills below, cementing his feet in place. He listened, head cocked toward the night sky. When the whoosh of airbrakes silenced the mockingbirds' call, he dashed up the porch steps.

First, Vinny slouched on the bench with his arm propped along the back. Then he sat forward and rested his elbows on his knees. Finally, after a mental reminder about the hazards of dorkiness, he lit a joint and drooped against the armrest.

A truck's door slammed shut, and his heart skipped. Beads of sweat pooled on his palm at the sight of Sasha. Her long brown hair tapped her leather jacket as she floated across the compound, baggy cargo pants dragging in the dirt.

Vinny hit the joint when Sasha's boot landed on the porch, casting a red glow around his face and luring her stare.

"Hey," he said, a stream of smoke following his voice.

"Yes! Weed me." Sasha plopped beside him, plucking the joint from his fingers.

Vinny watched her eyes drift shut, lips scrunching to kiss the end of the sticky paper. To be that joint right now, trapped in her soft grasp, lingering on her skin, creeping inside her…

"Is my mom still up?"

"No." His voice cracked, and he cleared his throat. "She went up to the big house about an hour ago."

"Otis?" After another puff, Sasha handed Vinny the joint.

"Yeah. He's in there."

She flashed a smile, hopping to her feet. "Keys go straight to the prez or road captain the moment you get back. Got it?"

Vinny nodded, and Sasha turned toward the clubhouse door.

"Hey, Sasha."

When she looked back, his body grew stiff. He wanted to say so many things. Tell her how beautiful she looked, ask to spend the night, confess his chest-shattering love, but simply said, "See you tomorrow."

"Goodnight."

Sasha's voice trailed off as she strolled through the threshold, but her smile hung in Vinny's mind. He dropped his head into his hands, rubbing his forehead. Any hint, the tiniest signal that she wanted him, and he'd jump, but Sasha was the queen of mixed messages. Lustful leers laced in angst. That's all he got from her.

Vinny rose from the bench, his fists tight at his sides. Wood planks creaked as he thumped down the small steps. While breathing in crisp mountain air, he walked to his truck.

Chapter Ten

Sasha

A motorcycle revved, pulling Sasha from the cusp of sleep. She sat up in bed, looking around her room. A crackle of fire echoed outside her window, and an orange glow lit her walls. She fought to untangle from blankets, rolling out of bed. Her hip bumped the nightstand, glass bottles clinking as she peered out the window. Sharp flames licked the sky, spreading down the line of tractor-trailers parked across from the clubhouse. Her jaw inched open, only the smallest of gasps seeping out.

Most of the fleet had disappeared behind a wall of fire. Most, not all. Sasha turned from the window, running out of her room. Splintered wood dug into her bare feet as she dashed down rickety stairs. Her long t-shirt rode up her thighs, frosty air chilling her skin. She glanced at her mother's house atop the hill, catching a silhouette in the window.

"Thank God," she muttered. If Satan's Crew had tried to burn her mother alive, she'd have to kill them slowly. It would've taken months to torture them all. At least now she could slaughter them quick.

Sasha turned back to face the roar of flames, running toward it. Fire streamed from the long gas tank of the green Peterbilt before it exploded, blowing the truck off the ground and Sasha's hair back. She skidded to a stop outside the clubhouse, dodging bits of fiery gas tank. Swirls of groaning flames, which had lifted the once-majestic Peterbilt into the air, spread out as the semi slammed back to the ground. A firestorm devoured the fleet. The green truck, now a mangled pile of blazing metal, infected the trucks beside it with its raging inferno.

A window shattered in her father's black International, the rig that inspired the club, and Sasha ran forward only to have a strong hand grasp her arm.

"No key," Kev yelled, holding her back while cupping a deep gash on his forehead.

"What are you doing here?" Sasha yanked herself free, shielding her face from swells of blistering heat.

"I passed out on the pool table and—Fuck! The trucks."

"Sasha!"

Sasha spun toward the sound of her mother's voice and the jingle of keys.

"Black truck," Sasha yelled. She caught the key that sailed toward her chest then sprinted to the rig. "Call the guys," she hollered to Kev. "They might be targets."

Another explosion rocked the ground as Sasha

reached for the driver's door, flinging her to the gravel. Flames poured from beneath the truck, climbing atop one another in a rush to gobble her up. "Shit," she yelled, springing to her feet.

Heated metal singed her exposed legs as she climbed into the cab. Her fingers shook, missing the ignition before cranking the engine to life. Sweat poured from her chin, the fire's roar vibrating her eardrums. The shifter scorched her palm when she gripped onto its steel ball. Even though it stung like road-rash, she grinded the truck into gear then drove from flashes of fire bursts.

Sasha jumped from the truck, wincing as jagged rocks scraped the bottoms of her raw feet. The sight of her mother frozen in front of the clubhouse, gawking, was more unsettling than the blaze. She'd never seen that woman hesitate before.

"I heard motorcycles," Sasha said, limping to her mother's side.

"The fleet," Ellen said, her eyes reflecting the fury of the flames.

"Get inside." Sasha took her mother's arm, hurrying into the clubhouse.

Kev rushed forward, and the phone's cord yanked him back to the wall. "Chewy and Vinny didn't answer."

Panic struck Sasha's chest harder than a fist. "Fuck. Otis?"

"I'm trying him now."

Sasha left her mother beside the pool table, snatching the phone from Kev's hand. "Go get me some clothes and bring my pickup around."

Kev ran toward the door, disappearing into curls

of smoke. Otis's groggy voice sang in Sasha's ear.

"We've been hit," she said, ignoring the tremble that disrupted her words.

"What? Are you—I hear motorcycles," Otis said in a hushed voice.

"Grab a gun and get low," Sasha said, clutching the phone's cord.

Pops burst through the receiver, followed by a grunt and the shatter of broken glass. Sasha flinched, and her mother hustled to her side.

"I need shotguns and ammo," Sasha said while listening to the stream of gunfire that blasted from the phone.

Ellen dashed into the backroom, and the line grew quiet, leaving Sasha with the crackle of fire. "Otis! Fuck, man. Otis!"

"I'm okay," Otis said. "My house just got lit up. Did you warn anyone else?"

"Kev's here, but Chewy and Vinny didn't answer."

"Ellen?"

"She's fine." Sasha glanced at her mother, who'd laid weapons on the pool table. "They firebombed the fleet."

Kev ran into the clubhouse, tossing clothes at Sasha's chest, and she propped the phone against her shoulder while dressing.

"I'll head to Chewy's," Otis said. "You and Kev get to Vinny's house."

"Be careful." Sasha hung up the phone and jammed her sore feet into tight boots.

"This is your fault," Ellen said, glaring at Sasha. "Our fleet, the crew, fucked. All because of that

91

stunt you pulled with Satan's Crew last month."

Sasha grabbed two shotguns, shoving a tin of shells at Kev's chest. "Get in the truck." Kev scurried from sight, and Sasha backed out the door. "Lock up and grab a gun," she said to her mother before sprinting to her running pickup.

"Otis?" Kev asked as she drove through the now-busted front gate.

"They shot up his house, but he's okay." Sasha cut the corner, flooring the gas. "Goddamn motherfucker!" She pounded her fist against the steering wheel, but it didn't stop a flood of rage from creeping into her mind. Her crew could be lying in puddles of their own blood right now, which reminded her.

"You okay?" Sasha asked, looking at Kev. "Your head?"

Kev wiped the streaks of blood from his forehead. "Fuckers hit me with something while I was passed out."

"This is my fault. I firebombed their warehouse. I started a war."

"They took out our men first." Kev sat up when they turned onto Vinny's street. "Oh shit."

Police cars lined the road, red and blue lights flashing off the tightly packed houses.

"Stash the guns," Sasha said, shoving her shotgun under the seat. She slowed the truck to a crawl, bobbing to see beyond the uniformed men who eyed her as she drove by. "Someone's on a stretcher." Her hand tapped Kev's chest. "Who is it?"

Kev sat up, looking over Sasha's head. "It's

Vinny. He's moving, talking."

"Thank God," she said. "Dez?"

"His truck's not here. He left with Debbie tonight."

Sasha busted a right, flooring it toward Main Street. "This is so not good, man. Now the fuzz is involved."

"Good thing you got those pictures of the sheriff."

"Yeah." Sasha stopped in front of the diner, shutting the engine. When Kev reached for the door, she seized his arm. "Wait."

After a second of looking and listening to nothing, she released her clutch. "Okay. Let's go."

They both grabbed a shotgun and inched to the stairs that led above the diner. On a small landing, Sasha lowered her gun and Kev covered her back. She knocked hard, then returned her hold to the barrel.

The steel slab cracked open, and Dez peeked out. "Sasha!" He ripped the door open, shrinking back when glimpsing the gun in her hands.

Sasha pushed by Dez, barging inside. "There's been a...thing."

"Don't freak out." Kev shut the door, resting his gun on his shoulder. "Vinny's okay. We think."

"What the fuck happened? It's four in the morning!" Dez shouted.

"Is everything all right?" Debbie asked, clutching Dez's jacket to her naked body.

Sasha's head twisted toward the squeaky voice, and Dez took hold of Debbie, ushering her backward from the room. "Hey, babe. Why don't

93

you go gather up my clothes? I gotta talk with my crew for a minute."

"Yeah, sure," Debbie said softly.

"Actually." Sasha looked beyond Dez, grinning at Debbie. "The club could really use your help, Deb. Do you mind?"

A wide smile spanned Debbie's lips. She bumped Dez aside, prancing forward while nodding.

***

Ellen

A big block engine purred, holding steady at one hundred miles an hour, and Ellen pushed the gas harder when she crossed the state line. Her Chevelle SS stood out like a sore thumb, sure to get her pulled over, which was exactly what she needed. Every cop in eastern Tennessee worked for Satan's Crew. Now to hook one.

After twenty minutes of speeding down Route 81, lights flashed in the rearview mirror. Ellen pulled to the shoulder, tucked a knife down her boot, and killed the engine. When the officer neared, she climbed from the car, slow, hands at her sides. "I need to see Dante."

"Ellen!" The cop inched closer, his hand on the butt of his holstered gun. "You're a little far from Kentucky, aren't ya?"

"Cut the shit," Ellen strolled past the man, stopping to pluck his nametag, "Miller." While waiting by the passenger door, she hardened her glare, which she directed at the gawking man.

"Let's go," she barked, and he jumped, hurrying to open her door.

***

Sasha

Sasha stood in the hospital's parking lot, watching Dez verge the threshold of a full-on freak-out. His body coiled tighter with every detail he learned of the night's events. He must've reached the end of his tension rope because now he was unwinding at a frantic pace. It was a miracle he hadn't punched anything yet.

Dez crashed his fist onto the hood of Sasha's pickup, denting the metal. "I can't believe my brother's laid up and I'm out here, hiding like a fucking pussy."

"There's probably mad cops in there," Sasha said, leaning against her bumper.

A low growl rumbled past Dez's lips, and he raised his finger, waving it in both Sasha and Kev's face. "I'm gonna gut me some douchebag biker faggot mother—"

"Look," Kev said. "Here comes Debbie."

They crowded around the tall blonde in the short leather skirt whose chain belt jingled every time her stillettos touched the ground.

"Piece of cake," Debbie said. "Told the bitch at the desk I was Vinny's fiancé. Spaz let me right into his room."

"And?" Sasha said, flapping her hand at the

wrist.

"Vinny has a message," Debbie said, leaning forward. "He says it's just a flesh wound. Ellen took care of the heat, and someone better be waiting around back 'cause he's gonna grab some pills and sneak himself out."

Debbie grinned, her jaw slapping at the gum that rolled in her mouth.

"Did you do the other thing?" Sasha asked, straining to mask her annoyed tone.

"Oh yeah." Debbie rifled through her large leather purse. "They totally leave those medical charts just laying around." She pulled out a wad of crumpled papers, frowning. "Oops! Had to hurry. Anyway, here're Vinny's records."

Dez snatched the papers, smoothing the creases while he read. "GSR to the shoulder, through and through."

"Dude must have a guardian angel," Kev said with a grin.

"I'm going around back to fetch him." Dez hurried toward his truck, which was parked beside Sasha's pickup in the near empty lot.

"Wait," Debbie cried out. "I need a ride home."

"Kev can take you." Sasha tossed her keys to Kev. "Take my truck, and meet us back at the clubhouse when you're done. I'll ride with Dez." She smiled at Debbie, patting her lightly on the arm. "The club owes you, big time."

"Bitchin'," Debbie said over the clank of her heels as she flounced away.

Dez revved his engine, and Sasha hurried into the cab. He floored the gas, thrusting her back into the seat.

"Vinny's fine. You can simmer down."

"The fleet, drivebys on our homes…" Dez hit the brakes, cutting around the back of the hospital. "What the fuck's been going down, Sasha?"

Sasha looked away, shaking her head. Dez slammed on the brakes, stopping in the shadow of a giant oak tree, and grabbed her arm.

"Don't." Sasha yanked herself from his grasp, glaring.

"Don't what? Touch you?" His large hands clutched the sides of her arms, pulling her close. "Why? 'Cause you like it too much?"

"Fuck off." She shoved Dez away, moving as far from him as possible. "You're sergeant at arms. Shouldn't you already know everything about everything?"

"Don't be a bitch, Sasha."

"Don't be a dick, Desmond."

Dez stared at the hospital's back door, his fingers strumming the steering wheel. "All I want to do is protect the club, like you. We have to trust each other. We only have each other."

The sincerity in Dez's voice grabbed and held Sasha's attention. Affection blazed behind Dez's chilled gaze, luring her toward its heat, but she fought to keep her body still. It didn't matter how hard she resisted, though. His soft gaze alone was enough to draw out her deepest secrets.

"You're right," Sasha said, unable to stop herself from rambling. "There is a lot you don't know. None of the guys know. My mom's been—"

The back door banged against the hospital wall,

and Vinny snuck out. Sasha jumped from the truck, running across the parking lot.

"I'm okay," Vinny said, cradling his shoulder. Sasha reached out when Dez brushed by and wrapped his arms around Vinny, who groaned.

"Jesus Christ, little brother."

"Ah." Vinny wiggled away. "Careful." He adjusted his sling and headed toward Dez's truck. "It was Satan's Crew."

"I know," Sasha said, hovering at Vinny's side. "They hit everyone, took out the fleet. We only have one rig left."

Vinny stopped short, his eyes bouncing from Dez to Sasha. "Is everyone all right?"

"I think so. I couldn't get a hold of Chewy." Sasha hopped into Dez's truck, sliding to the middle of the bench seat. They climbed into the cab, one brother on each side. The air seemed to grow thick, not suitable for proper breathing. Two different legs pressed against her own, both radiating a very different type of chill. Waves of lust collided with the flutter of love, exploding into a painful ache at the center of her chest. She didn't want to look at either of them, afraid her eyes would give it all away.

"Everyone should be back at the clubhouse by now," Sasha said into her lap. "I'm sure my mom already has a plan in the works."

A quick peek through her hair and she caught Dez's leer. Part suspicion, but mostly disappointment. She clasped her fingers, and her leg flinched against Vinny.

Chapter Eleven

Ellen

Ellen kept her back stiff, chin high, while walking through the flagship bar for Satan's Crew. Laughs dwindled under the crackle of a jukebox, a few guns cocked as bulky men rose to their feet, yet she walked on by. These jokers were no use to her. She wasn't seeking a half-assed lackey. Ellen pushed open the door to the backroom, stepping inside the room that tried too hard to resemble her clubhouse.

The man sitting at the desk that was an obvious knockoff of her antique desk flinched. Ellen forced a smile into a sneer.

"Dante," she said, closing the door behind her.

"Ellen! You look pissed." Dante snickered, leaning back in his chair. "Bad day?"

"You blew up my fleet."

"Tell me." Dante planted his elbows on the shiny desk in front of him, his muscles flexing under his tight shirt. "Did the trucks actually lift off the ground?"

"Still playing games, huh? Well, I'm done."

Dante chuckled, and a strand of his thin black hair drifted down to block his glare. "See, I pictured this giant ball of flames lifting the—"

Ellen stomped toward the desk, swinging her fist. Dante seized her arm without moving from his chair. Slowly, he rose to his feet. His body slithered along her chest, gaze locked on her glare.

"So you *do* wanna play?" Dante slammed Ellen's back against the wall, pinning her under his weight.

The smallest grin escaped her grasp, but she reeled it back. "We had a truce." She ripped his belt out of its pant loops, dropping it to the floor.

"Which you broke," his hands rode up her hips, jacking the skirt around her waist, "when Sasha firebombed my warehouse."

Dante thrust himself deep inside her, and she gasped. She clutched her fingers into his neck, nails digging into skin.

"That was an accident," Ellen whispered while staring at the chalkboard across the room.

"What about hijacking my coke shipment?" Dante lunged harder, faster. "That an accident too?"

Ellen shoved Dante off her, yanking her skirt back down.

"Dammit, Ellen." Dante pulled up his jeans, fastening the button.

"You're not my husband anymore, so you don't get to cum inside me." Ellen strolled toward the door, pausing to glance over her shoulder. "Stay the fuck outta my state."

Dante's chuckle followed Ellen out of the room,

but that didn't slow her steps. This time she glared at every man on her way out the front door.

***

Sasha

The second Dez parked in front of the clubhouse, he grabbed Sasha by the wrist. Vinny stumbled into the cool morning air, leaving her with Dez and his crushing grip.

Their eyes met, his steeped in fury. "You—"

Otis leaned in the open passenger door. "They got Chewy. He's gone."

Sasha's arm slipped from Dez's grasp, and she scurried from the truck.

"He was on his front porch," Otis said, staring at the smoldering pile of metal across the lot. "Took five to the chest."

Sasha closed her eyes, tilting her head back. Her teeth grinded under her clenched jaw, but she couldn't stop it. It was the only thing holding in the tears. "Where's my mom?"

"The place was empty when I got here," Otis said.

Boots crunched gravel, and Sasha opened her eyes. Everyone was standing in front of her.

"We were hoping you knew where she was," Kev muttered.

Hard eyes glared at her, seeking answers Sasha couldn't give, and her feet shuffled backward. "I don't know. Maybe." She rounded the truck, passing the tailgate. "What? It's been, like, two hours, right? Give it another hour. If she's not back, I know where to look." Sasha turned on her heels, her gaze locked on the stairs to her room. "Don't nobody go no where."

In a near run, she took off for the garage. Five minutes of peace and a big fat joint. That's all she needed. She didn't get it, though. Two seconds alone and a hit off a small roach was what she got before Dez barged through her door.

"You fucked my brother!"

"What?" Sasha froze. Shock came on so strong her mind was too stunned to whirl.

"The way you looked at him tonight, how you flinch when he touches you." Dez crept closer, face twisted in rage. "That's what you do with me."

"I…It's not…We're just friends."

"But you fucked him."

"What do you want me to tell you, that I fucked your brother?" Sasha charged forward, glaring up into Dez's cruel eyes. "That I fucked half this town? How about that I fucked Ronny?"

Dez gripped onto Sasha's arms, squeezing. "You better be lying."

It had to be a lie. She couldn't tell him the truth, that she'd tried to fuck herself straight for six years and not one of those many men did anything for her, except him.

"You make me do crazy things, say stupid shit," Sasha said. When Dez's hands loosened, Sasha darted away. "For a long time, it's been just me and Vinny. I love him in a weird way, but our relationship isn't about sex."

Dez ran his hand through his tangled hair. "He

has the parts of you I want."

The words lit a firestorm in Sasha's chest. She'd jump into his arms, feel his warm skin against hers, but his anger created a bubble that forced her back.

"That's not Vinny's fault. Don't let it ruin what you got with him." An engine's roar shook the floor as her father's Chevelle pulled into the garage below. "You gotta get this shit outta your head, Dez. We got club business to deal with." She brushed past him, avoiding the anguish that gripped his face, and walked out her door.

***

Once everyone settled at the table and prayed for Chewy, Ellen laid out three warped emblems of semi-trucks. "We're gonna get a little payback on Satan's Crew tonight."

Heads nodded, but Sasha glared down the long table. She stared at her mother, noticing that her face was dolled up and she was dressed to kill. She knew exactly where that woman had been.

"They only have one buyer left in their sorry attempt at trafficking." Ellen lit a joint and took a long hit. She looked at the empty chair on her right then passed the joint to Dez. "We're gonna intercept their cargo and snake their buyer. Not only will we shut them out, but we'll have the potential to add a new client to our roster."

"I like it," Otis said. "What's the plan?"

"Sasha."

Sasha looked at her mother through the billow of smoke that wafted from her mouth.

103

"Is the old black truck still operational?" Ellen asked.

"Yeah. Just a few melted fenders and a broken window."

"Good. I pulled some strings with our friends south of the border, got the Crew's shipment moved to our dock for pickup at eight tonight." Ellen glanced at the clock on the wall. "It's still early. If you leave now, you'll have two hours to spare. Take Vinny with you, for backup."

"I don't know," Dez said. "Vinny's kinda fucked up. Maybe I should go with Sasha."

Ellen turned toward Dez, narrowing her eyes. "I need you and the boys to hijack their truck. They owe us a few rigs." She rose to her feet, glancing at Vinny. "You're good, right? Can shoot a gun?"

"Fuck yeah," Vinny said.

After grabbing a briefcase, Ellen headed to the safe, and Sasha hopped up from her chair. She hurried around the table, kneeling beside her mother in the corner of the room. "That's a lot of cash for a pickup," she whispered, staring at the case that had so much money in it, it barely clicked closed.

"It's a big pickup. Don't overthink things, and don't fuck this up." Ellen shoved the keys and briefcase into Sasha's hands, delivering a harsh stare.

When Sasha stood, her eyes landed on Dez. If rage had a face, he was wearing it. A cyclone of liquid fire churned in her stomach. She dropped her head, tapping Vinny's arm on her way out the door.

"Grab your pain meds and a handful of joints."

***

Taillights zoomed by. The tires of the last big rig of Ashby Trucking hummed against pavement as they tore down the freeway, and Sasha glanced over to the passenger seat.

"I'm okay, really," Vinny said, brushing chucks of shattered glass from his seat.

"I didn't say anything."

"You keep looking at me."

"Sorry." Sasha sunk behind the wheel, hiking her foot onto the cushion. "It's just…it's good to see you in that seat."

"After I took that bullet, I was huddled on the floor. It was like the fourth of July, loud, but all I could hear was your voice."

"Vinny, I—"

"Not like that." Vinny turned to face Sasha, wincing when his shoulder rubbed the seat. "I could hear you telling me to stop being a little bitch, get off the floor, and grab a gun."

"Sounds about right." Sasha smirked.

Vinny sat back, groaning. "Can you pull over for a second?"

"Yeah." Sasha hit the brakes, veering to the shoulder. "You okay?" The truck rocked to a stop, and she reached for Vinny then pulled back, afraid a single graze would break him. "What's wrong? Maybe you should chill in the sleeper."

"Here, just," Vinny inched closer to his armrest, "come here for a second."

Sasha maneuvered to her knees, slanting toward the passenger seat, and Vinny yanked her onto his lap with his good arm.

"What are you doing, freak?"

"Careful now," Vinny said through a grin. "I'm injured."

A smile took Sasha's lips by surprise. Her tense body withered against his chest, her legs tight on his sides. "I thought it was just a flesh wound."

"Still, it requires a lot of attention." His hand glided down the arch of her back. "Someone has to take care of me."

"Really?"

Vinny's lips floated atop hers, so close she could almost feel them.

"Yeah," he said with barely a sound.

The heat of his breath traveled throughout Sasha's body, cloaking her thoughts in a fuzzy tingle. Her jacket fell to the floor, and a tongue slipped into her mouth. Vinny groaned from the bullet hole in his shoulder, and Sasha winced from the bruise on her side, but that didn't stop them from fumbling with each other's belts.

***

Dez

Dez sat behind the wheel of his pickup truck, staring down a curvy, desolate road. His right hand gripped the barrel of a shotgun, left tapping the walky-talky in his lap. He looked across the cab, finding Ellen's eyes fixed on him.

"How do you even know they're coming through this way?" he asked, shifting under Ellen's sharp glare.

"What's up with you and my daughter? I told you to keep her in check, not fall in love with her."

"I'm not...What the—"

"Oh, please. I have eyes."

Dez rubbed his forehead. For some reason, he actually thought he could wipe the notion from his mind, but Sasha's eyes wouldn't fade.

"You must really be something," Ellen said, leaning back to stare Dez down. "I've been trying to push Sasha onto your brother for years, and you get her all twisted up in days."

"What do you mean?"

"Of course." A smirk lifted Ellen's cheeks. "You can't see it. She's been different since you came back around, less mouthy, more...chill. I like it."

Before Dez could chew on Ellen's words, a diesel engine whistled in the distance.

"Get ready," Ellen said, zipping up her leather jacket.

Dez looked at a garbage truck, parked only yards away. He couldn't see Otis and Kev inside its dark cab, but he knew they were waiting for his signal.

"Incoming," Dez said into the walky-talky. Airbrakes whooshed as a Mack truck rounded the bend, missing his truck, which was hidden in the woods. When the long trailer rolled from sight, Dez pressed the button on the walky and said, "Go."

As Dez drove out of the woods, Otis parked across the road, blocking both lanes. The brakes of the mark, a shiny new Mack truck, locked up, lighting the trees in red. A squeal rang out, smoke wafting from the eighteen wheels that rubbed against the road. The Mack truck skipped to a halt, a few feet from Otis's stolen garbage truck, its trailer jacking slightly to the side.

After closing off the rear, Dez seized his gun and nodded to Ellen. They crept down the road, splitting off at the back of the trailer. Ellen's boots shuffled along the passenger side as Dez crouched below the driver's door.

Otis and Kev pointed rifles at the windshield, yelling for the men inside the semi to get out. The door flung open, nearly clipping Dez upside the head. A shaky arm popped out and he latched on, yanking.

A man crashed to the ground, and Dez planted his boot on the quivering body, aiming his gun down. Two blasts rang out from the passenger side, and Dez pulled the trigger. Blood splattered the pavement in a spray of pink-laced crimson, splashing his face. He leapt over the headless body and followed Otis around the front.

Ellen stood over a pool of blood oozing from the dead man at her feet. She shoved empty shells into her pocket then reloaded her shotgun. "Dez, check inside." Her barrel clicked shut, and she stood behind him as he climbed into the cab.

"It's clear," Dez called out, jumping to the ground.

"Otis, Kev, check the trailer," Ellen said, lowering her weapon.

Dez looked at the stiff convulsing in the dirt, the decal on his jacket blasted to shreds. "We got two. Chewy was worth ten of these biker fucks."

"For sure."

"It's empty," Kev yelled, closing the cargo door. "Just a bunch of chains." He rested his gun against his shoulder, strolling back toward Ellen. "What should we do with the bodies?"

"Drag 'em into the brush. Dez, help him." Ellen looked at Otis then gestured to the garbage truck in the center of the road. "Park it out of sight. You and Kev get to be the first to take our new semi for a ride."

"It's nice," Otis said, his hand gliding along the deep blue fender. "A brand new Mack."

Dez dragged a body into the tall grass. When he loosened his clutch, dead weight thumped to the ground. He wiped his hands on his jeans, turning toward the road. Beyond Kev, who struggled to haul a bloody corpse, Ellen smiled at him. That leer in her eye made him feel like a canary caught in a cat's gaze.

"Fuck," Kev panted, dropping the body beside Dez. "I need to start lifting."

"A few years in the pen will do the trick," Dez muttered, heading for his pickup.

Chapter Twelve

Sasha

Sasha slid back into her seat, latching her belt buckle. "We really should hit the road."

"Yeah." Vinny struggled with his pants, one arm still bound in a sling. "Fuck this." He tore the sling off, tossing it behind him.

"Dude!" Sasha yelled.

Vinny curled his fingers, shot them straight, then curled them again. "I can't even do my belt. I need two hands."

"Jesus, you're hopeless." Sasha reached over and fastened Vinny's belt. Her stare drifted up. That bump on his throat, smooth cheeks, crystal clear eyes...the same shade of blue that lay in his brother's glare.

Sasha lurched back. Her shriveled shell of a conscious threatened to rear its ugly opinion, and she chased it away with the puff of a joint. A quick check in the mirrors and she was back on the freeway, running through seven gears.

"So," Sasha said, glancing at Vinny. "Don't tell anybody about this. Ever."

"What? About just now?"

"Well, yeah," she droned. "But you know...we should probably just pretend we've never had sex."

The silence lasted maybe ten seconds, but in Sasha's mind, it had been two eternities.

"You're embarrassed."

"God no." She looked at Vinny, his gaze fixed on the trees whizzing by out his broken window. "I sort of got mixed up with this crazy dude. He's got a really short temper and—"

"You fucked my brother."

Sasha cringed. 'Fucked' and 'my brother' were now three words she never wanted to hear in the same sentence again.

"I, umm—"

"Damn it, Sasha." Vinny slouched against the door, his hair blowing in the breeze. "Why him? You said you weren't into dudes."

"I'm not." Never had Sasha been so happy to have the distraction of the big road before her. "It just sorta happened. This'll all blow over. I just gotta shake the guy."

"That's gonna be hard to do." Vinny leaned on his armrest, glaring. "He's our sergeant."

"Yeah." Sasha rubbed the side of her neck then plucked another joint from the ashtray.

"You really know how to create a shitstorm, don't ya?" Vinny snatched the joint from her grasp, inhaling hard. "Sometimes," he said through a stream of smoke, "I think you do this shit on purpose."

111

Her jaw hinged open, and she fumbled around the cab for her cigarettes since Vinny obviously planned on hogging the doobie. "Why would I do that?"

"I don't know. 'Cause you're bored." Vinny lit a cigarette, holding it out.

Sasha grabbed the cigarette and sat back, twisting the butt between her fingers. It could've played out differently. A lot of things could've played out differently, if she cared enough to fight the flow.

When she glanced over, Vinny looked away. That feeling returned to her stomach, nagging, roiling, scorching. How many times could she dick over her best friend? How many times would he forgive her, when she'd never said sorry?

"Are we cool?" Sasha muttered, the words left hanging in the spacious cab.

The chain of Vinny's wallet clinked, and Sasha flinched when he gripped her leg. She looked at Vinny, and he held out a freshly lit joint.

"What do you think?" he said.

Sasha glided her hand along Vinny's arm until her fingers found the joint. She plucked the doobie from his grasp, flashing a half-grin.

***

Dez

Dez leaned against the threshold of the clubhouse door. Heavy clouds masked the moon's light, covering the charred remains of their once-remarkable fleet in shades of gray. Otis snored on the couch behind him, stretching farther across the cushions. With Kev sleeping in the cab of the new truck, the spots for crashing dwindled.

Thunder clapped as Dez walked off the porch. While lighting a cigarette, he looked at Ellen's huge house on the hill. Wind rustled the curtains in its many windows, wide columns gleaming. She must have five guest rooms in that place, at least. He didn't know, had never been asked inside.

His gaze drifted to the dark room above the garage. Sasha had hours of road ahead of her. A shame to let that big, comfy bed of hers go to waste. Dez flicked his cigarette onto the gravel and headed toward Sasha's room.

The door squeaked opened, and her scent rushed in, provoking a grin. He searched for the light switch, and with a click, the mess that was Sasha's room fell under a soft glow.

Dez kicked piles of clothes aside, walking to Sasha's dresser. His fingers glided atop leather chokers, an array of brass knuckles, and bottles of perfume. Pictures lined the round mirror, all of Sasha, Vinny, and some redhead chick.

"What are you doing in here?" Ellen's bark flowed from the doorway.

Dez turned, and Ellen stepped into the room.

"I, uh…" His eyes stuck to bare skin. Ellen's silky dress hung low on her chest and high on her thighs. "I was gonna crash in here. I didn't think Sasha would mind."

Ellen chuckled, slinking closer. "Really? Wouldn't mind a strange man in her bed?" Her eyes wandered up to Dez's face. "You don't know her very well."

She reached for his chest, and he seized her by the wrist. "What are you doing, Ellen?"

"I want to see what makes you so special. You got the whole tough guy act down pat, but there has to be something more." Her other hand latched onto his belt, tugging. "Something bigger."

Dez pushed Ellen's hands aside. "Stop fucking around."

"Ooh. Watch your tone with me, boy. I'm your president." Ellen leaned against the dresser, gripping onto Dez's shirt. "Technically, you should be on your knees."

Ellen's leer trailed Dez as he knelt to the floor. His hands slid up her legs, hiking the stretchy fabric to her waist. He grabbed Ellen by the hips and lifted her atop the dresser, smirking before he leaned forward.

***

Sasha

Sasha pulled beside the dock and killed the engine. She leaned against the steering wheel, staring at Vinny's sleeping face. In the gentle glow of the moon's light, a tranquil beauty overtook his rough features. She reached out to him when the kink returned to her stomach. A burning sensation rose in her throat, the dashboard lights blurring. She rubbed her eyes, her fingers trembling. The spin clutching the world twisted faster, pulling Sasha to the side, and she banged her head against the window.

"Sasha!"

Vinny gripped her, but she couldn't focus on his face.

"Breathe," he said.

Her breath came out in shuddering waves, and the wild spin slowed to a wicked sway.

"What's wrong?"

"I'm gonna be sick." Sasha opened her door, nearly falling out of the cab. Her legs buckled, and she dropped to her knees, dry heaving. Vinny gently rubbed her back, and she looked up, taking a deep breath.

"You're scaring me," Vinny said, his arm encircling her waist.

"I'm cool." Slowly, Sasha rose while clinging onto Vinny's good arm. "Jesus. I feel like I slammed a pint of JD."

"Did you?"

"No." She chuckled.

Vinny ran his palm along Sasha's forehead, ending on her cheek. "You're all clammy and pale. When was the last time you ate?"

"I don't know."

"Come on." He helped Sasha back into the truck. "There're some chips in the back."

She shut her door, and Vinny climbed into the passenger seat. He handed her a bag of chips then searched through a cooler. A moment later, she was holding an ice-cold bottle of Coke.

Cramps accompanied every swallow, but the fuzz cleared, so she kept eating.

"Better?"

"Yeah," Sasha said between chews. "That was weird. Probably some kinda flu." She closed her eyes as she drank the cool soda, its heavy syrup coating her gut. She sank into her seat, looking out the window. "I wish I didn't have to—"

Lights flashed offshore, and Sasha groaned. "Do this." She blinked her running lights then rolled down her window. "Stay in the cab. Keep low with your gun on them."

"But your uncle—"

"I don't think I'm meeting with my uncle." Sasha grabbed the briefcase, pausing once her hand grazed the truck's door. For some reason, she wanted to kiss Vinny. Instead, she glowered. "Just be quiet. And stay in the cab, no matter what."

Sasha jumped from the truck, slapped on a hard leer, and walked forward. The boat docked, and right on cue men hurried toward her to shove rifles at her chest.

"*Paso a la luz*," a deep voice called from the darkness.

Sasha did as the man said and inched under the dock lights, lifting her chin.

"Ha!" A man pushed through the crowd, his dark eyes fixed on Sasha. "It *is* you, the ghost of Guadalajara." His long black hair waved in the sea breeze as he stared down at her. "They still call you that to this day. Did you know?"

Sasha shook her head, scanning the symbols inked on the man's dark skin. Each tattoo told the story of this man's rise to leader of the Call of Death, mostly due to her actions with a sniper rifle.

116

"You made quite a name for yourself, Sasha Ashby. That's hard to do in my *barrio*, especially for a *pote de la leche*."

"Oh." Sasha dropped her head to hide the scrunch of her face then peered back up at angry eyes. "You must be Tito. Look, what happened with the *Llamada de la Muerte*—"

"My crew," he sneered.

"Was not personal. I was hired to do a job, and I did it."

"It's funny." Tito's large hands landed on Sasha's shoulders, the slap when his hands collided with her arms masking her flinch. "Women always have the biggest balls." He released his grasp and leered over his shoulder. "*Vámonos*."

Men scurried away, and the back door of her trailer squeaked open.

"The case," Tito said.

Sasha gawked as the line of people bound by chains loaded into her trailer. "People?" Her voice cracked, the word barely escaping her lips.

"*Sí*. Twenty Orientals." Tito cracked open the case, thumbing through the bills. "See the one on the end?"

Sasha stared at a teenage girl, covered in filth. Her scraps of burlap, meant to be clothes, scraped her bruised thighs as she climbed into the truck.

"That one's supposed to be special. Blue eyes. It's rare in their country."

"I, umm—"

"Don't worry. We chained them to your trailer nice and tight. They won't be going nowhere." Tito placed a key in Sasha's hand and nodded. "Every

117

six months, I'll be here at this time." His cruel glare held firm as he backed away. Then he turned, following his men to the boat. "See you April first, *fantasma de Guadalajara*."

Moonlight glistened off the key in Sasha's palm, shining, sparkling. Her fingers closed into a tight fist, pressing the key's sharp edges into her skin. A thin piece of metal, yet it had the power to trap twenty people and scrape her soul at the same time. To climb back into that truck and drive away would take a shit-ton of ignorance, which was in no short supply. Sasha dropped her eyes to the dirt, walking to the rig.

Chapter Thirteen

Dez

Ellen walked out of the room, closing the door, and Dez dropped his head into his hands. "Stupid, weak bastard," he sputtered. Half his life had been wasted on fantasies of Ellen. What it might be like to have her. How great that dirty tongue of hers must feel on flesh. He never thought it would leave him so hollow.

He scanned the mounds of clothes, his somewhere among them. When spotting his jeans, he leaned forward and pulled them close. He fished through the pockets until he found a pack of smokes and a zippo.

As the flow of nicotine surged though his veins, he settled back against the dresser. Curtains blew in front of an open window, exposing the darkness beyond. The sky looked empty, cold, bleak. It never looked that way when he stared up at it with Sasha.

"Fuck! Sasha."

It didn't happen. He didn't just fuck Sasha's

119

mother, in Sasha's room. At least, he'd never admit to it. Anyone who said otherwise would end up with a mouthful of broken teeth, even if that person was Ellen.

Dez gathered the rest of his clothes, walked into the bathroom, and turned on the shower. His eyelids fought to stay open. It felt like days since he'd last slept, but he couldn't crawl into Sasha's bed smelling like two kinds of pussy.

After a quick scrub down, his head hit the pillow. One big lungful of Sasha's scent and the world clicked off.

***

Sasha

"People!" Vinny exclaimed. "Did you know about this?"

Sasha gripped the steering wheel harder, mashing down on the gas pedal. "No. I thought we were getting coke or maybe heroin, but…Jesus."

Vinny looked behind him, unable to see beyond the sleeper cab. "What kind of people?"

"I don't know. They were Chinese or some shit. Twenty women and children."

"Live cargo. You know what that means? As soon as we get back, Ellen's gonna send us out to…where do they go?"

"Not the warehouse." Sasha shook her head, the motor roaring as she pushed a hundred.

"You better ease off," Vinny said, checking his side mirror. "We don't wanna get pinched with this load."

Sasha lifted her boot from the gas pedal, and the engine wound down along with the race of trees but not the pound in her temples.

Vinny lit two cigarettes, then passed one to her. "What do you think will happen to them?"

"I don't wanna think about that. My stomach's already twisting."

"Still? Pull over."

"Why?" Sasha glanced at Vinny, smirking. "What are you gonna do to me now?"

Vinny smiled, popping a painkiller in his mouth. "I wanna drive. You can sit back and chill for a while."

"Awesome." Sasha parked on the side of the road, hopping over Vinny's legs as he slid into the driver's seat. The truck rolled forward, and she sank back. A cool breeze tickled her skin, lulling her eyes to a close. She leaned against the broken window, breathing in the scent of wisteria and honeysuckle.

"I want you to stay on the compound." Sasha closed the flaps of her jacket, wriggling into the seat. "Until this shit with Satan's Crew simmers down."

"In your room?"

Sasha peered over, attempting a scowl that ended in a smirk. "No. In your old room."

Vinny answered, but his words fell under the thump of tires. The cab's gentle rock stole Sasha's senses, carrying her body into its swing.

***

Ellen

Ellen sprawled atop her king-sized mattress, satin sheets caressing her skin. She looked at the clock on her nightstand and grinned.

"Four a.m., closing time."

She rolled onto her stomach and reached for the phone. Her finger spun the rotary, soft clicks singing in her ear. When the phone rang, she fought to suppress a giggle. Then Dante's voice flowed through the receiver, sparking a giddy blaze inside her chest.

"Dante, are you waiting up for that shipment?"

"Fuck!" Dante's shout streamed through the phone. "My chalkboard. You dirty cunt."

"Language, sweetie." A smile spanned Ellen's lips. She could almost see the anger puffing his tanned face. "I took your route and the semi. You won't be needing them anymore anyway. When my new rig shows up to make a delivery in a few hours, with my man behind the wheel, your brother is going to be so disappointed in you."

"One of these days, I'm gonna cut up that pretty face of yours," Dante said in a near growl. "That way, everyone can see you for what you really are."

"You say the sweetest things. Have a good night, Dante." Ellen hung up the phone, swinging her feet to the floor. After strolling to her closet, she laid a halter-top and a pair of jeans on her bed. She glanced back at the nightstand and the small pile of white powder beside a little silver straw.

"Gotta stay on the ball." Ellen hurried forward, cutting out two thick lines. "Gonna be a long day."

Her hair fell in a circle around her face as she bent, like a silky cloak to hide her depraved deed. Tiny silvery granules disappeared as she snorted, pumping life into her tired veins. Her head snapped up, and she exhaled before heading back down to take another round.

As she leaned against the nightstand, her palm fell atop a large hunting knife. The blade slid from its sheath so easy, its weight a comfort in her hand. The sight of her glare reflected in the smooth metal shocked her. So harsh, bloodshot, wired. Those eyes weren't the ones she remembered, wrinkled and steeped in hate.

Ellen thrust the knife back into its sheath, turning to dress.

***

Sasha

Sasha could hear Vinny fidgeting around the cab of the semi and the light hum of tires rubbing road, but she held her eyes shut.

"You alive?" Vinny asked, nudging Sasha's arm.

"No," she said, swatting his hand away. A hint of daylight snuck in, and she yanked her jacket over her face. "Fuck. It's morning, again."

"We'll be home in ten minutes."

"Good. I can't wait to stretch my," her knees cracked as she uncurled from the seat, "ah, my legs. God."

Vinny's chuckle pulled Sasha's leer.

"You look better," he said, glancing between her

and the road. "Your color, at least."

Sasha stuck her middle finger in the air, moving it in front of Vinny's eyes.

"Yeah, yeah." He shoved her hand back. "By the way, you suck at ridin' shotgun. I ran out of smokes two hours ago."

"You should've woke me, stupid." Sasha pulled a pack of cigarettes from her pocket, lighting one for Vinny then herself. "That's, like, an emergency."

"Ahh." Smoke flowed from Vinny's mouth, circling the air before it zoomed out the window. "I hope we get a few hours turnaround. I'm wiped."

"I can take the load myself," Sasha said, leaning against her armrest. "There're twelve gauges of backup under the seat."

"We have a jacked shipment of slave people going God knows where, and you think you're ridin' solo. Ha!" Vinny shook his head, puffing on his cigarette.

"See," Sasha bobbed her finger his way, "and I was trying to be nice, but fuck you, bro. You can suffer." Her words came out between chuckles, and Vinny laughed.

Air whooshed from the brakes, the truck rounded a sharp bend, and sunlight shimmered off their dented gate.

"Home sweet home," Vinny said, turning onto the compound. He pulled past the blackened heaps of twisted metal, parking across from the garage.

Sasha cracked open her door, pausing at the sight of her mother. A long breath slowed the pound of her heart as she closed her eyes. The darkness provided a temporary release. Orders weren't barked in her face when Sasha was hidden behind closed eyes; friends weren't killed while Sasha lingered in the depths of her mind. Just memories of soft skin, red hair, and sweet giggles. Her door flew open, but she stayed in a daydream of wandering fingertips.

"What are you doing?" her mother damn near barked, blowing her happy thoughts to bits.

Sasha looked to the driver's seat. It was empty. Her head rolled to her open door and right into her mother's irritated glare. "Where'd Vinny go?"

"Up to the house. You've been sitting here for five minutes. Are you on something?"

"There are people chained in the back of this truck."

"Really, Sasha? You've chosen *now* to sprout a conscience?"

A jolt of surprise nearly robbed the air from Sasha's lungs, mostly because she had no idea her mother even knew what a conscience was. "You put me in so much danger." Sasha narrowed her stare as she climbed out of the truck. "Do you even know who met me at the dock? The Call of Death. I spent all of last summer killing those motherfuckers for Felix."

A laugh, that's what her mother offered. "Looks like your shit's starting to pile up. Oh relax, this was a one-time thing."

"No, it's not. They expect me to be there every six months for the same kind of pickup." Sasha anticipated shock, disbelief, maybe a fraction of concern, but all she saw were money signs in her mother's eyes.

"Guess you got your new route after all," Sasha said, leaning against the slightly melted fender of the truck. "Do I even want to know who our clients are?"

Pebbles crunched under Ellen's fidgety boot, her stern eyes low. "The Lazzari Family, out of New York."

"That's Italian mafia!"

"Yeah," Ellen said, as if it were no big deal.

"We don't go that far east. You said it's trouble."

"I'm mending fences, expanding our horizons."

"Do our horizons include your biker boy-toy?" That one got a reaction. Watching her mother's feathers ruffle left such a warmth in Sasha's chest until that glare returned with a vengeance.

"Have you been following me?" Ellen asked through gritted teeth.

"Maybe."

Ellen jabbed Sasha's chest, and Sasha scurried back.

"You never could mind your own fucking business, girl."

"You *are* my business." The sudden growth of backbone surprised Sasha more than her mother, who gasped. This temporary lapse of courage would fade, but while it was here Sasha planned on rolling with it. "This club, my life. It's all tied to you."

"That's how you knew where their warehouse was," Ellen said with wide eyes. "You followed me."

Sasha looked away. She should've seen this coming. A person could only shove so many skeletons into a closet they're hiding in before pieces got loose.

"This is so typical of you," Ellen said in a sneer. "Did you see your mommy doing some naughty things and lash out?"

"Stop it." Sasha shrank down, eyeing the steps that led to her room.

"There's that childish temper again. You never think, you just do. That's the reason we're trafficking people. It's the consequence of your firebomb escapade."

A shiver ran through Sasha. She crossed her arms, held tightly onto her sides, but she couldn't shake the chill left by the truth of her mother's words.

"You know," Ellen said softly, almost in sorrow, "I'm getting really sick of waiting for you to grow the fuck up." She backed away, gesturing to the garage. "Get some rest. You're on the road again first thing tomorrow. And take a shower; you look like shit."

Sasha stood under warm rays of sun, a fire raging deep inside her gut. She looked away from her mother, who was strolling toward the clubhouse, and stared at the long white trailer of the truck beside her. She thought about the starving, sweltering people locked within breathing stale air and all the bullshit that led to this end. It wasn't the right path. This wasn't the club's vision, her vision.

Sasha turned away from the gentle breeze, the chirp of birds, things you couldn't experience while trapped inside a tractor trailer, and hurried up her stairs.

***

Vinny

Vinny leaned against a marble column of the big house and watched Sasha cower under Ellen's glare. The door opened behind him, and Otis stepped to the edge of the porch.

"What's all this?" Otis asked, pointing to the two women far across the lot.

"Sasha never backs down," Vinny said, keeping his gaze straight ahead. "Six-foot bikers, Mexican gangsters, but she crumbles with Ellen. I don't get it."

Otis snickered. "What would you do if Ellen got in your face like that, poking her finger at your chest?"

Vinny sank against the wide pillar. If Ellen ever barked at him like that, he knew exactly what he'd do. He'd run and hide behind Sasha.

"That's her president and mother." Otis turned toward Vinny, tapping an unlit cigarette on his zippo. "She's extra hard on Sasha. She has to be. It's how you mold a leader."

"What?"

"Sasha's gonna have to run all this one day, but Ellen can't just give it to her. Sasha has to work her way up, know every aspect of the club. She has so much potential." Otis lit his cigarette, nodding to the open front door. "The girls are in there cooking breakfast. You should grab some grub and hit the sack."

Vinny searched for Sasha beyond the rocky hill

but only found an empty lot. So bare, this compound, without her smile to fill it. He considered giving chase, until the scent of bacon encircled him like a lasso. The aroma and the sounds of muffled laughter and low music beckoned him. He tore his gaze from Sasha's little room above the garage, walking inside the big house.

Chapter Fourteen

Sasha

Sasha had to do a double take. The sight of Dez crashed out in her bed, naked, didn't sink in the first time. Quietly, she shut her door and crept inside. Sun spilled through the side of her shaded window, lighting the muscles hidden under Dez's bright ink. Flames, skulls, barbed wire. His body, a skin canvas of wicked art.

While backing away, she slinked out of her jacket and turned toward the bathroom.

"Sasha?"

Her light steps halted. She peeked over her shoulder as Dez wormed under the covers.

"Hey," Sasha said. A smile snuck onto her lips, and she tried so hard to hold it back that it turned to a frown.

"I'm sorry." Dez sat up, gesturing to the bed. "Your door was unlocked and I—"

"It's cool. You can crash here as long as you need to." Sasha turned away, rolling her eyes. That just slipped out. She didn't want him crashing in her room. Her gaze drifted back to Dez's solid chest, those rippling abs.

"I'm gonna shower," Sasha said, hurrying into the bathroom.

After shutting the door and blasting the water, Sasha slumped against the wall. "What the fuck was that?" she mumbled, ripping off her clothes.

Halfway through the shampoo cycle, it hit her. She hadn't tossed Dez out on his ass because she wanted to crawl in bed next to him. She actually needed his strong arms to hold her defeated body and strengthen her will.

"Oh God," Sasha groaned under the rush of flowing water.

In near record time, she shaved, washed, and dressed. Then she stood there, in front of the bathroom door, staring at the brass knob. Droplets tumbled from her tangled hair, splashing her toes, but she just stared. The lump in her throat wouldn't budge. Grumbles, huffs, nothing unclogged her airways.

Two failed attempts and a slap on the forehead later, Sasha yanked the door open. Her tight shoulders sagged, lips bunching when finding an empty room. Relief rushed in, overshadowing the disappointment and bringing her back to the usual hollow shell.

She grabbed her brush and sat on the edge of her bed. The door squeaked open, and Dez walked in, holding a plate of food.

"Hungry?" he asked, flashing a short stack of pancakes.

"Dude!" The brush slipped from Sasha's hand as she jumped up. She wrapped two pieces of sausage in a pancake then took a big bite. "This is, like, the best ever," she said between chomps.

"You eat like an animal."

Sasha closed her mouth, wiping her lips with the back of her hand. "Sorry." This time, she finished chewing then swallowed hard. "It's just so good."

Dez held out the plate, and Sasha snatched it from his hand, dropping back onto the bed.

"Where's Vinny?" Dez asked, peering out the window.

"He's crashing in his old room, at the big house. Didn't you see him when you went up there?"

"I didn't go up there. Some chick put that in my hand when I was having a smoke."

"Probably Lacy," Sasha said, crossing her legs to balance the plate in her lap. "She's always here. Carts the girls around, cooks like a goddess."

"Vinny has a room in Ellen's house?"

"Yeah. He lived here for a while." Sasha nibbled on a piece of bacon, gazing up at Dez as he stared out the window. "After you went away and your mom split, he was on his own. We took him in before the state could get him. Didn't he tell you any of this?"

Dez shook his head, eyes low.

"What do you guys talk about?" Sasha asked, wiping her hands on her pants. "When you're alone."

"I don't know," Dez said, turning away from the window. "Rebuilding motors and shit."

She snickered, plopping the half-eaten plate on

her nightstand. "Dudes are ridiculous."

"Did he graduate?"

"No." Sasha walked into the bathroom, grabbing her toothbrush. "I couldn't go back to school after...you know, with my shit all busted up, and Vinny didn't want to go without me. We just hung out here, doing chores until we made prospect. Then the chores got dirtier."

Sasha gazed at Dez's reflection in the mirror while brushing her teeth. He looked so sad. All these years, he never once crossed her mind. His name was unspoken in the club, but he'd been thinking about them.

"Sasha. I'm sor—"

"No!" She rinsed her mouth, walking from the bathroom. "I don't hold a grudge about that day. You guys just did what you were told. I get that now."

"You shouldn't have to get that. You and my brother should've finished high school, went to prom together, and got hitched."

"What crazy world are you living in? That was never gonna be my life or his." Sasha crept closer, but the levels of rage in Dez's stare held her back. "You couldn't have changed much, if you were here." She reached for his hand, just as he stomped toward the door. "Where are you going?"

Dez flung open the door, stopping in the threshold. "I'm supposed to work up a strike plan with Ellen. Half of Satan's Crew is combing the roads for your truck. We're gonna hit 'em hard, draw 'em back so you can move out tomorrow morning."

"Dez…"

"Don't worry, I'll find somewhere else to sleep."

Glares of sunlight veiled the sour look on Dez's face as he stepped outside, slamming the door behind him. Sasha stood in the middle of the room and shrugged. "Dudes. Are. Ridiculous."

Sleep could take her where she stood, and she'd let it. A long sigh flowed from her chest as she stretched, falling backward onto her bed. Two seconds of fluffy pillows. That was all it took to root her in place.

***

Nails tore at Sasha's insides. A tiny hand pressed on her stomach from the inside, raising her skin as little fingers ripped from within.

Sasha sat up in bed, gasping. She yanked up her shirt, running her palm along her stomach. Smooth skin, ripples of muscle, no hand.

Relief only lasted seconds, replaced by a burn that rose from her chest and settled in the back of her throat. She bolted from the bed and slid across the bathroom floor, lifting the toilet's lid just in time for her breakfast to come back up. Her shaky hands clutched porcelain as she pushed herself off the floor.

Sasha leaned over the sink, flipping on the faucet. The rush of flowing water pulled her stare, calmed the shudder of bones, and soothed her mind. She splashed her face then peered into the mirror.

"Uh, gross." Dark circles puffed the skin under her eyes, refusing to fade despite her many attempts to rub them away. She shut off the water, grabbed a towel, and walked out of the bathroom. The whirl in her stomach slowed, strength returning to her limbs with every step. A few hits from that doobie on the nightstand and her head would be on straight.

Before Sasha's fingers could graze the tightly wrapped paper, a red light caught her eye. Somewhere beneath the clutter of empty cigarette packs, dusty bandanas, and unopened mail, a light blinked from an unseen answering machine. Sasha reached for the mess, doubled back for the joint, lit it, and then dove in to find her lost machine.

Two quick puffs and a press of a button later, soft clicks filled the room before the message played. "Hey, Sasha. It's Candy…I heard about the fire and stuff. I just wanted to hear your voice, make sure you're okay. Sorry I bothered you." And with a click, the hum of a tape rewinding replaced Candy's silky voice.

Sasha stared at the phone, smoke rolling from her mouth. Candy. Her first love and constant source of misery. She'd taken two beatings and a million crooked glares for that girl, but the damn feelings, which she told herself not to feel, only grew stronger.

Twice Sasha reached for the phone, her fingers never making it to the receiver. She took another hit, grumbling through the exhale.

"Fuck it," she said, picking up the phone.

The now-tiny roach burned away in the ashtray as Sasha punched buttons. When the line rang, her throat sealed closed. She moved the receiver away from her ear, slowly lowering it toward its base when Candy answered.

Sasha thrust the phone to her head, clunking plastic to skull. "Hey, Candy."

"Oh, Sasha! God, I was so worried. Are you okay?"

"Yeah, I'm good. Busy."

"The whole town is talking about the fire and the shootings. I just, like, wish I could see you."

"You're not banned. You can stop by any time you want." Silence lingered, and Sasha searched the mountain of cigarette packs for a fresh one. Something told her she'd need a smoke for what was about to come streaming through the phone. "If you don't want to come around anymore—"

"No! I do," Candy said, pausing for the inevitable but. "But Otis said I should lay low for a while, that things aren't safe around the clubhouse right now."

"Otis?" Sasha froze, her lighter inches from the unlit cigarette in her mouth. "So, what? Are you guys, like, a thing now?" After another bout of piercing silence, she lit her cigarette and drew in the thick smoke. "Hello?"

"Yeah. We're sorta, kinda together. He's really sweet to me. Sasha—"

"Don't." Sasha shook her head, which did nothing to soothe the sting left by betrayal. "It's cool." The words came out through clenched teeth but thankfully sounded casual, at least in her head. "And Otis is right. It's probably not a good time to chill here." She hopped up, pacing within the cord's limit. "We'll have another party soon. I'll just see you then. Later."

Before one syllable could stream through the phone, Sasha slammed the receiver down. Glass bottles clinked together as she mashed her cigarette out. "Sounds about right. Who could turn down a road captain?"

Sasha tore through heaps of dirty clothes, stopping at the first pair of tan cargo pants. "I don't care. Why should I care?" After sliding into the pants, she pulled off her t-shirt and flung it across the room. "Bitch didn't waste no time." She grabbed a black tank top and lifted it to her nose. The stench of blood and whiskey, a combination she once loved, turned her stomach. She pitched the shirt over her shoulder and snatched another near identical top. "Whatever. She can live that lie." In a huff, Sasha pulled the tank down over her chest. "Got me talking to myself like a fucking freak."

Empty beer bottles rattled in every corner as Sasha stomped across the room. She yanked her door open, a cool breeze sweeping along her bare arms. The chill went straight to her heart, spiking in waves. Sadness, regret, anger topped in a rolling crest and nearly crushed her. She looked at her leather jacket crumpled on the floor, orange flames riding along its sleeve.

"Don't forget your skin," Sasha muttered. Her body wilted, and she trudged back into her room, scooping her heavy coat off the floor.

***

Thin beams of sunlight cut through the trees up the hillside, leaving Sasha in the remnants of day.

137

She strolled across a deserted lot, avoiding the pile of blackened metal to her right, and crept up the clubhouse steps.

She stopped just outside the threshold and peeked inside. It seemed…bigger without hairy-assed locals parked on barstools and lonely in the absence of long legs and tight minis. A step closer and she glimpsed into the backroom. Her eyes zeroed in on Dez. A lock of his tangled hair glided down his wide shoulder, and the corners of her lips raised. She cringed, backing away. Butterflies? That couldn't be butterflies in her stomach at the sight of a…man.

"What the fuck?" Sasha mumbled into her palm.

"What?" Vinny said from behind her. "What the fuck?"

A gasp carried Sasha around in a whirl. "Vinny!" Her balled fist loosened, and she whacked him on the chest. "You scared the shit outta me."

"What's going on in the backroom?"

Vinny stepped toward the door, and Sasha grabbed onto his arm, pulling him outside.

"It's just club BS," she said, practically dragging Vinny across the porch.

"Shouldn't we be a part of that?"

Sasha slumped onto the bench, staring at the town's lights in the distance. "I'm not ready to deal with all that yet."

"I know what you need."

Wood shifted as Vinny sat beside her. She turned to face him, finding a freshly rolled joint and a smile.

"Awesome." Sasha leaned over, bumping Vinny

with her shoulder. "Spark it."

They puffed and passed as the last of the sun's rays fell under darkness.

"You look better," Vinny said, leaning forward to better stare at her in the low light.

Sasha turned from the glimmer of fireflies and blew a cloud of smoke in his face.

Vinny exhaled, blowing the smoke back her way. "You even got a little pink in your cheeks."

His finger drifted toward her face, and she slapped it away.

"That's because I'm pissed," Sasha said, handing Vinny the joint.

"What's new?"

"Asshole." Sasha snatched the roach from Vinny's grasp, grinning as she took a hit. The smile faded when the cherry reached her fingertips, burning skin. "I talked to Candy." She squished the red-hot tip between her fingers, grinding its heat into tender flesh.

"She tell you about Otis?" Vinny asked in a near whisper.

"You know about that?" Sasha wiped her hand on her pants, a black stain remaining on her thumb and forefinger. "We spent fourteen hours alone in that truck, you didn't think to tell me?"

"Chill. I just found out this morning. Big mouth Betsy."

"You know, gossip isn't the only reason they call her big mouth Betsy." Sasha shook her head when Vinny's wide eyes veered to her. "Or so I've heard."

"I know. I found that out this morning too."

The giddy look on Vinny's face forced a chuckle from Sasha's lungs. A light clicked on overhead, and her mother walked onto the porch.

"Finally awake," Ellen said with full-on attitude. "Would you two like to join us now, or should we all keep waiting?"

Vinny jumped to his feet, and Sasha snickered. She rose from the bench, wiping her face clear. Her mother's scowl wouldn't burst her high, not yet. She kept her stare on Vinny's back, clumping past her mother's outstretched arm and into the clubhouse.

Chapter Fifteen

Sasha dropped into her chair. She nodded to Kev, raised her brow at Otis, then settled back. Her plan to avoid Dez lasted about two seconds. Like a joint to the flame, her gaze went to him, though he leered at her mother as she sat beside him at the head of the table.

"We're gonna burn their shit to the ground." Ellen lit a cigarette then poured a shot of whiskey. "Vinny, you're with Kev. I want you two to douse their bikes and that ghetto bar they call a clubhouse in gasoline." She downed the shot, slamming her glass on the table. "Me, Otis, and Dez will boost the rest of their semis. They still owe us a few."

"Where do you want me?" Sasha asked, leaning forward.

"Here. Just relax, watch the place. You got a long run and you're ridin' solo. Rest up 'cause I want you on the road at six a.m., give you time in case of traffic." Ellen looked at the clock, grumbled, and then poured another shot. "It's only eight. We still got five hours until we move out for Tennessee.

Grab some grub; load up the pickups with gas cans and shotguns. Everyone cool with this?"

Everyone around the table nodded their heads, except for Dez, who snickered. "No. This ain't no solo run. Sasha needs backup."

Ellen turned, her glare hardening on Dez. "This was your plan."

"Yeah, and I planned it so we'd be back in time to tail Sasha on the run."

Tension seemed to build an electric field between the two, creeping into every inch of the room. Neither backed down, which made Sasha's legs fidget.

"Do we need to take a vote?" Ellen seethed, her jaw clenched.

"No," Sasha said, tapping her zippo on the table. "It's a solid plan. Let's get ready."

"Good." Ellen rose from her seat, ripping her glare from Dez. "Kev, Vinny, head down to Gussie's and fill five or six gas cans. I'll be in the big house if anyone needs me. Sasha, walk with me?"

"Sure." Sasha hopped up and followed her mother from the room. "What's—"

Ellen lifted her hand, stopping Sasha's words. It wasn't until they hit gravel and the clubhouse lights dimmed far behind them that her mother's steady pace slowed.

"I called in my markers with every lawman from here to Albany. They're on full alert." Ellen stopped beside the lone semi, and her frosty glare melted. "You will have backup out on the road. You just won't see them."

Sasha nodded, dropping her smile from view. Fingers grazed her chin, and she flinched, raising her eyes.

"You didn't think I'd let my girl head out alone, did ya?" Ellen reached out and patted the fender of the semi beside them. "This was your father's favorite truck, the symbol of this holler. She needs to be protected."

An invisible hand of stupidity slapped Sasha in the face. She had actually thought her mother was talking about her, not a ratty old truck.

"Right." Sasha backed toward the garage, blinking away tears. "Important truck. I gotta make some phone calls. I'll catch you guys before you leave." She spun on her heels, making a beeline for the stairs.

Sasha gripped the railing and glanced back. Her mother glided up the hill, her outline blending with the darkness created by the big house's shadow.

"God, I'm a freakin idiot." Sasha took the steps to her room two at a time, but it wasn't fast enough to shake the hurt. "And now I'm talking to myself again."

Sasha slammed her door closed, sealing herself inside the sanctity of her room. The mess, the scent of stale beer and marijuana, stole the edge from her bones. Just as her tight muscles uncoiled, the door swung open and Dez stomped inside.

Reflex carried Sasha away from the angry man in front of her, and the stiffness returned. "What the f—"

"Where are you going? Who are you meeting up with?" Dez yelled.

He moved closer, and Sasha inched away. Her back thumped against the dresser, but she didn't crumble. Her chin lifted, frost hardening her spine. "What do you care?"

"I wanna know where you are, when you'll be back, what kind of danger you're in."

Dez stepped close enough for his chest to brush against hers, trailing sparks in its brief contact.

"Why?" The word barely made a sound, but Dez heard it. He had to have, with their lips so close.

"Because…"

Icy blue eyes pierced Sasha's strength. She wanted to look away, gather her wits, but Dez's stare held her prisoner.

"I…I'm your sergeant at arms. It's my job to make sure you're safe."

The snicker that burst from Sasha's mouth couldn't be stopped, even if she wanted it to. "Right." Her shoulder bumped against his as she walked to the center of the room. She had to be the most clueless person alive, yet everyone brought their shit to her. "For some reason, you think I have the answers." Her arms rose then flopped back at her sides. "I don't know shit! About anything, apparently."

"Sasha—"

"Go ask your president. She might give you what you want."

"She can't give me what I want."

Dez's deep voice boomed right behind Sasha. She tilted back, and arms slid around her waist. Lips brushed her cheek, warm breath drawing her in. Those large, rough hands skated under her shirt, and she wilted against the solid body behind her.

"You're what I want." Dez wrapped his fingers around the collar of her jacket, sliding the leather off her shoulders. The jacket fell to the floor, and his lips landed on her skin. "All of you." The light breath on the back of her neck came with shivers, which crawled beneath her flesh. "Every inch of you." His fingers snaked down her pants, forcing a gasp from her mouth once he snuck inside.

Sasha spun, locking onto Dez's kiss like a magnet. Every time she grinded against him, she hated herself a little more for liking it so much. This wasn't a punishment, a lesson she needed to learn. It was a true connection, an electric vibe that pulled her deeper into its clutches.

Dez's shirt dropped atop her jacket, and she bit the side of his neck. The moan that flowed from his lips, low and throaty, ignited a fiery blaze inside Sasha's chest. She ran her tongue down rock solid pecs, beyond the ripples of his stomach. Her knees hit the floor, and her hand landed on the gun fastened to his belt. She pulled the Colt from its holster, her eyes drifting up. Every muscles turned to rubber once she spotted Dez's half-smirk and the desire that drove his stare. The gun thumped against wooden planks, and Sasha unlatched Dez's belt.

***

Vinny

The moment Kev parked the truck, Vinny opened his door. He walked from the pickup,

145

peeking into the clubhouse. His gaze lingered on the flock of women who set out cold cuts on the bar, their long legs flaunted by tight little skirts. A nod and a wink later, he backed away.

Light shined behind Sasha's curtain, and Vinny headed toward the garage.

"I wouldn't do that."

Vinny stopped on the first step, turning toward Ellen's voice.

"Now's probably not a good time." Ellen pointed to her ear then up to the window.

Between an owl's call, Vinny heard a long moan. He knew that sound. He'd pulled it from Sasha's mouth the day before. His shoulders slumped, and he fought to keep his face straight.

"My brother up there?"

"Sorry, kiddo," Ellen said with a light shrug.

Vinny plopped down on the stairs, pulling a pack of cigarettes from his pocket.

"Looks like you're used to your big brother sticking his fingers in your Kool-Aid."

His smirk fluttered the zippo's flame as he lit his cigarette. "Something like that." He took a drag, glancing up to the window. "I used to hate Dez. Everything always came so easy for him, women, friends, respect. When he got sent away, I was happy, like the universe finally came to collect its fee for giving out too much awesome. It only took me two weeks to realize it didn't come easy. He just made it look that way."

"I don't know," Ellen said, sitting beside Vinny. "You might be right. Things do seem to come pretty easy for Dez." She snatched the cigarette from

Vinny's hand, taking a quick puff. "And he likes to throw his weight, even when he knows it's wrong. It's gonna be hard without Chewy. The club really needed a level head and a firm hand. With that VP chair empty, there's no one to keep our sergeant in check." After another drag, she handed his smoke back.

"It'll have to be Otis," Vinny said.

"No. His duties as road captain are too important. I need someone else, someone I can trust, someone I've known for years."

Vinny's mind drew a blank. Other than Kev, there was no one besides Sasha.

"I'm talking about you, stupid."

"What?" Vinny lurched back, shaking the rail. "From prospect to VP in a week? The guys will never go for that. I wouldn't get the votes."

"I can get the votes." Ellen leaned closer. "Would you get my back, no matter what?"

"Ellen," Vinny flicked his cigarette across the lot and grabbed her hand, "you're like a mother to me. Even if I were still sweeping the floors, I'd have your back. No matter what."

"And Sasha?"

Vinny's neck crooked, but he stopped himself from looking up at Sasha's window again. "Sasha isn't always…in tune with reality."

Ellen chucked, nudging Vinny with her shoulder. "You're good people, Vincent Archer. I knew it the first time I saw you. Knee high to a smurf, no front teeth, tryin' to say, 'Yes, ma'am.'"

Vinny rubbed his lip, hiding a grin.

"The girls laid out one hell of a spread." Ellen

rose to her feet, stepping toward the clubhouse. "Why don't you come grab a sandwich?"

"In a bit. I wanna hang out here, give 'em both the guilt trip when they come out."

"That's my boy." Ellen slanted forward, narrowing her eyes. "No talk of this VP business, to anyone. Got it?"

"Yes, ma'am," Vinny said through a smirk. Ellen grinned then walked down the gravely slope.

Vinny leaned back, elbows propped on the step behind him, and stared at the night sky. Clouds drifted overhead, flashing glimpses of stars between their thick swirls. His chest felt like those clouds, heavy, ominous, except he couldn't sail away on cool winds.

Floorboards creaked overhead as the bathroom door slammed. Vinny sat up and lit another cigarette, honing his disappointed leer.

Chapter Sixteen

Sasha

Sasha rolled onto her back, sinking into the mattress. Her fingers shook, lips numb; but somehow she controlled her breathing from running wild. When Dez's eyes fell to her, she looked away. His stare pierced her nerve, judged her every move, and added to the stockpile of shame she already carried on her shoulders.

Her arm twitched, but she kept that palm from slapping her forehead. She should hop up, say something quirky, and then rush out of the room. That's the routine. Her mind knew. She was just waiting for her goddamn body to catch up.

"Come here, you," Dez said, drawing her back to his chest. His strong arms held her body tight, lips tickled her neck, and that pesky layer of humiliation blew to tiny bits of tingles.

"We should go before someone comes looking for us." Her words sounded right, yet they felt so wrong. The last of her willpower teetered, and those hands traveling along her skin didn't help.

"Just let me live this dream a little longer."

"Dream?" Sasha peeked over her shoulder, tearing Dez's lips from her back.

"Yeah. One thousand nine hundred and ninety-eight nights, I dreamt of a soft bed and a beautiful woman. This is much better than my imagination."

Sasha turned in Dez's arms. His eyes hit her again, but her immunity must have built up because she didn't shy away. The heat Dez's body generated felt too good, infiltrating her with the most pleasant burn. She withered against his solid chest, kissing him softly. Her tongue snaked along his top lip, bringing him in as she pulled back. "Dream's over. Time to wake up." Sasha pushed off Dez's chest and climbed from the bed.

"Harsh," Dez mumbled, sinking into the pillows.

A shirt snagged Sasha's footsteps, Dez's shirt. She scooped it off the floor and tossed it at his face.

"Way harsh," Dez said without moving a muscle.

Sasha smirked, grabbing her clothes on the way to the bathroom. Once shut inside and surrounded by unshared air, she felt free to exhale. Not bad. She was only about fifty percent spaz.

Two minutes flat and she was dressed, teeth brushed, bandana tied atop her head. This time, waves of hesitation didn't force her back. She lifted her chin and strolled out of the bathroom. Dez greeted her with a lit cigarette and leery expression.

"Vinny's outside," Dez said, pointing to the window. "Just sitting on your bottom step."

"Fuck. Really?" Sasha maneuvered to the window, peeking out.

"You said nothing was going on. I'm not trying to move in on my brother's girl."

"I ain't no one's girl." Sasha hurled a glare, tripping over a mini-mountain of clothes on her way to the door. "He's probably just…just wait here."

Sasha pulled open her door, stepping onto the landing. "Hey, Vin."

Vinny stood and curved to stare up at her. Hurt shined in those baby blues, gleaming even in the low beams of moonlight.

Sasha opened her mouth, and Vinny turned his back, walking away.

"Nothing my ass," Dez shouted from behind her. "What the fuck, Sasha? You playin' me?"

"No!" She spun, nearly face planting Dez's wide chest. Panic sent her legs into a backward scramble, and Dez grabbed her by the arms.

"The stairs," Dez said, a tremble cracking his voice.

Sasha glanced over her shoulder at the steep set of stairs that she almost fell down trying to untangle from her own web of lies. Dez pulled Sasha close, backing them toward her room.

"I swear." She slid her hands up his chest, stopping him mid-step. "We're just friends." His grip on her arms tightened, and she racked her brain for a distraction.

"Vinny's just pissed about the run, about what's in the back of that truck." Her words just flew out, hanging in the air. If she could reach up, pluck the words from existence, and cram them back into her mouth, she totally would.

"What's in the back of that truck?" Dez asked,

his clutch loosening a tad.

"I can't." Sasha wiggled from Dez's grasp, and he latched onto the front of her coat. Leather wrinkled under his fist, squeezing her chest. "Dez." She looked at his hand then straight into his eyes.

The second Dez let go, Sasha scurried back though her gaze remained locked on his hard stare. "Please. Don't push this. You have no idea what my mother is capable of. If you ask too many questions, piss her off, you'll disappear."

His face changed, a skeptical type of fear flooding over the rage. Sasha crept closer, slapping on one of those glares that worked so well for her mother. "It's best to just mind your own business 'round here."

Dez walked out the door, the thump of his boots echoing over a concert of night critters.

She stepped outside, watching Dez tear-ass toward the clubhouse. If he had half as many brains as muscles, he'd take her advice. If not, she'd be watching that impressive body drop down the cellar.

***

Sasha never made it off her bottom step. She took up residence in Vinny's spot. His scent was long gone, but a bitter sadness still clung to the air. She counted the cigarette butts piled at her feet, almost half a pack. Vinny must've been sitting there awhile.

The sound of gravel crunching and giggles interrupted the tranquil rustle of leaves, and Sasha looked at the clubhouse. A trail of women glided off the porch, piling into a sedan. Even in the dark, their bright clothes glimmered. Sasha's view of long legs and high hair ended when Otis walked toward her.

"The girls were asking about you." Otis handed her a beer then leaned against the railing.

"Guess it's a good thing I stayed out here then."

Otis uttered a low groan as he slumped against the railing. "I thought we had a talk about this anti-social bullshit."

Sasha picked at the label on the ice-cold bottle in her hand. "I did what you said, slutted around."

"Oh yeah. Did you find the magic cock?"

Sasha shrugged, taking a sip. "Maybe."

"So, which Archer brother is it?"

The entire staircase shook as Sasha spun to face Otis, gawking.

"Think you're slick, don't ya, girl?"

"Okay, smartass. You tell me, which Archer brother is it?"

Otis chuckled, pulling a joint from behind his ear. "Knowing you, you'd go for Dez, even though you belong with Vinny, just 'cause you like to touch the fire." His zippo sparked to life, its glow masked by the gray smoke rising around it. "I think you were safer when you just fucked chicks."

After a second of silence, Otis crouched down. His stare turned hard, locking Sasha's eyes with his. "You better not drive a wedge down the center of this club."

He handed her the joint then walked away.

***

Sasha stepped inside the clubhouse, happy to find the place empty. Voices trailed from the backroom, and she snuck closer, peeking through the cracked door. It was almost like old times, when she'd spy on club business as a child, except Vinny wasn't huddled at her side. He was sitting at that glossy table, next to her vacant chair.

She turned toward the pool table, cluttered by sawed-offs and revolvers. In near silence, she loaded the guns while listening to her mother's edgy tone.

"…you two will ride with Otis. I'll go with Dez. When you hear the semi's start, light the fires. Vinny takes Dez's Ford and leads. Kev, you bring up the rear in Otis's pickup."

"We should head out."

Dez's voice snapped Sasha's spine straight. She tried to pinpoint the feeling in her chest, spawned by his deep rolling tongue, when the door tapped against the wall.

"Sasha. Well-rested, I hope," Ellen said.

Sasha clicked the barrel of a shotgun closed and placed it on the pool table. "As cherry as pie. Can I talk to you?"

"We're getting ready to move out."

"It'll be quick."

Ellen dipped her head toward the backroom then strolled inside. Sasha followed, slamming the door closed behind her.

Before her mother could flash that irritated glare, Sasha stomped forward. "You're totally zooted out."

"You better back up outta my face, little girl."

Sasha inched back half a step, lifting her brow. "What the fuck?"

"That's right, Sasha. What the fuck?"

"You're losing your shit, making crazy decisions. Last month, you tell me we're merging with Satan's Crew, 'combining our interests,' and now we're, what, wiping them off the map?" Sasha tried to hold back, but her tongue wagged too fast for her brain's liking. "Did your boy-toy rub you the wrong way?"

The slap came as expected, though much harder than Sasha remembered. Blood soured her mouth, and she took a full step back.

"I swear, if you had an ounce of common sense, you'd be dangerous. Stupid little bitch," Ellen said on her way to the door.

***

Once taillights faded down the mountain, Sasha hurried toward her mother's house. Those huge white columns gleamed brighter the closer she got, inciting the urge to flee in the opposite direction. Seventeen years of torment dwelled inside that house. It was a place where a woman she loved shredded her heart with sharp, hate-filled words. Since moving above the garage, Sasha hadn't stepped foot within the walls of the big house. She swore she never would, though tonight she'd make an exception.

The second step of the porch squeaked, just as she remembered, and the door, as always, was unlocked. Sasha walked inside, bright light stinging her eyes. Pictures hung along the foyer, a couple in love and their child in pigtails, but she kept her head low. No point in looking at the past. It wouldn't be returning.

She strolled through the parlor, sliding her fingers across the dust-ridden baby grand, and into the kitchen. Not a thing had changed. Pots hung above a wood-burning stove, herbs lined a little shelf, and the tile floor glistened. So many nights, she scrubbed that ceramic on hands and knees with a toothbrush while her mother listed all the things she hated about her. This place felt like home and hell all wrapped into one.

After flinging off a shiver, Sasha grabbed a milk crate from the corner. "Leave women and children in the back of a truck to starve. Fricken inhuman." She loaded boxes of cereal and bags of chips into the crate, grabbing two gallons of water. "Coked-out train wreck of an operation."

It took two tries with her foot before she figured out, *You put down the water to close the front door.* Her mother was right. Not a drop of sense had pooled in that brain of hers. She stormed down the gentle slope, eyes fixed on the cargo doors of a semi's trailer. The crate thumped at her feet, and she fished a key from her pocket.

When the ridges slid into the padlock, Sasha froze. Her mind screamed no. It wasn't her mother's wrath or Otis's disapproval that stunted her task. It was the dread she felt about what lay beyond that door. After a deep breath, she popped the lock. Metal hinges screeched as the door swung open, revealing only shadows. Sasha leaned closer, hit by the stench of piss and shit. A clink of chains echoed from within, and she eased back.

The second she lifted a jug of water, hands broke through the darkness. Blood-tipped fingers clawed the air, reaching toward her. The cries and moans ricocheted in her ears, soaking into her core. It left an ugly stain, bright enough for all to see. Her legs fixed to run, but she forced her spine to stiffen. She rolled the water inside the trailer then lifted the crate of food.

A woman crawled into the dim light, her face bruised, hair matted with brown clumps. She could've been any age, impossible to tell under all that filth and misery, but her blue eyes sparkled like those of a sunny teenager.

"Help…me."

Sasha gasped, stumbling back. Words that she could understand made this nightmare very real. Women, children, human beings sat chained in the back of her truck. The boxes rattled against the crate in her grasp, and she looked down to see trembling hands.

"Help. Me."

Within the woman's twisted face, Sasha glimpsed what could be her future. Bound in the dark, left in her own filth. That would be her fate if she saved these people.

"I'm sorry." Sasha placed the crate on the edge of the trailer. "I…I can't." Her gaze dropped, and she pushed the crate inside. Groans, chains, a soft whimper, they all drowned under the hammer of her heart's beat. She clicked off the switch for compassion, engaging the autopilot. A means of survival, which carried her though childhood. Just turn it off.

After she slammed the metal door closed and snapped the padlock, Sasha shook a cigarette loose and slid it between her lips. A gust of frosty winds stole the flame of her zippo, and she dropped her arm, trudging toward the clubhouse.

Chapter Seventeen

Ellen

Ellen slouched against the passenger door, glaring at Dez. Her fingers drummed the tight jeans that clung to her thighs, jaw clenching.

"What?" Dez said in a short, rough tone.

His eyes didn't leave the road ahead, which only fueled Ellen's temper and sparked her desire. "What was that shit you pulled in the meeting?"

"What shit?"

Finally, for the first time in sixty minutes, Dez glanced her way. His harsh eyes, probing her body, melted her stiff muscles.

"You challenged me at the table."

"No, I didn't."

Ellen snickered. The lost look plastered on Dez's face was too funny not to enjoy. Such a dumb bastard, hurling his power without even knowing it.

"Wait," Dez said, followed by a sarcastic chuckle. "You mean that Sasha shit?"

"Yeah, that Sasha shit. If I didn't know any

better, I'd swear you set me up."

"Set you up," he muttered.

"You laid out that plan with me then shot it down in front of the club. It's a pretty tired cliché, even for you. You'll have to be more creative if you want my seat."

"You need to slow your roll, woman. I didn't challenge you. If I had, you'd know about it. And if I wanted your seat…"

Dez glanced across the cab of the pickup, slinging a leer that could pierce flesh. "I'd do something a little more permanent."

Ellen sat up straight. A smirk crept onto her lips, and she chewed it back. It took mountains of self-control to keep from jumping in his lap and fucking his brains out while zooming eighty miles an hour down the freeway.

"I am sorry, though." Dez shifted in his seat, almost like he felt the pressure of her stare. "I might've spoken out of turn. I just thought…one of us would go with the cargo."

"There you go, thinking again." Ellen scooted closer, almost catching a whiff of his bullshit. Always the perfect toy soldier, obedient and silent, until Sasha came into play. Then his face changed. Love or lust? A few games and she could find out.

"I get it," Ellen said, sliding her finger down Dez's arm. "You've been away for a while. It's tough to fall back in the swing of things." She took his hand, guiding it between her legs. "There's still time for a proper apology."

Dez yanked his hand from her grasp, slapping his palm on the steering wheel. "Stop fucking around."

"Why? Because I'm not Sasha?"

His eyes flew to her, laced in different levels of fear.

"No. Because you're my president. The other night was a fluke. That shit can't happen again."

"So club members shouldn't fuck each other. Is that what you're saying?" Ellen turned toward Dez, her brow raised. Watching him squirm under her paw was more fun than riding him, for now.

"Ellen…" Dez shook his head, his grip tightening on the steering wheel.

"Right. I'm hearing ya." Love. It seeped from his body like a noxious fume. "Dull as a box of rocks."

The truck veered onto a ramp, heading away from lanes of traffic, and Ellen reached under her seat, fishing out a long chain.

"What's that for?" Dez asked.

Ellen stopped fumbling with the strand of linked metal and looked at Dez. "I'm gonna have your brother chain the front door shut before he lights the fire."

"You said the place cleared out by two a.m. Why lock an empty bar?"

"I might've been a little off on my times. Probably more like three-thirty, four." Ellen leaned back, her glare locked on Dez. "Now that I think of it, the place is usually jammin' at this hour."

"Yep. That sounds about right for you." Dez chewed on a smirk as he glanced at Ellen. "Don't worry. I warned Kev and Vinny this might happen before we left, figured you took care of Otis."

That smug half-grin on Dez's face sparked

161

Ellen's temper. She should be the one smiling. He just handed her a stone inside the glass house they share.

"You can't keep your big ass from making waves, can you?" Ellen said, managing to keep her voice at an even keel despite the anger brewing inside her chest.

"What's in the back of that Peterbilt?"

Ellen nearly choked on the rage that climbed up her throat. Heat prickled her skin, and her lungs pumped the wall of her chest. She rubbed her nose, her hand landing on the vial inside her pocket.

"There are so many things I could have your little brother do for me. As his president and somewhat of a surrogate mother, he just throws blind faith at me. And my daughter. God, she'd be devastated if she knew you stuck your dick in me."

"How'd you get to be such a vicious bitch?"

Ellen smirked then grabbed a shotgun from behind the seat. "The luck of the draw."

***

Sasha

Sasha sat on the steps of the clubhouse, puffing on her third joint. Headlights turned onto their dirt path, stopping at the locked gate. The flood of lights cut out, and Sasha grabbed the shotgun beside her.

While creeping into the shadows, she lifted the barrel. Candy ducked under the gate and scurried up the driveway. Her heels wobbled on tiny pebbles, arms out to grasp invisible rails. Sasha chuckled.

Just that one sight was enough to take the edge from her bones. She lowered the gun and stepped from the darkness.

"Whoa! Don't shoot." Candy stopped short, lifting her hands up in front of her chest.

"For real?" Sasha leaned the gun against the porch and returned to her spot on the steps.

"What's up with the sawed-off? You sounded really upset on the phone." Candy inched closer, glancing around. "Is everything all right?"

"Nobody's here. You can come sit down."

"Nobody?" Candy wormed toward the stairs, peeking through the open door. "Not even Otis?"

"They're all out on business. How'd you get here?"

Candy sat beside her, their hips grazing. When Candy batted her green eyes, Sasha dropped her gaze.

"I stole my mom's car," Candy said softly.

"You shouldn't have done that."

The look on Candy's face reflected fear, but the girl shrugged. "It's no big. She booted up right before you called. Probably won't wake up for a while anyway."

"I didn't mean for you to come here. I just wanted to hear your voice."

"I know. You said that on the phone." Candy reached for Sasha's hand, stopped short, and then scooted away. "What's wrong? You're acting weird."

Sasha moved back, taking in the vision beside her. Somehow, those lips had gotten fuller, stomach tighter, legs longer. "I've had a bad week, that's

163

all."

Candy took a deep breath, then grabbed Sasha's hand. Sasha pulled away, but the girl had one hell of a grip, or maybe she didn't struggle that hard.

"And you called me," Candy said, gliding her thumb along the back of Sasha's hand, "to make it all better?" The smile that followed those words could light the world on fire. "I can do whatever you want to make it all better."

It would be too easy, too right, to fall into Candy's arms. Gliding her tongue along that smooth skin could only do harm, and not just to her sorry excuse of a heart, but to her entire club.

"Can you just sit here with me, pretend to be my friend?" Sasha asked. It was possibly the most pathetic request she had ever made.

"Well, that'll be a cinch."

Candy latched onto Sasha's arm, cuddling tight, and Sasha let her weight fall to the girl's side. Evil saturated her soul. She feared it might spill over, but Candy stayed attached to her arm. The town's distant glow fought to claim the dark sky, and they sat in silence, feeding off each other's misery.

***

Vinny

Vinny squirmed in the passenger seat of Otis's truck. He looked at Otis sitting tall behind the steering wheel. If only he could absorb a fraction of the strength his road captain reflected, then he'd be a fraction of a man. At least he wasn't the only one.

By the sound of Kev's tapping foot, which thumped louder the closer they got to Satan Crew's bar, the guy needed a double shot of strength. Vinny turned, glaring at Kev in the backseat of Otis's four-door pickup. "Dude, stop kicking my seat."

Otis killed the engine, and Vinny turned back to scour the road ahead of them. The truck coasted to the side of the road, creeping to a stop behind Dez's pickup, and Vinny rolled down his window. From beyond thick bushes, music streamed from a small bar. A motorcycle rumbled over the muffled beats of speakers, and Vinny ducked low.

"Heads up, Kev," Otis said, slouching down.

Kev lay across the back seat, cocking a shotgun.

Light cut through the trees, beaming in front of Dez's truck. Chrome shined as a motorcycle rolled out of the driveway and turned onto the street.

Vinny sank below the dashboard, loud chops of exhaust thundering by. "Fuck," he said, peeking his head up.

"There's a shit-ton of motorcycles in that parking lot," Kev said, leaning into the front.

"Then I guess you better grab two gas cans." Otis turned, staring at Kev.

"Oh. Right." Kev hopped out, pushing the back door to a close in a soft clunk.

"Lose the jacket." Otis glanced around then opened his door. "You're a walking ad for Ashby Trucking." He picked a handgun off the seat and climbed from the truck.

Vinny peeled off his coat, taking a deep breath. His heart raced, a slight tremble invading his fingertips. It didn't make sense. He'd done much worse than light a few fires, yet a chill crept through his insides.

He stepped into the humid night air, eyeing his crew. It only took a millisecond to realize why spiked knots twisted his chest. No Sasha. He'd never done a job without her. That's what was missing, her energy and the smirk that told him they were unstoppable. Vinny shook his mind clear, grabbed a gas can from the bed of the truck, and walked toward Dez.

"You good?" Dez asked.

"Yeah," Vinny said, faster than he wanted. That should've pissed him off. He didn't need to be coddled, like a child, but it actually felt nice to know someone gave a shit.

Ellen shoved a jumble of chain in Vinny's arms then tucked a padlock in his pocket.

"I want you to chain the front doors shut before you gas the bar. Got it?" she whispered, glaring up with those callous eyes.

"Got it."

Ellen looked at Dez, and he pulled a hunting knife from his belt. They crept along the trees, down a thin driveway, Otis glued to Ellen's side.

Vinny glanced at Kev, as if seeking a command to follow. Kev must have heard his silent plea because he nodded, gesturing for him to move.

Vinny took light steps, keeping his head low. Ellen's arm hit his chest, rattling the chain in his grasp. He looked up as Dez skulked behind a man, his knife glinting in the streetlight. Dez dragged the blade along the man's throat, guiding the body to the ground, and a woman jumped up from her knees. Her mouth opened wider, to scream, and Dez thrust his hand over her lips.

"Shh." Dez lowered his arm slowly then pointed to the street with the tip of his blade.

She got maybe two steps before Ellen jammed a long knife in the side of her neck. Ellen caught the woman by the hair before she could thump to the ground.

"Idiot," Ellen said, as quiet as one could growl. She aimed her blood-tipped knife at Dez's face, dropping the woman in her clutch.

"C'mon," Kev whispered, nudging Vinny's arm.

Vinny walked alongside a row of motorcycles, trickling gas atop high handlebars and deep seats. The chain clinked when he stepped up to the front door. Laughter echoed from behind the thick wood, music all but bursting from its seams. He set the gas can down and slid the chain through both handles. In his mind, the jingle of metal blasted louder than a jet engine. He expected a horde of seething bikers to erupt from the bar and stomp his face to mush, but the lock snapped shut and nothing happened.

The scent of gasoline stung his nose, wiping the smile from his face. He glanced back, into an empty parking lot. Not a crewmember in sight, just the shuffle of footsteps around back.

Vinny grabbed the gas can, dousing the wood beside the front doors. Guilt never showed up. He backed away, splashing the landing, and didn't feel shit except relief.

Kev jogged from behind the building, and Vinny followed him to the street, trailing a stream of liquid death.

"I got the whole perimeter," Kev said through pants. "And they're in the trucks."

"I'll light it up." Vinny pulled a zippo from his pocket, gliding his thumb along its smooth case. The ignition of a diesel engine gave off a loud click right before the motor roared to life. Not many people knew the little quirks of a semi-truck. Most people didn't spend countless nights watching big rigs roll in and out of a gravel lot, but he did. So he held his breath, waiting for the key to turn and the ignition to click.

He flipped the lighter's lid open, his fingers moving on their own, as if his body had sensed a shift in the air. The ridges of the flint wheel dug into his thumb. Then he heard it. *Cl-Click*. Vinny lit the zippo, motors whistled, and he dropped the lighter. Flames shot out in front of him. Heat radiated from the ocean of fire, but it couldn't penetrate the icy shell that coated his skin. The solid doors banged against the chain before a blaze rose up, consuming his view.

Headlights shined through smoke, large stacks towering above flames. Vinny tore his eyes from the firestorm and bolted toward Dez's pickup. Screams cut into the night, mixing with the growl of fire. The sound stuck in his ears, even after he drove away.

Vinny's eyes bounced to the rearview mirror. He was counting headlights when an explosion filled the dark sky with orange light. He cringed, the shudder of the explosion making him slump. A tiny piece of filth wormed its way into his gut, but he ignored it and looked back at the mirror. In the flash of streetlights, Vinny could've sworn he saw Ellen grin. He pressed down on the gas and took a deep breath. The crackle of flames and shrills of terror faded under the hum of tires. He sat up straight, the way Otis would, the way Sasha would, and led the convoy onto the freeway.

Chapter Eighteen

Sasha

Sasha stood at the front gate, long after Candy left. It wasn't until a ray of sunlight gleamed off the shotgun in her hand that she turned back.

The double barrel thumped her shoulder with each step as she walked up the hill. Restless jitters crept in with the sun's rays, assaulting her joints. The road called, its silent invitation luring her like a siren's song. She should get ready, load the cab with necessities. One didn't need much to traffic slave people. Guns, ammo, more guns, knives, brass knuckles, and enough pre-fabs to smoke the whole ride home. Half that shit she already had stashed somewhere on her body, so she was already off to a good start.

In the light of day, a fresh coat of black paint shined on her father's semi. The sparkly decals lay in shreds on the dirt, stopping Sasha short. All trace of Ashby Trucking had been stripped from the rig and painted over. Rage came quick, and the windows of the clubhouse looked awfully appealing to her fists.

On the first step of the porch steps, a stupid idea hit Sasha. By the second step, she'd convinced herself the idea was pure genius. She loosened her balled fists and strolled through the open front door. There was something that would hurt her mother much more than broken glass, something that bitch would run for when she got back.

Sasha opened the top drawer of her mother's desk. Her fingers slid along the sides, and she lifted. An insert popped out like a tray, revealing a secret compartment. The baggie of cocaine tucked within gleamed like a snow log.

"That's a lot," Sasha said, holding the packed bag in front of her eyes. If she took this, she'd be sorry. Her mother would find every way to make her sorry.

"Fuck it." Sasha shoved the bag in her pocket, grabbed all the weed in sight, and put the desk back in order.

Her smile all but carried her from the clubhouse. She hurried to her room, clearing a space on her nightstand. After cutting herself out a fat line, Sasha started rolling joints. Hell, she might even throw some powder into the spliffs.

***

The twenty-second joint landed on the pile when a rumble shook the floor. Sasha peeked out her window, watching puffs of black exhaust rise into the air as semis pulled into the lot behind the garage. Vinny jumped out of Dez's truck, his eyes shooting straight to her room.

Sasha jolted back, turning away. Vinny's stare seemed cold, arctic, when it found her. Normally, she'd call him up here. They'd smoke a bone and do a few of her mother's lines, but it didn't feel right. He'd probably ignore her anyway.

A pout fell onto Sasha's lips, and she wanted to slap her own face. She grabbed a jean backpack stuffed with fully loaded handguns and packed the tiny mountain of joints into the front pocket.

Morning hit like an iron fist when Sasha opened her door. She doubled back for her shades then trotted down the stairs. Dez walked her way, but she kept her head down. Today, she'd operate on the assumption that if she couldn't see it, it didn't exist. It nearly worked, until she rounded the now dull black semi and glimpsed her mother's face.

"Perfect," Sasha said in near silence.

"Heading out already?" Ellen asked.

"Yeah. Traffic's gonna be a bitch." Sasha bumped her mother aside, reaching for the semi's door.

"Hey." Ellen clutched onto Sasha's arm, yanking. "What's with the 'tude? And yes, our run went great. We are all okay. Thanks for asking."

Sasha ripped her arm back, fighting to keep it at her side. "You stripped the decals off daddy's truck, slapped on an ugly flat black."

"I had to."

"Right. 'Cause you wanna erase his memories from this place."

"No, so you wouldn't be spotted on the road."

172

Ellen moved closer, sliding the sunglasses from Sasha's eyes. "It killed me to do it, but I have to protect you. You're my baby girl."

"I…" Sasha pushed her glasses back up, hiding the shock that swallowed her guilty stare. "I got pissed and took your blow and a bunch of weed. It's in my nightstand, top drawer. I'm sorry."

Ellen snickered, her head shaking. "Of course you did. Go on, get." She waved her hand, taking a step back. "Call me once you dump the cargo and clear the city, okay?"

Sasha nodded, climbing into the truck. Shame forbid her from speaking or tearing her gaze from the steering wheel. She turned the key, that old motor chugging and whistling with power. After stashing guns around the cab, she grinded the shifter into first. Airbrakes burst and metal rattled. Soothing sounds that reminded her of childhood, of a freedom that came with ignorance. She could never return to that place of imagination and wonder, but when the pavement glided by, she could pretend.

The truck eased down the slope, past the clubhouse, but Sasha kept her eyes ahead. Just beyond the front gate, wide open road beckoned. Her leg twitched, wanting to barrel down on the gas, when Vinny stepped out of the trees.

Sasha hit the brakes, rolling down the window. Vinny climbed up the side of her truck and poked his head inside.

"Hey." His grin lit up the cab as he slouched on the windowsill.

"Hey." Sasha leaned toward his icy blue eyes,

soaking in a warmth she thought would never burn again.

"Careful out there." Vinny ran his hand through Sasha's hair before climbing off the semi's step.

"My finger's on the trigger."

Vinny couldn't see it, but Sasha's palm rested atop the revolver in her lap. She flashed a smile then drove from the lot.

***

Dez

The edge of the clubhouse porch provided a great view for Dez. From here, he could watch his brother flirt with Sasha and Ellen sneak up the garage stairs. The shit that went down on this compound was enough to make one miss the simplicity of prison life.

"Hey, Dez," Kev called out from behind him.

Dez tore his gaze from Sasha's taillights and looked at Kev.

"Is it cool for me to go home now?"

"I don't know," Dez said, waving Kev off. "Why you asking me?"

"You're the sarge. You're supposed to know when shit's safe." Kev squirmed, wood planks creaking under his boots. "So…is shit safe?"

Dez glimpsed Otis move into the doorway and lean against the threshold. For the first time, Dez wished Sasha were there. She always had some smart ass shit to say. He always knew what to expect with her.

"I'd say we have at least twelve hours before Satan's Crew can regroup," Dez said. "If they can regroup. I think you'll be all right, but keep a gun close and listen for the phone."

"10-4."

Kev got into his pickup truck, and Otis stepped onto the porch.

"It was right," Otis said, creeping closer to Dez, "to burn those fuckers alive. They'd do it to us."

"I agree." Dez turned to stare Otis in the eyes. "I would've agreed from the jump, if anyone bothered to ask."

"Just keeping you on your toes." Otis knocked Dez on the shoulder then strolled off the porch. "You'll thank me later, brother."

Dez snickered, reaching for the pack of smokes in his pocket. "You headed out?"

"There's a feisty redhead I got a hankering to see. I'll be back in a few hours."

Long after Otis left, Dez waited. His cigarette burned down to the filter and still no Ellen. Five minutes of pacing at the bottom of Sasha's steps should've done the trick, but no. That woman and her games. He was done playing.

The pound of heavy boots had to announce his presence, yet Ellen looked surprised when he opened the door.

"Can I help you, Desmond?"

Ellen sat on the edge of Sasha's bed, and Dez fought the urge to toss her off.

"I'm crashing here for a little while."

"Oh, really." Ellen stood up, biting back a laugh. "This is my place. *I* let Sasha stay here. No one said

175

anything about you."

"What's your angle?"

"Huh?"

Dez shut the door, leaning against Sasha's dresser. "If you just tell me what your plans are for me, I'll do it. No complaining. It's the lies and tricks I'll fight, not you."

"Okay." Ellen picked a fallen joint off the ground, popping it in her mouth. She leaned back on the bed, gesturing for him to join her.

The moment Dez's ass hit the mattress, Ellen busted out with, "I want you and Sasha hitched."

Dez almost jumped back to his feet, but the aroma of a freshly lit joint clutched his body to Ellen's side.

"I..." Dez hit the joint two, three times. "Yeah, maybe. Sometime down the line, I could see us—"

"Sasha's a big-ole dyke. You do know that, right?"

"That's stupid. She likes—" Dez stopped himself. Not even Ellen would appreciate being told her daughter loved cock.

"Trust me," Ellen said, snatching the joint. "She's had her hands down little girls' pants since she was ten. Don't get me wrong, she's been with lots of guys and she did fuck your brother, but her eyes always stray to them girls. Until you breezed back in. Now her eyes are always on you, following your every move like a schoolgirl high on puppy love."

"You're seeing shit." Dez slanted his head and stared at Ellen. "When I look into her eyes, all I see is hate. It's cold, just like your stare."

"You're wrong. About her, not me." Ellen snuffed out the joint in the ashtray and took Dez's hand. "You can tear her away from herself, make her forget everything she thought was important."

"I don't wanna break her."

Ellen got up and walked across the room. "Then you'll have to put her down." She opened the door, glancing over her shoulder. "You're the sergeant."

The door slammed shut, leaving Dez alone with the scent of weed and vanilla. Little buttons clicked inside his mind. Each one triggered another thought until a switchboard of flashing lights erupted within his brain. Sasha's eyes did wander every time a short skirt traipsed by. He never questioned it before. Everyone else around him did the same. He did the same. For Sasha, though, it was different. And the beating...Ellen said she'd caught Sasha where her hand didn't belong. They all thought Sasha stole drugs, money. Not a feel.

Dez flopped back on the bed, a long breath sinking his chest. A gay, right in front of him. He should've seen it, but he didn't want to see it.

It would have been easier if Sasha just loved his brother. Then they could duke it out. High noon in front of the clubhouse, and just like in the old westerns, the victor gets the girl. A fantasy. Dez dropped his head onto the pillows, breathing in a lungful of Sasha. The thought of her hands on another person's body, any person, turned his stomach. If she wanted him and only him, it wouldn't matter, but he wouldn't force her to change who she was inside. Not for Ellen, the club, or himself.

177

Dez closed his eyes, and Sasha's curves popped into his mind, luring him to the brink of sleep.

***

Otis

Otis pulled into Candy's driveway and killed the engine. Glass shattered from within the house as he stepped out of his pickup, followed by a low shriek. He rushed to the door and burst inside. Candy's mother froze, like a strung-out deer in headlights, her fingers coiled tight in Candy's hair.

"Let her go, Betty."

"What the fuck, Otis? This ain't none of your business." Betty twisted Candy's wrist and yanked down.

Candy cried out, dropping to her knees. A trickle of blood seeped from the corner of her mouth as she looked up at Otis.

"It is my business. That's my girl you're gripping up on." Otis stomped forward, Betty cowering with his every step. Even though Betty let go, Otis pushed her aside. He held his hand out in front of Candy, a smile raising his lips. Her palm slid into his, and he pulled her up into his arms.

"She's coming with me, and she won't be back."

Otis looked at Candy's face, finding a sparkle beneath the scatter of bruises. "Is there anything you need to grab?"

"Just wait one sec."

Before Candy could trot from sight, Betty latched onto Otis's arm.

"Why do you want a little bitch like her? She's young, dumb, and full of cum. You could have me, baby." She rubbed her hard nipples against Otis's back and wrapped her hands around his chest. "I'll let you stick it wherever you want, honey, whenever you want."

Otis pried Betty's boney arms from his body. Scabs brushed against his skin as she tried to move closer, but when his hand hit an open sore, he dropped his grip.

"Nasty." Otis shoved Betty onto the couch, glaring down. He wanted to spit in her sunken face, but by the looks of her stringy hair, a bunch of people beat him to it. "For Christ's sake, clean yourself up."

Betty giggled, slipping her hand inside her ripped spandex pants. "You gonna teach me a lesson, Daddy?"

Otis grabbed Betty by the back of her neck, dragging her kicking and screaming to the mirror in the hall.

"Look at yourself." He squeezed until she lifted her eyes to the glass. "You used to be Miss Kentucky. Now you look like a five-dollar whore."

He unclasped her, and Betty stayed in front of the mirror, gawking at her own reflection. Candy moved into view, and Betty snatched a lamp from the table, smashing the mirror before chucking the broken base at Candy's head.

Candy ducked, clutching onto a duffle bag. She scurried behind Otis. "Crazy bitch," she yelled, peeking out from behind his solid body.

"Get the fuck outta my house!"

179

More glass broke. Knickknacks sailed around the room as Otis pulled Candy toward the open front door.

"You can buy that little slut her tampons and hair dye and watch her fuck up all your shit. Good luck, motherfucker," was the last thing Otis heard before his truck's door slammed Betty's voice out.

He turned to face Candy, and she looked away. That one second of guilt Otis glimpsed told him what he needed to know. Sasha brought this on.

Without a word, he backed out of the driveway, and they drove away. After fifteen minutes of silence, Otis parked in front of his house and shut the motor. He looked at Candy, and this time, she stared right into his eyes. Her body swayed, as if she'd spring forward and fasten onto his lips at any moment.

"What tripped her fuse?" he asked, amazed at how casual he was able to sound.

"I took her car last night. Guess I stayed out a little too long."

"Where'd you go in the middle of the night?"

Candy shrank back, and Otis chuckled. The girl was a master of the doe eyes.

"You were with Sasha?" Otis said. It was more of a statement than a question.

"It's not what you think—"

"Did you run to her, or did she call you?"

"Look," Candy reached out then pulled her arms back, "Sasha called me, but she didn't want me to come over. I just did, 'cause she sounded…wrong."

"Let me guess. Sasha got all right when you showed up?"

180

"No." Candy dropped her gaze. "It wasn't anything like that. Some heavy shit must've crept up on her. It didn't have anything to do with me. I think she was just lonely. If I didn't know any better, I'd say she was scared, but that's ridiculous. Nothing happened." She looked up, scooting closer. "Nothing will ever happen again, for reals."

Otis wrapped his arm around Candy, and she slumped against his chest. "I got you now, babe," he said, running his hand through her hair.

"You're like a prince from a fairy tale, rescuing damsels from wicked witches and junk." Candy gripped Otis's cheeks, kissing him softly. "My prince," she whispered, climbing onto his lap.

Chapter Nineteen

Sasha

Water glimmered outside Sasha's window, stealing her gaze for just a second. On the top arch of a wide bridge, the whole city stretched out before her. The Big Apple. She didn't get it. Didn't look like they grew apples here. Must be fancy city talk for some metaphoric apple no one could see or ever bite into.

Traffic got thicker, streets smaller the deeper Sasha roamed through a concrete maze. Between the many red lights, she tussled with a map. After circling two wrong blocks, she found a row of warehouses. At the end of the street, two men holding assault rifles pointed her toward an open bay door. Sasha drove past a sign that read **'*Lazzari Bros. Meats'*** and parked her truck inside the dark building.

This was no different from any other drop. Same type of warehouse in the same kind of rundown neighborhood, yet her hands wouldn't stop shaking.

She grabbed a gun, staring down at its worn handle. A first impression was key with new clients. To wear this gun on her hip would indicate fear, which would be more dangerous than going in unarmed. Sasha stashed the gun back under her seat then opened her door. In slow, easy movements, she climbed from the cab and stretched.

"Ms. Ashby." A round Italian man filled her view, his hand tugging at the Uzi strapped across his chest. "Mr. Lazzari would like a few words."

"Yeah, sure." Sasha stopped to adjust her bandana in the truck's chrome before hurrying to catch up. A series of tunnels and four guarded doors later, she walked into a bustling restaurant.

Her steps slowed at the loud flow of voices and smooth vibes of jazz, every table packed with propers decked out in sequined dresses and tuxes. She pulled at the ends of her leather jacket, looking at her baggy cargo pants.

"It's all right," the man said, taking Sasha's arm. "The mooks don't notice anything. They just drink and keep to themselves. Right up those stairs, miss."

Sasha walked by large round tables, not one head turning her way. It left an odd taste in her mouth. It was a comfort to float around unseen yet a chill to be faceless. She could be killed in this room and not one of these people would look up from their china plates.

Three small steps stood between her and a lone table of finely dressed men. These men didn't laugh into their cups and stare at silver spoons. They eyed her. Straight lips, hard glares, taking her in from

183

head to toe.

"Well, look at you," the widest one at the head of the table said, only sparing a second to part from his heaping plate of lasagna. "The spitting image of your mother. Sit."

He gestured to the empty seat across from him, and the other men moved their hands under the table. They were trying to intimidate her by holding their holster guns, and it was working. Instinct told Sasha to drop her stare, but she forced her chin up and sat at the table.

"Your mother," the man at the head of the table said, waving a butter knife Sasha's way, "she must have a lot of confidence in you to send you here. Or she hates you."

The men around the table chuckled, and Sasha leaned back.

"Probably a bit of both," she said.

More chuckles, until a tall man walked over. A hush befell the table, maybe the entire room, as people exchanged whispers.

The tall man walked away, and the round man who headed the table stared at Sasha. "You fed them?" he asked. He dropped his silverware into the lasagna, and everyone tensed up.

Sasha cleared her throat, removing the lump that crept up to rob her of breath. "I'm sorry, sir—"

"Antonio."

Now Sasha's eyes dropped. She couldn't help it. "Antonio Lazzari." Don of the largest crime syndicate in America. "I, umm…because of the last minute nature of this delivery, there were delays. I didn't want your stock to get ruined, so I had to

184

improvise." Sasha glanced up, unable to read Antonio's blank face. "It won't happen again."

"They left quite a mess in your trailer."

"It's no big. I'll hose it out at a rest stop. I'm sorry for the inconvenience, sir—I mean, Mr. Antonio."

He chuckled, his big belly jiggling, and the tight grip in the air loosened. "That's why I love you southerners, so polite." He waved his arm and, like magic, a woman in a tiny black dress placed a glass of wine in front of Sasha.

Sasha took a sip, watching the woman's hips sway as she walked away.

"I was surprised to get a call from Ellen," Antonio said between chews. "She turned this place upside down when she left. Broke my poor brother's heart when she ran off with that Ashby punk and twenty-G's of my money."

Antonio's eyes locked on Sasha. All the men's eyes seared holes through her nerves.

"Your brother?"

"Of course." Antonio pushed his plate aside and reached for a pack of cigarettes. "It's just like Ellen to toss someone in a viper's nest without a mention why. Your mother was married to my brother, Donatello. You might know him as Dante."

"Dante's a Lazzari?" Sasha downed her cup of wine.

"Smoke?" The man at Sasha's right slid a pack of cigarettes in front of her. How nice. Maybe she'd get a few puffs in before they whacked her.

"So," Sasha lit her zippo, gaze on Antonio, "I guess you know about the...scuffle that's been

185

going down."

"Probably more than you do." Antonio nodded, and the men got up from the table, leaving just the two of them. "It must be hard for you, in your mother's crew. She's very intolerant."

"I don't know what you mean."

"I saw the way you looked at the young lady who brought the wine. It only took five minutes of sitting across from you to see what you're all about." Antonio flicked his ashes in a crystal tray, leaning close. "I reached out to a few associates of mine, asked about you. The ones who didn't fear you respected you. That's a rather large feat for a girl of only...?"

"Nineteen."

"Huh. Nineteen? You don't say."

Antonio sat completely still, staring at the smoke rising from his cigarette. When he finally moved, crushing out his butt, Sasha flinched.

"I like you, Sasha. You're honest, smart, civil. Those are hard qualities to come by these days." He smiled, much like a man who was trying to lure a child into his van. "If you worked for me, you could be whoever you want. You wanna sit here every night with a different girl on your lap, no one would say a thing. The boys might bust your chops, but hey, that's just what we do." He dipped his head to the side and shrugged. "No pressures, messy turf wars. Just a few jobs here and there and the freedom to live your life the way you want."

"Wow. I..." Sasha slouched in her chair, looking around the room. Diamonds and rhinestones glittered in the low light, a mesmeric dance of shimmering flickers.

"You have no idea how tempting that offer is." What a good life she could have…for maybe two months until her mother came to burn the city to the ground. "I really appreciate this, really, but I can't abandon my club."

"And loyal, I like it."

Antonio rose from his seat, and Sasha scrambled up. She stood tall as he stepped closer and placed a briefcase in her hand.

"My offer stands anytime," he said, patting her on the arm. "I hope to see you for my next shipment."

"Me too. Thank you, sir." Sasha shook her head then grinned. "Mr. Antonio."

***

Twenty miles of pavement and a little rest stop off I-78 lay between Sasha and the glow of city lights. She hosed down the trailer, the water's stream sending a wave of filth pouring out the back door. The stench caught in her throat. It took all she had to keep from gagging. Her mother's voice played on a loop in her mind. *This is what you get for being nice, you stupid little bitch.* She hated that the words rang true. Every time she sacrificed for the comfort of others, she ended up standing in a pile of shit.

Sasha jumped from the truck and shut the faucet, taking a long gulp of fresh air. A quick call home then nine more hours of open road. Her eyes zeroed in on a phone booth when a young woman strolled in front of her.

"Hey there," the woman said. Bells jingled from her flowing skirt, a long stretch of skin between its waistband and a tiny suede halter-top. "Are you a trucker?"

Sasha stepped back, scanning the woman over. Chipped nails, worn flip-flops, ratty hair littered with dreads and braids. It looked like the road had chewed her up and the seventies spit her out.

"Yeah. Why?"

"So awesome!" She took a half-spin, clutching her fringed bag. "Say, how come truckers shove their hands up your skirt at the twenty-mile mark?"

"Excuse me?" Sasha said, crossing her arms.

"Oh no." She waved her hands, more jingles trilling from cheap bracelets. "I'm not trying to be rude. It's just every single trucker I've ever rode with stuck his hand up my skirt. And it's always at the twenty-mile mark. I started keeping track. Is it, like, some unspoken trucker law?"

"Yeah, it is." Sasha held a straight face, even through the woman's gasp. "It's how you're supposed to pay for the lift."

"Really?"

"No," Sasha said with a snort. "Men are just pigs. That's probably how long it takes before their hard-ons overpower their brains."

She giggled, holding out her hand. "Misty."

"Sasha." Soft palm, too silky to match the rough ensemble. "You waiting for someone?"

"I am. Maybe it's you. Are you going to D.C.?" Misty asked, flashing a cute smile.

"No, sorry. I only cut through the western edge

of Maryland."

"That's close enough. Do you think I could hitch a ride? I mean, it's cool if you can't. I just thought…you know, you won't try to put your hand up my skirt."

Sasha tried to hold it in, but a laugh burst from her lips. This woman, she couldn't be more wrong. Maybe men weren't pigs, just truckers, no matter what sex.

"I guess that's cool." Sasha backed toward her truck. "Just wait right here for a sec." After shutting the trailer door, she hopped into the cab. Guns decorated every surface, not to mention the suspicious briefcase. She shoved the shotguns under the seats, stuffed the handguns into her backpack, and loaded a revolver into her holster. The briefcase slid into its secret compartment in the floor, and she moved a cooler over the seams.

Before leaving the truck, Sasha peered into the side mirror. Misty stood in the same spot, dancing to music only she could hear.

Sasha jumped to the pavement, stopping Misty mid-spin.

"I just gotta make a call," Sasha said, heading for the phone booth, "then we'll hit the road."

***

Ellen

Ellen jumped when the phone rang. She dropped her straw on the desk, hurrying from the backroom of the clubhouse. By the third ring, she lifted the receiver from the wall.

"Sasha?"

"It's me," Sasha's voice streamed through the phone. "Everything went fine."

"Where are you?"

"I'm about twenty miles outside the city. I should be home by first dawn."

"All right, good." Ellen slumped against the wall, the knot in her chest unraveling. "Wake me when you get here."

"Okay. Later."

The line clicked, and Ellen squeezed the receiver. A dial tone blasted in her ear, humming in its steady tone. "Love you, baby," she whispered, hanging up the phone.

Her heel dug into the floor, and she turned toward the backroom when a motor revved. She marched to the front door, grabbing a shotgun from the pool table on her way. When spotting Otis, his arm around Sasha's favorite trucker slut, she chuckled.

"Hey." Otis dropped a grease-soaked paper bag on the nearest table. "I brought food."

"Nice." Ellen set down the gun, stepping toward Candy. "What happened to your face, darlin'?"

"Oh." Candy darted her eyes to the floor. "I might've upset my mama."

"It don't take much with that woman." Ellen pointed to the bar. "Why don't you flip on those neon lights and call some of the girls? Let's get this place rockin'."

"Hell yeah," Candy said, the clack of her heels filling the room as she hurried to the bar.

Ellen shifted her gaze to Otis then strolled into the backroom.

"I gotta take care of some business, babe," Otis said, glancing at Candy.

Candy waved her hand while gabbing into the phone, and Otis followed Ellen, shutting the door.

"You got that look on your face." He walked to the end of the table, leaning against the solid wood. "Did something happen with the run?"

"No. Sasha called a bit ago. It's all good," Ellen said, keeping her eyes low. In a minute, she'd play Otis like a fiddle, and he wouldn't catch on until after she got her way. Unless she looked into his eyes. Then he'd spot the guilt in her stare.

"It can't be all good."

Ellen snaked across the room, placing her palms on Otis's chest. "The VP chair is gonna need to be filled now that Chewy's in the ground." Her hands wandered down, and she unbuckled his belt.

"You want me to be VP?" Otis asked, his smile spreading wide.

"Oh honey," her fingers grazed the soft yet hard flesh inside his jeans, "you've been my VP for a long time. The title's symbolic. It doesn't actually mean anything."

Otis clutched the sides of Ellen's arms and positioned her so her back was against the table. His hands slid to her hips, and he lifted her atop the glossy surface, sliding her leather skirt up.

"So you're fucking me." Otis twisted his fingers into Ellen's hair, thrusting himself inside her.

A moan pushed passed Ellen's throat, trailed by a chuckle. "Looks like you're fucking me."

Otis ran his tongue up Ellen's chest, along her neck, and to the soft spot behind her ear.

"Whatever it is, I got you." He slowed his pace, hands coasting down her back. "I always got you."

Chapter Twenty

Sasha

Sasha reached into her backpack, pulling out a joint. Tiny bells clattered from the passenger seat, a hint of patchouli floating on the breeze. The scent brought back fuzzy memories. Arms holding her tight, a kiss on the forehead, her father's smile.

"You have some awesome tunes in here," Misty said, picking through a case of eight-track cartridges. She popped out Def Leppard and slid in the Allman Brothers. "Yes!" She smiled, bobbing her head to the beat. With her bare feet propped onto the open window, she reached for the joint.

Sasha tensed up when Misty's palm slithered along her skin. Tingles followed the light touch then it was gone, along with her joint.

"What's in D.C.?" Sasha asked, her stare alternating between the road and the skirt riding up Misty's thigh.

"Things I haven't seen yet." Misty took a long, slow hit, her face scrunching. "Your grass tastes funny."

That didn't stop her from taking two more hits before passing it back.

"I put coke in it," Sasha said between puffs.

"Cocaine?" Misty drew her legs into the cab, crossing them underneath her body. "No wonder I feel so wired. I wish I could dance. There are so many stars out here, in the middle of nowhere."

"Hold on a second." Sasha slowed the truck, turning down a dirt road in between two cornfields.

"What are you doing?" Misty asked, an edge of panic trembling her voice.

Airbrakes whooshed, and Sasha shut off the engine, leaving the radio on. "I wanna show you something." She cranked the volume up and opened her door, climbing onto the steel running board. "Slide over here."

"Okay."

Sasha helped Misty out the truck, balancing on the grated step. "Climb up this ladder, careful for the exhaust. Those stacks are hot."

When they got on top of the trailer, Misty gasped. She lifted her arms at her sides and tilted her head back to look at an endless abyss of twinkling stars. "Wow! This is amazing." She twirled, her skirt fluttering out. "This must be what Heaven looks like."

"Yeah." Sasha sat down, leaning on her elbows. A beautiful woman swayed and floated atop her favorite truck, an infinite supply of sparkles to brighten the silky blackness beyond. "Heaven," she said in a long, drawn-out breath.

Giggles, jingles, and flowing cloth melded so

194

well with the faint music. Sasha slipped a joint from behind her ear, twisted it in her fingers, and then popped it in her mouth.

"You're like magic, Sasha." Misty knelt down, her eyes shimmering in the zippo's flame. "Is this what it's like to be with you every day?"

"Ha." A puff of smoke trailed Sasha's snicker. "No. That would be more like…*The Rocky Horror Picture Show.*"

Misty giggled, swiping the joint. She drew deep, inching closer. Her eyes drifted to a close, and she dipped low, blowing smoke into Sasha's mouth.

"Come dance with me," Misty whispered, her lips grazing skin.

"No way." Sasha leaned back, shaking her head. "I don't dance."

"Everybody dances." Misty shoved the joint into Sasha's mouth, tugging at her arm. "C'mon."

Sasha allowed herself to be guided up. Starlight cast a gentle glow, adding a silvery tinge to Misty's long blonde hair. This moment did feel like magic. The numb haze that swelled from every joint's hit, a melodious beat hanging in the background, and a beautiful creature on her arm. Magic. Sasha forced the burdens from her mind, making room so music could flow in.

Before the smile left her lips, she fell under the rhythm of tambourines and guitars. Her hips swung, hair blowing in the breeze. A laugh rolled freely from her chest, and Misty pulled her close. They twirled in each other's arms, alone beneath a million twinkling lights.

***

Ellen

"Vinny! As VP." Otis buckled his belt, glancing up as Ellen hopped off the table. "You got something going with Dez?"

Ellen readjusted her skirt, lit two cigarettes, and handed one to Otis. "Not me."

"What's the angle?"

"Sasha and Dez are pulling away from each other. This'll bring them closer together, give them something to relate to." Ellen sat in her president's chair, looking up at Otis. "They're hatred for me."

"I don't understand why you give a shit."

"Because I need Sasha tame, levelheaded."

Otis snickered, sitting on the table in front of Ellen. "And you think Dez can do that?"

"Maybe. He's the only person who's ever backed her into a corner before." He smirked, dropping his head to one side.

"Besides me." Ellen ashed her cigarette, taking a long drag. "If Dez don't get them reins on that girl, she's gonna end up with her fingers in your tall stack of redhead out there."

A grumble left Otis's mouth as he crossed his arms. "I'll get Kev onboard, but I'm gonna tell you straight up. If this shit backfires and we gotta pick between those two brothers, Dez is going in the cellar."

"Agreed." Ellen nodded, managing to quash half the grin from her lips.

***

Dez

Dez sat on the porch of the clubhouse, stretching out on the bench. So far, five carloads of people had crammed into the clubhouse, a full-blown party erupting within. Every one of those jokers stopped and smiled at him on their way to free liquor, spouting shit like, "Hey, Dez!" and "What's up, sarge!" They all knew his name, face, but he couldn't point them out if he tried.

The music died out between songs, and his brother's voice took its place in the night air. Dez leaned forward, propping his elbows on the rail. Vinny strolled down the hill, a curvy blonde tucked under his arm. They walked up the steps, and Vinny stopped, turning toward Dez.

"I'll catch up with ya." Vinny slapped the girl on her ass, and she giggled before trotting inside.

"Waiting for someone?" he asked, walking in front of Dez.

"You." Dez sat back, pulling a flask from his inner pocket. "I don't know anybody in there. All my friends from the old days are dead."

"Oh wow." Vinny leaned against the railing, his brow raised. "So it's a pity party, then."

"Fuck you." A smile cracked Dez's lips, lasting only seconds. "Sasha said something about Mom splitting on you?"

Vinny groaned, sitting beside Dez. "Yeah. I came home one night and her shit was gone. Of course, I went running to Sasha 'cause she…always knows what to do."

"Is, umm…" Dez dropped his gaze to the shining flask in his hand. The concept was too stupid to think, let alone look someone in the face while voicing. "Is Sasha a dyke?"

"What?" The bench wobbled as Vinny jolted back, shifting against the armrest. "Why would you ask that?"

"Some shit Ellen said."

"Ellen," Vinny muttered, shaking his head. "You know I heard you having sex with Sasha, right?"

"Yeah."

"Did she seem like a virgin to you?"

"Fuck no." Dez chuckled.

"And I'm sure she went down on you."

That broke Dez's smile, triggering his fist to curl.

"I'm just saying," Vinny lifted his hands, as if pleading innocence, "she has some skills that no dyke can master."

The words soothed Dez's mind and riled his temper at the same time. "Yeah, all right. I get it."

"So you done feeling sorry for yourself?"

"Yeah, I am. Asshole." Dez took a swig from his flask before stashing it away.

"Good. Let's go shoot some pool." Vinny got up, glancing back as he headed for the clubhouse door. "You woman-stealing bastard."

"Aw. That's harsh, little brother." Dez rose from the bench, walking toward the sound of cackles and booming speakers.

***

Sasha

Sasha barreled down on the gas pedal. Only two hours had been lost to fun, and she could easily make that up by driving a hundred miles per hour. She looked to the passenger seat, catching a glimpse of Misty's smooth skin in the passing streetlights. In a little while, this beautiful distraction would be gone. Her real life waited four hundred fifty-four miles away, ready to sucker punch her in the gut. Nothing could stop that, not even Misty with her haunting eyes and jingling bells.

"We just crossed into Maryland." Sasha kept her gaze straight ahead, though she felt the woman beside her slink closer. "Where should I drop you at?"

"The next rest stop is fine," Misty said softly.

A bitter taste rose in Sasha's throat. Ugly visuals filled her mind, all of them ending with Misty being gangbanged in the back of a trailer.

"How long have you been hitching?" Sasha asked.

"A few days, maybe a week."

The sour sting turned to a full churn, and Sasha shifted in her seat. That girl had no idea what kind of trouble awaited a sweet, young woman on the big open road. "You know, most of the truckers I've met are pretty...dangerous."

"I know," Misty said with a snicker. "It's been intense, but I just wanna see new things before I have to go back to school."

"Where's school?"

"Ohio State. The first two weeks were a total

bitch, so I ducked out. I'm almost ready to go back. I just need a few more days to decompress, take in as much awesome as possible before the establishment converts me into another Ikeman."

"Have you ever seen the mountains of Kentucky?"

"No!" Misty twisted to face Sasha, bouncing to her knees. "What do they look like?"

"Steep. The rocks sparkle when the sun hits 'em just right. In the spring, there're flowers on the trees. Pink, purple, white pedals raining to the grass. Now the leaves are turning so at sunset it looks like the hillside is lit in flames."

"Wow!" Misty sank back into her seat, keeping her gaze locked on Sasha. "That's where you're from, Kentucky?"

"Yep. Down in a holler."

"A holler?"

Sasha smirked. It had been so long since she had an actual conversation with a non-club member. She'd have to tone down the mountain-men lingo. "It's a flat spot between two peaks. I don't know why they call it that. I think the old hillbillies used to yell out and listen to their own voice echo off the cliffs. There ain't much to do in the middle of nowhere."

"Unless you have a backpack full of joints and a Mack truck."

"Yeah. That sure does help." Sasha glanced over, caught by the upward curve of Misty's lips. The steering wheel vibrated, and she darted her eyes ahead. "I, umm…" Her fingers drummed the side of her leg, left foot tapping. "I have a run to Ohio next week. If you wanted to, you could crash with me for a few days and I can bring you back to school when I hit the road."

"Really? That sounds far out. Kentucky, here I come," Misty said, cranking the radio up and dancing in her seat.

Sasha grinned until her mother's face flashed into her mind. Then she thought of Dez, most likely curled up in her bed. This was the worst time for company. Her mother would blow a gasket, which would be hilarious until it wasn't.

That's when she reached into the backpack and fished out another joint. Her gaze wandered to Misty, and she plastered on a smile. It'll be all good. A little bitchin', maybe a slap. It'll be like an average Tuesday.

***

Dez

Dez eyed the eight ball, leaning down to take his shot. A hip bumped his side, and the tip of his pool stick nicked the cue, sending the white ball rolling along green felt.

"Ha! I win," Vinny said.

"Son of a bitch!" Dez slammed his fist on the table, turning toward the asshole who just fucked him out of a hundred bucks. A woman backed away, her bright green eyes growing wide.

"Oh my God. Dez! I'm so sorry. I'm such a klutz. Here." She thrust her beer into his hand. "Peace, mercy, or some junk."

201

Dez chuckled, giving the beer back. "It's cool, uh…"

"Candy. I'm," her head tilted to the side, "Otis's girl," she said, her voice raised as if posing a question.

"What happened to your face?" Dez lifted his hand to Candy's bruised cheek, and she pulled away.

"It's nothing. My mama gets ornery. Say, was it hard to get used to the outside? You know, after being away for so long?"

"What?" Dez asked, trying but failing to hold back a hard glare.

"I'm sorry, it's just…My dad's away, upstate, and I wonder what he'll be like when he gets out."

Dez stared at the timid girl who nibbled on her lip while twirling her fiery red hair. A forbidden fruit, Otis's maybe girlfriend. Dez looked at Vinny. The open-mouthed gawk and grim stare should've been enough to ward him away, but it only piqued his interest more.

"Why don't we cop a squat?" Dez draped his arm over Candy's shoulder, ushering her toward the couch. "Talk a little more."

***

Ellen

Ellen belted out a laugh, setting her bottle on the bar. She turned from the group of men, still chuckling, and scanned the clubhouse. Her smile dropped, muscles tightening. She watched Dez wrap his arm around Candy and stroll toward the sofa, shooing a couple away.

Her eyes locked on Vinny, who was leaning against a pool stick with a dumbass look on his face. The levels of annoyance in her body spiked. She pushed through the crowd, stepping beside Vinny.

"What the fuck is this shit?" she asked, joining Vinny in his gawk.

Vinny shrugged without tearing his glare from Dez. "I don't know. It was weird. They bumped into each other and just started talking."

"About what?"

"Stupid shit. Not…her or anything."

"This could go sour," Ellen said, cringing as Candy laughed under Dez's arm.

"I know," Vinny said, his foot tapping the wooden planks. "But if I drag him out of here, he's gonna know something's up. Where's Otis?"

Ellen peeked over her shoulder then turned back to the scene on the couch. "At the bar, shootin' the shit with a few locals."

"I could start a fight." Vinny curled his fingers into a fist, glancing around the room. "That guy in the corner looks shady."

A snicker brought Ellen's anxiety down a notch, and she patted Vinny on the back. "That's why I love ya, kid. You know what? Fuck it. Let's get a drink."

"But—"

Ellen took Vinny by the arm and pulled him toward the bar, pool stick and all.

Chapter Twenty-One

Sasha

A ray of sunlight bounced off the chrome mirror, and Sasha squinted. Her eyes already burned, the lines of the road in front of her crossing. Two more turns and a trek up the mountain, then she could peel her ass off this springy seat. Her hand pawed the center console, spilling empty cigarette packs to the floor.

Misty rubbed her eyes, sitting up in the passenger seat. "Do you need something?"

"My shades," Sasha said, tossing a handful of empty potato chip bags into the sleeper cab behind her. "They should be right here somewhere."

"This place is a wreck." Misty rummaged through maps and receipts, shoving her hand under the seat. "Oh. I found them and this."

First, a pair of blue-tinted sunglasses fell into view then came the butt of a Colt .45.

"Shit." Sasha slipped the plastic rims up her nose and grabbed the gun. "It's for protection. I told you, truckers are dangerous."

"I guess so." Misty scooted away, leaning against her door. "It was really heavy, but I guess that makes sense. I mean, it's a thing that takes people's spark from the world, so it should weigh a lot."

A chill ran through Sasha, the gun in her hand seeming much heavier than before. "I never thought of it that way. The types of people I would use this on, they don't have any spark. Just different shades of darkness."

A burst of air gushed from the brakes, and Misty flinched then giggled. "Are we here?"

"Yeah." Sasha stopped the truck, eyeing the open gate. Beyond the gentle slope, her compound looked quiet. Almost peaceful. If they killed enough bikers, it could stay that way forever.

"Is something wrong?" Misty asked.

Sasha looked at Misty then to the gun pressed against her palm. "No. I thought the gate would be locked." She laid the weapon in her lap, pulling into the driveway.

"Ashby Trucking," Misty said as they passed the sign that towered above a chain-link fence. "This is where you work?"

"Work?" It took Sasha a minute to make the connection. People only saw the outside of Ashby Trucking, the business, not the front for drug trafficking it really was on the inside. "Oh, no. This is my family's business. I have a little apartment above the garage."

Misty stayed glued to her window, turning to stare into the clubhouse as they passed. Through its open door, a light shined above the pool table.

"That looks like a bar."

"It's just a hangout for our…employees and friends. There're a lot of people who live farther up the hill and on the next one over. This way, they don't have to drive all the way down the mountain to get a drink."

"Groovy," Misty said in a long flowing breath. "I like it here already."

Sasha parked, and Misty reached for the door's handle.

"Hold up." Sasha grabbed Misty by the wrist, quickly letting go. "Can you wait here for a second?"

"Sure. I—"

"Just stay inside the truck until I come back. Okay?"

Before Misty could utter a word, Sasha was out the door and across the lot. No one called her name. The path remained clear of any bizarre obstacles. It might've been the first time ever that the universe cooperated with her plans. If she opened her door and found an empty room, it'd be a sign of a good day.

"Damn it." Sasha stood in the doorway, staring at Dez's bare thigh wrapped around her blanket. Cuts of muscles gleamed in the thin sliver of daylight. The urge to crawl beside Dez crept up, and she choked it back, loathing the feeling the instant it infected her body. Sasha slapped on a hard glare and stomped toward the bed.

"Dez. Get up."

He groaned, rolling onto his back. A hint of a

smile swept his lips even though his eyes stayed shut.

"Come on, man," Sasha said, kicking the side of the bed. "I'm beat."

Dez lifted the blanket, scooting back. "Get in here. I won't bite, much."

"Stop fucking around." Sasha picked Dez's clothes off the floor, dropping them in his lap. "I've been on the road for twenty hours. I wanna stretch out in my bed, alone."

"Damn." Dez sat up, swinging his legs over the edge of the mattress. "You're one cranky motherfucker after a run."

"Yep. Don't you have shit to do? There's three burnt up semi carcasses out front, and Vinny's house is full of bullet holes. Shouldn't you guys get on that?"

"Fuck." His belt clinked as he jumped up and pulled on his pants. "Yes, ma'am." Dez slung his shirt over his shoulder, grabbed his boots, and stormed into the blinding rays of sunshine. A minute passed then two, with only a sparrow's call echoing from the open door.

Sasha hurried to the window, peeking out. A part of her expected to find catastrophe. Angry bikers with Molotov cocktails, a scorned lover hunkered down on the steps, her mother. However, the horrible things she usually glimpsed when looking out this window remained hidden today. Since tranquility only lasted seconds in this place, Sasha turned and dashed out the door.

***

Dez

Dez sat behind the wheel of his pickup, searching his jacket pockets for his smokes. Two knifes, a glock, spare clips, but no fucking cigarettes. He reached for the ignition, glancing at the rearview mirror. His jaw inched open, and his throat sealed shut.

He turned, glaring out the back window as Sasha snuck a blonde chick up the stairs.

"You gotta be fucking kidding me," Dez said through clenched teeth.

When a sharp sting pierced his palm, he looked down to see his fingers caught in a fist. He took a breath, but it wouldn't unravel. A red tinge crept over the world, clouding all thoughts in waves of fury. It was his fist. It wouldn't unravel. He sat, betrayed by Sasha's lying mouth and his own body's refusal to obey the simplest of commands to unlock his goddamn fist.

Dez swung the fist that refused to unclench, slamming it into the radio. First, the sound of a crash tore him from a rage-filled haze. Then came the pain. Hard plastic dug into his skin, pieces of dashboard raining from his knuckles. He pulled his arm back and the radio fell to the floor, taking the overflowing ashtray with it. His hand finally decided to loosen, and a burning sensation shot through his arm. Warm streams of blood seeped between his fingers, dripping onto the seat.

He reached for the door, stopped by his reflection in the mirror. It was enough to scare himself. So much violence lay in his eyes, the wrath warping his face into one of a monster. That's what he'd be if he stepped foot outside his truck, a monster who pulls a girl from her bed to deliver an old-fashioned stomp down in the parking lot, again.

His brain pounded so hard its thump echoed in his ears. He started the truck. A coffee and a cigarette. If that didn't calm him, then he'd come back and beat Sasha's ass.

***

Sasha

The shower's roar streamed from the bathroom, and Sasha picked up the phone. She dialed her mother's line, eyeing Misty's bag as the phone rang.

"Sasha?"

Her mother's voice cracked, followed by a series of coughs. Sasha wanted to laugh, make some crude remark about old ladies who party like teens, except that old lady would whoop her teen ass.

"Yeah, it's me. I'm home."

"Why didn't you come up? The front door's unlocked."

Sasha sat on the floor, leaning against her bed. The truth, that she was busy entertaining a guest, wouldn't fly, so she spouted out the next best thing. "I'm spent. My bed was calling. I gotta crash out for a few."

"Get some rest. We're having a meeting at noon."

"Yeah, all right." Sasha hung up, looking at the bathroom door. Misty seemed as gentle as the song she hummed while showering. Sasha wanted to trust the strange woman she picked up at a truck stop, but this was 1984 and people were freaks.

Before her mind could think up a rebuttal, she snatched Misty's purse and pulled back the zipper. No severed heads or weapons of mass destruction, just tampons, makeup, and a mini pharmacy of pills. She opened a little brown wallet, staring at Misty's smile on her student ID. A regular person, playing hooky on a regular life. The things that happened on this compound could devour a norm like her. These next few days had to be handled just right.

Sasha pulled the tape from her answering machine and unplugged the cord from the phone. No calls, in or out. After tossing the receiver and tape under her bed, she stashed the phone's base in the closet.

A faucet squeaked, and the shower cut off. Sasha dashed to the center of the room, realized how awkward she looked, then sat on the edge of the bed.

"Hey, Sasha?" Misty called out from within the bathroom.

"Yeah." Sasha jumped to her feet, walking toward the closed door, and it flew open. Beads of water dripped off Misty's bare shoulders, trapping Sasha's stare. "Yeah," she repeated in a low mumble.

Misty gestured to the towel wrapped around her body. "Do you have a t-shirt I can borrow?"

"Sure." Sasha turned to her dresser, pulling out an extra-large black tee. "All my shit's baggy. I hope you don't—" Her words bunched in her throat as the towel dropped to the floor. White lace panties with little pink flowers, the only stitch of clothes on the tanned flesh in front of her. A perfect vision of beauty. What a shame, to cover this sight with such plain fabrics.

"Geeze, stare much?" Misty grinned, taking the shirt from Sasha's hand.

"Sorry." Sasha lowered her gaze, turning her back.

"It's like you've never seen a naked woman before."

"Yeah," Sasha snickered, opening her little fridge and grabbing a beer. Before its cap could hit the ground, she downed half the bottle.

"Or maybe you've seen too many."

Sasha shook her head at the ridiculous notion. One could never see too many naked women. "Nah. I, uh...I'm gonna take a quick shower. There's some snacks and shit. Help yourself." Beer in hand, Sasha barged into the bathroom and shut the door.

***

Otis

Otis rolled over in bed, reaching for Candy. Scratchy sheets grazed his fingertips, not the silky skin he was seeking. He opened his eyes, and sunlight rushed in to stun his brain. A clink of glass echoed from outside his bedroom door, drowned out by Candy's squeaky voice attempting to sing "Sweet Home Alabama."

After a quick trip to the bathroom, Otis followed

a light giggle to his kitchen. He stood in the doorway, watching Candy's ass shake as she mixed pancake batter. A softly spoken "Oopsy" or "Shit" streamed from her mouth every time batter spilled over the brim of her bowl, splatting to the floor. This would be the point where Otis showed the floozy to the door. It should be, except he wanted to lock the door and keep Candy safe inside forever.

If he strolled behind her and wrapped his arms around her tiny waist, she'd melt like butter in his hands. He could have her right there. She'd let him bend her little body over the counter and she would like it, but goddamn he was hungry.

"Candy."

She jumped, the cutest yelp slipping from her lips.

"It's the perfect name for you."

"I know." Candy smiled, lifting her chin high. "That's why…" Her grin dropped, carrying her gaze along with it. "I picked it," she mumbled, turning back to the stove.

"Sasha named you Candy?" Otis took a step closer, stopping when Candy's shoulders tensed.

"I'm sorry. I know I'm not supposed to talk about her." Candy shrunk down, as if waiting for a strike from behind.

"Babe." Otis ran his fingers along Candy's cheek, drawing her stare. "When we're alone, you can talk about whatever you want. And you won't be getting hit 'round here, but that don't mean you can mouth off, right."

Otis didn't think it possible, but Candy's green eyes lit up even brighter.

"I won't be mouthing off." Candy lifted her gaze. When her eyes hit Otis's face, she dropped her stare. "I mean…I like you."

Her pouty lips taunted him, and the strand of crimson hair that fell between her breasts tortured his mind. Fuck pancakes, he needed a piece of Candy.

Otis slid his hands around Candy's waist, backing her against the counter. The silky robe that barely covered her curves slipped open. He caressed every inch of skin. His teeth dug into the side of her neck, and she moaned, grinding into him.

"What are you doing?" Candy whispered, pushing down his boxers.

"I want some dessert before breakfast."

***

Sasha

Sasha walked from the bathroom and into pitch black. "Whoa!"

"A lot of light shined in through your curtain," Misty said from somewhere in the darkness of her room. "So I hung a blanket over your window. I hope you don't mind."

"It's awesome." Sasha's eyes adjusted to the darkness, and she caught the outline of Misty's body in her bed. She stumbled over piles of clothes, tripped on a boot, and flopped onto the mattress.

"I thought your truck was messy, but this place takes the cake." Misty giggled, scooting closer to Sasha.

"I'm on the road a lot and—"

"You don't have to explain yourself. No judgment, just an observation." Misty rolled onto her stomach and buried her face in the pillow, inhaling deeply. "Your bed smells like a man."

Sasha turned onto her side, resisting the urge to run her fingers through the golden hair sprawled across the pillows. "Judgment or observation?"

Misty propped on her elbow, staring into Sasha's eyes. "I saw you chase that dude out of here. Is he your old man?"

"No. Just a friend. He's in between pads right now, so I told him to crash here while I was away."

"You're a nice person," Misty said, running her fingers along a strand of Sasha's hair. "I'll bet you're an Aquarius. They're the most generous of the zodiac."

"I don't know what sign I am."

"When's your birthday?"

"June sixth."

"Oh." Misty fell to her back, glancing away.

"Is that bad?"

"No," Misty said in a hell yes tone. "You're a Gemini, the twins."

"What does that mean?"

"Gemini's can be tricky. They're, like, two different people rolled into one. They always fight themselves 'cause they never know which version they want to be. The good twin or the bad."

"What are you?"

"I'm a Cancer. We're very in tune with the Earth. Gentle, delicate souls who seek out connections."

214

"Huh." Sasha flopped to her back, staring up at the ceiling. "It fits, all that zodiac shit."

"So which twin are you right now?"

Sasha grinned. If there were any part of her that didn't contain pure evil, she'd never met it. Although, in comparison to what she usually does in this bed with half-naked women, her behavior could be much worse. "The good one, I guess."

"Is the bad one gonna come out to collect her payment for the ride?"

"What?" Sasha raised on her elbow, staring down at Misty's smile in the low light. "You want me to stick my hand up your skirt?"

"I'm not wearing a skirt."

The words sparked a frenzy in Sasha's chest, one that kicked her lungs into overdrive. "You don't have to do that with me."

"What if I want to?"

Misty's blue eyes fluttered, and Sasha smirked. Her hand flinched, yearning to stroke the freckled skin beside it. "Do you want to?"

Misty squirmed, and their legs brushed against one another. "I don't know. I kinda do."

Sasha glided her palm to the nape of Misty's neck, leaning down. Their lips met, and Sasha tasted strawberries. Her hand wandered. A curve of a waist, hip, the silky flesh of the inner thigh, they all withered under her grasp. Every sweet moan that flowed made the blood in her veins pulsate. She ran her tongue down a smooth neck while pulling Misty's shirt up, slow and tender.

"I've never done this before," Misty said between pants. "I mean, with a…"

"Do you want me to stop?" Sasha hooked her nails around Misty's lacy panties and looked up.

"No! Don't stop," Misty said with a shudder, curling her fingers into Sasha's hair.

Chapter Twenty-Two

Dez

Dez stood on the edge of the clubhouse porch. The ground shook when a bulldozer dropped its bucket onto the gravel. He grinned, turning to glare at Sasha's door.

"What the fuck is this shit?" Ellen grumbled over the racket of heavy machinery. Dez didn't bother to look. He could see Ellen's sour expression clearly in his mind.

"You know Sasha's trying to sleep," Ellen said, stepping in front of him.

"Is that what she's trying to do?"

"What?"

Ellen tugged on Dez's arm, and he jerked away, steering his glare to her. "Sasha wanted it done now, so it's getting done," he said in a low growl.

"What happened to your hand?"

Dez looked at his knuckles, decorated in puffy red scabs, and sneered. "You're wrong. Nothing can change who a person is inside. Not me, not even

217

you, can undyke Sasha."

"Hey!" Ellen glanced around, pushing Dez to the farthest corner of the porch, "I was wasted yesterday. Some of the things I said might've—"

"No." Dez pushed Ellen's hands off his chest. "You were actually honest yesterday, maybe for the first time in your life." His eyes shot back to Sasha's door before honing in on Ellen. "It doesn't matter how many times you beat her or how hard I fuck her. If pussy falls in her lap, she'll take it."

Dez pushed past Ellen and stormed into the clubhouse, heading for the bar.

***

Otis

Otis caught the look on Ellen's face before he even parked his truck. He knew that expression. Every time she made it, someone he cared about had died.

He cut off the engine and walked up the clubhouse steps, standing beside her on the porch. Ellen didn't look over or nod. Not even a flinch when the machine across the lot dumped a tangle of metal into a steel dumpster.

"Do you know where Candy is?" Ellen asked, glancing at Sasha's door.

"In my living room, watching soaps and smoking all my pot. Why?"

Her eyes drifted to him, her stare losing its sharp edge. "It's been a strange morning."

Otis followed Ellen's stare through the

clubhouse window to Dez, who was pounding shots at the bar. "We still doing this vote?" he asked, hoping to get a fuck no for an answer. Dez already held the look of a man ready to gut a biker, but Ellen could never resist a chance to poke a cage bear.

Ellen reached into Otis's jacket pocket and took his pack of smokes.

"Why not?" she said, knocking a cigarette loose. "At the least, it'll be entertaining."

After seizing the zippo from Otis's hand, Ellen strolled inside. He leaned against the threshold, watching Ellen's hips sway as she strolled across the clubhouse. On her way into the backroom, she snatched the bottle of whiskey from Dez's grasp and clicked on the radio.

***

Vinny

Once the bulldozer cleared the lot and the dumpsters were hauled away, Vinny walked his *friend* to her car. He couldn't remember her name, but he'd never forget her ass. The perfect size to fit in his hand. Tight yet soft, and so sexy when it bounced in his lap.

Before Vinny could open the chick's car door, she shoved her tongue in his mouth. He slid his hands right to that sweet ass, squeezing.

"Call me anytime," she said, dragging her nails across his neck.

If he knew who the fuck she was, beside the

brunette with huge tits, he might just do that.

"For sure," Vinny said, guiding her into the driver's seat of a yellow bug.

He puffed on a joint as she drove from the compound. Right now, he should be feeling pretty damn good. The sun shined on his skin, a calm buzz radiated throughout his body, but an edge clung to his bones.

In less than five minutes, the club would gather for a meeting. He'd be voted vice president of Ashby Trucking, betray his best friend, humiliate his brother, and he didn't know why. Power meant nothing to him. The burden of responsibility scared the shit out of him, but he wanted that spot so bad.

If he were the man with the plan, Sasha would finally see him. He could crawl from beneath her shadow, stand in the light, and she'd notice.

"Nancy, huh?" Otis asked.

Vinny turned, and Otis walked off the clubhouse porch.

"Nancy, that's right." Vinny smirked. "I was trying to remember that."

"You seen Sasha yet?"

"Nah." Vinny walked closer to Otis, peeking up at Sasha's door. "I'm surprised she didn't start shootin' out the window when that dozer scraped dead semi off the ground. She must've slept right through it."

"It's past noon, and everyone's here," Otis said, gesturing to the clubhouse. "We're just waiting on her."

Vinny rocked in place. On any other day, running to fetch Sasha would be a highlight. She'd spout out some hilarious rant, they'd blow a quick bone, he'd see that glimmer in her eyes. He could pull that off. One last time, before the big vote changed everything.

"I'll go get her," Vinny said, hurrying toward the garage.

***

Sasha

"Wake up."

Sasha grinned. Warm breath tickled her ear, and a hand clutched her waist. She scooted back, into the soft body behind her, and pulled the arm around her tight against her chest.

"Someone's banging on your door," Misty whispered.

"What?" Sasha sat up. Over a steady knock, Vinny's muffled voice flowed through her closed door.

"I'll be down in a minute," Sasha yelled, falling back into the pillows.

"Why is your door locked? Open up," Vinny said, jiggling the knob.

"Oh my God," Sasha mumbled. "Dude," she shouted, "I'll be down in a minute."

After the thump of boots trailed off, Misty rose to her knees. "Are you not supposed to have people here?"

"No. I just...don't usually have people here, that's all." Sasha tossed the blanket aside, draping her legs over the edge of the bed. "Whoa." Her head spun, and a surge of fire jetted from her stomach to the back of her throat. "Not again."

Sasha dashed to the bathroom. Her knees hit cold floor, and she dry heaved into the toilet.

"Are you okay?" Misty asked, rushing to Sasha's side.

Misty brushed Sasha's forehead with her silky hand, and Sasha backed away. "I'm good. It's just some weird stomach thing."

"And it usually happens when you first wake up?"

"Yeah," Sasha said, slumping against the wall behind her. "Is there something going around?"

"Umm, yeah. It's called pregnancy."

"What!" Sasha jumped to her feet, ignoring the sway of the room. "That's just, no." She pushed past Misty, stopping in the middle of her room. "No. It's not…It can't…"

"When was the last time you had your period?" Misty asked softly.

Days melded into weeks, flying by like the lines of the road. Sasha looked at the calendar on the wall. Almost two weeks of X's stood between this day and the day she was supposed to get her period. A few days late was understandable, a week was sweating it, but nine days? She dropped her head into her hand, slapping her palm against her forehead a few times. "No fucking way."

"It'll be okay." Misty spoke in a soothing tone while rubbing Sasha's shoulder, but it didn't help. Okay was the last thing any of this would be.

"There are places that," Misty shrugged, leaning close to whisper, "that take care of this sort of thing.

Maybe some of the local women can point you in the right direction."

"Yeah. Fuck! I have a meeting. I gotta go." Sasha pulled on a pair of cargo pants and grabbed her jacket. "Just chill here. I'll be back in an hour. Sorry."

Before Misty could speak, Sasha scurried out the door. Her steps slowed at the sight of Vinny. He leaned against the rail, smiling up at her from the bottom of the stairs. She wanted to punch that look right off his dumb face. If he had any idea about the spawn growing inside her body, he'd choke on that bobble-headed grin of his.

"It's about time, princess," Vinny said.

Sasha's plan to play cool crumbled. A snarl lifted her lip. She stomped down the last few steps, shoving Vinny out of her way. "You're an asshole," she shouted. His smile dropped into a frown and her stomach retched even harder, so she stormed toward the clubhouse.

"What'd I do?" Vinny ran in front of Sasha, blocking the path that would lead her away from explanations.

"Nothing. I'm just…" *Pregnant with either your or your brother's baby.* "Cranky. I'm sorry." She forced her scowl into a half-smile, gesturing to the clubhouse. "We better go before my mother comes out here breathing fire all over the place."

Vinny moved aside, and they strolled toward the porch.

"That reminds me," he said. "Dez had the burnt-out trucks cleared away this morning."

"Oh yeah." Sasha looked across the now-empty

lot then to her feet. Dez, the latest of the many people she treated like shit for selfish reasons. This one stung more than usual. Vinny was used to her shit, but Dez put her on a pedestal. He'd created a flawless version of her inside his mind, one she could never live up to, a self she never even wanted to be, until now.

Her footsteps went into double time. It didn't make sense, but she knew one glimpse of Dez's frosty eyes would calm her riled soul. She stepped into the backroom, and all eyes went to her except for the ones she wanted most. Not a glance. Dez sat in his spot, hands clasped, jaw clenched, his glare fixed on the solid table.

"Sasha," Ellen said, the way one would address a naughty child.

Sasha tore her gaze from Dez, turning to face her mother.

Ellen sat at the head of the table, narrowing her glare on Sasha. "Are you gonna join us?"

Vinny had taken his seat, leaving her alone in the doorway. She considered shaking Dez until he acknowledged her presence, but she settled for a loud slamming of the door. He still didn't look over.

"All right." Ellen pushed an ashtray full of joints to the center of the table. "Everyone, light one up for Chewy." She waited until five halos of smoke rose into the air, took a long drag of her own doobie, and then leaned forward.

"I know it's soon, but with everything going down, we need to fill the VP seat. And discuss bringing in some new blood."

Sasha uncrossed her legs, banging her boot to the

ground. "Chewy's body is barely cold."

"We need a strong front," Ellen said, looking around the table. "Satan's Crew might be out, but others will come. We need to be prepared for the next pack of loudmouth douchebags who roll onto our turf."

Otis sat up in his chair. "I nominate Vinny as VP."

"What!" Sasha and Dez thundered, almost in sync. Now Dez was looking at her, but not the way she wanted. She wanted a longing gaze and got a seething glower.

"I'll second that," Ellen said, directing her harsh leer at Dez.

Sasha grated the legs of her chair against the floor, turning to face Vinny. "What the fuck?"

Vinny shook his head. He opened his mouth, but no sound came out.

"Let's vote," Ellen said in a chirpy, giggly tone. "All in favor?"

"I," Kev muttered, his gaze low.

"Opposed?" Ellen asked through a grin.

While caught in Vinny's apologetic stare, Sasha fought the urge to laugh. The words *Hell no* bunched in her throat, and for the life of her she couldn't push them out. Dez didn't make a peep. Sasha couldn't bring herself to look at Dez, to see the hurt in his face.

"That's three in favor and two undecided. Congratulations, Vinny, you're our new vice president." Ellen smiled, pointing to Chewy's vacant chair. "Why don't you come take your position?"

Shame. Sasha caught shame in Vinny's eyes as he rose to his feet. He walked around the table, behind Kev and Otis, and sat at the other end—opposite his brother, next to her mother, and far from reach.

"Are we done here?" Sasha tapped her foot, glancing at the door.

"No," Ellen said. "There's still the matter of choosing two new prospects."

"I vote yes to whomever you've chosen to be our prospects." Sasha jumped up from her chair, latching onto Dez's arm. "So does he."

It didn't take much of a yank to get Dez on his feet. The muscles beneath his skin flexed and she let go, but he grabbed onto her hand as they walked out the door.

Chapter Twenty-Three

Dez jerked his hand away the moment they walked out the clubhouse's front door, and Sasha flinched. She followed him onto the porch, stumbling when he spun to face her.

"I saw you sneak that girl into your room."

Sasha fought to keep a blank expression as her brain scrambled for a suitable explanation. Since her mind was too high to produce a witty comeback, her instincts kicked on. She stood tall, slapping on her game face. "I didn't sneak shit."

"You threw me out on my ass for some skank."

"She's not a skank."

"Did you fuck her?" Dez asked with a deep growl that sent shivers.

Sasha took a step back. She looked at his scabbed hand, curling into a fist. "No. Why would I fuck her?"

"Don't stand here and try to play me. Your mother told me about you, about what you are."

"What I am?" Right there, Sasha should've decked him, except Dez wasn't who she wanted to punch. That person floated around this compound acting like the president of the world and not a two-bit club of dimwitted thugs. "Jesus Christ, Dez. In case you haven't noticed, my mother likes to start a lot of shit."

His body loosened, and the anger that seemed to sizzle the air around them faded. Sasha inched closer, taking Dez by the hand. The cracked skin on his hand drew her stare, and she rested her palm atop his knuckles.

"I was a bitch to you this morning," she said, looking up into his eyes.

"Yeah, you were."

She rose to the tips of her toes, her chest gliding along his. "You should probably get used to that."

Dez snickered, wrapping his arms around Sasha's waist. "Why don't you go bounce that hippie bitch on *her* ass and sneak me into your room?"

Sasha groaned. "She doesn't have any place to go."

The stiffness returned to Dez's body, and he pushed Sasha away. "What is it with you and strays?"

"Two, three days tops and she'll be gone forever."

"Fuck!" Dez waved his hand, walking away. "I'm not okay with this."

"Dez."

He turned away from her and jumped into his truck. The engine revved, and he sped off, showering the lot in tiny pebbles.

***

Sasha tore into her room, and Misty jolted up from the pillows. A hint of fear lit Misty's eyes, and guilt sliced into Sasha's stomach. It was like she had an asshole cloud hovering over her, absorbing her misery to rain it back down on the suckers who got too close.

"Bad meeting?" Misty asked, scooting to the edge of the bed.

Misty's blonde hair shimmered in the light of the open door, more so when Misty ran her fingers through her hair. Sasha wanted to dive into Misty. Those silky strands could run all over her body, cleanse the filth from her spirit, except bum-rushing the woman without a word would probably be another asshole move.

"I've had worse." Sasha swung the door closed, and it bounced back open.

"Can we talk?" Vinny stepped into the doorway, stopping short. His eyes shifted between Misty and Sasha, ending on his boots. "Wow! Are you...busy?"

"What do you want?" Sasha yelled, giving Vinny a little shove. "And by the way, now you really are an asshole."

"I didn't know that was gonna happen." Vinny glanced at Misty then gestured to the landing.

Sasha crossed her arms, raising a brow. "Bullshit."

"Dammit, Sasha." He pulled her outside, shutting the door. "You're right, I am an asshole, because some part of me actually thought you'd be happy for me."

"Happy," she sneered. "Whatever my mother told you, it was all lies. She tricked you into believing you want this to use you as a pawn in her stupid games. And you fell for it."

"You're just a selfish bitch. If it's not about Sasha, you don't give a fuck."

Vinny turned, just in time to miss her gasp.

"Hey," Sasha yelled, and Vinny spun to face her. "You don't get to talk to me like that. You might be my *superior* now, but I brought you into this life. If it wasn't for me, you wouldn't be shit."

Tears rose inside her eyes, higher with every disgusting word that flew from her mouth. She fumbled for the knob and stormed into her room, locking the door.

***

Vinny

Vinny sped down the mountain, his truck bouncing along the narrow road. Five miles, a small town, and two rocky hillsides stood between him and the holler, yet Sasha's word rang loud and clear in his mind. He turned onto his street, and there was Dez's truck, parked in his driveway. His house rolled into view, along with Dez hanging a new front window.

"Great," Vinny muttered, climbing from the pickup.

"I'm almost done," Dez said between hammer swings.

"You don't have to do this."

"Yeah, I kinda do." Dez dropped the hammer and grabbed a caulk gun without casting a single glance Vinny's way.

"Can you stop fucking with that shit and come inside? Let's have a beer, talk about this club shit."

Dez stood up straight and turned toward Vinny, staring down. "Is that an order from my VP or a request from my little brother?"

"C'mon, man. It doesn't have to be like that." Vinny peered up, finding that look, the one Dez reserved for those about to taste their own blood. Maybe now, it did have to be like that.

"Your brother," Vinny said, his shoulders sagging, "who might have no idea what he's gotten himself into."

The sharp edge drained from Dez's face, and he dropped the caulk gun into the toolbox. "I could use a cold one."

***

Sasha

Sasha sunk into her mattress as Misty's soft hands ran up her bare back. Misty's thighs clung to Sasha's sides, squeezing as Sasha propped on her elbows.

"Can you feel the shiatsu technique lift away your tension?" Misty asked, her breath tickling the nape of Sasha's neck.

"Fuck yeah." Sasha looked over her shoulder, staring at the beautiful woman massaging her back.

It was worth living through a fucked-up day to get an ending like this. Misty's palms slid down Sasha's arms, and her nipples pressed into her back. The thin top that trapped Misty's breasts separated their skin, blocking the electric vibe. It drove Sasha's mind into a frenzy. Their eyes connected, and her fingers twitched. God, how she wanted to tear that shirt to shreds.

"You're amazing." Sasha bit her bottom lip, crinkling her nose. That was supposed to be a thought, but it rolled off her tongue so easy.

Misty slinked away, dropping onto her side. "No, I'm not. I'm," her eyes fell to the checkered sheets, and she tugged on a loose thread, "trouble. You should get me out of here, drop me off at the nearest rest stop."

Sasha sat up, tossing on a tank top. "If you really want to go, we can leave right now. I'll take you wherever. Ohio, D.C., you name it."

"It's not like I *want* to go, but I probably should, before I ruin your life."

Candlelight flickered, showing glimpses of fear and guilt in Misty's stare.

Sasha leaned back, studying the woman's eyes in the seconds they flashed to her. "What are you talking about?"

"I don't know." Like a switch flipped, the confident air returned to Misty's face. "Things got crappy for you when I showed up. Maybe I'm your bad luck charm."

"My shit was fucked long before you got here. It's this room." Sasha hopped up, glancing around. "A lot of mistakes happen in here. It has bad karma.

You wanna go do something?"

"Sure." Misty pushed aside the blanket she'd hung over the window, peering outside. "It's getting dark. There's a line of cars driving in."

Sasha squeezed behind Misty, staring at the convoy coming up her driveway. Any minute now, music would seep through her walls and rattle the beer bottles scattered on every surface. A party for the new VP, a major event. Half the state would trample this compound in a few hours. Busy bee, her mother, slapping together a huge blowout in only hours. It'd be crazy to think she had days to plan this.

"Looks like the bar's open," Misty said, gawking at a guy with a bright green Mohawk.

"There's a party tonight. That dude from earlier—"

"The one you tossed out or the one you yelled at?" Misty asked with a smile.

Sasha started to chuckle, but she covered her mouth. "The one I yelled at. He got a big promotion today. Festivities must follow, in the form of trucker sluts, unending shots of whiskey, and copious amounts of drugs."

"Trucker sluts?" Misty cringed, moving away from the window.

"That's what they call themselves. It's just a group of chicks who only date truckers."

Misty giggled. A cute, nervous smirk followed. "Truckers have groupies? That's excellent. Can we go to the party?"

"Yeah, but…" Sasha eyed Misty over. The whole package, suede halter top, billowy skirt, right down to the silver bells that encircled her ankle, all screamed sore thumb. "Your outfit is awesome, but—"

"I don't fit in." Misty lifted the sides of her long, flowing skirt before her arms flopped to her sides.

"Do you trust me?" Sasha asked, flashing a smile.

This time Misty's laugh, even cuter than the last, held a sarcastic edge.

"I let you take me to new places, didn't I?"

Misty's lips, eyes, and silky shoulders floated within Sasha's grasp, teasing Sasha's fingertips. Misty was an apple given that one could not eat, existing only to torment Sasha's mind. She had to turn away or risk taking another bite.

"This'll be different and much more uncomfortable," Sasha said, opening the bottom drawer of her dresser.

***

Dez

Dez grabbed a beer from the fridge, sitting at the little round table in Vinny's kitchen. He took a sip, staring at Vinny. His little brother, not so little anymore. He hadn't noticed, until now. It could've been the harsh kitchen lights, this VP bullshit, or the fact he was done chasing his dick around, but he noticed the man who stood in front of him.

"I didn't know about this." Vinny leaned against the sink, twisting the bottle in his hand. "Actually, I did know. Ellen set the whole thing up a few days ago. Sasha said it's just part of some crazy plan her mother cooked up, and she's probably right. I always dreamed of holding this spot but not like this. I don't know, man."

It took every ounce of strength for Dez to hold back a smile. Even with all those muscles and brains, his little brother still needed him.

"Ellen wasn't like this before," Dez said, taking another swig of his bottle. "Not when Charlie was alive."

"You knew Sasha's father?" Vinny sat across from Dez, leaning on the table.

"He recruited me as prospect. A few months later, he died. After Ellen was voted president, I made runner. She was always shady, but now she's just cruel." Dez dropped his elbows on the table, rattling the empty beer bottles around its edge. "There's ten-percent truth in everything Ellen says. If you can decipher her mind, you can turn the tables on her game."

"I wish you never went away. You'd be in that VP seat right now."

"I never wanted that position. You need a certain kind of...patience, and I don't have time for that shit. You're perfect for this seat. I wouldn't trust anyone else to be my VP."

Vinny tapped his bottle against Dez's, taking a long gulp.

"So when's your party?" Dez asked.

"Oh shit! Right now." Vinny jumped up, disappearing into the bathroom. "We gotta get going. I'm gonna get laid twenty ways 'til Sunday tonight."

"Then you better stop and get twenty packs of rubbers," Dez called out, finishing his beer.

Vinny popped his head into the kitchen, toothbrush hanging from his lips. "Good idea, man."

Chapter Twenty-Four

Sasha

Sasha stepped back, admiring her masterpiece. Misty's bangs were teased up at least two inches, cresting to the side in a blonde wave and held in place by half a can of Aquanet. A thick band of black eyeliner stood out over bright blue eyeshadow, complementing her cherry-red lips so well. And that wasn't even the good stuff. The tiny outfit clinging to Misty's body showed more skin than fabric.

"I feel weird." Misty tugged at the tight black mini, unable to pull it any lower. "Naked."

"You look outrageous."

"I know, right? It's stupid." Misty fidgeted with the leather tube top, crossing her arms.

"No. That means you're sexy as hell. Hold up, we gotta put you in some fuck-me pumps."

"What! Sasha, you know how sometimes in movies the girl ends up on a pool table, surrounded by guys pulling down their zippers?"

237

"Oh my God. We're truckers, not bikers. That kind of stuff don't happen 'round here. You can change back if you want, but come here first."

Misty trudged forward, and Sasha turned her toward the mirror. "Take a look."

At first, Misty took small glimpses. Every time she stole another eyeful of her new self, the curve of her lips raised.

"You can be anyone you want to be tonight. Have a million different stories." Sasha glided her hand down Misty's arm, holding out a pair of red stilettos. "And you're safe with me."

"I do look kinda hot, huh?"

"You have no idea."

Misty slipped on the heels, adding an extra inch that brought her up to Sasha's eye level. "I think I understand what they mean by liberation now. You know, why those women burned their bras."

"What?" Sasha giggled. "You don't even have a bra."

"Never mind. Let's do this."

Sasha slid a joint under the brim of her bandana and opened the door. "After you." Instinct kicked on her manners, and the desire to see that rear view kept her manners in high gear. Once they hit the parking lot, Misty latched onto Sasha's arm.

"There're so many people here."

"Yeah." A spectacle, really. Close to two hundred heads, and that was just those gathered around the bonfire out front. They all knew her name too. Their smiles and greetings blended as she strolled by, not one of their names popping into her mind.

"Everybody knows you. You must be important."

"Not really. Just a small county." Sasha took Misty by the hand as they squeezed into the over-stuffed clubhouse. Her eyes scoured the smoky room. No crewmembers stared her down, and her mother didn't pop out of the woodwork. It could turn out to be a nice, relaxing night.

"Sasha!"

Candy's voice cut above the music, and Sasha shook off a chill. She dropped Misty's hand, turning to face Candy. Candy's green eyes fluttered, shaming all the other colors in the world and piercing Sasha's heart.

"Who's this?" Candy did that thing where she puffed her chest up, crossed her arms, and lifted her chin. Her tough guy stance, fucking adorable.

"This," Sasha pulled Misty to her side, "is my friend—"

"Friend?" Candy asked in a short tone.

"Yes. Just a friend."

"Hey, I'm Misty. I just moved to town, and Sasha's showing me around."

"Ooh, fresh meat." Candy's face lit up. She bumped Sasha aside, taking Misty by the arm. "Come on, honey. Honey, that actually works. Maybe we'll call you that from now on."

"Dude," Sasha called out. "What the fuck?"

"Take a chill pill." Candy waved her hand, pulling Misty closer. "I wanna introduce her to the girls."

Sasha stepped forward, but Misty shook her head, flashing a smile. Candy and Misty slipped into the mob scene, and Sasha's body grew tense. This could go wrong a hundred different ways with no right path in any direction. She leaned against the wall, taking the joint from beneath her bandana and popping it into her mouth. Before she could reach into her pocket for a lighter, a flame ignited in front of her eyes. A soft glow shined on an inked arm. Skulls and demons ripping through shards of flesh, fire and chains. She had spent countless hours staring at that ink over the years, at Vinny's ink. Sasha lit the joint, straining to keep her glare off of Vinny's face.

"I can't believe you brought her here," he said, clicking his zippo shut.

"She's just a friend."

"You have friends?"

"Dick!" Sasha looked at Vinny. His grin melted her icy stare and uncoiled her tight muscles.

"That's not what I mean. I just thought I knew all your friends."

"Obviously not." Sasha pushed off the wall, walking past Vinny, and he grabbed her by the wrist.

"Wait." Vinny pulled Sasha to his chest, loosening his grip.

Sasha stared up into eyes that begged to be forgiven. It chipped away little pieces of her heart to hold a grudge against him. She didn't want the vice president position, and she didn't want anyone except for him in it, but he broke the cardinal rule. He played her, just like her mother always did.

"Congratulations, Vinny. Enjoy your party, and stay away from my friend." Sasha yanked her arm from Vinny's grasp, bulldozing her way out the door.

***

Dez

Dez flicked a cigarette over the railing of the porch. He walked toward the clubhouse door, bumping into a bony shoulder. The scent of weed and roses hit him before any other senses could kick on. "Sasha."

Sasha smirked. She pressed her body against his chest as she pushed him from the doorway.

"This place is nuts." Sasha hit a joint, lips parting just a crack, eyes drifting to a close. If only she knew what that did to him, the shivers it sent beneath his flesh.

Some asshole stumbled into her, driving her hips into his. Dez could slug the douchebag, maybe thank him, or just grab Sasha's ass. His hands glided down the curve of her back, and he ushered her into the far corner of the porch. "Yeah, it is."

"Are you drunk?" Sasha asked through a smile.

Her eyes sparkled when she looked up at him, even though every other part of her was a blur.

"Maybe." Dez leaned down, dragging his lips along her cheek to her mouth. When Sasha's warm tongue tickled his own, all the people and sounds faded away. Everything he needed was in his arms. As her hands rode up his chest, he appreciated the silky skin under his fingertips. She was the key to his survival.

His blood surged, prickling his veins. There was nothing he could do about the bulge in his pants except grind it into her.

"Damn, hello," she whispered into his ear.

"Let's go somewhere."

"Where?"

"Your room." Dez slipped his hand under Sasha's shirt, and she didn't push it away. "Your bed."

"I can't just leave my friend in there."

Dez gripped onto the front of her pants, tugging. "Shit, girl. I'll fuck you right here."

Even though his voice held a serious edge, Sasha giggled. His brow lifted, and he unclipped her belt buckle.

"Okay. Jesus." She fixed her belt then took his hand. "Come on."

Her little fingers slid between his, and she led him into the clubhouse. They cut through the crowd like ghosts. Drunken cackles and wild drumbeats mingled to a dull buzz. This room could've been empty. All he knew was his thumb circling the soft skin of her palm.

Sasha pulled Dez into the bathroom, and two dudes looked up from the white lines piled on the sink.

"Out," Dez barked, and they flinched, scurrying out the door. The sound of Sasha's laughter snapped the last shred of self-control left inside Dez's body. He locked onto her lips, tearing the jacket from her shoulders. A moan filled his ears when her back hit the wall. She whipped open his belt in one swift move, and his knees quaked. How his zipper didn't burst, he'd never understand. He hated pants more than anything right now. He needed them gone, to feel her warmth against him, to dive inside her.

"Oh God, Dez." Sasha gasped as Dez dug his teeth into her neck. He bunched up her top, moving his mouth down. No bra, just full breasts and pink nipples. His hands worked both her belt and his jeans, a mouth full of Sasha. The whole process of unbuckling both their belts at once would've been amazingly smooth if it wasn't taking him so fucking long.

Sasha's pants hit the tile with a thud, and Dez looked up into her eyes. "Gun?"

"Brass knuckles."

Dez grinned, lifting Sasha off the ground. She drifted in his arms like a feather, but her thighs clung to his waist like a vice. Their eyes connected as he slowly slipped inside her. The way her lips curved into an O. That carnal leer penetrated his soul. He almost lost it on the spot, but the need to have more of her, all of her, held his concentration firm.

Sasha ran her fingers through his hair, electricity vibrated his skin, and Sasha's sweet moans echoed in his head. He drove into her harder, faster. His body couldn't get enough of her touch, smell, taste. Sasha surrounded him.

Her fingers trembled on his neck, her back arching against the wall. He clutched her hips tighter, and she squirmed, forcing the air from his lungs. A whirl took his mind by surprise. Sasha cried out, and Dez lost the power to resist the ecstasy that called to him. A deep thrust and surrender came easy. Chills replaced the fire in his veins, her lips landing on his. He lowered her feet back to the ground, never breaking her kiss.

Sasha bit Dez's bottom lip before gliding away. A soft tingle shot from his head to his toes, and he slumped against the wall, pulling up his jeans.

"God. Damn." Dez looked at Sasha, who was fidgeting with her belt. Even with messy hair and crumpled clothes, she looked perfect, good enough to throw against the wall again.

Sasha narrowed her eyes and tilted her head. "What?"

"What?"

"You're looking at me all funny and junk."

That's 'cause I wanna rip your clothes off and throw myself into every part of you. "Sorry." He reached out, straightening her top. "There."

A new look crossed Sasha's face. Insecurity. It made her even more beautiful. She shrank back, scooping her bandana and jacket from the floor.

Dez held in a grin, glancing to the sink. "Those assholes left their blow. You want a bump?"

Sasha took a step forward, but her hand landed on her stomach. "Nah. I'm good. Are we good?"

Hell yeah almost flew from Dez's mouth, but the sting in his knuckles brought the memory of betrayal back. "No. I'm pissed. Not because you lied or picked some chick over me, but because you twist the simplest of tasks into a jumble-fuck of danger."

"What the fuck are—"

"I don't know this bitch, if she can be trusted. It's my job to keep this club and its members safe."

"She's just a girl. If anyone's in danger here, it's her."

"Who is she?" Dez asked, his voice growing louder with every passing syllable. "Where did she come from? How long have you known her?"

"See, that's why I don't want you near her. She thinks we're a bunch of hillbilly truckers right now. You start with the interrogation and she'll know something's up."

"I want her out of here. Now."

"Yeah," Sasha snickered, crossing her arms, "and I want a million dollars."

"I'm not joking. I'm your sergeant at arms, and I'm telling you, she goes."

"Or what? You gonna take it to the president?"

"Why do you have to put me in this position?" Dez had to stop himself from grabbing Sasha. If shaking her would do any good, he'd latch on and go to town.

"Do whatever you have to. Sarge."

Sasha unlocked the door and stormed out, leaving him alone in a stifling room. The air must've followed her, the way his skin boiled. He should be used to this, but the presence that surrounded Sasha left a hollow void in its absence.

The door cracked open, and a scrawny dude popped his head inside. "Is it cool if I get my blow, man?"

"Have at it." Dez grabbed the knob and yanked the door wide open, walking into the crowd.

Chapter Twenty-Five

Sasha

Sasha squeezed her way to the bar. Misty's arms flopped around her neck.

"You're back," Misty slurred, wobbling on those high heels. "Candy's awesome."

"Yeah. How many shots did she give you?"

"All of them," Misty snorted, leaning to the side.

A snicker broke Sasha's scowl for half a second, then her glare rolled to Candy.

"What?" Candy said in a cute little huff. "She wanted to play quarters."

"Awesome," Sasha grumbled, fighting to keep Misty's hands off her body. A high-pitched laugh drew her gaze. Through the sea of faces, Sasha spotted her mother in a corner chatting it up with a bunch of locals. If that woman looked her way, it'd be a fitting end to this fucked-up night.

"Dance with me, Sasha," Misty breathed into Sasha's ear, the words laced in one hundred twenty-five proof Kentucky whisky.

"Sure. Come on." Sasha slipped her arm around Misty's waist, guiding her toward the front door. She looked back at the corner, and Vinny inched through the crowd, blocking her mother's view. Her eyes must've screamed thank you because Vinny nodded, flashing that mischievous smirk she loved.

Once outside, Misty took a deep breath. Her clutch on Sasha's neck tightened, much like a noose.

"It smells so good here, like freedom," Misty said, practically shouting. "Where are we going? Did you want to dance under the stars again?"

"No. Well, yes, but not right now." Sasha ushered Misty from the porch and toward the garage.

"Ooh. We're going back to your room. Are you gonna show me some more *new* things?"

Sasha chuckled, moving Misty's hands from her body to the step's railing. "Maybe in the morning, once you've sobered up."

"You're such a gentleman, except you're a woman. You're a gentlewoman!" Misty flung a smile over her shoulder, teetering on the edge of a step.

"Careful." Sasha gripped onto the unsteady woman's hips. "Just a few more steps."

"I wish you were a man. I'd run away and marry you."

"I'm gonna remind you of that tomorrow," Sasha said, snickering.

"Okay!"

Sasha inched onto the landing, her hand sliding up the curve of Misty's waist. She reached for the door, brushing Misty's chest. Misty's lips glided along her neck as she ran her hands down Sasha's sides.

"I had fun tonight," Misty said, flashing those dangerous eyes. "I knew every day would be like magic with you."

"We'll see how magical you feel when you're praying to the porcelain God."

Misty giggled, and Sasha pushed open her door. Before she could click on the lamp, Misty wiggled out of her top.

"Yes! I can breathe."

The leather skirt flew through the air, landing on the dresser, and Sasha looked away from the stretch of bare skin just within her grasp. "Do you want a t-shirt?"

"No." Misty dropped onto the bed, wrapping herself in the blanket. "I'm good." Her words came out in one long roll, trailed by a giggle.

Sasha turned on the light in the bathroom, shutting the lamp by her door. "I'll be right outside, having a smoke."

The music lulled, and a soft snore erupted from the pile of blankets on the bed. Sasha backed away as drum beats kicked up again, growing louder with the blow of the wind. When her door creaked shut behind her, about a hundred and ten pounds of stress lifted from her shoulders. A momentary lapse of bliss, so light and free. She should soak it in, latch onto every shred of peace before chaos breezed in to claim it.

The flame of Sasha's zippo flickered as she plopped down on her top step, lighting a cigarette.

Across the lot, two figures leaned against the trailer of her father's truck. A red cherry glowed from the joint that passed between them, cutting through the night. Vinny strolled toward the big house, one chick tucked under each arm. He looked at the stairs as he passed by. It felt like he was staring right into her eyes, even though shadows cloaked her in darkness. Sasha didn't move a muscle, and Vinny didn't break his stride toward the big house, not that she expected or even wanted him to.

Her stomach retched, and she flicked the cigarette over the rail. No drugs, whiskey, cigarettes. For what? She wasn't going to keep the creature that grew inside her, the tiny piece of life that thrived with her heartbeat. A baby, her baby.

Sasha pulled a pack of Lucky Strikes from her pocket, staring down at the cigarettes that poked out from atop the soft pack.

"Fuck!" Sasha shoved the cigarettes back into her pocket, climbing to her feet. Tomorrow would be a better day to think about this baby problem, or maybe the day after. She opened her door, greeted by a loud snore, and walked inside her room.

***

Dez

Dez heard fragments of the conversation around him. Something about Whitesnake or maybe a Corvette. He didn't know, didn't care. His mind had wandered to Sasha's *friend,* and that's where it stayed.

"Hey, Dez." Otis snapped his fingers, pulling Dez from his own jagged thoughts and dropping him in a crowded clubhouse. "What do ya say, man?"

"Ah…" Dez looked at Otis, who waited for an answer to his unheard question. "I don't know. Whitesnake is kinda faggy."

"No," Otis chuckled. "I asked if you wanted to go for a walk, burn one."

"Oh, shit. Hell yeah!"

The crowd parted when Otis strolled through, nearly crashing around Dez as he followed. It had always been that way for Otis, even back in the day. The man held a certain glare in his eyes, brutal, vicious, but to Dez it was the look of an old friend.

"It's been a day, huh?" Otis said, leading Dez from the porch to a patch of trees. "The vote, this party," he lit his zippo, puffing on a joint, "Sasha running around with that blonde."

Dez froze solid, only his head tilting toward Otis. "Who is she?"

"Who? The blonde?" Otis passed Dez the joint, shrugging. "Never seen her before. Don't look like Vinny knows her either. Strange, the timing, with everything going down lately."

For years Dez had known Otis, yet he still couldn't crack the man's cryptic tones. This could be a warning. Sasha could be in line for another beat down or worse, the cellar. He'd drag his blade across Ellen's neck before he'd let that happen. Otis's too if it came down to it. If he played this just right, he might get something useful from this conversation.

"Did Ellen recognize her?" Dez asked, straining to sound nonchalant.

Otis grinned, exhaling a stream of white smoke. "I haven't talked to Ellen about this. She forgets what it's like to be young and stupid. Hell, she might've been birthed full grown and evil."

A snicker floated on the cusp of escape, but Dez didn't let it out. A light grin would suffice; keep the poker face.

"But Sasha..." Otis looked at the leave-strewn ground, and a hint of sorrow peeked from behind his mask of confidence. "Sasha never had a childhood, wasn't allowed to make mistakes. Now that she's strong enough to stand up for herself, she's making up for lost time. It's a shitty reason to put a bullet in someone or give up on them."

Dez hit the joint, using its smoke to hide his smile. "I hear that, and I'm glad you said it."

"Yeah. Well, I'm glad I'm not the sergeant at arms," Otis said, snatching the bone from Dez's fingers and taking a big hit. "To have to stay up all night, watching and waiting in case the stranger on our compound tries anything. That would suck." He handed Dez the joint, backing away. "I would help out if I knew anything about any of this, which I don't."

"Hey," Dez called out.

Otis stopped and Dez nodded. "Thanks, man."

"Don't mention it," Otis said with a wink. "Seriously."

***

251

Ellen

Ellen stood in the doorway of the clubhouse, watching the last car drive off the lot. The quiet seemed to rumble, louder than the music it replaced. These seconds, when a stillness gripped the valley, were a special treat in her wild life. There was no one around to look at her for answers. In the silence, she could pretend people weren't depending on her decisions for their survival. It was a rare opportunity to be herself, the woman who gazed up at moonlit clouds and smiled, the person stopping to smell the light hint of mist flowers in the air. That's who she was.

Empty bottles scattered across the floor as Ellen moseyed back inside, the tip of her boot grazing a different brand of drained beer with every step. The Tasmanian devil could've tore through this clubhouse and she'd never know the difference. Perfect time to break in a new prospect. Good thing Kev had an unending hoard of cousins, all dying for a spot at her table.

Ellen clicked off the light in the backroom just as the phone on the wall rang. Her hand hovered over the receiver. The phone's loud ringing filled the room, lifting the hairs on her arms. Another ring vibrated her palm, and she lifted the phone to her ear.

"Finally alone, baby girl."

"Dante? What the—"

"You think I can't see you," Dante's voice boomed through the phone, "standing there in that little red skirt, white boots to your knees. You know

252

I love that tube top on you."

"Where the fuck are you?" Ellen asked, clutching the receiver.

"In your living room. From here, I can see into your clubhouse window, your daughter's crap-shack, and some guy is fucking a screamer down the hall. Did you know one of your men just parked his pickup behind the clubhouse and is watching Sasha's door?"

Ellen slammed the phone back on its hook, storming into the night. Her heart pounded. Gravel crunched under her boots as she tore across the lot, past the garage, and up the hill. On its own, the front door of her house cracked open as her foot swept the porch step. Anger spread heat through her body and carried her feet faster. It wasn't until after she crossed the threshold that fear slowed her steps.

Floorboards creaked as Ellen crept inside. Not one light shined on the bottom floor. The only sound was a soft flow of music from Vinny's room. Ellen inched down the hall, and a hand cupped her mouth. An arm slid around her waist, pulling her into a firm body and squeezing tight.

"Umm. You smell dirty, baby girl."

Ellen fought the quiver in her bones, biting into the skin that covered her lips.

"Ah. Bitch!" Dante yelled, pushing her away.

Before Dante could grin, Ellen grabbed him by the shirt and shoved him against the wall. "What did you do?"

Dante clutched onto Ellen's hips, pulling her close. "Nothing. Yet."

A smirk lit Dante's dark eyes, which made

Ellen's heart pound. She fell against Dante's solid body, wrapping her arms around his waist. "You cut it close at the bar. If I had shown up five minutes sooner, you'd be roasting in hell right now."

"I bet you would've liked that," Dante whispered, skating his tongue along her neck.

"Come to my room." Ellen pushed off Dante's chest, took him by the hand, and headed toward the stairs. He caressed the arch of her back as they walked. His touch, spreading icy tingles along every inch of skin it grazed, lulled the revulsion of what had to come next. She had to kill him. The things you love destroy you unless you wipe them out first. A few more nights lost in his strong arms, then she'd kill him.

Ellen flipped on her bedroom light, dropping onto her bed. Dante gripped his belt, shutting the door, and her teeth dug into her bottom lip. Such large hands. They should be clutching her body.

"Come here, honey," Ellen said, patting the mattress beside her.

"Why? So you can stick a blade in my back." Dante smirked, leaning against a tall dresser. "I should come over there and fuck you, since I took the knife from under your pillow."

Ellen slid her legs over the side of the bed, looking at the nightstand.

"I got the handgun from your nightstand too," Dante said, holding a smug leer. "And the shotgun in the closet and the machete under your mattress. Is all that for me, or do you make friends everywhere you go?"

"I don't need all those weapons for you. You're

not that scary."

"You haven't seen my best side yet."

"Oh, I think I have." Ellen climbed off the bed, flashing a grin.

"That shit with Ashby wasn't nothing. If you fuck me over—"

"Dante." She reached out, but he pulled away. "Okay, I'll admit it. I did consider slitting your throat tonight, but every time I look into your eyes, I...I already let you take out half my crew. When are you gonna trust me?"

"When the rest of your crew is dead, like mine. Tell you what." Dante pulled her handgun from his pocket, loading a round into the chamber. "I'll get the ball rollin'. Take care of the guy downstairs."

"Wait!" Ellen latched onto Dante's wrist, hurrying in front of him to block the door.

"I knew it." He tossed the gun to the floor, ripping his arm from her grasp. "We had a plan. I gave you my resources. Let's finish off your crew and we can start building a new, stronger club. It's what you wanted."

"It's what I still want." Ellen backed Dante toward the bed, pushing him onto the mattress. His dark eyes locked onto her face as she crept between his legs. "I took out all the weak links. The ones left are the strongest—"

"No," Dante yelled, shoving her away and jumping to his feet. "Only Sasha and my cousin. The rest eat a bullet. That was the deal."

"Keep your voice down."

"Your men will never follow me," Dante said, grabbing onto the sides of Ellen's arms. "They'll turn on you. They have to go for this to work."

A tiny piece of Ellen wanted to say yes, let someone else run the show, except the only show she cared about was the one starring her crew. "Give me a few days. I can bring them around."

"Fuck that and fuck you." Dante gave Ellen a firm shove, knocking her into the wall. He opened the door, stopping to hurl a glare. "I told you I'd burn your world down if you screwed me over one more time. Remember that when you're rolling in flames."

Dante walked into the shadows of the hall, and Ellen rocked in place. Her gaze fell to the gun on the floor, but she ran past it, rushing to catch Dante. The front door thumped against the wall as she hurried onto the landing, peeking over the banister. Through the open doorway, beams of porch light spilled into the house. Soft, yellow light cast an eerie circle in her foyer, the wind carrying dry leaves through the threshold.

Silence crept through the air, settling over Ellen like a frosty layer of ice. "Vinny," she whispered. A chill hit her spine, and she ran down the stairs. At the end of the hall, Vinny's door sat cracked open. Ellen's heart jumped into her throat. The bare wood floor stretched out before her, growing longer with every step. If she opened Vinny's door and saw red, if that boy's blood painted her walls, the world would burn.

Ellen reached for Vinny's door, and her lungs sealed shut. No air would pass. Her body wouldn't allow for a breath, not until she looked beyond that door. Her fingers wrapped around the brass knob and she pushed. Candles flickered, throwing slivers of light around the room.

On the bed, tangled beneath two naked women, lay Vinny. His chest rose up and down, a tiny grin stuck to his sleeping face. Relief washed over Ellen, and her breath flowed out as a loud chuckle. The brunette snuggled against Vinny's side, and Ellen backed out of the room, closing the door.

Chapter Twenty-Six

Sasha

Sasha lifted Misty's arm, squirming out of bed. The clock on her wall read 4:20. It always read 4:20, since the batteries had died over two years ago. She didn't need that gadget to know the time. Every new morning carried with it an electric vibe, one that shocked her core and wiped clear her muddy slate.

In the beams of sunshine that radiated beneath the front door, Sasha searched for her pants. Much to her surprise, the usual whirl of her stomach steadied to a low rumble. Not that anything could come out. She'd have to put something in for it to upchuck.

After sliding on her jacket, she glanced at the bed. Misty's leg was curled around her blanket, her golden hair spraying the pillows. She reached for the door, pausing. Her instincts said to dive back in bed and replace that blanket in Misty's grasp, but her gut screamed for food. In an hour, when Misty crawled from her drunken slumber, only a grease-soaked breakfast sandwich would combat the hangover in store.

Sasha opened her door, recoiling from the sting of the bright sky. She stopped grumbling when the thick plastic frame of her shades hit the bridge of her nose. She hurried outside, locking the door behind her. While trotting down the stairs, she searched the lot for Dez's pickup but found only gravel. It was stupid to think he'd be camped out on her bottom step, just as stupid as wanting such a bother. After her rejection, and with nowhere to go, he probably found his way to another woman's bed. She shouldn't care. They had no ties, and Dez was a total dick. His safe arms could clutch someone else. Some other bitch could feel his soft lips skate along their flesh.

Sasha's jaw clenched, and her hand balled to a fist. Rage boiled into a blinding fury. It had to be released before it burned away the last tatters of her sanity, but there was no one to hit. She hurled her arm outward, punching thin air. A wave of stupidity rushed in, chilling the heat that prickled every inch of her skin, and she shook her fingers free. After a quick glance around, Sasha hopped in her pickup and drove toward the front gate.

***

Dez

Dez inched back behind the clubhouse as Sasha opened the front gate. He leaned against his truck, stashed in the trees, listening to her big block engine purr as she floored the throttle. A smile lifted his cheeks. That little display, her hissy fit…she was looking for him. Up until now, he couldn't tell what Sasha's game was. Her lustful leers held an edge of scorn and every word she spoke stung, but this was proof. Somewhere beneath that hard shell, a heart did beat his name.

His grin dropped when Sasha's door squeaked open. Blonde hair glistened through thick leaves, and Dez crept forward, glimpsing Sasha's friend prance down the stairs. He crouched low, backing against the clubhouse wall. His glare locked onto her body. The way she moved, stiff, eyes on every corner, it clashed with her dime store hippy getup. This girl was a pro.

Dry flakes of wood crumbled as Dez slid under the strategically cracked-open window. Her sandals clacked every time they hit the ground, making it easy to follow the woman's steps. She scurried through the clubhouse, right into the backroom. The slam of desk drawers rattled the front windows as Dez snaked toward the porch.

In near silence, he hopped over the railing and snuck beside the front door. A click echoed from inside, and papers shuffled. He pulled his zippo from his pocket, using its shiny surface to spy through the door. Shapes and colors blurred in the metal, and he groaned. That dumb spy shit always worked for James Bond. It didn't matter who that woman was or what she was planning to do. He had to stop her right now.

Dez peeked into the clubhouse, staring at her

back. She clung to the phone on the wall, whispering in the receiver, and he edged inside. His steps fell lighter than he thought possible. He held his breath, and her voice streamed over the pound of his temples.

"This is Rebecca Prescott, agent 5327. Connect me to the director."

The words stopped Dez short. This bitch wasn't a spy for some other crew; she was a goddamn fed. He crept up behind her, catching a whiff of Sasha's shampoo on the woman's hair. He lifted his arm, and for a split second, their eyes connected. The fear he glimpsed struck him, paralyzing his muscles. Papers fell to the floor, and a man's voice streamed from the phone in the woman's trembling hand. Dez pressed down the lever on the base, ending the call. She staggered back, and he seized her by the throat, bashing her head against the wall.

Her body fell into a heap, and Dez took a step back. The hate he felt for this woman left the taste of bile in his mouth. She'd already carved a wedge between him and Sasha. What he had to do next might finish them. Anger spiked in waves, shrouding his vision in red. Dez grabbed the woman by the arm and dragged her into the backroom, closing the door.

***

Ellen

A thump jolted Ellen from the pillows. Her bedroom door pounded under a barrage of knocks, and she flung the blanket aside.

"Yeah," Ellen yelled, pulling on a pair of jeans.

"We gotta get down to the clubhouse, now," Vinny shouted through the closed door, "Dez called and—"

Ellen pulled open her door, and Vinny stumbled back, then ran down the stairs.

"What happened?" Ellen hurried down the staircase, fumbling with her boots, but Vinny was already out the front door.

Sunlight shocked her brain once she stepped off the porch. She shielded her eyes from the day's harsh glare, rushing to catch Vinny. Before climbing up the clubhouse steps, Ellen looked at the garage. Panic swirled in the pit of her stomach. Sasha's door sat wide open, her truck gone.

"Ah fuck, Dez!" Vinny's raised voice pulled Ellen's stare into the clubhouse. Vinny gawked at Ellen from the backroom, a white shade overtaking his face.

Ellen marched across the room, pushing past Vinny only to have her legs lock up once she stepped into the backroom.

In the corner, Dez hovered over a young woman duct-taped to a chair. Blood speckled the floor below her, dripping from the bruised cuts under her eye and flowing from her split lip.

"What the fuck is going on?" Ellen steered her glare to Dez just as he pulled a knife from his belt.

"Sasha brought her home on the last run," Dez said, pointing the tip of his blade to the woman taped to a chair.

"So you decided to torture the bitch?"

"I caught her in here, going through your desk. She had your gas logs and maps. She's a fed. I heard her on the phone." Dez dragged his blade along the woman's cheek, and she cried out, squirming in her chair. "Rebecca Prescott, agent 5327," he sneered.

"No," the woman sniveled. "My name's Misty Jeffers. Ask Sasha. She knows me."

Ellen turned from the swollen eyes that pleaded up at her, staring at Dez. "Are you sure about this?"

"Positive," Dez said, the knife trembling in his hand. "I heard it, Ellen."

The regret on Dez's face spoke louder than his words. He knew what this meant for Sasha, how she'd be punished. Oh, how that girl would be punished.

"Where's Sasha?" Vinny asked, pacing in the doorway.

"She left," Dez called out, his glare locked on the woman whimpering in a chair, "about twenty minutes ago."

Vinny stomped across the clubhouse, staring out the front windows. "She could be back any second."

Ellen snatched the knife from Dez's hand. "And I'll deal with Sasha when she gets here." She placed the tip of the blade under the woman's fingernail, pressing lightly.

"No, please don't."

"What's your name, honey?" Ellen asked in the softest tone her fuming body could muster.

"Mist—"

Ellen jabbed the knife forward, peeling the woman's nail from her flesh. The scream that

263

followed filled Ellen's mind with rage. She stepped back, glancing at Dez. "Hit her."

Dez's large fist rocked the side of the woman's face, teetering the chair before it slammed back on its legs. The woman's eyes rolled back, and Ellen slapped her across the cheek, holding the knife to her neck.

"You're gonna die, darlin'. There's no way out of it. Tell me your name, and I'll end you quick. Fuck with me, and I'll make it last days."

"Please, please," she whimpered.

Ellen back away, nodding. Dez grabbed onto the woman's shirt, holding tight while hurling punches. Between the crack of bones, and in a watery croak, bits of words echoed.

"Hold up." Ellen caught Dez's arm mid-swing, leaning close to the bloody mess that was once a woman's face.

"Rebecca Prescott, agent 5327," she mumbled, over and over as though all other information had been beaten from her head.

"Sasha's here," Vinny said, looking from Ellen to Dez.

"Good." Ellen cut the tape from the chair, and the bitch flopped to the floor. "Bring her," she said, pointing to the woman whose blood stained her floor. She tossed the knife aside and grabbed a handgun from her desk, walking out of the room.

***

264

Sasha

Sasha leaned against the steering wheel of her pickup truck, staring up at her open door. "Oh fuck." Her truck bounced as she sped past the clubhouse. Rocks kicked up as she skid to a stop outside the garage. Sasha jumped from the cab and ran up her stairs. Inklings spawned in the back of her mind, warning her of danger, telling her to run away from this entire compound, yet her legs pushed on up rickety steps.

An empty bed mocked her. No sweet smile, fringed leather bag on the dresser, sandals by the door. Just a hint of patchouli, the only trace that Misty had ever been there. Sasha backed onto the landing, and the shuffle of boots filled her ears. A chill sucked all the warmth from her body, leaving a bone-jarring shiver. Her eyes drifted toward the clubhouse, stopping on her mother's glare. It was that look, the stuff of nightmares, a glower that said four men she trusted were going to stomp her face into the gravel. At first, her legs resisted the urge to move. Then she saw Misty, slumped over Dez's shoulder and trailing a stream of blood.

"No," Sasha cried out, running down the stairs. "What did y'all do?"

Dez tossed Misty to the ground at Sasha's feet, and Ellen stormed forward. The side of a pistol slammed against Sasha's cheek, flashing the world to black.

Sasha dropped to her hands and knees, blinking back a haze. Blood gushed into her mouth, and a buzz bounced around inside her head. Thick fluid trickled down the back of her throat, and she hacked until she heard the sound of a gun being cocked, its click silencing her cough.

This was it, the end of a bumpy line. Sasha rose to her knees, and the barrel of a gun was pressed into the back of her head.

"You brought a federal agent onto our property?" her mother all but growled, shoving the gun harder against her skull.

"What? No. She's just a college girl from—"

A kick sent Sasha face down onto the ground. Rocks dug into her palms, and Misty's blood pooled beneath her fingers.

"Listen to her, Sasha," Dez said, his shadow falling over her.

Sasha pushed herself back to her knees, keeping her eyes low. Ellen stepped forward, grabbed Sasha by the hair, and yanked her closer to Misty's twitching body. Sasha closed her eyes, but she couldn't block out Misty's garbled voice as she repeated a name and a badge number.

"My only child, a disgrace," Ellen sneered, releasing Sasha in a shove. "I tell you to cool it, and you bring in the heat. I warned you, girl."

The gun's barrel returned to the back of Sasha's head, and she opened her eyes, looking up at the deep blue sky. "Do it. Fucking kill me."

A gunshot jolted Sasha's body, echoing off the green hills. Her heart pumped, fast, strong, but a bullet didn't pierce her skull. She dropped her gaze, and Dez lowered a gun from Misty's head.

"It's done," Dez said, moving behind Sasha. "Ellen."

Sasha couldn't move. Splatters of bright red held her gaze. Misty stared at her through vacant eyes until blood covered her battered face.

"Yeah," Ellen muttered.

Boots shuffled all around, but Sasha stayed on her knees. The lake of blood beneath Misty's head, ripped off nail on her delicate finger, crimson-stained blonde hair trapped her stare. A beautiful person, an ugly lie, a gory heap. Sasha didn't know what she was looking at.

An icy prickle ran through her veins, and she shivered. She knew that feeling well. It spawned every time her mother grew near.

"I'll deal with you later," her mother's voice growled from behind her. "Clean this shit up."

Minutes dragged. It could've been hours. Sasha couldn't tell. Time dwindled under the fiery ache that scorched her insides. That split she felt in her chest, it had to be the last fragment of her soul breaking. She was broken.

"Sasha." Vinny glided his hand up her arm, and a tear rolled down her cheek. "I'm sorr—"

"Don't." Sasha shrugged away from his touch, climbing to her feet. "My mom's right; I am a disgrace. I wanted her," she said, her stare caught on the hole in the back of Misty's head. "I put the club at risk because I wanted her."

"I'll get a tarp, to wrap her in."

"Don't waste a tarp. Just help me throw her in the back of my truck." Sasha turned, avoiding Vinny's face like the plague. One dose of his gentle eyes might cause a full out breakdown, but without him at her side, she'd still be on the ground like a

267

pathetic rat.

Sasha opened her tailgate, and Vinny gripped her shoulder.

"I'll get her," Vinny said, blocking Sasha's view of a corpse that was just starting to twitch. "You go start the truck."

Her instinct to argue didn't kick on. Broken. Vinny must have seen it, the shatter of the self she'd pieced together. She must be marked. Now, when the world looks at her, they'll see another broken girl, and she didn't care. She couldn't care, or she'd never be able to leave her bed again.

The motor roared to life, and Sasha flinched. She looked down to find her hand on the key and foot on the brake. Vinny hopped inside, nodding. For a second, life seemed normal. Just another day with her best friend, out for a joyride up the mountain, except he wasn't her best friend anymore, this was no joyride, and a body was leaking brain matter all over the bed of her truck.

Autopilot stayed engaged, directing her hand to the gearshift and foot to the gas. Without a word, she drove up the hill, toward the cellar.

Chapter Twenty-Seven

Ellen

Ellen hung up the phone, marching into the backroom. She stood over Dez, glaring down as he scrubbed blood off the floor.

"What'd the sheriff say?" Dez asked without sparing a glance.

"That it'll take a few days to find out anything concrete."

"Shit. We could all be in jail in a few days."

Ellen kicked the bucket beside Dez, splashing soapy water over its brim. "Who the fuck do you think you are?"

His cruel eyes veered to her, but she stood firm. If Dez actually expected to intimidate her, he'd have to practice that glower in the mirror a few more times.

"Don't you ever come between me and my daughter again," she said, wagging her finger in his face. "This club, that girl, they're mine to control. Just like you, motherfucker."

Dez rose to his feet. This time, his stare held a vicious edge. A slight improvement, though still the look of a boy playing man.

"You can run this club into the ground for all I care," Dez said, inching closer. "But I won't let you put a bullet in Sasha's head."

"If I wanted to put a bullet in my little girl's head, nothing would stop me, especially not a punk-ass kid like you."

Dez curled his fingers into tight fists, and Ellen lifted her hand to the butt of her holster gun. One excuse, that's all she needed to end this man's self-designated reign over her club. Boots rattled the floor, but neither one of them dared to look away. A wisp of Old Spice filled Ellen's lungs, bringing a smile to her lips.

"What's going on in here?" Otis asked, walking into the backroom.

A smug glare lit Dez's eyes, as though he had the upper hand, and it set Ellen's blood to boil. His nerve superseded what little patience she possessed, but she refused to give him the power to know he rattled her. His death could only provide moments of satisfaction. The suffering she had in mind for him could deliver years of spiritual pleasure.

Ellen lowered her hand from the gun on her belt, stepping aside. "Go on, Dez. Swoop Sasha into your arms. Ask her to run away with you. I just wish I could be there to see your face when she shoots you down."

Dez bumped Ellen's shoulder as he strolled by like a stubborn child walking through the clubhouse, with his fists clenched, legs stomping out the door.

"Whose blood is on the floor?" Otis asked, sitting at the far end of the table.

For the first time since Ellen's rude awakening, the tight strands that tugged at her every muscle loosened. She dropped into the chair beside Otis, slouching onto the table. "Spark a bone and I'll tell you all about my shitty morning."

***

Sasha

Dry leaves whirled around Sasha. A cascade of colors rode on the mountain breeze, but she couldn't see them. A fog stole her vision, tunneling it to dead eyes. It was strange, how quick the sparkle faded. The cellar door squeaked open, but her gaze remained a prisoner to Misty's cold, empty eyes.

Vinny knelt down and grabbed Misty by the shoulder, looking at Sasha. "Did you want to say something?"

"Yeah." Sasha took a step back, but she still couldn't lift her stare from the swollen, ripped skin of Misty's face. "She was good. Nobody ever played me like that before and never will again, I swear it."

Leaves rustled as Vinny dragged the body toward a dark hole in the ground. Then, in the slip of a second, Misty was gone and Sasha could finally look away.

She closed the cellar door, its thud carrying

across the valley, and clicked the padlock shut. "Everything you did today, standing back so my mother could do what she needed to, comforting me after. It's what Chewy would've done." She stood, lifting her eyes to his regret-filled face. "I'm glad you're VP, and I'm sorry I didn't tell you sooner."

"Sasha, I—"

"I'm pregnant." Sasha slapped her hand over her mouth, regretting the release of words even though it felt so good to let them go. Poor Vinny. She might have stunned him stupid. He just gawked, looking like he could puke at any minute.

"I, uh…I don't…" His jaw hung open, waiting to catch flies. "Is it mine?"

The question stung, but he had a valid reason to ask it, so she didn't slug him. "You or Dez."

Vinny shook his head, rocking in place. "It has to be Dez."

"Jeez, asshole, way to pass the buck."

"That's not what I mean." He rushed forward, grabbing her hand. "He'll kill us both, but for real. He blacks out, sees red. It has to be his. Besides, we weren't fucking around. Remember?"

"It doesn't matter whose it is." Sasha yanked her hand away, walking toward her truck. "I'm getting rid of it."

"What? No, you're not," Vinny shouted, grabbing her arm.

She twisted from his grasp and shoved him, hard. "What do you care? We were never together anyway, remember."

"Sasha."

Whatever Vinny was about to say, she didn't

give a fuck. He had no idea what was best for her life, her body. She opened the driver's door, nearly clipping his side with its edge. "I'm not bringing a baby into this shit. What a good life it'll have, spending hours on the road doing drug runs and dropping bodies down a mine shaft. Are you fucking crazy?"

"Are *you* fucking crazy? Half the women that go into places like that don't come out alive. I don't want you to do this. Please, don't make me stop you."

"Oh yeah. Good luck, because I'm doing it today, and nothing is gonna change that." She slid into the cab and started the engine. "Get in."

Vinny held tight to her door, his legs cemented in place. "Just give it a few days. It couldn't hurt. Maybe you'll feel different."

Sasha revved the motor then put the truck in reverse. "You wanna walk back?"

Every one of her days for the past eleven years, she spent with Vinny. Not once had she seen that look in his eye. That look belonged to Dez, right before he put his fist through someone's face.

Vinny staggered back, slamming her door shut. "I'll walk."

"Come on, man."

"Go," he yelled, waving her off. "Take care of yourself, like you always do."

The anger that trembled his voice, the tinge of disappointment in his stare, it hit harder than a backhand. Sasha punched the gas, shooting a rooster of dark earth from her tires. The truck bounced and clunked backward down the trail, but

273

she didn't let off. Another second was too many to dwell in these woods, on this compound, in her own blood-speckled skin. She tapped the brake and cut the wheel, spinning the truck around to face her mother's house far below the hill. Without a glance in the rearview mirror, she drove past the big house and toward the puddle of blood at the foot of her steps.

***

Dez

Dez paced in Sasha's bedroom. He had no idea what he was doing in there or what he'd say when she returned. Words couldn't reverse what he'd done. He took something from her, something more important than a piece of ass. The confidence was gone from her stare, and he took that.

When Sasha's truck's engine rumbled the floor, his legs froze in place. If he had a decent bone in his body, he'd throw himself out the window, slip from her life, and never look back. But he didn't move, which meant his inners were soaked in decay. The thump of boots on stairs rivaled the pound of Dez's heart. He inched away from the door just as Sasha stormed in. She jumped at the sight of him, her hip crashing into the dresser beside the door.

"Goddammit, Dez!" Sasha shrank down, backing toward the doorway. "What are you doing in here?"

Dez took a step, and Sasha flinched, her back hitting the threshold. "I'm not gonna hurt you," he said, feeling like a total dick for attempting to defend himself. "I had to do that. You understand, right? If I didn't shoot her, Ellen would have killed you. Sasha, I—"

"You should have let her kill me." Sasha rushed forward, her tiny fists striking Dez's chest. "Why'd you stop her? Why!"

"Because I love you." Dez seized Sasha by the wrists, holding tight. "I love the shit out of you. I can't sleep another night without you in my arms, wake up another morning and not see your smile."

Sasha fell against Dez's chest, and he wrapped his arms around her. He could stand there and hold her forever. She belonged to him, covered in blood and dirt, shaking in his grasp. The missing half, ripped from his soul five years ago, back to make him whole again. Her lips glided along his cheek, brushing his mouth, and his grip on her body grew tighter.

"Dez, I...I'm..." Sasha pushed off Dez's chest, staring into his eyes. "I...need to get out of these clothes." Her gaze dropped, and she rubbed her forehead.

"I got you." Dez scooped Sasha into his arms. A light shiver ran down his spine as her weight fell against his chest. Her fingers twisted into his hair, warm breath floating along his neck as he carried her into the bathroom.

***

Vinny

Vinny ran down the hillside. Branches snagged

his jacket, scraping his skin, but that didn't slow his sprint. He jumped a fallen log, weaving through dense trees. Day, night, he could run this narrow trail down the mountain blindfolded. These were his woods, the home of his childhood, the place where he first kissed a girl, an eternal keeper of his murderous secrets.

He rounded a bend, picking up the pace. The snap of twigs echoed over his heavy gasps as he broke through thick brush. His boots dug into rocky dirt, skidding to a stop. Beyond the grand Victorian house that dominated the hillside, Vinny glimpsed Sasha's truck parked in its usual spot.

"Thank God," he said between pants, hunching to combat the burn in his sides. He eyed her tires, his fingers drumming the sheath of his knife. It couldn't be that easy. If he slashed the tires in Sasha's pickup, she'd just hop in a big rig and take off. Her bull-headed determination was admirable and annoying as hell.

Vinny considered pulling the fuses from every vehicle on the compound when Ellen strolled onto the porch of her house.

"Ellen," Vinny shouted, hurrying down the hill. Halfway to the house, his brain clicked on. Of all the moves he could make, this would be the stupidest. Ellen would eat Sasha alive, twist her into submission. A scorching blade of self-loathing sliced into his chest, but he ignored its burn, running up the porch steps. He was okay with Sasha hating him, if it meant she'd be alive to do it.

"Oh Jesus. What now?" Ellen asked, rushing toward Vinny.

"Please, don't freak out." Vinny sucked in a long gulp of air, leaning against the doorframe. "Sasha's about to make a horrible mistake."

Chapter Twenty-Eight

Sasha

Hot water rained down, washing over Sasha and clearing the fog from her mind. She tilted back, leaning against the hard muscles under Dez's soft skin. Hands slid over her shoulders and down her chest, trailing a path of soapy bubbles. Dez's fingertips beamed strength. The energy shot beneath Sasha's skin and spread into every fiber of her being, recharging her weakened essence.

Dez skated his lips on the back of Sasha's neck as his hands moved lower, tracing her hips, creeping to her inner thigh, and sneaking between her legs.

"There you go," Dez said, biting Sasha's ear. "All clean."

"You missed a spot." Sasha pushed Dez's hand farther and his fingers slipped deep inside, igniting an onslaught of white-hot sparks. The feel of water flowing over her skin and his touch spanning the deepest parts of her was too much to bear. Her knees wobbled, and his grip tightened. Water splashed Sasha's face, and she turned her head, connecting with silky lips. Dez's kiss drove her blustery passion into a wild frenzy, and she spun, gliding her chest against his. She reached down, gripping onto the hardness that throbbed in the tiny space between them.

Dez slid his hands down Sasha's back, gripping her ass. "Let's take this to the bed."

"Yeah," Sasha muttered into Dez's chest. The faucet squeaked, bringing her back to the steam-filled tub. She pushed the shower curtain aside, and her eyes connected with her mother's glare.

"Shit!" Sasha yelped, snatching a towel off the rack and covering herself.

Ellen leaned against the open bathroom door, holding that ornery stare she'd mastered so well. "That was very entertaining, but Dez, I'm gonna need you to get dressed and get the fuck out. My daughter and I need to have a little chat."

Dez smirked. He didn't flinch or try to hide any part of his naked body. "I'm not going anywhere."

"Oh really," Ellen said, narrowing her eyes. "You wanna test me?"

"I'm not leaving you alone with her."

"How romantically heroic of you," Ellen sneered, tearing her gaze from Dez for the briefest of seconds to glance at Sasha. "Are you afraid to be alone with me, Sasha?"

"No." Sasha looked between her mother and Dez, both locked in a venomous leer. "Can't this wait?" She pushed her mother from the bathroom, closing the door just enough to block Dez's bare ass.

279

"I don't think so." Ellen crossed her arms, looking at Sasha's stomach. "It's kind of time sensitive."

Sasha threw her towel to the floor. "Fucking Vinny," she muttered, pulling on a long t-shirt. She peeked into the bathroom as Dez buttoned his jeans. The questions in his stare could've filled the room, and she couldn't get him out of it quick enough. She grabbed his shirt and boots from the floor, thrusting them at his chest.

"It's cool. I'll catch up with ya later," Sasha said, ushering Dez to her front door.

"Sasha?"

Sasha opened the door, shoving Dez outside. "Later, dude."

The confusion that clouded Dez's face warped to a mask of shock, and Sasha shrugged, slamming the door closed. Only after the thud of footsteps faded did she turn to face her mother. "What did Vinny tell you?"

"That you're a giant slut." Ellen plopped onto the bed, stretching out. "I'm not surprised you got yourself knocked up. You are pretty careless. But the whole not knowing who the father is, scandalous! I thought you were better than that."

"I'm glad you're having fun with this." Sasha dropped onto the far corner of the bed, pulling her legs in beneath her.

"You do know there's no way on God's green Earth I'd let you take an unborn life, right?" Ellen said in a low, firm tone.

Sasha looked at her mother, darting her stare away at the first glimpse of a glower. She wanted to scream, tell her mother to shove it, that this was her body and she'd do with it as she liked, but it would be lies. Everything she had, all that she was, belonged to her mother.

"So help me, Sasha, I'll chain you up in the basement for the next nine months."

"Please don't," Sasha all but begged, knowing exactly how serious her mother was.

"I don't want to."

Her mother slid closer, and Sasha kept completely still, only the slightest of breath escaping. It wasn't until her mother's arms wrapped around her that every muscle quivered. Many hands had gripped her body—men, women—but their embraces could never match this one. A hug from her mother was like touching the sun, terrifying yet soothing. Definitely a once-in-a-lifetime event to be cherished.

"Don't cry," Ellen said, which brought a wall of waterworks to the brim of Sasha's eyes.

A soft palm wiped tears from Sasha's cheek, and she fought to keep the rest inside, to be strong.

Ellen held Sasha tight, kissing the top of her head. "We can make this work. My baby and her baby. Now, just tell me who you want the father to be and I'll make the other guy disappear."

"Mom." Sasha pulled back, gawking. "That's not funny."

"I wasn't trying to be, as long as you pick Vinny."

Sasha chuckled, and the only embrace she ever dreamed of drew her back into its graces. Whatever fluke befell the world, she didn't care. She'd bask in this affection for as long as it lasted and call for it again once it left.

"I want it to be Dez," Sasha said, the words igniting a whirl in her stomach as they left her lips.

"Then it will be." Ellen rubbed Sasha's arm, squeezing tight before letting go.

"What about my runs, this shit with the Lazzari family? The *Llamada de la Muerte* won't deal with anyone but me. I know Tito. He's a crazy motherfucker."

"You'll only have to make that one run pregnant. Vinny can handle the rest until you spit the baby out. Then, afterward, I'll help Dez with the little one so you can get back on the road. Do whatever it is that you need to do out there, and when you come home, you play the good wife and mother."

"Wife?"

"That's right." Ellen rose from the bed, lifting her chin high. "Welcome to your fairytale, princess. You should've used a rubber."

In the time it took for a smile to turn to a scowl, her mother returned to usual form. Sasha made a mental note of the date, October 13, 1984, the day her mother almost said I love you.

***

Dez

Dez flicked his cigarette onto a small patch of grass beside the garage. He'd already hosed away the blood from the foot of Sasha's steps and the bed of her truck, smoked four cigarettes, and still not a peep sounded from the room above him.

Just as Dez shook loose another smoke from his pack, Vinny crept up beside him.

"What's going on up there?" Dez shouted, pointing to Sasha's room.

"I don't know. What's going on?" Vinny asked, darting his eyes away.

Dez growled. Before he could stop himself, he clutched Vinny's jacket. "Don't feed me no bullshit, brother."

"Back off, man." Vinny pushed Dez's arm aside, straightening his crimpled leather. "Chill. This isn't about earlier."

Dez teetered on his limits of *chill*. Club ranks, secrets and favoritism, he'd had enough.

"If you don't start talking, you're gonna be eating teeth."

"Fuck!" Vinny rocked in place, looking up at Sasha's room. "Umm, well, it looks like Sasha's gonna have a baby, so I guess, congratulations. You're gonna be a father. And you suck for making me tell you."

"I don't..." Dez staggered back. His brain searched for the words, for any words, but none came into play. None, except for father.

"I'm gonna be a...father?" Dez continued backing away, toward his truck.

"Hey," Vinny called out, lifting his arms at his sides. "Where you going?"

"I'll be back."

Vinny shouted some shit, but Dez didn't have time to listen. He needed some air, and this place had just run out.

***

Sasha

Sasha stayed curled at the foot of her bed, long after her mother had gone. Her mind had finished contemplating options. She had a few, but she didn't want any of them. Part-time Suzie-Q homemaker and weekend road dyke sounded like two parts of an ugly façade. She could run the streets of Little Rock with Carmen, tear up New York City under the Lazzari rule, but that would only add more blood to her already marred soul. Plus, she'd be killing for two.

Her stare gravitated to the nightstand and the joint she knew rested in the ashtray. One hit couldn't hurt. Hell, with the amount of pot she smoked, it might help.

A knock shook the door, and Sasha closed her eyes. There was only one person she wanted to see right now, and she doubted a curvy redhead was at her door. The slow creak of hinges rang out, followed by light jerky steps. It was Vinny. She didn't have to look; he practically vibrated beside her.

"Sasha."

"Dick!" Sasha hurled a pillow across the room, striking Vinny's chest.

"I'm sorry," Vinny said, tossing the pillow aside, "but I had to tell her. You left me no choice."

"What about my choice, or don't I get one?"

"I don't know." Vinny sat on the floor in front of Sasha, looking up into her eyes. "Maybe you'll think differently, later. Thank me."

"Doubt it." She glanced at the nightstand then back to Vinny. "At least you didn't tell Dez."

"Ah, shit. Sasha."

"You didn't," she said, leaning forward.

"He was gonna make me eat my teeth."

Vinny sank down. One hand shielded his face while the other protected his balls, and Sasha snickered.

"Double dick," Sasha hollered, hitting Vinny with a much larger pillow. "So what'd Dez say? Did he freak?"

"He left."

"Oh wow." Sasha lowered her head, rubbing her temple. "And we never saw him again."

Vinny chuckled, and Sasha laughed, in a nervous kind of way.

"What do you keep looking at?" he asked, following her gaze to the nightstand.

"That doobie in the ashtray. I wanna smoke it, but I don't know."

Vinny grabbed the joint, pulled out his zippo, and fired it up.

"And now you're gonna smoke that in front of me, harsh."

"No." Vinny scooted closer, raising to his knees. "I'm gonna smoke it with you. You pretty much breathe pot; it's already in your system. How much damage can one more joint do?" His arm lifted, sending a halo of smoke high into the air. "It's a choice."

Sasha grabbed Vinny's hand, sliding her fingers between his. Her legs draped over the side of the bed, landing on either side of him. "I'm sorry." She leaned toward him, and his warm forehead rubbed against hers. "You got a raw deal."

Vinny dropped the joint, gliding his rough palm along the side of Sasha's neck. "As long as you're around, it's a good deal." He slid his fingers into her hair, and his lips brushed against her mouth. "Can you promise me you're not going anywhere?" he asked in a whisper, his voice trembling.

"I can't promise something like that."

"At least say you won't split. Leave me here with Dez and Ellen."

Sasha smiled, caressing the stubbly skin of Vinny's cheek. Then, before she could think, their lips drew together. She might've leaned in, or he lunged for her. Either way, the kiss felt right and still so wrong. Sasha tried to push Vinny away but ended up pulling him closer.

Her back hit the mattress, and his body covered her. A haze of soft lips and wandering hands crippled all rational thought. His fingers skated along her sides, hiking up her shirt, and the fog thickened. Maybe she could have him, this one last time. Her love for him would fade, but only after a proper sendoff. Although it sounded good, it was lies she told herself to disguise the dirty.

"Vinny. We shouldn't," Sasha said, driving her hips even harder against his body. "Not here, not now."

"You're right."

Vinny moved off Sasha, and cool air rushed in to sting her heated skin.

"I'm sorry, Sasha. I don't know what I was

thinking."

After a minute of silence, and once the flush left Vinny's cheeks, he jumped up. "I'm gonna go."

"Hey, wait." Sasha reached for Vinny's hand, but he dashed for the door. "Vinny—"

"Don't." Vinny gripped the doorknob, looking over his shoulder. "Words just fuck shit up. I'm cool. We're cool." He mustered a half-smile before walking into the blinding daylight.

Chapter Twenty-Nine

Ellen

Ellen picked up the phone on the clubhouse wall, staring at the keypad. She had dialed every number, talked to all her contacts, and still no word of Dante. An hour ago, she would've let him burn this compound to the ground, but a baby. That changed everything. Leave it to Sasha to fuck up one's strength of mind. That girl would be the death of her or salvation. A loud beep streamed through the phone's receiver, and Ellen crashed it down on the hook.

"You need to relax," Otis said, leaning over the pool table and sinking a ball into the corner pocket.

"I need to find Dante. I have no idea what he's gonna do."

"He's one man with no crew or trucks." Otis shrugged, lining up his next shoot. "What could Dante really do?"

"A lot." Ellen turned, glaring out the window as Kev and two younger carbon copies of him strolled toward the clubhouse. "What the fuck is this shit?"

Otis laid the pool cue on the table, stepping beside Ellen. "Our new prospects. Remember, Kev's cousins?"

"Shit. Great timing. This place could use a little sprucing." Ellen swung her leg, and glass bottles clinked as they rolled across the floor. "Look at 'em. It's like they were all plucked from the same cabbage patch."

"Yeah." Otis chuckled. "Right down to that same dumb-ass grin. Let's hope they got all the brains in the family, 'cause if they're any dumber than Kev, they're going right back to the farm."

Kev stepped inside, motioning for the two men to stay behind. "What's up?" he said, walking to the other side of Ellen to join in on the ogle of the two nervous men on the porch. "So what'd you think?"

"They got names?" Ellen asked, glancing at Kev. "Or should I just call them one and two?"

"Cash and Cory."

Ellen snickered, crossing her arms. "Really?"

"They're twins," Kev said with a shrug. "Not the sharpest nails, but they know when to keep the lip shut and how to take orders."

"Good. Have 'em whip this place into shape, then send 'em out to restock the bar." Ellen looked at Otis as she backed away. "I'm going out for a few. Look for our friend."

If a stare could freeze a person in time, his would have, but it didn't, so she walked out the front door. "Tweedledee, Tweedledum," Ellen said as she glanced at the near-identical men while heading off the porch. Right on cue, Vinny pulled her Chevelle from the garage and parked beside her. The motor's rumble cut through her body, knocking loose a grin.

Vinny jumped out, holding the door open. "All gassed up and ready to go."

"Thanks, kid. Listen," Ellen grabbed onto Vinny's arm, looking him dead in the eyes. "I want you to stay on the compound while I'm gone and…be ready."

"Is there something I should be ready for?"

"Yeah." Ellen slid into the cool leather seat of the Chevelle, shutting the door. "Everything."

In a purr of finely tuned engine, she sped down the lot and out the open gate. Tires squealed once hitting pavement, the rear end fishtailing. Ellen punched the gas, taking off down the mountain.

***

Sasha

Sasha ran down her stairs as the roar of a Chevelle faded into the hillside. "Where the fuck is she going?"

Vinny stepped in front of Sasha, blocking her view of round taillights. "Your bandana is crooked."

"God," she said in a long drawl. Vinny stared down at her, like a robot waiting for the proper command before he could continue. A series of muffed obscenities flowed from her lips. Sasha twisted the fabric that covered the top of her head, tugged at the ends of her jacket, and shifted the belt of her pants. "Am I pretty enough now?"

"You're always pretty, but that'll probably change after you get fat."

"Asshole!" Sasha lifted her fist, and Vinny ducked down. He chuckled, until the back of her hand whacked his gut. Then he groaned.

"Where did my mother go?"

"I don't know," Vinny said, rubbing his stomach. "She didn't say."

"Is Dez back?" Her eyes screamed *desperate girl,* at least she thought they did. Just in case, she cast them down.

"No, not yet. He's coming back."

It was too late to hide the stench of despair, so Sasha rolled with it. "You don't know that. Your dad took off."

"My dad was a loser alcoholic. Dez is the complete opposite of that scumbag. He'd never just roll. He wants this. You should've seen his face."

"I wish I could have." Sasha glared, forcing Vinny back a few steps. "Come on," she said, walking past him. "I need a drink."

"You can't drink," he said, following her toward the clubhouse.

"Not liquor. Coffee."

"I don't think you're supposed to have that either."

"Jesus Christ." Her pace quickened, but she couldn't shake Vinny or his list of don'ts. She popped a cigarette in her mouth and lit it. Before she could get in a full drag, Vinny yanked the butt from her lips.

"You definitely don't wanna smoke these." He puffed on the cigarette before flicking it to the

291

gravel.

"Come on, man." Sasha stopped at the foot of the steps, her arms out.

Vinny turned Sasha toward the clubhouse, ushering her up the stairs. "Let's get you a soda pop."

"Jesus fucking Christ."

She got maybe a foot into the door when some dude blocked her path.

"Hey, Sasha."

"Who the fuck are you?" she asked, leaning back to better hurl a glare.

"I'm Cory, that's Cash." The dude pointed to a near-identical guy behind the bar working a mop. "We're your prospects."

"What the…?" Sasha squinted, eyes bouncing between the pair. "Kev, what the fuck is this shit?"

Kev hurried from the pool table, stick in hand. "What? What'd he do?"

"How am I gonna tell them apart?" Sasha asked, crossing her arms. "They look exactly alike."

"Nah," Kev said, waving his hand. "Cory over there is taller, wider."

"That's Cash," Cory said, looking down.

"Ah shit," Kev cried out, banging his pool stick on the wood-planked floor.

"Make 'em wear signs or something." Sasha headed to the nearest stool, slapping her palm atop the freshly wiped bar. "Hey, tall, wide one. Get me a Coke, on ice."

The guy sprang into action, fumbling with the ice chest, as Vinny sat beside Sasha. She leaned toward him, shielding her smirk. "Prospects are awesome."

"You better watch it. You sounded like your mother for a second. It was scary."

"Blasphemy!" Sasha's grin spread into a full-blown smile. "You deserve a slappin' for that one."

A glass of ice-cold cola landed in front of Sasha. She nodded to the man whose name she couldn't remember and spun in her seat, watching Otis spank Kev at a game of nine ball. Over Kev's whine, a pickup truck revved. Sasha jolted upright, her fingers twisting together. A knot pulled at her chest, squeezing her airways when the sound of a truck door slamming shut echoed through the open door.

Vinny nudged Sasha's arm, popping the invisible bubble that suffocated her and letting the oxygen-filled room flood in.

"Told you he'd be back."

Sasha hurled a sharp leer Vinny's way then grabbed her glass, taking a sip. When Dez walked in and smiled at her, she lowered her gaze. Almost by instinct, she shoved a cigarette in her mouth. Her zippo flipped open, and Vinny plucked the cigarette away.

"S'up," Dez said, leaning against the bar.

"Where you been, man?" Vinny asked.

"Umm." Dez glanced around the room before turning his stare to Sasha. "Can I get a hit of this?" He snatched the glass from her hand, took a long gulp, then cringed. "It's just soda."

"Yeah. Tell me about it."

"Oh. Right." Dez put the drink down, sliding it away. His hand fell to Sasha's thigh, and he squeezed. "You wanna go outside, have a smoke?"

"I would love to have a smoke," Sasha said, rolling her head toward Vinny.

Dez took Sasha's hand, and she stole back her cigarette while hopping off the stool. It wasn't until they hit the porch that she noticed how tense Dez's shoulder were and the sweat on his palm. She jerked her hand away, and his flustered eyes shot to her.

"You're pissed, right?" Sasha leaned against the wooden rail of the porch, staring at her feet. "I was gonna tell you. Fucking Vinny."

"Sasha," Dez said, his voice cracking. He reached into the inside pocket of his jacket, pulling out a small felt box.

The world took a quick spin before crashing down on Sasha. Air grew thick, like cement, she couldn't breathe. Then, as if to push the limits of her sanity, the lid flipped open and Dez dropped to one knee.

"Sasha Ashby."

Sounds, light, her breath all vanished under a high-pitched buzz. She closed her eyes then opened them, but Dez was still down there.

"Will you marry me?"

A huge diamond sparkled in the sun's rays, casting a rainbow of light and bewitching Sasha's mind. "Get up," she muttered, tearing her gaze from the ring and Dez's hopeful face.

"Not until you answer me."

"Hey, Sasha." Otis walked onto the porch, took one look at Dez on bended knee, and dashed back the way he came. "Never mind."

"Oh my God, get up." Sasha latched onto Dez's jacket, pulling him to his feet. "Just, no."

"What?"

Sasha snapped the lid to the ring box closed, pushing Dez's hand away. "We don't need a shotgun wedding. I'm not gonna keep you from your baby."

"That's not..." His jaw clenched, head rolling back. "Why do you have to make everything so fucking difficult? Here." Dez shoved the tiny box in Sasha's hand, inching so close she could almost feel his heart pound. "I love you, you loopy bitch. If you love me, you'll marry me."

Sasha stood, paralyzed, as Dez walked away.

"No hurry," he called out from the clubhouse door. "But you might not fit into a hot dress in a few months."

"Dress?" Sasha muttered. Finally, the grip over her body released, and she looked at the clubhouse door, but Dez was gone, except he hadn't left her alone. The smooth box that pressed into her palm successfully smothered her in his absence. Amazing, how something so small could carry with it the weight to make her hand tremble.

The floorboards shifted beneath Sasha, footsteps drew near, but the damn box bound her to a state of shock. A zippo clinked from what sounded like a mile away, and smoke wafted by in a thick, gray cloud. It's smell and the promise of nicotine called to her, and still, she couldn't move a muscle.

"Hey, kiddo," Otis said softly.

Sasha flinched, breaking the chains of whatever spell had ensnared her. She could hug Otis for freeing her from the trance Dez and his stupid ring put her into.

"Crazy day, huh?" Otis said, plopping onto the bench.

"You could say that." Sasha shoved the ring in her pocket and sat beside Otis, taking the cigarette from his hand.

"I hate to add to your bucket of shit," Otis said in a completely unregretful tone, "but I have some questions that can't wait."

She'd been waiting for this. The interrogation, followed by the *I'm so disappointed* speech.

"Okay," Sasha said, keeping her stare on the faded wood of the porch's railing.

"This woman, where'd you pick her up at?"

"A rest stop, about twenty miles outside the city."

"Was she already there, or did she show up after you?"

"I don't know." Sasha took a long drag of her cigarette, replaying that day in her head. "I had to take a hose to the trailer, the cargo…excreted, so I was there for a little bit before I saw her. She just walked up to me, spouted out some cute shit, and the next thing I know she's riding shotgun."

Otis sat back, the bench squeaking under his shifting weight. "Did you see her make any phone calls?"

"No. This morning was the only time she left my sight, except for last night at the party. But she was with Candy, so I don't think she could've made any calls. I followed the road protocols, checked for tails the whole way home, switched up routes midway. I wasn't shadowed."

"What I don't understand," Otis said, turning his

glare to Sasha, "is how can you be so smart and so stupid? What did you think was gonna happen here?"

"I don't know." Sasha flicked the cigarette over the railing and leaned forward. "I was just gonna give her a ride, but she was so full of spirit, carefree." Misty's easy flowing smiles, the woman's laid-back attitude. It was everything Sasha could never become. "I wanted to be her," she said, the words barely making a sound as they trickled out her mouth.

"It was just an act, Sasha."

"I know." She sat back, straining to force the images of golden braids and soft blue eyes from her mind. "People like that don't exist in real life."

Otis didn't say anything for a while. Perhaps he wanted to save the lecture, lay it down while a baby ripped its way from her birth canal, or maybe he could see she'd had enough. Regardless of the reasons, Otis didn't scold and she wasn't complaining.

"Do you think I brought the heat down on us?" Sasha asked, avoiding Otis's eyes and the truth that lie within them.

"I think the mess with Satan's Crew brought the heat on us. You were just the one who walked them through our door."

Shame pulled Sasha into a slump. "What should I do?"

"Nothing." Otis knocked a fresh cigarette against his lighter, packing the loose tobacco into its sleeve. "If you get hauled in, you picked up a girl at a rest stop, and she wanted to do drugs so you dropped her off at the next service station. Got it?"

"Yeah."

"I'm gonna grab a gas can and head up to the cellar, do our yearly burning a little early." Otis got up, pointing to her jacket. "What are you gonna do about Dez?"

Her hand flew to the lump in her pocket, which created an even bigger lump in her throat. "I don't know. What do you think I should do?"

Otis shrugged, lighting his cigarette. "You could always tell him to go fuck himself, marry me."

The slow nod of Otis's head and the playful gleam in his eyes pushed a smile onto Sasha's lips. "Don't tempt me."

"You already know you're gonna say yes. Now it's just about how long you wanna make the poor guy suffer."

Sasha snickered as Otis strolled off the porch. A few more minutes as a single woman then she'd go inside and end Dez's suffering, essentially starting a new phase of torment.

Chapter Thirty

Ellen

Rocky cliffs rose higher, and Ellen leaned back in the Chevelle's bucket seat, loosening her grip on the steering wheel. Four hours, two states, and every dive bar in between, but not one hog in sight. She was actually afraid, not of death or the destruction of her tiny empire. Her fear stemmed from the thought of losing Dante.

The train wreck of her brain settled once she turned onto the compound. Stiff drinks and the quiet countryside sat just up that hill, the two things that could salvage this hellish day. However, when she glimpsed the amount of cars scattered around the lot, she knew only one of those two things would be possible.

Ellen parked in front of the garage, killing the engine. Music and laughter replaced the rumble of horsepower, provoking her last proverbial straw to bend. Some dude leaned over the clubhouse's rail, regurgitating about a pint of JD, and that straw snapped. An all-out party tonight. If Otis hadn't lost his mind, she'd beat it out of him.

Red tinges clouded her vision. Somewhere between plotting Otis's death and scouring the sea of faces for Dante, Ellen found herself standing in the middle of the clubhouse. Her eyes zeroed in on Otis, and he cringed. People crowded all around her, and the word congratulations echoed in the air, a lot.

"Shit, Ellen," Otis said, weaving through the mob to reach her side. "You had me worried."

"So you threw a party? Are you fucking serious?"

Otis shook his head, pointing to the small group at the bar. "It wasn't me. This is all Sasha and Dez's doing. I tried to get them to hold off but," he drew her close, his lips grazing her ear, "without telling them the truth, I had no solid reason."

"When's the wedding?" a woman yelled over the thump of speakers.

Ellen pulled back, gawking up at Otis. "Wedding?"

"They're getting hitched," Otis said through a grin.

The room faded to black, only Sasha shining through. Ellen watched her little girl smile and sparkle. In that moment, her child held the radiance of a fierce woman. The spoiled brat would return, like always, but for this moment, she'd enjoy the glimpse.

"Did you find what you were looking for?" Otis asked.

"No."

"Come here," Otis said, cutting into the crowd.

Ellen followed him into the backroom, shutting the door on a large percentage of the racket. "I'm so pissed and so happy, which is making me pissed off even more."

"It's all right." Otis pulled a flask from his pocket, handing it to Ellen. "This party is also a trap. Kev, Vinny, and the prospects are stationed around the compound. They're loaded up and on the prowl."

"What did you tell them?"

"To stay low, keep an eye out for anyone creeping into the big house. Or anywhere else they shouldn't be."

"Smart." Ellen took a step toward Otis. The ridges of his chest looked so inviting, a perfect place to rest her frantic head. "Otis, I don't know what I'd do without you." Her arms circled his waist, and he held her close.

"Let's hope you don't have to find out."

Otis's deep voice echoed in his chest, singing in Ellen's ear, and she squeezed him tighter. "I'm sorry to drag you into this mess with your cousin, but Dante, he gets under my skin."

His big, safe hand cupped her cheek before gliding down the side of her neck. "I tried to warn you about him, twenty years ago when you saw him at my party that night."

Ellen grinned, peering up into deep, brown eyes. "Yeah."

"And when you said you'd marry him."

"Right." The comfort of his touch grew cold, and she slinked away.

"Then, when you ran off with Ashby."

Ellen plopped into a chair, kicking her feet onto the table. "If you're so intuitive, why'd you follow me?"

"You know me, I'm a masochist. Can't get enough of the pain." Otis grinned, heading for the door. "You coming? It's your daughter's engagement party, hopefully her only one."

Ellen settled back, the legs of her chair creaking. "I'll be out in a minute."

Otis nodded then slipped out the door, into the blare of music and excited voices. The sounds of celebration usually quelled her never-ending stream of thoughts. Not tonight, though. A moment she'd been dreading had come to pass this night. The choice. After years of slinging angles, she had to pick between the man who drove her wild for the last two decades and the club that kept her sane.

She reached for a bottle of whiskey, her boots thumping back to the floor. Hard liquor burned its way down her throat, replacing the scorch of regret. If she had a soul, she'd sell it for five minutes with Dante. She could sway him. Given time, he'd fall right into the fold, and he knew it. That was the reason he stayed away.

A cheer sliced into her solitude like a knife. Ellen sunk down against the wooden back of her seat, clutching the bottle to her chest. The party could wait. She needed a few more swigs of whiskey and to make a life-altering decision.

***

Sasha

Sasha lingered in and out of the conversation. She really did want to know about the property for sale up the mountain, but her attention couldn't break from the backroom. Dez squeezed her leg, and she looked at him. His glare demanded an answer, which she would gladly give if she had any idea what the fuck he'd asked.

"You feeling all right?" Dez asked, running the back of his hand over Sasha's cheek.

"Yeah." Sasha pushed his arm away, jumping off the barstool. "I'll be right back."

A usual five-second walk to the backroom took five fuckin' minutes, thanks to the bombardment of people Sasha barely recognized. The barrage of well-wishers ended with Otis, who guarded the door to the backroom like a pit-bull.

Sasha gestured for Otis to move aside, and his eyes narrowed. A snicker flew from her lips, as if he could stop her. She hip-checked Otis from her way, opened the door, and strolled inside the backroom.

"Hey," Sasha said when her mother looked up from the bottle in her hand. She closed the door and crept toward the table. "Can we talk?"

"That's never a good opener." Ellen kicked the chair beside her out, its legs grating the wood as it slid toward Sasha. "Take a load off."

On the drop into the chair, Sasha eyed the joints in the ashtray that centered the table.

"Did you stop smoking?" Ellen asked, grabbing a joint and lighting it up. "You don't have to. I smoked my whole pregnancy, and you came out

303

just fine."

"Awesome." Sasha took the joint, drawing in a long hit before passing it back. "I wasn't sure," she said through a tunnel of smoke. "When I was in New York, I had a talk with Antonio Lazzari."

Ellen snickered, taking a gulp of the near empty bottle in her hand. "And what did Tony say?"

"That Dante is his brother and that you were with him, before you met my dad."

"Yeah. That was a long time ago."

Two men and one woman, the subject hit a little too close to the collar for Sasha. She didn't want to ask her mother these questions, didn't care to know the truth, but needed to figure out how to find her own answers. "You must really love him, Dante. To still be messing with him after all these years."

Her mother leaned forward, narrowing her eyes. "What are you getting at?"

"I guess, I'm just wondering. If you could go back, do it different, would you have picked Dante instead?"

A smile spread across her mother's lips but not the happy kind. More like a lost-to-destitution simper.

"I don't give much thought to what if's and should have's." Ellen hit the joint, handing it to Sasha. "We gotta live in the now and what's to come."

"Dante wasn't in that fire, was he? You wouldn't burn him alive."

A far-off gaze gripped her mother's stare, one Sasha had never seen before, one that scared the shit out of her.

"No, he wasn't. But you're wrong. I would burn him alive, if I had to." Her mother rose, the typical cool glare breezing in to blow away the hint of sadness. "Come on, we're missing your big party."

Sasha smiled when her mother's hand slipped into her own. A small tug and she was on her feet, moving toward the door.

***

Dez

Dez scanned the crowd, looking for Vinny or Kev. He'd even settle for one of those weird lookalikes right now, but all he got was more freeloading rednecks.

A hand ran up his back, rough and sloppy. Not Sasha. Dez turned, latching onto a soft wrist without bothering to look at its owner.

"Ooh. Feisty," a silky voice all but breathed on his neck. The first thing Dez saw was tits. Huge, overflowing, way too tight halter-top tits. Right, the brunette with blue eyes.

"So, Dez," she said, sliding her finger down his chest. "Why don't we duck out of here real quick, while you're still single?"

The chick rubbed on him like a cat in heat, and he inched away. "I'm not single."

Candy stepped beside Dez, crossing her arms. "You better back off, Nancy, or you'll be picking your crooked teeth off the floor."

Nancy waved her hand and stomped into the crowd, stopping to throw a wink Dez's way.

305

"Sorry, Dez. That bitch is going for the grand slam," Candy said with a cute little huff.

"What's that?"

"You know. When you ball all the club members? I'll scalp the bitch if she gets near Otis. Word is, she's only gotten Vinny and Kev so far."

Dez nodded. A grand slam, it seemed like a noble accomplishment for a woman. That's when he remembered one of his clubmates was a woman. "How's that gonna work with Sasha? She's a runner."

"If you want a real grand slam, you gotta get her too," Candy said, as if Dez were dense. "I guess I'm closer to a grand slam than Nancy."

"What?" Dez said with a bark that made Candy flinch. "You were with Sasha?"

Her jaw dropped, but those green eyes grew wide. "Oh shit. You didn't know? I'm not a giant slut or anything. We were together for years, but she broke up with me a long time ago, like two whole weeks."

"What!"

"Oh shit. I gotta run, Dez. Congratulations?" Candy shrugged, scurrying toward Otis.

Broke up, dated. Dez understood a little fun here and there, but for Sasha to date a chick for years. That meant something.

A rush of voices erupted from all sides, laughter stinging his ears. Too tight, too many people. He staggered, lost in a flock of eyes, when an icy breeze grazed his cheek. The sliver of crisp air promised a chance at escape, and Dez barreled toward it. His legs didn't stop once outside the front door. He kept going, down the porch, across the lot, and toward his truck.

"Dez! Wait up," Otis called out, jogging after him.

"No. No more pep talks."

Dez opened the door to his truck, and Otis slammed it shut.

"You don't know Candy," Otis said, blocking Dez's reach from the pickup's door handle. "She over-exaggerates. What she calls dating, a normal person would call the occasional screw."

"You're lying to yourself." Dez took a step back, waving his arm toward the clubhouse. "You're all lying to yourselves, especially Sasha."

"Dez, listen—"

"Two weeks ago, that's when Sasha decides no more women. Out of the blue and when I just happen to come around. She's using me as a cover, to keep her mother happy, to get my spot at the table. Probably planned this whole pregnancy shit."

"You're wrong." Otis grabbed Dez's arm, holding tight. "She did change when you came around. You changed her. You can't see it, but you clear up all the confusion in her mind."

Dez yanked himself from Otis's grasp, backing away. "No. I'm confusing her more. Why do you think she's picking up chicks at rest stops?"

"That bitch targeted Sasha."

Otis dropped his head, and Dez glimpsed Sasha on the porch steps. Their gaze met, her lips curved up, and a pang shot through Dez's chest.

The view of a dark angel fell behind Otis as his stare raised. "When you look in her eyes, you see love. Nothing else should matter."

Sasha stepped beside Dez, peering up at him.

"Is everything cool?" she asked.

Dez saw the shimmer in her eyes. More intense than concern, yet softer than lust. True love.

"Yeah." Dez looked away, hiding the bit of rage that still lingered in his stare. "Just getting some fresh air."

"Wanna sneak off with me?" Sasha took Dez by the hand, a sly smile crossing her lips. "Get into some trouble."

Sasha inched closer to Dez, her chest gliding along his own. It felt right. Heat still surged with her slightest touch, and his hands still wanted to grip her ass.

"Yeah, I do."

"Weird." Sasha wiggled her shoulders. "I just got a chill." Her grip on Dez's hand tightened, and she led him toward the garage.

Chapter Thirty-One

Vinny

Leaves crunched, and Vinny raised his shotgun. High up on the hillside and tucked between dense trees, he could see the entire compound. The people who traipsed in and out of the clubhouse, a wide stretch of gravel where their big rigs rested, the porch of Ellen's house, but not the woods around him. Under a moonless sky, so far from the lights of the compound, Vinny stood blind in the darkness. Just him and his twelve-gauge.

Branches cracked behind him, and he spun, lifting his gun. A hand seized his barrel, pushing it down.

"Yo, man! It's me," Kev said, creeping closer.

"Fuck, dude. I almost shot you."

"No, you didn't," Kev snickered. "I totally had the jump on you."

Vinny shook his head, turning back to stare at the compound below. "You're supposed to be on the east side."

"How many times have we had to stake out the woods during a party?" Kev asked, nudging Vinny's arm. "Never. What's going on, man?"

"What makes you think I know?"

"'Cause you're our VP."

"Shit," Vinny muttered beneath his breath, "that's right." He'd forgotten he was supposed to be the man with the answers, except he never thought to ask any questions. Otis said watch so he watched. Probably not the makings of a great leader. All the right stuff for a perfect bitch-boy, though. In times like these, there was only one thing he could do: fake it.

"There was an article in the paper this morning, about a bar fire in Tennessee. Said eight members of a local biker gang were killed, along with eleven other men and women."

"Only eight," Kev said, crashing the butt of his gun on the rocky path. "That leaves what, five, six douchebags? That's enough to regroup and do some damage."

"I think that's what Ellen's afraid of."

"Please." Kev waved the notion off. "Ellen ain't afraid of shit."

Vinny chuckled. Truer words had never been spoken. "Okay, well. On the lookout then. Hold up." Two figures walked up the hill, and Vinny slanted forward.

"What is it?" Kev whispered, lifting his gun a hair.

The garage light shined on wavy black hair, and Vinny stepped back. "It's just Sasha and Dez."

"Umm. I guess I'll head back now. Go be on the

lookout."

"People are already starting to leave." Vinny smirked. He was about to give his first order as vice president of Ashby Trucking, and it stirred every part of his body. "After everyone's gone, we'll head down."

"Yes, sir," Kev said, slipping back into the night with barely a sound.

"Sir," Vinny mumbled. It sounded stupid. He stared down at the little outlines that buzzed around his clubhouse, adjusting his belt. Tight. His pants were suddenly too tight. He had the position, respect of his peers. If only he'd gotten the girl. Could have been the trifecta. No worries, his patience held no bounds. Knowing Dez, and he did, dude would fuck it up in no time. Sasha, the Rubik cube of his life, might never be his, but at least she wouldn't belong to his brother.

***

Sasha

Sasha sat on the edge of her bed, watching Dez study the pictures that lined her mirror. After the interruption in the shower, he should be all over her.

"You looking for something?"

"This redhead, Candy." Dez pulled a photo of Candy kissing Sasha's cheek off the mirror, staring at it. "She's in every picture."

"Yeah. I've known Candy a long time. She's the girl, the one my mom caught me with, that day."

Dez sat on the opposite end of the bed, far from

311

grasp. "And you kept hanging with her, in front of your mom?"

"We dyed her hair from blonde to red, changed her makeup and name. My mom didn't even know, just another girl running in and out of the club."

"Why would you do that?"

"Because I love her." Sasha drew back. She was more shocked at her own words than Dez looked. That thought should've stayed in the brain, but the air around Dez vibrated in passion, creating a type of truth serum. She couldn't lie to him. What was worse, she didn't want to.

"You love her?" Dez asked, as if he just stumbled onto the impossible.

"Candy is…special to me. I treated her like shit, always. I was angry for a long time, took most of it out on her, and she's still so sweet to me. I love her for that."

A sour looked scrunched the bridge of Dez's nose, much like he'd been chewing on lemons. Sasha could tell harsh words lingered on the tip of his tongue, and she had a good guess as to what they might be.

"Did Candy say something to you?" Sasha asked, regretting the question before it even left her mouth.

"She said you guys dated for years, and you just broke it off with her two weeks ago."

The groan that broke loose carried Sasha's eyes to the ceiling. "There was no dating. We messed around. That's it."

"Are you…are you a…?"

Sasha took a deep breath. Any minute now, the

word dyke would fall out of Dez's mouth, and she'd have no control over her fist. Not how she imagined the night's end.

"I've been with a bunch of women and men," Sasha said, hoping a little preemptive strike would end the conversation.

"That's not normal, Sasha."

"Is anything we do normal?"

"I want some things to be." Dez tossed the picture onto the nightstand, finally looking at Sasha's face. "Do you plan on fucking other people after we're married?"

"Do you?" For the first time in a long time, Sasha felt lost. She'd never set terms of a relationship before. In hindsight, it might have been a good idea to get this out of the way before the engagement.

"No, I don't," Dez said firmly.

His hard stare cut straight through her. If the right hands caressed her in the right way, would she be able to say no?

"I don't plan on it either." The gold band on her finger grew tighter, the diamond heavier. Sasha twisted the ring, tugged, but it didn't relieve the pressure. "We don't have to do this, so soon." Thanks to the gallon of sweat that coated her palm, the ring slid off with ease. She ran her thumb over the sharp ridges of the pointed stone, then held the ring out. "You can give it back to me when you're ready. I'm not going anywhere."

Dez reached out, his fingers drifting toward the ring. His hand closed around hers, pressing the rock into her skin. He scooted closer, holding her arm to his chest.

"I'm ready now," he said, his lips brushing her cheek.

Warm breath flowed over Sasha's skin, and every emotion spiked. Love mixed with hate, desire and disgust blended, and they all tore at the seams of the flesh that kept them contained.

Dez pried open Sasha's fist, took the ring, and slipped it back onto her finger. It might've been the tingles that stemmed from his touch or the cool metal that hugged her skin, but her restraint shattered. She crashed into his arms, driving his back into the mattress. His kiss was rough yet gentle, hurling a wave of white fuzz over her mind. This wasn't her. She wasn't a vulnerable, frightened little girl who quivered inside strong arms. Unless she was and never knew it.

Lips skated along Sasha's neck as Dez pulled at her shirt. She could feel the affection in his fingertips, the hunger, even when he manhandled her. Such a force could only be one thing, love. She could sacrifice a bit of herself, be that scared girl for love.

"Dez," Sasha called out before her mouth could stop the word from slinking loose.

The grip on her body tightened, and he spun her, laying her back against the mattress. A kiss snuck in, intoxicating, bringing an ache. His hands slid up her arms, guiding them over her head. Their fingers laced, and he squeezed while rubbing harder between her legs.

"Too much clothes," Dez said, releasing his clutch to fumble with her belt.

Sasha stared up, into the frosty eyes that shined behind thick strands of wavy hair. The words I love you almost slipped out. She wanted to say it, let Dez know how badly her body craved his, but the declaration refused to leave her cowardly grasp.

Dez stopped battling with Sasha's pants, a half-grin striking his face. That gleam caught behind his stare; it was as though he could hear her thoughts. He leaned down, and she felt his kiss before it landed on her lips.

***

Vinny

Vinny cringed as he walked past the garage. The sounds that spilled from Sasha's room, especially with her window open, hit his gut like a sucker punch.

"That's beat, man," Kev said, looking at Vinny and then to his feet. "Losing your girl to your brother."

"She wasn't my girl." Vinny picked up the pace, but he couldn't outrun the sting of the truth. Sasha never really was his girl.

"Yeah, but you guys were fucking."

"No," Vinny said casually. "We weren't like that."

"Bullshit. You lived in the same house with her, steps from her bedroom. I know you guys fucked around. I would've."

"She's like my sister, my clubmate. Sex would just make things weird." The words sounded alien

315

to Vinny, but they came out so natural he almost believed them.

"I guess," Kev said with a shrug. "You got some willpower. Must be why you're VP and not me."

Vinny snorted. He'd have to work on the whole discipline thing, since everyone thought he's the responsible one. It should be easy, as long as Sasha's not in reach.

"What's this?" Otis asked, walking down the clubhouse steps.

Kev hung back with the prospects, leaving Vinny alone to stare into Otis's hard eyes.

"Everyone split," Vinny said, straining to keep his spine stiff under the weight of Otis's stare. "So I thought we'd do a perimeter check."

Otis hardened his glare, and Vinny fought the urge to scurry back up the hill. He made a call and technically, he outranked Otis. It felt kind of cool and totally sucked.

"Yeah." Otis nodded, slow. "Good idea. You can send Kev and the prospects home when y'all are done. I'm gonna crash at the big house tonight, in the spare room. I hope you're a light sleeper."

After a hard whack on the arm, Otis brushed by, but the gravity of his face hung in the air.

"Hey, Otis!" Vinny cut around Kev and trailed Otis up the hill. "What's going down?"

"What do you mean?" Otis glanced at Vinny but didn't stop his stroll toward Ellen's house.

"You never sleep here unless there's trouble. And the whole guarding the house during the party shit. Did something happen last night?"

Otis stopped, turning on his heels to stare bullets.

"Did you hear something last night?"

"I thought I saw Ellen in my room." Vinny inched closer to Otis. If his voice could manage to project a fraction of the command his position stood for, he might get some answers from his road captain. "If you tell me what's up, I can help. Don't keep me in the dark. This is my family."

A twinge of compassion shone in the porch light. It almost worked, but the softness drained from Otis's face the instant it appeared.

"Someone's always waiting to storm in here and take what we got. Bikers, street thugs, the feds. It'll just get worse the bigger we get." Otis gestured to the clubhouse below the gentle slope to the three men who stood just outside, shooting the shit. "It'll get quiet again then all hell will break loose. That's the life we signed up for. From now on out, shoot everyone first and sort details later. Colors, badges, patches, all of 'em."

Vinny shook his head. What Otis said, the way the man's voice slightly trembled, left a bad taste in Vinny's mouth. The taste of bullshit. "Otis—"

"We have a run scheduled for tomorrow afternoon," Otis said, holding a blank glare. "The club needs to vote on whether to restock or lay low. You should call a meeting before Sasha heads out, don't you think?"

Vinny smirked. He'd gotten all he could from Otis, a big fat nothing. "Yeah," he said, easing backward down the hill. "Ten a.m."

"Sounds good. I'll tell Ellen; you let the others know."

Vinny turned, trudging down the hill. His eyes

flew to Sasha's room. Everything he wanted dwelled within that room, and this time it wasn't her body he desired. It was the information stuffed inside her brain he needed.

"So." Kev held his arms out at his sides, shotgun in one hand and a joint in the other. "Back to the woods or what?"

"Nah." Vinny stopped in front of Kev, snatching the joint from the man's hand. "We'll take a quick look around and call it a night. You two," he pointed to the prospects then to the woods behind him, "take the east side and we'll meet up at the front gate."

Without the slightest hint of protest, the prospects crept into thick brush and slipped behind the trees. Vinny slapped Kev on the shoulder, taking a few hits of the joint before handing it back. "Having prospects is awesome."

Kev chuckled, following Vinny around the backside of the clubhouse. "That's how I felt when you and Sasha made prospect. I had just spent a year being club bitch, earned my runners patch, and thought I was hotshit. That's why I was so brutal on you guys."

"You call that brutal." Vinny took the joint from Kev's fingers and smiled. "As your new VP, I promise to show you the real meaning of brutal."

"A tyrant already, I should've known. It's always the quiet ones."

Chapter Thirty-Two

Sasha

Sasha wiggled under Dez's arm, which had grown so heavy it squished her into the mattress. He slept soundly, despite the morning's glare that beamed through her curtain. Not her, though. An incessant chirp had woken her twenty minutes ago, firing up the burn in her stomach. She now wished all birds would die and the sun would fade away. These symbols of a new day only meant dry heaving and twelve hours behind a wheel. Hidden in shadows with rough hands on her body, that's where she longed to stay.

A knock rattled Sasha's door, and Dez flinched, rolling away.

"Meeting in an hour," a deep voice echoed behind the closed door before boots thumped down her stairs.

"Who the fuck was that?" Dez asked, taking his hand off the gun on the nightstand.

"One of those prospects." Sasha crawled out of

319

bed and dashed into the bathroom, slamming the door to shut behind her. A whirl took her knees to the tile. She hugged the toilet, and this time, her stomach made sure to save a bunch of its contents to bring up.

"Are you all right?" Dez asked.

The bathroom door inched open, and Sasha kicked it shut. "I'm good," she yelled between gasps. "Just head down. I'll catch up."

Dez spouted out more words, but the solid wood of the wall separating them and the flush of the toilet blocked them out. Chills made Sasha's teeth chatter. Strange, since she was so hot her flesh felt like it was damn near boiling. She sat on the cold floor and leaned against the wall, listening to footsteps shuffle around her room. Once the front door clicked and Dez's boots thumped away, she drew her knees to her chest.

Nine months of this shit, with no cigarettes or liquor to boot. A punishment. Her body yearned for a woman's soft touch, mind always on supple curves, yet she'd given herself to Dez so freely. The penalty for betraying her true nature was the fracture of her soul, given to the life that grew inside her. It didn't seem fair for the baby. What could it have done to deserve a mother like her? If she couldn't figure it out in the next fifteen minutes, she'd peel her ass off the floor, slap on a brave face, and plunge into ignorance.

***

Vinny

When Sasha's door opened, Vinny jumped up from the bottom step. He stared up the narrow staircase, and Dez paused before thumping down the steps.

"What's up, brother?" Dez asked, standing close. A little too close. "You weren't at the party last night, and you haven't said one word to me or Sasha since we got engaged."

"Oh!" Vinny inched back, but Dez stayed inside his comfort zone. "No. It's not like that. I'm really happy for you guys, seriously."

"Yeah?" Dez glared, searching Vinny's eyes for a buried truth.

"Yeah, man." Vinny pushed his secrets down deeper and tossed a firm stare back. "I'm pissed about missing the party last night, but I had some club business to deal with."

Dez smirked, backing away. "Listen to you. Big-time VP, dealing with business and shit." He pointed to Sasha's room while continuing to back away. "She's up there, but I'd wait if I were you."

Vinny waited until Dez disappeared into the clubhouse and then dashed up the stairs.

"Sasha?" After two quick knocks, Vinny opened the door and barged inside. He braced for barbed insults to fill his ears, but Sasha's voice didn't flow. An empty room greeted him, made even more hollow without her presence. "Sasha?"

The bathroom door creaked open, and Sasha looked up at Vinny from the floor. Misery clouded her honey-tinged eyes. She'd never looked so pathetic, so cute.

"Morning sickness." Vinny sat beside Sasha, and she dropped her head onto his arm.

"You know a lot about this shit. How many chicks have you knocked up?"

Vinny chuckled. "None. I picked up a few books at the library yesterday. Did some reading."

"Say what?" Sasha leaned back, staring at Vinny as though they'd just met.

"Well, somebody needs to know what the fuck is going on and..." Vinny's fingers flinched. He wanted to reach for Sasha's hand. "Help you through this."

A bright smile lifted Sasha's pale cheeks, and she wrapped her arms around Vinny. Her head fell to his chest, its weight filling a void he'd been trying to seal for days.

"Is that why you're here?" she asked into his chest. "You sensed me puking and ran up to hold my hair."

"No," Vinny snickered, resting his chin atop Sasha's head. "I actually came up here to pump you for info."

"Ooh. That sounds dirty."

Sasha pinched Vinny's side, and he squirmed away.

"C'mon, I'm serious."

"Yeah, you are." Sasha sat up straight, turning to face Vinny. "What?"

"Do you know why I wasn't at your party last night?"

Her stare dropped, and she nodded. "Yeah."

"Does everyone know everything but me?"

"Maybe."

"That was rhetorical," Vinny grumbled, looking down at his jittery hands. "Who are we gearing up for? How many people should we expect? When? Are we gonna fucking die?"

"Jesus Christ," Sasha said, the rise of her voice echoing around the tiny bathroom. "Did you go see that *Terminator* movie? 'Cause I told you it was gonna screw with your head."

"No. It's not even out yet, and I am going to see it." Vinny looked at Sasha, captured by her deep eyes. "I got this feeling in my gut. It's like…every time I see you, I feel like it's the last time I'll ever see you."

"That's crazy." Sasha took Vinny's hand into both of hers, sliding so close their hips pressed together. "I'm not going anywhere, and if I do, I'll send you a postcard so you can join me."

"It's heavier than that, Sasha."

"It's really not."

Sasha tried to jerk her arm away, but Vinny held tight. His gaze screamed his desire to be delivered from ignorance. He could only hope she could hear the silent call.

"Vinny, you're putting me in a bad spot here."

It nearly killed his conscience, he knew what Ellen would do to her, but he held his tight grip and hard glare.

"Fine, asshole!" Sasha yelled, narrowing her eyes. "No one's coming after us. This is about my mom and some twisted foreplay she's got going on with her ex, Dante."

"Dante?" Vinny's arms went limp, and Sasha's

hand slipped from his grasp. "You mean Dante, president of Satan's Crew, Dante?"

"They've been mind-fucking each other for the last twenty years, among other things. He's not coming for us, just her. And not to kill."

"You sure about that?" Vinny asked, still trying to wipe the image of Ellen getting down with a biker from his mind. "Last night, Otis said shoot to kill, that everything would get sorted later."

"Of course Otis wants you to kill Dante. The man's his competition, but did my mother say anything like that at all?"

The look on Vinny's face must have done all the talking, because Sasha let out a huff.

"You're VP now. The only orders you take are from the president. If you kill her boy-toy without her consent…" Sasha covered her mouth, staring off for a second. "It would be bad. Worse than the cellar bad."

"I can't believe Otis would set me up like that."

"I don't think he meant to. He either doesn't know about my mom and Dante, or he just thought she'd let you slide since you're her favorite."

Vinny sneered, and Sasha's palm flew up.

"Please," she said in a long, drawn-out groan. "You're so her favorite, but I don't think she'd let even you slide on this. Oh, great. Look at your face, man." Sasha climbed off the floor, pulling on her pants and swapping out the long t-shirt for a tight tank top. "You're never gonna be able to keep your cool through a whole meeting."

"The fuck I can't. And seeing your tits just now really helped."

Sasha gasped, and Vinny grinned. She hammered his arm with her fist.

"Come on, perv. Let's get this shit over with. I wanna get on the road by noon."

Vinny took a moment to admire the sway of Sasha's hips before pushing himself off the bathroom floor. He stepped behind Sasha, and she spun, jabbing her finger into his chest. "Don't you tell anyone about what I told you."

"Ouch. I won't, jeez."

"I'm not kidding, asshole."

Sasha's bony finger poked Vinny again, right between the ribs, and he pushed her arm away. "Okay. I won't." Vinny opened Sasha's front door and held out his hand, presenting a rainy gray morning. "After you."

He liked to let her go first. It made him feel like a gentleman, and he got to watch her ass shake as she strutted on her merry way.

***

Sasha

Sasha walked into the clubhouse, and Candy looked up at her from the couch. A nervous look crossed Candy's face before she buried her nose in a magazine.

"Candy?" Sasha said, straining to keep from smiling at Candy's guilty expression.

"I'm so sorry, Sasha. I'm never gonna drink again; I say the stupidest shit when I drink."

Sasha plopped on the couch beside Candy,

hoping it would quiet the girl's loud mouth. "Shit, Candy, we talked about this."

"I know, I know. Your name doesn't pass my lips," Candy said in a near whisper. "Did I ruin everything?"

"No." Sasha stood up, flashing a smile. "And let's keep it that way."

Candy winked, and a chill ran down Sasha's spine. She backed away before her feet could carry her forward.

"I got a meeting."

With just half a turn, Sasha left Candy's red lips to glimpse her mother's frown.

"Last one at the table...again," Ellen said, leaning back in her seat.

Sasha bit her tongue and closed the door, dropping into her chair. At this point, Vinny would nudge her arm and attempt a snide comment, except the space beside her sat bare while the two men she loved hovered at her mother's side.

"Today, we need to vote on restocking." Ellen slid an ashtray to the center of the table, a circle of fresh joints peeking from its top. "After Sasha takes her run, the warehouse will be spent. Kev, you know about the undercover fed we took care of yesterday, right?"

"Yeah. Otis filled me in."

"Good." Ellen leaned onto the table, glancing at the crew members seated around it. "I talked to the sheriff this morning, and he doesn't think they have anything on us. They can't even prove their agent was ever here. That leaves us with a vote. We can pick up our supply tomorrow like scheduled, or I can push it back a few weeks."

Otis grabbed a joint from the ashtray and sparked it up. "If we hold the pickup, we'll have to delay our drop-offs. We could lose clients."

"We could lose a lot more than that," Dez muttered, shifting in his chair.

"Even if the feds are watching," Otis said from behind a cloud of smoke, "they couldn't know our pickup times and location. Plus, the warehouse isn't on our property or connected to any of us."

Dez crashed his elbows on the table, leaning forward. "You're not the one taking a risk on an eight-hour drive with kilos of drugs. Sasha is."

"All right," Ellen said, breaking the dick-wagging contest. "That's why we're gonna vote."

"Right now," Kev whined. "Shit, man."

"I have a run." Sasha looked at the dwindling pile of joints. In fact, she'd been staring at them this entire meeting. "There's no other time." That being said, she snatched a joint from the ashtray and lit her zippo.

"All in favor of business as usual?" Ellen asked.

Sasha's hand went up. Why wouldn't it? She brought the heat down on the club. The risk should be hers to take.

Arms raised on both sides of Vinny, and he scooted his chair back, its legs scraping the floor.

Kev looked between Sasha, Otis, and Ellen, all with their hands high, then slowly raised his arm.

"These votes are bullshit," Dez said, jumping to his feet. His chair crashed to the ground, and he stormed out the door.

"I guess the meeting's adjourned," Ellen

327

snickered, rising from her seat. "Careful on your run, Sasha."

Otis slid a set of keys across the glossy table, right into Sasha's palm. She looked at Vinny, who glared at the side of Otis's face.

"Vinny," Sasha called out, drawing Vinny's and everyone's attention. "Help me gas up the truck?"

"Yeah, sure," Vinny muttered, shooting Otis another quick glare.

Sasha waited until Vinny left the room before following him outside.

Chapter Thirty-Three

Dez

Dez slouched against the wide trunk of an oak tree, staring at the clubhouse. Smoke wafted from the cigarette in his mouth, clouding his view in a gray haze. This place was going down; he could feel it. If he had half a brain, he'd grab Sasha, throw her ass in his truck, and hit the road. Great plan, in theory. He'd get maybe five miles from the compound before Sasha beat the shit out of him and stole his ride. The club meant everything to her, much more than he did, maybe more than her own child.

Dez might not be able to take the club out of the girl, but he could change the club to save the girl. All he had to do was persuade Ellen. They could lay low, find other means of income. The porn industry was a fountain of wealth. The club could dip into that for a while. Sasha would love it, and maybe he could score a little three-way action.

A grin popped onto his lips at the thought of

him, Sasha, and a hot blonde in a big bed. He flicked his cigarette to the gravel. Ellen wasn't the only one who could use their mistake as leverage. With a drop of finesse and a ton of blackmail, he might just get his way.

After a hit from his flask, liquid courage hardened his veins and lifted his chin. He marched back up the porch steps, thanked God Otis was nowhere in sight, and strolled into the backroom.

***

Sasha

Sasha walked behind the garage, toward the large lot that housed four big rigs.

"Which truck are you taking?" Vinny asked, smoothing back his rain-soaked hair.

"The blue one."

"I gassed that one up yesterday."

"I know," Sasha said, continuing toward the row of semi-trucks.

Gravel crunched as Vinny stopped in the middle of the lot, but Sasha kept walking. Once in the cover of two long trailers, she turned and gestured for him to follow.

"Jeez, you're dense," she said when he finally reached her side.

"Sorry if I can't read minds like you."

Sasha rolled her eyes, which wasn't easy with the mist beading on her eyelashes. "I think you should come with me on this run."

"Why? I thought you said everything was cool."

"Everything is cool, except you. You're in there practically stabbing Otis with your glares. I should've known you'd spaz out."

"Hey, fuck you, man," Vinny yelled. It was a real yell, one of anger, not the usual shouts he flung in jest. "You're the only one spazzing out right now. I know what I'm doing, and I don't need a babysitter."

Sasha leaned back, eyes wide as she watched Vinny stomp up the hill and toward the big house.

"Damn," she drawled, opening the truck's door.

During Sasha's climb inside the cab, her ring clinked on the steering wheel. Cool metal pressed against her skin, triggering the worst of thoughts. Her days of hopping in a semi and taking off were over. The rules of legitimate engagement required notice before one could split.

Water splashed under Sasha's boots as she jumped back to the ground. While brushing clumps of wet hair from her face, she hurried back to the clubhouse. Her steps slowed once she crossed the threshold and entered a deserted bar. Not even one of those creepy lookalike prospects was lurking around.

Sasha inched farther inside, and her mother's voice rose from within the backroom. A little closer and words filtered through wood, loud and clear.

"You think Sasha will care about that, Desmond, after I tell her how your tongue felt when it rubbed up and down my—"

Sasha pushed the door to the backroom open, flinching when it slammed against the wall. So many wonderfully cruel slurs swarmed inside her mind. She needed to let them loose, but her throat sealed tight, and she could only stare at two pitiful expressions.

Dez stepped toward Sasha, and she stumbled back.

"Sasha."

His voice sent a spike through her heart. She wanted to return the favor, but lucky for him, she didn't have a blade handy. When her mother moved beside Dez, a stream of vulgar images flashed into her mind. She closed her eyes, but it didn't help. The dirty visions grew brighter in the darkness. Her mother wrapped her hand around Sasha's arm, and she jerked away, storming out the door.

***

Otis

Otis parked his truck out front of the clubhouse, and Sasha practically ran down the porch steps. When Ellen and Dez gave chase, he groaned.

"What do you think this is all about?" Candy asked, dropping a half-eaten burger into a paper bag.

"Go jump in Sasha's truck, the blue one. Try and calm her down."

"What's wrong with her?"

"I don't know," Otis said, even though he had a good idea, "but I'm sure you'll find out. You're good at that kinda shit."

"Okay." Candy planted a kiss on Otis's cheek and leapt out of the pickup, sneaking behind the garage.

***

Sasha

Sasha had her key in hand before the truck's cab graced her view. The pound of her temples did little to drown out the buzz of voices that chased her or the thoughts of jamming the rig's key in her mother's neck.

"Just wait!" Ellen shouted, louder than Dez's half-assed excuses of drunken mistakes.

Ellen tugged at Sasha's jacket, but Sasha yanked herself away without missing a single one of her rushed steps.

"This isn't what it sounds like," Ellen said, scurrying to keep up with Sasha's pace.

The bullshit had piled so deep that Sasha had to stop wading through it. She stopped in a skid of gravel, bouncing her glare between her mother and Dez. "You guys fucked, right? While I was out on the road?"

When both their eyes dropped, a bit of vomit crept up the back of Sasha's throat.

"You're disgusting," Sasha said, ducking to meet her mother's gaze. "Did you even want him, or did you just want to take something from me?"

No answer, no surprise. Her mother only spoke in insults and comebacks, but they wouldn't help here. Nothing in the whole wide world would help here.

"I'll take this run, 'cause I fix my fuckups. But

333

when I get back, I'm packing my shit and I'm gone."

"No," Ellen yelled, "you're not."

Her mother had the balls to grab onto her arm, and she shoved the bitch, hard. Of course, Dez caught his lover before she could land on her ass, spoiling any chance of satisfaction.

"I'll do whatever I goddamn please," Sasha said, unable to stop the quake of her every limb brought on by revulsion. "You two can go fuck yourselves or each other. I don't give a shit."

Dez lunged toward Sasha, and she rocked her fist against his chin.

"Brass knuckles is next," she said, reaching for the truck's door.

"I'm sorry, Sasha." Dez backed away, his hands up and eyes full of shame. "I'm just…sorry."

"Yeah. You are." Sasha climbed into the cab, locked the door, and started the engine. A second to slow her mind would be nice. So would peace on earth, an end to starvation, and a mother who didn't bone her boyfriend, but nice didn't belong to people like her.

Sasha glanced across the cab, yelping as Candy waved from the passenger seat.

"Hey," Candy said, like she was at the bar and not skulking inside Sasha's truck. "What's going on out there?"

"Get out," Sasha yelled, grinding the shifter into first.

Candy recoiled, grabbed the handle of her door, then sank into her seat. "No."

"I might not come back," Sasha said, easing off

the clutch.

"Whatever."

"Fine." Sasha drove from the lot, past the clubhouse, and out the front gate without a single glance back.

"What happened?" Candy asked, slinking as far away as possible.

"Didn't you hear?"

"No. I just got here and saw—"

"Dez fucked my mother." Tears blurred the road in front of Sasha, but she blinked them back.

"Eww," Candy cried out. "I don't think so."

"Ahh no, really. They did."

"Oh." Candy wiggled in her seat, glancing at Sasha. "Your mother probably raped him at gunpoint."

Sasha snickered, wiping a stray tear from her cheek. She didn't think pain like this existed, never imagined an ache that could slice her chest so deep, squeeze her heart and burn the air from her lungs.

"She takes everything from me." Sasha looked across the wide cab at one of the things her mother had stripped from her life. "Candy, will you—"

Tires squealed, the steering wheel shook, and the rig slid sideways. Sasha gripped the steering wheel with both hands, flooring the brake. Her palms slipped from sweat and vibration, but she held tight to the steering wheel, veering the truck's front end away from the twenty-foot drop off just beyond the road's edge. The trailer started to jackknife, jolting the cab before the brakes locked up. In a scream of rubber peeling onto road, the truck lurched to a stop.

"Oh my God," Candy yelled, still hugging her armrest. "What happened?"

"I don't know." Sasha looked into her side mirror, a long white trailer filling her view. She glanced at the passenger side, and the door flew open. A shotgun's barrel filled Sasha's gaze then white light. Reflex snapped her eyes to a close, and warm chunks pelted her face. The blast of a shotgun echoed off the hills, ringing in Sasha's ears, but she still heard the most sickening thud.

Her entire body shook, jarring her eyes open. The body heaped beside her didn't look like Candy, not with half its head blown off. If it wasn't for those incomparable legs, which twitched against the truck's shifter, Sasha would have never known her first love lay dead on the floor. She reached out, and a pink clump oozed from shards of skull, slapping onto the rubber mat. A shriek trickled out her mouth. Red splatters of blood surrounded her, covering her arms, clothes.

Sasha shrank back, and her door opened. A large hand latched onto her jacket and yanked. She fumbled for the door, but solid ground came fast and hard. Rocks dug into Sasha's side, her head bouncing off the pavement. She rolled onto her back, peering up as the butt of a gun crashed down.

Chapter Thirty-Four

Dez

Dez stood in the middle of the lot, jiggling his arm, but his fist wouldn't break free. "Why do you have to be such a cunt?" Although he looked at Ellen, the statement was meant for himself.

"This is your fault," Ellen shouted. She stormed up to his face then backed off. Smart woman. She must have figured out his tell because he was getting ready to swing.

Ellen lifted her finger but didn't dare step close enough to wag it in Dez's face. "If you didn't run in my office, flashin' your shit—"

"Do you even hear yourself?" Dez rushed forward, his hands hovering over Ellen's neck. "Nobody wants your position, this club. I just wanted to keep Sasha safe, with me."

His rage surged with such fury that when he heard a high-pitch screech, he thought he'd actually blown a gasket. Then a gunshot wafted up the mountain. Ellen's expression changed from one of anger to terror, and Dez's heart skipped a beat.

"Sasha," Ellen said, and Dez took off running.

By the time he reached the front gate, his legs burned. He slowed to a jog when Vinny's pickup sped down the compound, fishtailed out the front gate, and skid to a stop beside him.

"Get in," Otis yelled from the passenger side, pointing to the back.

Dez jumped into the bed of the truck, holding tight as Vinny floored the gas. Part of him didn't want to see what lay around the bend. It wasn't real if he didn't see it. This way, he could chalk it up to a silly accident. Sasha hit a deer and had to put the poor creature out of its misery. It wasn't even her, just some assholes hunting nearby. Dez held hope, but the sinking feeling in the pit of his stomach deepened with every passing second. Then he saw it. The backend of a tractor-trailer spread sideways across the narrow road.

Vinny locked up the brakes, and Dez leapt from the back of the pickup. His feet worked double-time to keep his face from eating pavement, crunching asphalt in search of grip. One glimpse. He just needed one glimpse of Sasha, but the wide trailer butting up to the steep mountain hid the cab from view.

With only one route open, Dez ran to the passenger side. A blood-streaked leg hung out the open door. Crimson droplets seeped to a puddle on the ground, only a taste of the red splatters that painted the inside of the semi.

Otis crept toward the body hanging half out the door, slipping on the pools of blood that painted the road. "Candy," he choked, grabbing her limp hand.

A pain-filled cry erupted from Otis's mouth, breaking Dez from a red-tinged stupor. He tore his stare from a blown open skull, backing away from the pink clumps that slopped to the ground.

"Where's Sasha?" Vinny asked, rising on his toes to peer inside the truck.

Dez scanned the empty road ahead while hurrying around the front of the rig. That tiny piece of hope within him roared into full-fledged expectation. It all shattered when he stepped beside an empty driver's seat. A dream, where Sasha sat against the mountainside and waited for his embrace, gone.

"Fuck," Dez yelled into the gray sky above.

"She's probably okay," Vinny said, scanning the truck's step then a small red puddle at his feet. "There's not enough blood here for her to be…We'll get her back."

"Get her back!" Dez grabbed onto Vinny's jacket. He didn't want to but couldn't stop himself. "From where, who?"

Vinny wrenched himself from Dez's grasp, marching back to the passenger side. "Otis?"

Otis didn't move. His eyes hung low as he caressed the back of Candy's hand, the only place that wasn't stained in blood.

"I didn't even know her real name," Otis said in a near whisper.

"Janice." Vinny placed his hand on Otis's shoulder. "Janice Holden."

An engine revved, and Dez pulled his gun from its holster, stepping in front of Vinny.

"It's Ellen's Chevelle," Otis said, dropping Candy's hand and walking away.

Ellen ran around the back of the trailer and slid to a stop. "Oh my God. Is she…?"

"That's Candy's blood," Vinny said, rushing to Ellen's side. "Sasha's not here."

Dez teetered on the verge of madness. The world should be in flames. People should be screaming and gagging on their own entrails until Sasha returned to his arms. A frenzy rushed in, forcing out the shreds of rational thought. Dez pushed past Otis and seized Ellen by the wrist, twisting. "Where is she? Who took her?"

"Back off, man," Vinny yelled, shoving Dez away and stepping between them.

"All the front tires are flat," Dez shouted, pointing to the blood-spattered Mack truck behind him. "Someone laid down a spike strip, blew Candy's fucking head off just to get to Sasha. Who?"

Ellen staggered back. Her hip bumped Otis, and he didn't budge, but she kept walking backward. "Come on. I know where Sasha is."

***

Sasha

Light filtered in, bringing with it a throb that pounded thoughts into sharp flashes of jumbled shapes. Sasha squeezed her eyes closed. She longed to return to the dark, where crushing pain didn't plague her head and warm streaks weren't running down her neck.

"Hey, little girl," a deep voice echoed over the pound of her head.

A slap rocked Sasha's face to the side, spreading razor-tipped prickles beneath her skin. She opened her eyes, and a violent glare blurred into focus. For a second, she thought a mirror sat in front of her. Then she glimpsed a smile, cruel, rough, far from those in her arsenal of expressions.

"Dante," Sasha said with a groan.

Dante stood so close, close enough to strangle, but Sasha's arms wouldn't move. Her wrists chaffed, burned. She sat up straight, jolting forward. Ropes held her to a metal chair, which refused to move from the concrete ground. A belt of laughter flowed over her growl. Strands of twine, the only thing keeping her from crushing Dante's windpipe, and they wouldn't hold for long.

"I've waited a long time for this," Dante said, wiping a smudge of blood from Sasha's cheek.

Sasha turned her head away, slanting back. "What? To tie me to a chair?"

"To look into your eyes."

Her stare veered to Dante, warping to match the vicious thoughts in her mind. "Do you see death?"

Dante took a step back, dropping his cocky leer. "Yeah, I do. It reminds me of your mother, the way I knew her. Except for the brown eyes and that wavy black hair of yours. If I remember correctly, your dad was a blond with bright blue eyes. Just like Ellen."

A subtle hint, which Sasha chose to ignore. Instead, she worked at the scratchy rope pinching her skin.

"Not very polite, is she?" A voice rang out from behind her.

She froze, peeking over her shoulder. The typical biker douchebag, with his cheap leather jacket and scuzzy hair, only held her glare for a second. It was the walls, a wide bay door, and hanging light fixtures that drew her interest.

"We're in my warehouse," Sasha said, letting loose a tiny chuckle. "You dumb motherfuckers. What's wrong, did you have a little fire at your place?"

The back of a hand struck Sasha's face, loosening the ropes just a tad.

"So ridged," the shitsack beside Sasha sneered.

Another man, just as ugly, crept up on her other side. "It's 'cause this bitch never had a real man, just faggot truckers." The guy ran his hand across Sasha's chest, slopping his tongue in her ear. She'd have to boil her skin after she stripped the flesh from these vile wastes of space.

Both men hovered over Sasha, groping and tugging at her shirt as Dante looked away. If rage didn't burn so hot, she'd feel sick right now.

"You wanna see what real men can do, honey?" the asshole squeezing her breast said.

Sasha's teeth damn near chipped under the pressure of her clenched jaw. She curved her stare to Dante, who looked as grossed out as she felt.

"Stop!" Dante stomped forward, and the creeps scuttled away from Sasha.

"What the fuck, Dante? She wants it, I can tell."

"That's my fucking kid, asshole," Dante yelled.

Sasha looked up, glaring at Dante. She'd been waiting for that, hoping it wouldn't be spoken out loud but still waiting. He didn't dare cast a glance her way.

"Sorry, boss. I didn't know."

"You're not my father," Sasha said in a near growl. "Charles Ashby was my father, you sick fuck."

"See, little girl, that's why I had to strap you down." Dante circled behind Sasha, resting his hands on her shoulders. "You're a wild pony, and I've been kicked enough."

"Whatever game you're playing, you won't win. My mother would hit this place with a rocket launcher with me inside just to get you." Sasha glanced over her shoulder, catching the fear that decorated Dante's face. "Tell you what," she said, tugging at the ropes on her wrists. "If you let me go, I won't stab you in the face. No promises for your buddies."

Dante's chuckle iced Sasha's veins. Now she'd make chop meat of all their ugly mugs.

"It's my turn for custody, little girl. The clubhouse, that property, all them connections. They belong to you, and you belong to me now." Dante slid his hand down Sasha's arms, bringing his lips to her cheek. "Didn't you know saint Ashby left it to you? It was the only reason we let him believe you were his."

The feel of Dante's hand on her skin, though light, pressed her body into the chair. She wiggled out from under Dante's grip. A mistake, because he moved right in front of her to stare into her eyes.

343

"I would've came for you sooner, right after I killed Charlie, but Ellen held guardianship over you. Now that you're of age—"

Sasha drove the tip of her boot into Dante's shin, grinning as he cried out. "I won't do shit for you."

"You already are, little girl." Dante hopped back, rubbing his leg. "You're my bait. When Ellen storms up this mountain with her crew, the men I got hidden in the woods are gonna pick 'em off, one by one."

Sasha flung her body from side to side, failing to free herself from the tight ropes that bound her to a metal chair. "The second I get loose, you're all dead."

A fist cracked Sasha's cheek, launching her into the armrest of the chair and sliding the ropes down her wrist. One, maybe two more hits and she'd be free. Free to grab the knife inside her boot. Free to slash and carve until sweet, sticky blood coated every stitch of her flesh.

Sasha rolled her head to the man who just cracked her jaw and smiled, even though it felt like chewing on glass.

"You hit like a little bitch," she sneered, spitting a wad of blood to the floor at his feet.

The large man, and his giant fist, turned to Dante. Sasha looked at the man who claimed to be her father, standing by to watch her get beat. The scenario fit, for her family anyway.

"Not the face," Dante said, inching farther away.

Sasha's heart jumped into her throat. Out of nowhere, for no sane reason, she sensed the baby inside her. Before she could yell out, knuckles flew toward her stomach. She hunched down, taking the blow to her chest.

In a blustery rush of fire, the wind left Sasha's lungs. She gasped for air, but only drops made it past the blaze behind her ribcage. A haze took her stare down, and she saw sneakers with neon green trim. Some real man this asshole was, wearing sneakers not even a punk would be caught dead in. Sasha slammed the heel of her combat boot on top the guy's foot, twisting.

"Ah!" He hopped back, glaring, and Sasha blew a kiss.

His face turned beet-red. The jab at his ridiculous male pride struck harder than all the other damage Sasha had inflicted while tied to a metal chair.

Just as Sasha hoped, a fist barreled her way. Instead of bracing, she lifted her chin to gain full momentum.

A brick wall hammered Sasha into darkness. It had to be a brick wall, since punches don't come that solid. Somewhere under the buzz that vibrated her brain, voices shouted. There should be gravel digging into her skin. Chewy should be holding Vinny back as he screamed her name. Where was Vinny?

"No, Dez, don't," Sasha slurred. Her fingers twitched. She rolled her head to the side, forcing the world's spin to slow. The club wasn't standing over her, delivering a beat down at her mother's whim. She wasn't a child, laying in the dirt on *her* own property. It would've been nice, though. A trip back in time and a beating was worth a glimpse of Candy as a blonde. Splatters of brains and blood flashed into Sasha's mind. Candy. Her sweet Candy, a crumpled body with half a skull.

Tears stung the cuts under Sasha's eye, and she lifted her arm, paused, and sat up straight. She'd been freed. Sadness turned to relief, then distorted into a wrath that held such fury it shook her core. She blinked through a red-tinged fog to glare at Dante. The men argued across the room, like children, too busy insulting each other to notice her wandering hands.

Sasha hiked up the leg of her pants. Thick blood drooled from her swollen lip, a throb battered her brain, but nothing would keep her grasp from the switchblade in her boot. Metal grazed her fingertips, and Dante's neck became so appealing.

Chapter Thirty-Five

Dez

Dez squirmed, barely able to move in the cramped backseat of Ellen's Chevelle. Leather crinkled as he turned to look out the back window. He couldn't see Sasha's truck or the gate to the compound, just curves and cliffs lined by leafless trees. His gaze drifted to Vinny, who was stretched out in the seat beside him while loading a shotgun. The kid's hands were more steady than his own. He needed to get his shit straight.

"We can't just leave the truck in the middle of the road like that," Otis said, as if just realizing they had driven away from a blood-covered semi loaded with pounds of weed and bearing their club's name.

"Kev and the prospects are on it," Ellen said, turning onto a dirt road. "Load up. We're almost there."

"Where?" Dez asked, leaning toward the front seat. "There's a gun pointed at your back, Ellen." He wasn't lying and wasn't afraid to shoot. His

347

thumb slid over the safety, clicking it off. "The shit that rolls out of your mouth next better have one hell of a truthful tone."

"Knock it off, Dez." Vinny snapped the barrel of his gun closed, raising an eyebrow.

"Really," Dez said, holstering his weapon.

Vinny shrugged, laying the gun across his lap. "I didn't aim it at ya."

"We're going to the warehouse," Ellen said. "It's the last place I'd look so it has to be where he took Sasha."

"Who?"

"Dante," Vinny blurted before pressing his lips tight.

"You know what?" Ellen sat tall, moving her hand from the shifter to the butt of her holstered gun. "Yeah, I am fucking Dante. And I was trying to ease him into the club."

"Are you insane?" Dez shouted. "That motherfucker took your daughter."

"He's just trying to get my attention."

"He killed Candy," Vinny said, a tremble raising his voice. "If Sasha hasn't gutted him by now, I will."

Dez could hug his brother. Until now, he'd been convinced Vinny was Ellen's bitch-boy.

"Stop the car," Otis said. "It's too loud. We should go in on foot, catch 'em by surprise."

Ellen pulled to the side of the dirt road and shut off the engine. "We can vote on my dismissal when we get back, but you guys need to know…" Her gaze fell to her lap, and she shrank down. "There are two men with rifles in the bushes at the base of the trail and another two by the bay door."

"Fucking bitch," Dez said in a roar, holding back his fully cocked fist.

"This was a trap for us," Vinny muttered.

"How long have you known about this?" Otis asked, slanting toward his door.

"Don't play innocent, man," Dez snorted.

"Otis, please." Ellen reached for Otis, and he slapped her hand away. "Dante called right before the meeting. I was gonna tell you, so we could stop him before he nabbed Sasha, but fucking Dez distracted me with his bullshit."

"No!" Vinny bobbed in his seat, like a teakettle ready to burst. "This is your doing. We're nothing to you, just objects to use in your sick games." He pushed on Otis's seat, dropping his head. "Let me the fuck out."

Dez slid over when Vinny got out, gaining a better view of Ellen's face. Blank, cold, full of contempt. This new light tainted her beauty in a shadow of ugliness, more so than ever before. He could strangle the life from her in minutes. It might take even less time and the world would thank him for it, but not Sasha. Ellen remained an eternal Goddess in Sasha's eyes, at least for now.

"Sasha's gonna see you for what you really are after this. I'll make sure of it." Dez smirked, grabbed a shotgun from the floor, and climbed from the car.

***

Kev

Kev gripped the wheel as the airbrakes let out a whoosh. Without a trailer, the semi hopped like a frog on a hotplate. Tires chirped as the rig lurched to a stop, just beside Vinny's abandoned pickup.

"Oh shit," Cash said from the seat beside Kev. "She jackknifed?"

"Sasha's the best driver I know," Kev said, opening his door. "Something must've happened."

"What do we do?" Cory asked, popping his head up from the back cab.

"Follow me." Kev jumped to the pavement, glancing around. "And keep your eyes peeled."

"For what?" Cash climbed from the truck, creeping forward.

"I don't know," Kev said in a huff, waving his arm toward the ghostly trailer. "Anything."

"There's blood," Cory yelled, hurrying to the passenger side.

"Wait!" Kev pulled his gun, jogging after the moron who would run into unknown danger.

"Oh, goddamn," Cory sputtered. "There's a dead girl in here."

Kev stepped over a river of blood, staring into the cab of the semi. "Candy?" If he hadn't spent years gawking at that girl's body, he'd have never known it was her with no face left.

"These tires are flat," Cash said, kicking the front tire.

"It was a hijacking." Kev backed away, checking the road up and down the mountain.

"The product?"

"No," Kev said. "They didn't have enough time to boost the product. I think they were gunnin' for Sasha."

"What should we do with all this?" Cory lifted his arms to the crooked tractor-trailer, which oozed a bloodbath onto the road it blocked.

"Push her leg inside and shut the door," Kev said, looking over the guardrail at the long drop to a rocky valley. "I'll straighten the rig out so you can unhook the trailer. Then we'll roll the cab off this cliff."

"What?"

"Yeah. There was a horrible accident here," Kev said, his stare locked on the treetops far below the road's edge. "The truck slid off the road. People died. We'll know exactly how many when Ellen and them get back."

"Umm, Kev, man." Cash's big hand landed on Kev's shoulder, rocking his body. "I'm sor—"

"Let's make this quick." Kev turned back to face the truck, cringing as pink chunks rained down from the body Cory pushed inside it. "We still gotta hook the trailer up to the other semi, get it and Vinny's pickup back on the compound."

Kev didn't wait for a reply. Any minute, some asshole could drive up the road and then he'd have to kill them. It'd be nice to get through this without a pile of vehicles at the bottom of the mountain. Not likely but nice.

***

Sasha

Sasha yanked the knife from her boot and wrapped her arms around the back of the chair. The talking stopped, and all eyes steered to her. Dante stayed far from reach, behind his lackey, but the one who liked to hurl his fists inched closer. Her thumb rubbed the button of the switchblade as she glared up at the man.

"What the fuck are you staring at, bitch?"

"Just taking a good look before you're mush." Sasha grinned, couldn't help it. The guy came to her like a moth to the flame.

"This is what's gonna happen," the guy said, standing beside Sasha. "I'm gonna stick my dick in every hole of your body." He grabbed Sasha by the hair, pulling her head back while rubbing his crotch. "And my friend over there is gonna make your daddy watch."

Sasha looked across the room, and Dante shrugged, nodding at the gun at his head. The blade flipped out of the handle in Sasha's palm, almost by itself, and she sprung to her feet. A fight broke out across the room, but she didn't care if Dante lived or died. She wanted to stick something of hers in the fucker who staggered in front of her.

It happened in flashes. The tip of a blade ripping open the flesh on a man's cheek. Sasha screamed she jammed her knife in the guy's neck and pulled. Her knees crashed to the ground when she slipped on blood. A body thrashed between her straddled legs, slower as its face disappeared beneath a scatter of deep gashes.

Sasha's arm burned. Blood flew up in spurts, drenching her neck, but she couldn't stop jabbing her knife in and out of mangled flesh. A gunshot rang out. The blast bounced around the wide open room, yet Sasha's arm wouldn't stop slicing, tearing, ripping. It was an improvement, really, of the ugly face that used to be there.

A shadow fell over Sasha. She brought her blade down, glaring up to see which asshole had survived the gunshot. Dante walked away from his now dead lackey and headed toward Sasha, lowering the gun that had found its way to his hand.

Sasha's legs wobbled, and the knife in her grasp shook, but she rose, standing tall.

"Sorry, little girl," Dante said, a hint of remorse breaking his cruel glare. "I'll catch you next time."

Dante smirked, which called upon the wildest of hellfires to scorch Sasha's insides. After a dip of his head, he took off running for the back door. Sasha didn't have the energy to chase Dante, so she chucked the knife in her hand. The force of the throw took her down. Cool concrete stung her palms as she hit the floor. She peered up, looking across the warehouse just in time to see her knife sink deep into Dante's leg.

Dante pulled the knife from his calf, tossing it across the room before he limped out the steel door. Sasha fell to her side, taking a deep breath. The soft pound in her temples filled her ears and lulled her eyes to a close. If only death would come, end the agony of a dislocated shoulder, silence the torment of knowing too much.

A sharp ache cut through her gut, and she

gripped her stomach. Another life depended on her now. She didn't have the luxury of lying on a floor and dying. Mothers didn't do that. Her mother would never do that.

Sasha rolled to her knees, and a cry burst from her sore chest, flying past her bloody lips. The walls teetered and the ground swayed, but she climbed to her feet. This warehouse had always been a reservoir of good memories. Chewy's laughter, her father's hugs, a time when smiles flowed. Those good times were gone, buried under crimson splatters. A face full of slashed skin and Dante's leer, that's what she'd see now when stepping foot in this place. Nothing a gallon of gas and a match couldn't fix.

Sasha staggered toward the front bay door, stopping to scoop a handgun off the floor. For destroying the last happy place she had left, Dante would pay. Her mother would pay. The assholes waiting outside her warehouse to shoot her family would pay. She loaded a round into the gun's chamber, slumping beside the metal bay door.

***

Vinny

Vinny ran through the woods, away from Dez's words and Ellen's sorry face. His right hand tightened around the grip of his shotgun, and he pulled a long serrated knife from his belt with his left hand. The two men at the base of the trail would bear the brunt of his rage. The other two by the door, they could have his agony.

A ray of the setting sun gleamed off metal, and Vinny ducked low. Through dense trees, the edge of a tall steel building shined. It had to be the warehouse. Now to find the biker fuckwads creeping around it. Vinny looked around, unable to see the trail he started on beyond clusters of bushes. Any one of those nests of briars could be hiding two men, ready to shoot him at the command of the woman he thought of as a mother. The second mother to steal his trust and trample his heart.

Branches rustled at his left, followed by a man's cough. Bingo. One sloppy dead douchebag coming up. Vinny's steps floated, barely touching the leaf-strewn ground. On the tips of his toes, with a gun in one hand and a blade in the other, he crept around the patch of shrubbery. His heart pumped as he stared down at a man's back. He raised the knife, ready to plunge down, when a gun cocked from across the trail.

Any second, bullets would fly at him. Luckily, there was a human shield at his feet. Vinny dropped the knife, yanking the jerk who was crouching in the dirt up and in front of him. Gunfire rang out, crackling the air.

Vinny shrank down, and shots battered the body that pressed against his chest, driving him back a few steps. The blasts stopped but their echo lingered in his ears. He had ten seconds, at best, before the asshole across the trail reloaded, but he only needed two.

In one swift motion, Vinny released the gagging man in his grasp and swung the shotgun up. His finger cupped the trigger, squeezing. Both slugs fired from his double barrels, rocking him on his heels. Through wisps of gunpowder, he glimpsed boots flop against the dirt. A garble and slurs of words streamed from the man at Vinny's feet. He bent beside the guy, who spewed blood from the many new holes in his quivering body, and picked up his knife from off the ground.

"Thanks, buddy," Vinny said, dragging his blade along the man's neck.

Sticks cracked, and Vinny tossed his empty gun aside, grabbing the rifle from the dead man's hand. He lifted the gun, peering down its scope, and Dez dropped low.

"What the fuck, man?" Dez said through pants. "You got a death wish?"

Vinny turned back toward the warehouse, slinking to the edge of the trail.

"Stop," Dez called out, louder than he should have.

Otis slid to a crouch beside Vinny, grabbing his arm. "There's still—"

"Two at the door. I know." Vinny pulled himself from Otis's clutch, kneeling down to take aim up the path. "I'm baitin' 'em," he whispered. "They'll pop out in—"

A face filled Vinny's scope, and he pulled the trigger. "A second." While lowering the gun to cock the bolt-action, he watched a man drop to the ground outside the warehouse. As he brought the rifle back to his shoulder, the last man took off for the tree line behind the warehouse.

Vinny shot, the action rumbling Vinny's bones,

and the target fell from his sights. He looked over the gun, squinting. In the last of the day's light, he scanned the four bodies on the ground.

"Damn kid," Otis said, glancing around the trees and up the trail. "Where'd that come from?"

Vinny looked at Dez then Ellen, who hung far behind. He loaded another round, jumping to his feet. "Sasha. She's a good teacher."

Dez walked onto the path, slowly creeping toward the warehouse. A clank of metal rang out, and he froze. "The bay door's opening."

Vinny raised the rifle and gazed into the scope. It was everything he wanted to see and what he feared at the same time. "Fuck," he said. The gun slipped from his hands, and he took off in a sprint.

***

Sasha

The gunfire ended, but Sasha didn't move. Her fingers wrapped around the chain of the bay door, yet she couldn't pull. The trap had sprung, and knowing Vinny, he'd run headfirst into it. They could all be dead, even her mother, who she wanted to punish not bury. If that were the case, and everything she cared about was bleeding out on the ground, she had a lot of killing to do.

Sasha yanked the bay door's chain, sending the thick metal up into the ceiling. Two bodies lay face down in the gravel. Their boots, jeans, even the flames on their leather jackets matched, but those weren't her people. She'd be able to feel it if they were.

Her legs fought every step her brain commanded, and her arm couldn't lift the gun in her hand. She dropped to one knee, spitting a mouthful of blood to the dirt.

"Get the fuck up, bitch," she muttered, pushing herself off the ground. Her shoulder grinded, eclipsing the cry that burst from her chest, and she sank back down to her knees.

"Sasha!"

"Vinny?" Sasha blinked back a haze. She'd heard Vinny's voice. That, or her battered mind was playing cruel tricks on her. Before she could look up from the swaying ground, strong arms wrapped around her body. Vinny's smell, musky like the forest after a rainstorm, filled her lungs before his face graced her view. He squeezed tight, and she winced. His embrace hurt like a motherfucker, but she'd take the pain just to have the strength of his touch any day.

"Fuck, Sasha," Vinny said, his voice quaking. "You couldn't have waited ten more minutes? I was coming to rescue you, Clint Eastwood-style."

Sasha snickered until the searing pain in her chest twisted her laugh into a groan. "You can totally carry me out of here if it'll make you feel like a big hero."

Vinny rested his cheek atop Sasha's head, caressing her back. The grate of pain dulled under his embrace, so she clung tighter.

"She used us," Vinny said in a tone that sent spikes into Sasha's heart. "This whole time, she was using us all."

"I know." Sasha pulled back from Vinny's grasp, gazing up at his face. A veil of sadness clouded his frosty-blue eyes. To see her best friend suffer at the hands of her mother rekindled the fires of rage inside Sasha's chest.

Otis knelt down, brushing a strand of blood-soaked hair from her face. "Are you all right?"

"No," Sasha said. "I'm not all right." Her eyes found Dez in the darkness, his sorry-ass stare shining through the night. Then she glimpsed her mother. How old, weak her mother looked now. Just another chick, controlled by another asshole dude. That's what Sasha glimpsed from the woman who straggled at the far end of the lot, looking beyond her bloody child on the ground to the bodies inside the warehouse.

"Help me up," Sasha said. She gripped Otis by the arm, and Vinny's hands clutched onto her waist, guiding her up. When she teetered, Vinny lifted her into his arms.

"You said I could." Vinny held Sasha tight to his chest, carrying her from the warehouse.

"Don't drop me." Sasha all but collapsed in Vinny's clutch, draping her hands around his neck.

"Me and Dez will stay back, clean up this site," Otis said as Vinny carried Sasha down the trail without a break in his steady steps.

Sasha avoided Dez's gaze. One more look at his desperate eyes, and she'd forgive him on the spot. Her body already wilted at the sight of him, but her mind wasn't ready to forget what he'd done yet. Her mother shrank down as they walked by, like a scared little kitten standing alone in a pack of wolves.

"Come on, *Mom*," Sasha said, leering over Vinny's shoulder.

Chapter Thirty-Six

Dez

Night rolled in quick, surrounding Dez in shadows. Otis dragged a body from the bushes and up the trail, but he just stood there, watching his brother carry Sasha away. That should be him cradling her broken body. Her hands were supposed to be clinging to his neck, and they would be, if he hadn't been such a pathetic excuse of a man.

"You gonna help or sulk like a little bitch?" Otis asked, dropping the body in his grasp atop an ever-growing pile of corpses.

"I fucked up." Dez trudged down the hill, toward the legs that poked out from tall blades of grass. "Sasha would've been better off if I never came back."

"Cut your woe-is-me bullshit." Otis seized the dead man by the ankles, yanking him from the weeds. "Your girl is still alive. You can go fix it."

The way Otis sagged his shoulder, the quiver in the man's lip. It looked like he might cry. Fuck. Dez

361

would hightail it right out of there if the dude started bawling.

"Otis, man…I—"

"Shut the fuck up and grab this asshole's arms."

Dez clamped his lips closed the entire time they hauled the body up the trail. He couldn't say a damn thing. Otis was right; Sasha was alive, and he could gaze into her deep eyes, catch a stray smile, touch her skin, even if she did punch him in return.

"Now what?" Dez asked, releasing the body so it could join the others in their heap.

"We wait." Otis strolled toward the warehouse and sat on the concrete slab outside the bay door. "When the prospect comes, we'll load them in the truck and get rid of 'em."

A strong voice flowed from Otis's mouth, betraying the crushed face that spoke it. That could've been Dez, miserable on a cold ground, thinking what if. It still could be.

Dez pulled out his pack of cigarettes, knocking two loose. After lighting them both, he sat beside Otis and handed one over. "I talked to Candy a few times. She was…really special."

Otis nodded, looking away, and Dez did the same. Grief radiated around them, creating an orb where crickets didn't chirp and light wouldn't shine. Just time, stripping happiness to tatters.

***

Sasha

Sasha curled into the backseat of her mother's

362

Chevelle. Vinny scooted closer, drawing her under his arm and into the refuge of his affection. Her imagination failed to capture the true sensation of his touch. In her wildest dreams, she couldn't replicate this type of connection. A cross between coming home after a long run and sliding into warm pajamas, but better. This moment would be fucken' awesome, if not for the throb in her temples, spasm of her shoulder, tingle in her fingers, and her mother's eyes scanning her over in the rearview mirror. On second thought, maybe she'd caught a chariot to hell.

"You trying to read my face?" Sasha glared into the front seat but didn't dare part with the only remnant of family in this car, Vinny. "I bet you're just dying to find out what I know."

"Sasha, I—"

"Here, let me." Sasha sat up, leaning against Vinny's chest. "If you would have known he'd beat me so badly…You had no idea his buddies would turn on him and try to rape me…Candy wasn't supposed to die."

Sasha's fingers curled around the bench seat that separated them, leather sinking under her nails. "I loved Candy." She heaved herself forward, just to make sure not one word was lost. "You wanna know why I loved her?" The closer she got, the more her mother cowered down. An incredible experience, worth every hit she took. "It was the way she squirmed when I bit her nipple. Her cute little gasps when I went down on her. She tasted like peaches and felt like Heaven when I slipped my fingers in—"

"Sasha!" Her mother hurled a leer that could only belong to a small-minded bigot.

For the first time, Sasha saw a chip in her mother's unbreakable armor, and she had the perfect-sized nails to drive into it.

"What's wrong, Mother? You don't like that?" Sasha fell back against Vinny's chest, and his arm circled her waist. "Then you're probably not gonna like the type of shit that I'll be doing on *my* property. The women I'll be kissing, touching, fucking. In fact, I don't think it's going to be the best…environment for someone like you."

Vinny's chest shook, his light smirk rustling Sasha's hair.

"I guess," Sasha said, rolling her eyes, "since you are blood kin, I'll give you twenty-four hours to get your shit and get off my compound."

"Who the fuck do you think you are?" The car skid to a stop, just outside the open front gate. "Some scribbles on a piece of paper don't mean shit. I made this club what it is. You'd be a trashy, pleather-wearing skank if it weren't for me. You should be thanking me right now, you ungrateful little bitch."

"Hey!" Sasha cocked her head to one side and wagged her finger in her mother's face. "If you don't give any lip, I'll let you take my Chevelle."

"You'll let me…Oh, you're gonna be one sorry—"

Sasha held up her hand, blocking her mother's red face from view. The most colorful slurs dribbled from her mother's mouth, Grade A shit Sasha would definitely reuse later, but she'd had enough for now.

In between, "You couldn't find your ass from your elbow!" and "Don't call me from prison!" Sasha pushed open the passenger door. She squeezed from the backseat, taking in a lungful of crisp night air. After Vinny crawled from the car, Sasha slammed the door shut. Her mother finally gave the viper-tongue a rest, but it wasn't a peaceful silence. The quiet held an eerie sense of danger, the way a sky would groan before a twister.

Their eyes met through the window, and Sasha winced. She expected to find a fury sharp enough to slice but only glimpsed sadness in her mother's stare, which cut even deeper. The engine revved, and Sasha backed away as her mother peeled wheels down the mountain.

"I can't believe you did that," Vinny said, walking into the road to stare at the taillights that glowed in the darkness.

"Was it fucked up?" Sasha stood beside Vinny, turning her back on the squeal of tires. "It feels fucked up."

"Who knows anymore? We're both idiots for believing her shit when we should've known better. Were you serious about her leaving?"

"I was, until she drove away." Sasha shook her head, as if that could jiggle out the crazy. There was something wrong with her. The most toxic element in her life had just driven away, and she wanted to chase it.

"You think she'll come back?" Vinny asked, glancing at Sasha.

"I hope so. If not, I know where to find her."

Vinny glided his fingertips over Sasha swollen cheek, almost as lightly as the breeze chilling her skin. "I was so—"

"Sasha?" Kev called out.

Sasha braced herself as Kev ran out the front gate, coming in for a hug. He squeezed her tight, and the bone in her shoulder crunched, forcing her to yelp.

"Hurt! Dude, I'm hurtin'."

"Oh shit!" Kev let go, giving her a light tap on the arm. "Sorry. I'm just...I didn't think I'd ever see you again." His smiled faded as he glanced around the empty road. "Where's everyone else? Are they...dead?"

"No," Sasha yelled, wishing she weren't so sore so she could slap Kev for being so stupid. "They're up at the warehouse."

"The warehouse?" Kev looked up the road, which narrowed as it stretched along the mountain. "Wait. The warehouse was right up the road this whole time?"

It didn't matter who knew now. Sasha would never step one foot in that warehouse again. "Can you get one of the prospects to go fetch my truck? I gotta go back, get the guys."

"You heard her," Kev yelled, without turning to look at the two men straggling at the end of the driveway. In a shuffle of footsteps, they hurried up the hill and melded into the darkness.

Vinny nudged Kev out of the way and took hold of Sasha's arm. "Come on, you need to get cleaned up. I'll go back to the warehouse."

"No." Sasha yanked her arm back, groaning as a

wave of what felt like broken razorblades rolled beneath her skin. "I have to go back. There's something I forgot, but I do need you to pop my shoulder back in its socket."

"Ah, fuck, Sasha."

"I'm out," Kev said, lifting his hands while backing away.

"The fuck you are," Vinny said. "Get your ass over here and hold her steady."

Kev cringed, but Sasha didn't know why. *He* wasn't the one about to have his arm bone slammed back into its socket. "Don't be a pussy," she teased as Kev walked behind her.

Vinny smirked, taking her by the wrist. "All right, let's see." His other hand landed on her shoulder, nice and gentle, yet a fire still surged in her chest. She looked at Vinny's face. A crinkled brow, beads of sweat. She was fucked.

Before she could utter a word, Vinny yanked her wrist out and pushed her shoulder down. Bones scraped. She cried out as a million red-hot needles shot through her arm. Her legs turned to jelly, but Kev held tight, keeping her boots on solid ground.

"You good?" Vinny asked, ducking to stare into her eyes.

"Yeah." Sasha shook the prickles from her fingertips, staggering away from Kev's grasp. "Dang that smarts."

Headlights flooded the road, and a rumble echoed off the high rock wall. Sasha's pickup turned off the gravel and onto pavement, idling to a stop beside her. The rusted truck sputtered as the prospect climbed out. A sad sound, one of looming demise, a reflection of everything she touched on her corner of the Earth.

"Where's Candy?" Sasha asked, glancing at Kev. "Her body?"

Kev inched behind Vinny, nearly squirming out of his skin. "I made it look like an accident. Tossed a rock on the gas pedal and let the semi plow through the guardrail."

It seemed as though Kev wanted to say more, like he wanted to apologize for dumping the most beautiful woman she'd ever seen over the side of a mountain to lay under twisted metal in the cold night, alone, as if it were his fault somehow.

"Okay," Sasha muttered, battling to suppress the image of a head bursting to pieces. There were so many memories of Candy stored inside Sasha's head. The way her golden hair shined the first time they spoke on the playground at school, the glimmer in her eyes when they first kissed. Those were the memories Sasha wanted to remember, not the feel of Candy's blood splashing her skin.

Sasha couldn't take the sympathetic stares of her clubmates or the pound of her heart any longer than she could stand in the middle of this cursed road.

The soreness of her body lessened as she limped around the back of the truck, heading for the open driver's door. Sasha dropped inside, and the prospect shut her door, leaning on the open window.

"I left something in there for ya," he whispered, nodding toward the center console.

An ice-cold glass of cola vibrated in Sasha's cup holder, and a freshly rolled joint sat in her ashtray. She grinned and shifted into first gear, glancing out the window. "You're all right, tall, wide one."

In a chirp of tires, Sasha took off up the mountain. Fate stole many people from her this night, and she planned to take one of them back. Tomorrow might be different, but right now, she couldn't breathe until Dez wrapped his arms around her. Just one touch, one night. It didn't have to mean forgiveness, only solace.

The motor revved as Sasha downshifted, veering onto the dirt path. Every bump spread waves of broken glass beneath her skin, scraping but doing little to slow her determination. She snatched the joint from the ashtray, pushing in the dash lighter. Two puffs and a steep bend, then she could breathe again.

***

Dez

Dez jumped up when a motor revved in the distance. "Did you hear that?"

"Yeah." Otis stood, clutching a shotgun to his chest. "There's headlights. Take cover."

It took only one step for Dez to realize he didn't give a shit who was coming up the trail. He had nothing left to lose beside his pride if he cowered in the bushes, and fuck that.

A click rang out as Dez cocked back the pump of the shotgun in his hands. He stood firm in the middle of the empty lot, aiming down the trail. A pickup truck cut around the curve, and a chill ran down his spine. He lowered the gun. Despite his mind's protests, his body wouldn't aim a weapon in that direction. Then the lights steered from his eyes, and he saw why. Sasha, his angel in a devil's costume. Their eyes connected as Sasha parked, and Dez could've sworn he glimpsed a smile, which meant he'd gone delirious or she was there to kill him.

"It's Sasha," Dez yelled over his shoulder, walking toward her truck. When she hurried toward him, he stopped short. A quick scan of her hands revealed no weapons, but he couldn't gauge the look in her eyes. It was an intense stare, not anger or hatred. Nothing he'd ever glimpsed in her eyes, or anyone else's, before now.

Dez stepped back, but Sasha kept moving toward him, all but collapsing against his chest. The gun slipped from his grasp, and reflex took his hands to her body. She floated into his grasp like air, numbing his lips with her kiss. It had to be a dream. He squeezed tighter, kissed her deeper as his fingers curled into locks of silky hair. A hell of a dream, one he'd gladly dwindle in forever.

Her soft hands skated along Dez's cheeks, trailing a wave of sparks. Sasha drew back but didn't get very far. Some magnetic force held her lips just above his, igniting the tiny space between them in electric fire.

"I forgot to tell you I love you," Sasha whispered, her fingers trembling on the back of Dez's neck.

Dez leaned closer to Sasha, his heart racing, and she jerked back.

"But I hate your fucking guts too," she said in a

dead-serious tone. Her brow crinkled, but that blaze still lit her eyes.

"I can take that." Dez lifted Sasha's chin, gliding his hand down her neck. Before his lips could touch hers, a throat cleared behind him.

"This is disgustingly sweet," Otis sneered, "but we got a lot of cleaning up to do here."

"Burn it," Sasha said, glancing at the warehouse. "The bodies too."

Otis stared at Sasha as though she'd just spoken a foreign language. "But the runs, our pickups."

"We'll have to get a new stash house." Sasha limped to the back of her truck, grabbing a gas can. "This place might as well be listed in the yellow pages."

"I guess." Otis shook his head, his gaze falling to the tall metal building. "It's a shame. You grew up here."

"Yeah." Sasha tightened her grip on the gas can, marching toward the warehouse. "I did."

Chapter Thirty-Seven

Sasha

Sasha squeezed against the driver's side door as Dez and Otis crammed into her truck. An orange glow lit the woods around her. Flames groaned in the quiet night, but she didn't look back. A fire had already devoured this warehouse in her memories. Witnessing the real inferno seemed unnecessary.

After shutting the passenger door shut, Dez dropped his hand on her leg, and she sped off down the trail. For just a second, she peeked in the rearview mirror then darted her stare to the road ahead. Now she couldn't look. It had become an issue of pride, a dare to prove her back still held a solid bone. Sasha cut around a curve, ignoring the red flicker that danced on every tree. A squeak rang out from under her palm, and she loosened her grip on the hard plastic steering wheel, her gaze coasting to the side mirror.

"Sasha," Otis said, pulling Sasha's stare just in time to keep her willpower in mediocre standing.

"We should talk about your mother."

"She's gone."

"What?" Otis grunted.

Sasha looked past Dez's stunned face and into eyes drenched in anger. This would be the point where she usually backed off, delved into la-la land, but she couldn't stand to live another second in lies.

"I sent her packing. Did you know I owned the entire compound and all its contents?" Sasha slowed the truck. It was getting pretty difficult to speed down a bumpy trail while sardined in a tight cab and keep track of Otis's guilty expressions.

"You do?" Dez asked, his eyes wide.

Sasha waved her hand in Dez's direction, bouncing her eyes between the road and Otis.

"I did know that," Otis said, leaning against his door, "but having your name on a piece of paper doesn't give you the right to toss your mother out of her home."

"Did you know Dante was my real father?"

That one must have hit Otis in the teeth, because he didn't say anything for a while.

"Sasha." Otis exhaled loudly, shifting in his seat. "I know everything. About everyone."

"Is that a threat?" Sasha asked, unable to stop the sneer that carried her words. Dez tensed up, but she didn't look at him. This time, her gaze reflected one of guilt, but she was better at hiding it than Otis.

"No," Otis said, matching her short tone. "You're my family. I don't throw family under the bus when things get rough."

The words struck a chord, a loud grating tune that plucked at Sasha's soul. She'd had her fair share of fuckups. In the old days, she wasted years tormenting her mother, and never once was she thrown out of her home.

"She'll come back," Sasha said, mostly to soothe her own heavy mind. "Then I can apologize."

"Apologize!" Dez yelled. "She was gonna let us get killed. All of us."

"You're wrong," Otis said with a low growl that disrupted the air around them. "You have no idea what you're talking about."

"Do you?" Dez said.

"Guys!" Sasha held out her hand, but it did little to ease the rise of tension in the cab. "Give it a rest. My fucking head is killing me."

She turned onto the compound, never happier to see the dented front gate. In a minute, she could park this truck then walk away. These two jokers could spend all night beating each other's faces in, but she'd had enough bloodshed.

Vinny walked down the clubhouse steps as she parked, Kev not far behind. Their eyes were fixed on her, seeking answers, directions, guidance. She never had those things to spare, not for herself or others.

When Otis got out, Dez moved away and Sasha grabbed his hand. "Stay with me tonight?" she asked, recognizing but ignoring the desperation in her question.

Dez smiled, warm and genuine, a sight as rare as a blue moon and just as stunning.

"I'll stay with you every night," he said without hesitation.

Every night. The thought was both tempting and

terrifying. "We'll just start with this one," Sasha said, and Dez's glower swept back in.

***

Vinny

Vinny turned his back as Sasha walked toward the garage with Dez. She said three words to him before strolling off with his brother, and they weren't the ones he wanted to hear. No, "I love you," "Thank you, Vinny," not even a, "Let's burn one."

All she said was, "Mom back yet?" Then she nodded and away she went. Not that he expected different, only hoped.

A zippo clicked, the porch steps creaked, and floorboards shifted beneath Vinny's boots. He peeked over his shoulder, groaning. The crew of eyes hovering at his back wanted something, and they wanted it from him.

"Where's Ellen?" Kev asked, shooing the prospects back.

"Good question," Otis said with a glare that matched his harsh sneer.

Vinny looked at the road far below their rolling hillside. It would've been great to see headlights. Then he could point his finger to Ellen, wander off, and wallow while she barked orders, which always seemed to flow easily.

"Ah…" Vinny shrunk down under Otis's glare, then puffed his chest up. He was VP of Ashby Trucking. These men answered to him, not the other way around. At least that's what Ellen would tell him.

"Ellen's out on business," Vinny said, nearly convincing himself. "She'll be back soon. Otis, can you crash here again tonight? You know, just in case."

"Sure, kid." Otis nodded, easing off enough for cool air to rush in.

"I can stay too," Kev said, cringing from his own eagerness. "I mean, if you need me to."

Vinny smirked. It was either that or cry. His friends were as sad and lonely as he was, lugging around their own loads. They should be together. No one else would have them.

"Yeah, man. You can have my room for the night. I'll sleep in Sasha's old room, but those two," Vinny pointed at the prospects who lingered nearby, "they're bunking in the clubhouse."

Tingles coursed through Vinny's veins, turning his blood to steel. He propped his head high and strolled off the porch, toward the big house. Tonight, he was the ultimate authority. It shouldn't feel so good. His rise came from Ellen's fall and Sasha's weaknesses. He could keep a level head, no problem. After all, this power was fleeting. Ellen would be back, and, like always, Sasha would spin the situation into gold. Everyone'll soak it up, and then it was business as usual, the blissful state of ignorance at Ashby Trucking. Not for him, though. He knew too many ugly truths and hadn't heard enough of the right words.

A giggle spilled from Sasha's open window as Vinny passed the garage. He looked up, stopping his stare before it reached her room. A glimpse of his brother's hands on Sasha's body was not a visual he wanted trapped in the ole noggin. The images already circling around in his mind, where Sasha ran her fingers through his hair, licked every inch of his flesh, were far better. It wouldn't be long now. When Dez fucked up and Sasha flipped out, he'd be standing by, her trusty friend on standby, the man who always held her heart in the end.

***

Sasha

Sasha drew the arm that circled her waist close to her chest. Minutes dwindled into hours while she lay adrift in Dez's warm clutch. He took to snoring a while ago and she'd kill for a few puffs of a joint, but her soft bed kept her shackled in its chains of refuge.

She nestled closer, floating on the cusp of a dream when an engine's rumble jolted her eyelids open. That sound disturbed her sleep so many nights. The smooth chops of a big block motor, deep bass of exhaust. Mother's home.

Electric vibes stirred Sasha's body. Sleep would never come now, not until she said everything she could to return things to some semblance of peace. She lifted Dez's arm, slinking away. Her shoulder pulsed, more so than her head, but this couldn't wait. If she didn't beg her mother to stay, she'd spend months tracking the bitch down just to plea for her return.

377

In near darkness, Sasha fumbled for her clothes. A heavy metal belt buckle clinked as she squirmed into her pants, echoing louder than it should in the thick silence. She grabbed the end of her belt, glancing at the bed. Dez grunted and rolled over. She inched backward. His arm flopped over the side of the bed, and a steady snore rang out. Sasha hurried to the door, snatching a leather coat from the floor along the way.

Frosty air shocked Sasha's skin when she stepped outside, filling her lungs with its wintery chill. She crept down the stairs, slinging the coat around her arms. The sleeves ran far past her wrists, and a musky scent tickled her nose.

"Dez," Sasha whispered, pulling the flap closer and taking a deep breath. A hard edge dug into her ribcage, knocking her chest with every step. She reached into the inside pocket, her fingers grazing the snub-nosed barrel of a revolver. A smile spanned her lips. Dez probably had a mini arsenal tucked away in these pockets, a thought that turned Sasha on too much.

She looked at the big house looming atop the hill and its many windows cloaked in black. Her loosely tied boots thumped as her foot tapped gravel. One apology. After losing so much, trampling on her self-respect should be a cinch. Her legs should carry her punk-ass right to her mother's feet, but they weren't budging. Instead, a call summoned her back to Dez's warm arms.

Sasha turned away from the big house, catching a beam of light in the woods. She headed up the hill, taking light steps. Muffled voices rose above the symphony of crickets, and she pulled the gun from her pocket.

Branches scratched her face, snagging her hair as she climbed the gentle slope into dense trees. A man shouted, stopping her short. She crouched low, glancing back at the compound far below. In the dead of night, through tight-packed trees, Sasha only glimpsed more trees. Twigs snapped behind her. She turned, lifting the gun when she heard the screech of metal hinges. The cellar, she must be near the cellar.

"Fuck that," her mother's voice rang out, cracking in fear.

Sasha jumped to her feet. Her mother's fright echoed in her ears, tuning out the inklings of danger and drawing her forward. She burst from the web of branches, her gun raised high. A flashlight shot to her face, blinding her in white, but she kept her finger on the trigger.

"Sasha?" her mother said. "What the fuck?"

The light dropped, but its glare stayed strong in Sasha's eyes. She blinked, moving toward her mother's voice. Blue dots cleared from her vision, and Dante's grin filtered in. She froze in place, swinging the gun to him.

"I was hoping you'd show up," Sasha said, clicking the hammer back.

"Your mother brought me here, to take you again."

"What?" Sasha lowered the gun, looking at her mother.

"He's lying," Ellen yelled, reaching for the gun in Sasha's hand.

Sasha backed away as Dante and her mother closed in.

"She wanted me to keep you locked up for nine months," Dante said, his eyes fixed on Ellen's face. "Apparently you're having a kid and your mother wants it, but not you, little girl."

"Don't listen to him, Sasha. He's insane."

They kept moving closer, like a magnet drawn to her pull yet repelled by each other. Sasha scurried backward. The gun rattled against her palm, and the ability to control her arm became iffy at best.

"When I told Ellen to go fuck herself, she pulled this gun on me." Dante lifted his hand, flashing a handgun. "Marched me up the hill. I think she was gonna toss me in the cellar. That's why I elbowed her in the gut and took this bad boy." He waved the gun before lowering his arm.

Sasha closed her eyes. She didn't know Dante. If he was a pathological liar like everyone else, she didn't have a clue, but this seemed like something her mother would do. She opened her eyes, finding her gun aimed at her mother's chest.

"You're not buying this shit, are you?" Ellen shouted, moving closer to Sasha.

"Stay back," Sasha yelled. "Both of you." She swung her gun back and forth, legs hurrying away. The whirl in her mind grew into a cyclone. She couldn't separate truth from lie. Still, they both slithered closer. "Just stop. Please, stop."

"It's okay, little girl," Dante's voice trickled in so smooth, silky, darker than night. "I couldn't do it before, but I'm ready now. I'll set you free."

Dante lifted the gun, and Ellen cried out, rushing

to Sasha's side. Sasha staggered backward as her mother ripped the gun from her grasp. An elbow hit her chest, driving her even farther back.

Roots snared Sasha's heel, and she fell as shots blasted through the air. She braced for hard ground, but the fall didn't break. Stars drifted away, stone walls zoomed beside her, and a darkness swallowed her whole. The cellar. She fell into the—

Ash spouted up in pillars as Sasha slammed onto concrete. Blood spewed from her mouth, showering her face in its warmth. She gasped for air, finding none. No oxygen, no light, just a churn of shattered glass in every inch of her body and a red-tinged sky so far above.

A velvety haze settled over her, bringing the aroma of lavender to her oxygen-stripped lungs. Pain left her body as quick as it struck. The intense fear of dying atop piles of burnt bones melted away next, leaving only cold. Her fingers twitched, every tiny breath held fire, yet her skin hardened in a frosty layer of ice.

Shapes swirled against the faint glow of stars. A person? Sasha tried to reach out, strained to kick, cry, move, but only a cold shell remained.

Her head rolled to the side without consent, and a set of bright teeth grinned behind chunks of flesh. The flaps of skin swayed, peeling. For a second, Sasha thought the skull was laughing at her, mocking her for meeting the fate she dished out to so many others. Then a swarm of maggots oozed through the cracks of rotted meat and spilled onto her face.

A blanket of white washed over Sasha's numb

body. In the blinding fog, she glimpsed bright green eyes. She couldn't see a face. No sound penetrated this barrier of pure bliss, just soft arms lifting her into a tunnel of rainbow light.

Chapter Thirty-Eight

Sasha clawed at the speck of white, which beamed through the cold blackness that surrounded her. A deep voice drove her, his voice. He spoke in tones of love, louder than ever before. This time, Sasha could trace it. The more she scratched at the dark, the clearer his words echoed. Vinny. His desperation fueled her fight, bringing a strength to her mind she'd long forgotten.

Fingers slid between her own, and she squeezed. Vinny called her name. His lips brushed her cheek, and warm breath sparked electric tingles along the back of her neck.

"Vinny," Sasha mumbled, leaning toward his touch.

"I'm here," Vinny said, gripping Sasha's hand tightly. "Open your eyes! Come on, Sasha, I know you can do it."

A rush of strange sounds filled Sasha's ears. High-pitched beeps, the low static of a television, laughter in the distance, but most importantly, Vinny. Her eyelids fluttered. The sting of bright light burned her eyes, cutting straight into her brain, but she wouldn't stop staring into the glare. Not until she glimpsed Vinny's face.

"Vinny." First, his eyes faded in then his smile. "Am I…?"

"You came back." Vinny collapsed against Sasha's chest, sprinkling her face with kisses laced in tears. "I knew you'd come back. They said it was impossible, but they don't know you."

"Who…? What…?" Sasha stuttered. Her throat seared with every word. She reached out, and her arm flopped back down to a soft mattress.

"Don't try to speak," Vinny said in a rush. "I'll get a doctor."

"No." Sasha swatted at the air, snagging Vinny's shirt. "Water."

"Right! Hold up."

Wires tangled around Sasha's arm, and she looked over. An IV? She followed the tubes to a metal pole, sitting beside a blinking monitor. The hospital. She was in a hospital.

"You ready?"

Sasha rolled her head to the side, looking right into Vinny's smile. It wasn't a dream. He was there with her. The back of her mattress raised, and she pushed to keep herself upright. It wasn't easy. Her arms were like jelly.

"Slow sips," Vinny said. He lifted a cup to Sasha's lips, and cold water rushed in, shocking her body with its chill. Her throat sealed shut, and she gagged, coughing water in a spray onto her lap.

"Oh fuck," Vinny cried out, slamming down the cup and patting Sasha on the back. "Are you okay?"

"What happened?" Her voice came out so raspy she hardly recognized it. After clearing the lumps from her throat, she signaled for more water. This time, she managed to hold her own cup, a feat that seemed to amaze Vinny. "Where's my mom?"

"What do you remember?" Vinny asked, sitting in the chair stationed beside the bed.

Sasha tried to think back, but memories jumbled in flashes. Dez's arms, holding her tight. Her mother and Dante, creeping toward her in dark woods. The cellar.

"I fell into the cellar." Sasha cringed. That was one memory she wished had never returned. She could still feel bones digging into her back, flesh of rotted skulls peeling beneath her fingernails.

Vinny kept one hand firmly planted on Sasha's waist, leaning closer to brush stands of hair from her forehead. "What were you doing up there?"

It took Sasha a minute to sort through her thoughts, which streamed into her mind all at once and in no particular order. So many cruel glares had been flung her way, and she relived them now in a blur. The image of Candy's sweet face bursting into bits of pink clumps stopped every other thought, forcing the horror story that was Sasha's life back into her brain.

"I saw a light, heard voices. My mom and Dante were by the cellar, arguing. The door was open. Dante said..." Sasha squeezed her lips closed. What Dante said to her on that mountain, how he was there to lock her up and steal her baby at her mother's request, would never leave her mouth. Ever. "I don't know. Dante said some shit, and my mom grabbed the gun from my hand. I think I tripped and fell into the cellar."

Sasha sat up, pushing Vinny's hand off her cheek. "Where's my mom? Dez?" She gripped onto her stomach. It felt different. Empty. "My baby."

"Sasha." Vinny took her hand, holding so tight Sasha couldn't jerk away. She didn't want to hear what was about to flow from Vinny's mouth. His face said it all.

"Your mother didn't make it. I'm so sorry."

"No." Sasha finally twisted her wrist free, sagging down. Her spine tingled, shooting prickles into her toes. It would've been the worst pain she ever experienced, but her splintered heart dulled it to a petty ache. Her mother was dead. That was why the world looked so dark, why a hollow void carved a hole through the center of her chest. Her mother's light wasn't around to fill the cracks of Sasha's soul with warmth. She could never be warm again.

"How?" was the only word Sasha could force from her mouth.

"Ellen took three bullets. By the time we got there, she was dead and you were in the cellar. Dez jumped in, broke his fuckin' ankle, but we hoisted you out."

"Am I broken?" Sasha flung the blanket aside and wiggled her toes, sighing as they waved in what might be the most beautiful sight of her life.

"No," Vinny said, sounding just as surprised as Sasha felt. "Nothing permanent, now that you're awake."

Vinny said the last part like it was a miracle. In fact, he looked at her as if she'd risen from the dead.

"I lost my baby." Sasha wrapped her arms around her stomach, as though she could hug the lost child she'd failed to protect. She'd been able to keep from breaking down, barely, but tears were pushing for release.

"The baby's fine," Vinny said, his voice raised as if to pose a question. "He's, umm—"

Sasha leaned away from Vinny's nervous stare, her side hitting the bed's metal rail. "He's?"

Again, Vinny went straight for Sasha's hand. The situation was turning creepy and starting to piss her off.

"This is gonna be really weird," Vinny said, nearly crushing Sasha's hand with his tight grip. "So just try to stay cool."

"Dude, you're about to get really punched if you don't start making sense."

Vinny snickered, his fingers shaking against the back of Sasha's hand. A glaze coated his eyes. It was the way he looked before he kissed her or cried.

"You were asleep for a long time, Sasha, but the baby kept growing inside you."

"What?" Sasha pulled up her gown, gasping at the sight of a wide scar running across her stomach. It was grotesque and fitting. Her outsides finally reflected the ugliness within.

"A few months after they cut him out, the doctors took you off life support, but you kept fighting."

Sasha ran her finger along the puffy line that mutilated her smooth skin. It couldn't be real. She would be able to feel something if a baby had grown inside her, some kind of connection. This had to be a nightmare. Sasha covered her eyes, but the beep of a heart monitor, the scratchy sheets beneath her didn't go away. A flood of tears snuck loose, pooling in her palm, and she dropped her arms to her sides.

"How long has it been?" Sasha asked, almost afraid to hear the answer.

Vinny's hands left Sasha's skin for the first time since she woke up.

"Four years," he said in a near whisper that hurled shivers beneath Sasha's flesh. "I've been here every day. Dez comes by when he can, but it's hard with running the club and chasing Tyler."

"Tyler?"

"Your son! I have a picture in my wallet."

Vinny reached for his pocket, and Sasha shook her head. She didn't want to see that picture, the creature they cooked inside her then carved out. The pinnacle of this hellish reality. Sasha squirmed back as Vinny shoved a photo in her face. It was just a baby. Curly brown hair, a dark stare, and a goofy smile. Another cute kid. Not hers, though. The baby she knew died in the cellar, along with Sasha Ashby.

"Here," Vinny said, waving the picture in front of Sasha's eyes. "You can have it. I got lots more."

"I don't—"

Before Sasha could utter another word, Vinny shoved the picture in her hand. A strong pull drew her gaze to the photo and that kid's smile. She turned the picture over, looking away. That damn kid haunted her with his deep eyes, Dante's eyes.

"He's got your eyes," Vinny said through a grin.

"No, he doesn't," Sasha snapped, flinching at her own nasty tone.

"It's a really old picture. Wait 'til you see him now. He's so big." Vinny jumped to his feet, nearly choking on his wide smile. "I gotta call the guys, get a doctor in here." He leaned over, kissing Sasha on the forehead. "Try to relax. I'll be right back."

The notion of relaxation was too funny to laugh at. She couldn't slow the pound of her heart. Nothing could be done about the room that spun around her, growing smaller with each whirl. Her mother died, taking the only world Sasha knew with her, and she was supposed to relax?

Somewhere outside this hospital room, a new life had her name on it, a bizarre life where Dez ran the club and a strange child waited. That life didn't belong to her. It belonged to her ghost.

Sasha had to get away before this new life came to claim her, run as fast as her weak legs would carry her, except her stupid legs wouldn't move. No matter how hard she strained, only twitches stirred her feet.

"Fuck!" Sasha cried out, crashing her fist against the bed's hard rail.

"What on earth?" A nurse strolled inside the room, stopping short. "Oh my! You're awake. I'll get the doctor."

"Wait!" Sasha reached out, wobbling on the edge of the bed.

The nurse ran to Sasha's side, pushing her back onto the pillows. "Try to be still, sweetie. Your limbs have been out of commission for some time.

You don't want to pull one of those tender muscles."

Soft fingertips glided to Sasha's wrist then to her neck. She peered at the nurse beside her, gazing into playful brown eyes. Her stare drifted down a silky neck, to the overflowing cleavage beside a nametag. It took a few seconds, but Sasha glanced over to scan the name.

"Nurse Baker," Sasha said, grabbing onto the woman's hand.

"Ginger," the nurse said, adjusting Sasha's IV. "I can't believe you pulled out of it. Must be all those fine-looking men. Give you something to wake up for, huh?"

"Listen." Sasha opened the flap of her hospital gown, pulling wires off her chest. "I'll give you five thousand dollars if you get me out of here right now."

"Out of here!" The nurse clicked off the heart monitor, silencing its screech, then tried to stop Sasha from ripping out the IV. "Sweetie, you're going to need months of physical therapy before your arms and legs cooperate properly."

"Okay. I'll give you another five g's if you get my shit working again." Sasha grabbed the woman by the arm, holding as tight as she could. "That's ten grand, cash." It was so close. The woman's eyes lit up then dropped. "Please, Miss."

"Ten grand, really?"

The woman's question made Sasha's pulse race. She'd pay anything, kill whoever, to get out of this mess. "I swear to fucking God."

After a grin then a frown, the nurse said, "I'll do

it. Let me go get a wheelchair."

The nurse walked away, her heels clacking, and Sasha ripped the needle from her arm, wiping a stream of blood on her blanket. The picture flipped over, its glossy surface drawing her stare. She lifted the tiny portrait, holding her breath. Those chubby cheeks, strong jaw. It reminded her of Dez and fractured her will.

Sasha slapped the picture on the nightstand, pushing it away. One more glimpse would crumble her resolve, drive her back into Dez's web of lies and lust.

"All right." The nurse breezed back into the room, pushing a wheelchair. "Your cute friend was coming back, so I sent him on a goose chase for the doctor. You sure you want to do this?"

Five times Sasha asked herself this very question, and five times she came back with the same answer.

"Hell yeah." Sasha shoved her dead legs over the side of the bed, waving the nurse closer. Her body slumped into the wheelchair, and she pulled the blanket over her, tucking it around her bare feet. A jitter spawned in her chest, creeping up to chatter her teeth. The wheelchair squeaked as the nurse pushed Sasha across the room, toward a brightly lit hall.

"You need anything before we go?" the nurse asked, slowing in the doorway. "There's a leather jacket hanging in the closet."

"No. I'm good." Sasha didn't look back. There was nothing behind her except agony, misery, and shame. Her eyes stayed ahead, eager to glimpse the next chapter of her new life as Sasha Lazzari.

The End

Acknowledgements

This book wouldn't have been possible if not for the help and support of so many others. Much thanks and big hugs to:

My husband, Shaun, who handles my editing rants with such tact and patience.

My son, Sabastian, as his very existence pushes me to strive for greatness in all aspects of my life.

My brother, Brett, whose positive outlook is a constant source of inspiration.

My sister, Nikki, who happens to be the strongest woman I know.

My best friend, Chris, who'll jump to get my back even when he thinks I'm wrong.

My dear friend, Brandie, whose constant encouragement, from the first of many query letters I sent to her, means more to me than she can ever know.

My amazing friend, Ruth, and her lovely mother in Puerto Rico who helped with the Spanish sections.

My critique partner and fellow author, Jadah McCoy, who is always around to deal with my freak-outs.

My extremely talented writer friend, Ty Martin, who is still the first person I run to when something writerly happens.

Everyone at Limitless Publishing for making *Ashby Holler* a reality, especially my amazing editor, Tiffany Cole, who helped me add depth to my writing.

All my #amwriting friends from Twitter, who

know the real pains of publishing and are 100 percent supportive.

Last but certainly not least, all the amazing people who volunteer their time and energy to host/mentor writing contests on Twitter. Michelle Hauck, Brenda Drake, S.C., Elizabeth Briggs, Michael Anthony, Jessa Russo, Tamara Mataya, Amy Trueblood, Laura Heffernan, and so many others have helped me and countless writers achieve their dreams, and I couldn't be more grateful.

About the Author

Jamie Zakian lives in South Jersey with a rowdy bunch of dudes, also known as family. A YA/NA writer, her head is often in the clouds while her ears are covered in headphones. On the rare occasions when not writing, she enjoys blazing new trails on her 4wd quad or honing her archery skills. She's a card carrying member of the Word Nerd Association, which means she's probably stalking every Twitter writing competition and offering query critiques so keep an eye out.

Twitter:
https://twitter.com/demoness333

Website:
http://www.jamiezakian.com/

CPSIA information can be obtained
at www.ICGtesting.com
Printed in the USA
BVOW03s2153281117
501513BV00001B/10/P